Also by Nicole Helm

South Dakota Showdown
Covert Complication
Backcountry Escape
Wyoming Cowboy Marine
Wyoming Cowboy Sniper
Wyoming Cowboy Ranger
Wyoming Cowboy Bodyguard
Wyoming Cowboy Justice
Wyoming Cowboy Protection
Wyoming Christmas Ransom

Also by Colleen Thompson

Passion to Protect
The Colton Heir
Lone Star Redemption
Lone Star Survivor
Deadly Texas Summer
Rescuing the Bride
Lethal Lessons
Capturing the Commando

Discover more at millsandboon.co.uk

le Helm grew up with her nose in a boo
m of one day becoming a writer. Luckily, a
d career choices, she gets to follow that
ng down-to-earth contemporary romar
ıntic suspense. From farmers to cowboys,
ıe West, Nicole writes stories about people
ıselves and finding love in the process. She
ouri with her husband and two sons and dre
eday owning a barn.

Texas-based author of more than thirty novel
llas, **Colleen Thompson** is a former teacher
ssion for reading, hiking, kayaking and the
ıce rescue dogs she and her husband have welc
their home. With a National Readers' C
ırd and multiple nominations for the RITA® A
has also appeared on the Amazon, BookSca
nes & Noble bestseller lists. Visit her onl
v.colleen-thompson.com

ISOLATED THREAT

NICOLE HELM

HUNTING THE COLTON FUGITIVE

COLLEEN THOMPSON

MILLS & BOON

First Published in Great Britain 2020
by Mills & Boon, an imprint of HarperCollins*Publishers*
1 London Bridge Street, London, SE1 9GF

Special thanks and acknowledgement are given to Colleen Thompson for her contribution to *The Coltons of Mustang Valley* series.

ISBN: 978-0-263-28035-7

0620

FSC
www.fsc.org
MIX
Paper from responsible sources
FSC™ C007454

This book is produced from independently certified FSC™ paper to ensure responsible forest management.

For more information visit: www.harpercollins.co.uk/green

Printed and bound in Spain
by CPI, Barcelona

ISOLATED THREAT

NICOLE HELM

For those who've learned to ask for help.

Chapter One

In the dark of his apartment, Brady Wyatt considered getting drunk.

It wasn't something he typically considered doing. He stayed away from extremes. If he drank alcohol, it was usually two beers tops. He'd never smoked a cigarette or taken a drug that wasn't expressly legal.

He was a good man. He believed in right and wrong. He believed wholeheartedly that he was smarter, better and stronger than his father, who was currently being transferred to a maximum-security federal prison, thanks to a number of charges, including attempted murder.

When Brady thought of his twin brother nearly dying at Ace's hands, it made him want to get all the more drunk.

Brady wished he could believe Ace Wyatt would no longer be a threat. His father wasn't superhuman or supernatural, but sometimes…no matter what Brady told himself was possible, it felt like Ace Wyatt would always have a choke hold around his neck.

Once he could go back to work, things would be fine. Dark thoughts and this sense of impending doom would go away once he could get out there and do his job again.

The fact he'd been shot was a setback, but he'd taken his role as sheriff's deputy for Valiant County, South Dakota, seriously enough to know being hurt, or even killed, in the line of duty was more than possible.

He'd been shot helping save his soon-to-be sister-in-law. There was no shame or regret in that.

But the fact the wound had gotten infected, didn't seem to want to heal in any of the normal ways no matter what doctors he saw, left him frustrated and often spiraling into dark corners of his mind he had no business going.

When someone knocked on his apartment door, relief swept through him. A relief that made him realize how much the darkness had isolated him.

Maybe he should go stay out at his grandmother's ranch. Let Grandma Pauline shove food at him and let his brother Dev grouse at him. Being alone wasn't doing him any favors, and he was not a man who indulged in weakness.

He looked through the peephole, and was more than a little shocked to see Cecilia Mills standing there.

Any relief he'd felt at having company evaporated. Cecilia was not a welcome presence in his life right now, and hadn't been since New Year's Eve when she'd decided to kiss him, full on the mouth.

Cecilia had grown up with the Knights, on the neighboring ranch to his grandmother's. Duke and Eva Knight's niece had been part of the fabric of Brady's life since he'd come to live with Grandma Pauline at the age of eleven—after his oldest brother had helped him escape their father's gang, the Sons of the Badlands.

While Brady had been friends with all the Knight girls, Cecilia was the one who'd always done her level best to irritate him. Not always on purpose either. They were just…diametrically opposed. Despite her job as a tribal police officer on the nearby reservation, Cecilia bent rules all the time. She saw gray when he saw black, and even darker gray when he saw white. She was complicated and they didn't agree on much of anything.

Except that their fundamental function in life was to help people. Which, he supposed, was what had made them good friends despite all their arguments.

Until she'd kissed him and ruined it all. She hadn't even *tried* to pass it off as a joke when he'd expressed his horror.

Still, he opened the door to her, even if he couldn't muster a polite smile.

She was soaked to the bone, carrying a bundle of blankets. The blankets let out a little mewling cry and Cecilia shoved her way inside.

Not just blankets. A baby.

"Close the door," she ordered roughly.

He raised an eyebrow but did as he was told, if only because there was panic underneath that stern order.

Her long black hair was pulled back in the braid she usually wore for work, but she wasn't wearing her tribal police officer uniform. Her jeans and T-shirt hung loose and wet and her tennis shoes were muddy and battered. Even with the panic on her face, and the casual clothes, there was an air about her that screamed *cop*.

He should know.

"What's all this?"

Goose bumps pricked visibly along her arms and she quickly began unbundling the baby. It was warm outside, even with the all-day rain, so he had the air conditioner running. He moved to turn it off.

"You got anything dry for him?" she asked.

Brady wanted explanations, but he could see just how wet they both were. So, he walked into his room and rummaged around for dry clothes for Cecilia, and a few things to wrap around a small infant. He grabbed some towels from the bathroom and headed back to his living room.

He handed the towel to her first. She knelt on the floor, placing the baby gently on the rug. She spoke softly to the child, unwrapping the wet layers, and even the diaper. Brady winced a little as she wrapped the baby's bare butt in the towel he'd given her, rather than a new, dry diaper, though she didn't appear to have any baby supplies.

"You need to get out of your wet clothes too," he insisted once the baby was taken care of.

She looked up at him, an arch look as if he was coming on to her.

Heat infused him, an embarrassment he didn't know what to do with. He did not *blush*, being a grown man. He was probably just feverish from this damn infection he couldn't kick. Again.

"I'm not going to jump you," Cecilia said in that flippant way of hers that always set his teeth on edge. "That ship has sailed. So unclench."

He had never appreciated Cecilia's irreverence for the rules of life. Or at least, *his* rules of life. One of which was nothing romantic between him and any of the Knight girls. Maybe some of his brothers had crossed that line, somehow made it work, but Brady had his rules. If there'd been a brief, confusing second on New Year's Eve when Cecilia's surprise kiss had made him wonder why, it was a moment of weakness he wouldn't indulge.

Cecilia didn't follow the letter of the law. She often advocated for wrong as much as right. She had *kissed* him. On the mouth. Very much against his will.

Then had had the nerve to laugh when he'd lectured her.

"Just go to my room and change," he grumbled. "I'll watch…" He gestured at the baby.

She looked back at the wriggling infant she was crouching over. Pain clouded her eyes, and fear was etched into her face.

"This is Mak." She stroked his cheek with the gentleness of a mother, but Brady knew Cecilia had not secretly been pregnant or given birth to a child. He saw her too often for that to be possible.

He sighed, sympathy warring with irritation. "What's going on, Cecilia?"

CECILIA COULD FEEL the shivering start to spread. It had been hot outside in the rainstorm, but Brady's apartment was cold. Pretty soon her teeth would chatter, no matter how hard she fought against it.

And she would fight against it. Showing weakness in front of Brady Wyatt wasn't something she could afford right now. She had to be in charge if this was ever going to work. If she was ever going to convince by-the-book Brady to go along with it.

"I'll go change. You can leave him there or pick him up. He can roll over though, so keep an eye on him."

She grabbed the stuff he'd brought out, helped herself to his room, and then once the door was closed, slumped against it.

She'd been a tribal police officer for seven years. She'd been afraid, truly afraid for her life. She had struggled to understand the right thing to do in the face of laws that weren't always *fair*. It was hard, stressful, at times painful work, and she intimately knew fear.

But this was new. Bigger and different.

She didn't want to die, so she feared for her own life when she had to at work. But she'd also accepted that she *would* die to save someone. That was why she'd gone into law enforcement, or at least something she'd accepted as she'd taken on a badge.

Now she had a *specific* someone. A tiny, defenseless baby. Poor little Mak. He didn't deserve the stress and panic of being on the run, and yet she didn't know what else to do. If Elijah got a hold of him…

Cecilia shook her head.

She needed help. She needed…

God, she did not need Brady Wyatt, but she didn't have any other viable options in the moment. And the moment was all there was.

It was that lack of options that forced her to move. She stripped off her wet clothes, then put on the dry, too-big ones that were Brady's. She paused at that. Brady had worn these clothes on his body.

And washed them, you moron.

She couldn't help the fact she had the hots for Brady. Couldn't help that the New Year's Eve kiss hadn't helped dissipate them any. Luckily the memory of his stern lecture afterward always made her laugh.

He was just so *uptight*. He drove her crazy. Yet, there was this physical thing that also drove her a different kind of crazy. She believed deep down it was just her dualistic nature. Of course she'd be attracted to someone whose personality made her want to pull her hair out.

That was her lot in life.

But that lot was way in the background now. Her only concern was finding a way to protect Mak. Cecilia had been trying to help her friend Layla through postpartum depression for the better part of six months, but a suicide attempt had landed Layla in the hospital with the state preparing to take Mak away.

Layla had begged Cecilia to hide him. The state would only take him to his father, who was rising in the ranks with the Sons of the Badlands.

The fact Ace Wyatt's gang had begun to infiltrate the reservation Cecilia worked and lived on, the place she'd been born, filled her with a fury that scared her.

So, she'd focus on this. Keeping Mak safe until Layla was given a clean bill of mental health.

Elijah had already threatened to take Mak, maybe more than once. Layla wasn't always forthcoming with what went down with Elijah, since there was still a part of Layla who believed she could save the man she loved from the wrong he was doing.

Cecilia didn't believe. She knew the world was gray—that black and white were illusions made by people who had the privilege to see the world that way—but anyone who moved up the ranks in the Sons was too far gone to change for the better.

She would save the innocent baby who'd had the misfortune of a terrible father and an emotionally abused mother.

She'd been that baby, more or less, and her aunt and uncle had saved her. Showed her love and kindness and taken her in when her mother had died. She'd been six years old. Aunt Eva was gone too now, but she still had Uncle Duke, and the four other women he'd raised who were her sisters regardless of biological ties.

Cecilia tied the sweatpants tight around her waist. They were too long by far, but she cuffed the ends, then did the same with the sleeves of the sweatshirt. She took the bundle of wet clothes with her as she stepped back into the living room.

She stopped short. Brady held Mak, cradled easily in his good arm. Brady wore a T-shirt, so she could see a hint of the bandage that was on his opposite shoulder.

Recovery from the gunshot wound he'd received when saving Felicity had been complicated.

There were six Wyatt brothers, any of whom she could get help from. Easier help. All of them understood, to a point, you had to bend some rules to save people from the Sons.

Brady was the one who didn't, or wouldn't, accept that. He was also the one who currently couldn't work. Who lived alone. Who could hide a baby.

Elijah might think to look at the Wyatt Ranch for Mak, but he wouldn't think to look into Brady individually. Not at first anyway. Not while she came up with a plan.

"Can I throw these in your dryer?"

Brady inclined his head, gently swaying Mak's body back and forth as if Brady had any practice with calming babies.

She'd spent some time in Brady's apartment. Not much. They'd all helped him out here over the past two months, trying to give a hand with chores that might hurt his shoulder. She'd come over with Felicity and Gage one night and made him dinner. She'd delivered some food courtesy of Grandma Pauline a few weeks ago when he'd been doing laundry, and despite how little she wanted to be alone with him when everything about him made her body *react*, she'd insisted on helping him move the clothes from the washer to the dryer.

She did so now, tossing her own clothes in the dryer. She wouldn't have time for them to get completely dry, but it would help. Hopefully the rain would stop so it wouldn't be a completely futile gesture.

She hesitated going back into the living room. Much as she wanted Mak in her own arms where his warm weight gave her a settled purpose, she knew she couldn't go back to Brady without a clear sense of what she was going to say.

She'd practiced on the way here. She'd just go with that. *Brady. I need your help. I know you won't approve, but you're the only one who can keep this innocent child safe and away from the Sons. I know you'll do the right thing.*

Simple. To the point.

But as Cecilia stood on the threshold of his small, stark living room, watching a big man holding a tiny baby, she could only say one thing.

"His father is a member of the Sons."

Brady's expression did that thing that had always fascinated her. It didn't chill. It didn't heat. It was like something inside of him clicked off and he went perfectly blank.

She envied that ability.

"His mother is in the hospital," she continued. "The state is going to award him to his father. I can't let that happen."

"It's not up to you, Cecilia."

He said it so coolly, so *calm*. She wanted to scream, maybe give him a good punch like he'd once taught her to do when she'd been thirteen and a boy at school was bothering her.

But rage and punching never got through to Brady Wyatt. So, she had to be harsh. As uncompromising as he always was. "Would you send this baby to survive *your* childhood?" Because Brady had spent eleven years stuck with the Sons, surviving his father—the leader of that terrible gang.

There was a flicker of something in his eyes, but his words and the delivery didn't change. "He isn't Ace's son."

"He could be," Cecilia returned, trying to match his lack of emotion and failing. "Ace is gone. Elijah is trying to move up, take over. He's recruiting people at the rez at a rapid rate."

"Elijah Jones," Brady said flatly.

The fact Brady knew him didn't soothe Cecilia's nerves any. "Yes. You know him?"

"Of him," Brady replied, still so blank and unreachable. "He has a record." Brady's gaze lifted from the baby to her. "The state wouldn't put a child with someone who—"

"You know what? Forget it." God, he infuriated her. After everything he'd seen as a police officer, everything he'd survived as a boy, he could believe the state would do the right thing. She marched toward him. "I don't need your help. I don't need you and your rigid, ignorant belief in a system that does not work. Hand him over." She held out her arms.

But Brady simply angled his body, keeping Mak just out of her reach. "No," he said firmly.

Chapter Two

Brady had seen Cecilia angry plenty of times. She was a woman of extremes. Completely calm and chill, or…this. Fury all but pumping off her in waves. If he hadn't been holding a baby, he was certain she would have decked him. Possibly right in the gunshot wound.

"You brought him here for a reason," he said in a tone of voice he'd learned and used over the years as a police officer. Calm, but not condescending. Authoritative without being demanding. It often soothed.

Not with Cecilia. "Yes, and boy was it a stupid reason," she returned through gritted teeth. He could practically see the wheels in her head turning as she tried to figure out how to get the baby away from him without hurting Mak.

"Why don't you calm down and—"

She bunched her fist and he winced because he'd made a serious tactical error in telling her to calm down.

"I swear to God I will—"

The baby in his arm began to cry. Brady blinked down at the little bundle wiggling against his arm. He'd dealt with babies before—not often, but he'd held them. Calmed a few after a traffic accident or during a domestic case. Babies weren't new or strange to him.

But little Mak was so tiny. His face wrinkled in distress as he cried, clearly disturbed by the sound of raised voices. He had a patch of dark hair, and spindly little limbs that reminded Brady of a movie alien.

Cecilia held out her arms, gave Brady a warning look, but Brady simply bounced the baby until he calmed, nestled closer. There was something comforting about the weight of him. Something real and…heavy, even though the child was light. Brady had been adrift for weeks, and holding Mak felt like a weight tethering him to shore.

Cecilia frowned, her forehead wrinkling in much the same way Mak's had. But she didn't argue with him any more. There was a kind of anguish on her face that had his heart twisting.

Brady nodded to the couch. "Sit. Tell me the whole story," he ordered quietly.

"I don't want to sit," she returned, petulantly if he had to describe it.

She would not have appreciated that characterization. She folded her arms across her chest and began to pace.

She was tall and slender and like a lot of the female cops he knew, played down everything that made her look too feminine. Her hair was simple—straight, black, braided. She wore no makeup, and the jeans and T-shirt she'd shown up in were on the baggy side, as if she might have to put her Kevlar on underneath.

Cecilia could flip the switch when she wanted to. Put on a dress, do up her face in that magical way women seemed to have—like she had on New Year's Eve, all glitter and smoke and fun. She even seemed to enjoy it. Or maybe she'd just enjoyed knocking him off his axis.

With Cecilia, he'd bet on the latter.

"His mother's in the hospital. She…" Cecilia hugged

herself tighter, then finally sat on his couch. "She's one of my oldest friends on the rez. She's been wrapped up in Elijah Jones for years now. I couldn't come out and say he was bad news, you know?" She looked up at him, an uncomfortable amount of imploring in her eyes. "If you say they're bad, it only makes some people want to hold on even more. Fix them even more. Some people don't understand that not everyone is fixable."

Brady nodded. He'd worked enough domestic cases to know that people of both sexes were often blinded by what they thought was love. Enough to believe they could change the worst in someone else.

Cecilia seemed to find some relief in his understanding. "So, I tried to be subtle. I tried to make it more about her. What she should have. What she *could* have if she only gave up on holding herself back." Cecilia shook her head. "Anyway, she was ecstatic when she got pregnant. Elijah stuck around more. He had plans. But they all involved the Sons." Her tone turned to acid. "Layla had the baby, and Elijah told her he'd be back once the kid was out of diapers so he could take him. *Make* him."

Cecilia popped back up onto her feet. "Take him. As if that boy was a peach that had to ripen before he ate it. Take him, as if he had any right." She shook her head vigorously. "Layla had already been struggling a bit, but that really sent her over the edge. I helped out, but I urged her to talk to her doctor. Something wasn't right. Finally I took her down to her doctor myself and wouldn't leave until she told someone how she was feeling. They said it was postpartum depression."

"Common enough."

"Sure. Sure. Since then I've done my level best to help her out. To do what I could to help Mak. I took her to her appointments, but we had a hard time scheduling them. Her insurance is terrible and she was already struggling financially. She didn't have any supportive family, and I tried to be that for her, but…"

"You're only one person, Cecilia." It came out gentler than he'd intended, and the look of anguish she sent him made his chest too tight.

She collapsed back onto the couch. "One person or ten, it doesn't seem to matter. The night I came to the hospital to talk to Felicity and Gage, that night you were shot? She took a bunch of pills. She called me. Told me, so I called an ambulance and it got there in time, but—"

"You know better than to blame yourself."

"Do I?" she snapped.

"You should," he replied, keeping his voice gentle even though he wanted to snap right back. She should know better, and she shouldn't be sitting here making him feel sorry for her. She didn't want his pity any more than he wanted to give it.

"Yeah, well *should* can bite me. I do blame myself, and I will," Cecilia replied with a sneer, though it quickly faded. "I also know if it weren't for me, she would have had no one to call and she would have died. So, maybe it evens out. I don't know. They let me see her and she begged me to take Mak. He was with a neighbor and Layla didn't trust the woman not to hand him over to the state or Elijah." Cecilia blew out a breath. "She just needs help. She needs to get through this. She won't if Mak is with Elijah. Or gets shipped off into foster care."

"Cecilia, there are laws and rules and—"

"I had to. I *have* to do this for her. I know you only care about your precious laws and rules, but—"

"Those precious laws and rules are the difference between people like us and people like Elijah." And Ace. Though he didn't say that aloud, he had the uncomfortable feeling she heard it anyway.

"Except when those laws are going to hurt an innocent baby," Cecilia insisted. "If they give Mak to Elijah, being abused by the Sons is all that boy has to hope for. Is that what you want?"

Of course it wasn't. He didn't want that for anyone. It wasn't that he thought the law was infallible, that people didn't fall through the cracks of it. No rule could possibly apply to everyone in every situation, but this wasn't so much about following the letter of the law as it was about consequences.

"We could both get fired for this. You far more than me, but it risks both of our badges. We are sworn to uphold and protect the law, even when we don't agree with it."

She closed her eyes, then buried her face in her hands. Brady was rendered speechless and frozen in place for a good minute as Cecilia began to cry.

He'd never seen her cry before. She'd broken her arm falling out of a tree when she'd been thirteen and she hadn't cried. She'd yelled and cursed a blue streak, but she hadn't actually cried. At least not while he'd stayed with her and Gage had run to get help.

"Stop that," was all he could think to say.

She looked up at him dolefully, her face tearstained and blotchy. "You're such a comforting soul, Brady," she replied, her voice scratchy.

He didn't know what to say to that, since usually he *could* comfort people. Usually he knew what to say, how to calm and soothe so the work could be done. If she was anyone else he would have sat next to her on the couch and patted her shoulder, or leg or something. He would have known what to do with her tears.

But when it came to Cecilia, all those options seemed dangerous, and he didn't want to figure out why. He wanted to keep his distance.

"I'm sorry," she said on a sigh.

"You don't have to apologize for crying."

She rolled her eyes, wiping her cheeks with her palms. "I'm not sorry for crying. I'm sorry because I shouldn't have brought this to your doorstep. It's just, I had to think of the place Elijah would be least likely to look for Mak. He's going to suspect I had something to do with Mak's disappearance—Layla's neighbor will no doubt tell him who took him even though I bribed her not to. So, he'd know to look at the ranches, and I thought Nina and Liza made them too obvious," she said, speaking of her foster sisters who each had a child in her care—Liza her young half sister and Nina her daughter. "But you're just a bachelor in an apartment."

"Just a bachelor in an apartment," Brady repeated, surprised at how much that appraisal hurt.

"You know what I mean. Besides, you're hurt. He'd think less of you because of it. He'd think I'd want Mak with someone..."

"Who could actually protect him." That feeling of everything that had gone wrong since the gunshot wound settled deeper. He nodded toward his bad shoulder. "I *can't* protect him."

Cecilia stood again. Though the traces of tears were still on her face, there was something powerful about the way she stood, the way she angled him with a doleful look. "I'd take an injured Wyatt over just about anyone else. You'll protect just fine."

Brady didn't want that kind of responsibility thrust upon him when he was so… Things weren't right inside of him, and if he looked too closely at it, he had to believe it had begun even before the gunshot wound.

"Now, I have to get going. I don't think Elijah would have tracked me, but the longer I stay here, the more chances there are. I have to get back to the rez."

"You're just going to leave the baby with me?"

Her expression went grim, but it softened when her gaze landed on Mak's sleeping form cradled in Brady's arm. "Unfortunately, I'm a liability to him right now. I have to leave him with someone I can trust."

"They could track your car."

She shook her head. "We walked."

"You…walked. In this rain?"

"I had to. I had to." She cradled her head in her hands again, though she didn't cry, thank God. "I didn't want to tell you this. I didn't want to… It isn't fair, but I can't worry about that when Mak's *life* is in my hands."

She looked up at him—desolate, apologetic. His heart twisted, though he tried to harden himself against that. Against her.

"Elijah idolizes Ace. He worships him. He wants to *be* him, and not in that Sons way where they'll do whatever Ace did just for power. In a real way. In a real, dangerous way. He wants to take Ace's spot, and he'll do anything to get there."

Brady felt no surprise, no hurt. He should be feeling both of those things, but he couldn't manage it with a soft baby curled up against him. He could only tell her the truth. "I know."

"YOU KNOW?" CECILIA blinked at Brady, at that harsh, final way he said those two words. "How do you..."

His jaw was set, and that blankness he'd perfected enshrouded his whole being. But his eyes told a different story. There was anguish there. Had she ever seen anguish in Brady?

"I've had run-ins with Elijah for the past eight years," he said, not offering any explanation as to what *run-in* might mean.

"Eight years," Cecilia repeated, just barely keeping the shriek out of her voice, and only for Mak's sake.

"It was happenstance. The first time."

"The first... Brady. What is this?"

"I arrested him. My first arrest actually. When he realized I was a Wyatt...it became something of a game to him. To poke at me. To try and get arrested by me specifically. I assume to prove he could get away with things—and out of jail over and over again. Nothing serious, obviously, but he made it pretty clear he was the next iteration of my father and there was nothing I could do to stop it."

"How come none of you ever told me?"

He turned away from her, Mak still sleeping cradled in his arm like the baby belonged there. "I'm the only one who knows. I didn't think it'd ever touch anyone else."

"Brady." She was utterly speechless. He had a secret from his brothers. She hadn't thought it possible. Oh, there were emotional scars they all kept from each other, anyone who'd grown up in the midst of them knew that. But not actual...secrets.

She'd thought.

"What do you mean—"

"It isn't the point right now. The point is if you really don't want anyone to know you stole this baby—"

"I didn't steal—"

"Then you can't stay. Do you have anything for him? Diapers? Food?"

"Not yet, but there's a plan in place."

"A plan?"

She looked at him for a second, trying to wrap her brain around what was happening. What she was asking, and what he was saying. She'd known Brady would have to go along with some of this because he understood what it was to be a child in the Sons.

But she'd had no idea he had a connection to Elijah. That her life, which had just taken the most complicated turn, would be even more complicated by the man in front of her. She'd always considered him pretty uncomplicated.

"You can't tell me there's something you've never talked to your brothers about, that ties to this child, and then change the subject."

"Except I just did."

"Were you *born* this frustrating or did you have to work really hard at it?"

"Says the woman who brought me a stolen infant."

"He is not stolen," Cecilia replied through gritted teeth. She'd done the right thing, knew that with an absolute certainty that had no room for doubt, and yet he made her feel shame for not finding a legal way to do it. "What would you have done differently, Brady?" she asked, though she was half-afraid he'd have an answer, and a good one.

He looked down at the sleeping baby for the longest time, then finally sighed. "I don't know."

Thank God.

"What's the plan for baby supplies?"

"Felicity and Gage are going to bring you dinner… but it won't be food in the take-out bags."

"And you didn't take the baby to them because…?"

"Felicity has already had her Sons run-in. Besides, she…" Cecilia trailed off. She was usually an expert at keeping secrets, but that one had nearly slipped out.

Brady raised an eyebrow, waiting for her to finish that sentence.

"She has a job. They both do. I know you'd love to be back at yours, but you can't. Trust me, if I could leave him with Liza or Nina, I would, but I think Elijah would expect that. He's going to look at my sisters harder than he looks into the Wyatts, what with it being my friend's baby and all."

Brady's face was impassive. "He'll look at us too."

"Maybe he will, but I don't trust anyone else." She hated being so baldly honest with him, hated the fact she'd cried in front of him. But she would do it over and over again if it kept Mak safe.

And Mak *looked* safe in Brady's arm. Sleeping against Brady's chest. Brady was too noble not to do everything in his power to keep Mak safe. She had to believe he'd bend some rules for *this*, if nothing else.

"I have to go. Gage and Felicity should be here soon. I'll be in touch." She moved for Brady and Mak. She looked down at the baby she loved and thought about Layla's desperate pleas. All that responsibility weighed heavy.

This small, helpless life was in her hands, and the only way to ensure his safety was to leave him in someone else's.

They were capable hands, though. She looked up at Brady, whose face was way too close for comfort. She'd had a few drinks that night she'd kissed him. Still, she remembered the kiss far more clearly than she remembered the rest of the night. The impulse, the need.

That split second where shock had melted into response before he'd firmly taken her by the shoulders and pushed her a step back. He'd looked furious.

But there had been that moment. It had scared the life out of her. Just like all the things jangling in her chest right now, looking up at his hazel eyes and knowing he'd take all of what she put on his shoulders.

She stepped back and then turned and headed for the door. She couldn't let herself look back, or even go back to the dryer and get her damp clothes. She had to keep moving forward until Mak was safe. For good.

Chapter Three

Cecilia was right. Felicity and Gage showed up not too long after she left and disappeared into the night. Brady opened the door, keeping the sleeping baby in his arm out of sight.

Gage and his fiancée stood on the threshold. It was still weird. His twin brother and Felicity. Engaged.

It wasn't all that long ago Felicity had had a crush on *him*. Brady had never seen Felicity as more than a little sister. He respected Duke Knight too much to look at any of his foster daughters and see… Whatever it was people saw in each other that made them want to get married, apparently.

Gage had no such qualms. It hadn't taken more than a few months for him to settle into being with Felicity, to propose marriage.

"We brought you dinner," Felicity said, smiling as she held up the bag. They both stepped inside, carefully closing the door behind them.

Without hesitation, Felicity moved across the room to the counter that ran between his kitchen and his living room. She pulled things out of the bags.

"Diapers. Formula. Bottles. We've got some more

stuff in a bag in the car. We'll go down and get that later when I leave."

"You mean, when you both leave."

"Nah. I'm bunking," Gage said, settling himself onto the couch easily. "You don't expect to care for an infant on your own, do you?"

"I'm not sure I expect the two of us to do it either."

"We'll figure it out," Gage said, all smiles. Gage liked to lighten a situation with a joke, but this smile was more than just that. It was aimed at Felicity. It was love. "Go on now," he said to her.

"You should," she replied, clasping her hands together.

Gage patted the seat beside him and Felicity went and sat there. They both looked up at him expectantly like he had any idea what they were doing.

"What is with you two?" Brady grumbled.

Gage slung his arm across Felicity's shoulders. "We're going to have a baby," he announced, grinning. Not Gage's typical grin meant to hide everything going on inside his head. No, this was a true smile. True happiness.

Brady blinked. It took a while to realize his brother had not spoken in a foreign language, but had in fact delivered a clear, concise sentence in English. "A baby."

"Real as the one you're holding."

"But… You aren't married yet."

Gage snorted out a laugh and Felicity smiled indulgently.

"Did you need a lesson about the birds and the bees?" Gage asked, with a smirk.

"No. I… A baby. Congratulations."

"I hope you'll be able to say that and mean it at some point," Felicity said gently.

Brady stepped toward them. Irritated with himself for not handling this the right way. "I *am* happy for you. I'm just shocked. It's been a day," he said, looking down at the baby he held. Who wasn't his, but was now his responsibility.

Mak began to squirm, fuss, then cry. Felicity popped off the couch, holding out her arms.

"Can I?"

He handed off the fussing baby and rolled his shoulders, trying not to wince at the pain in his injured one. Felicity rocked and crooned to Mak and Brady looked at his twin brother. They'd shared everything, or close to it. Not everything. Not the separate ways their father had tortured them.

Not Elijah Jones.

"You're going to be a father," Brady offered helplessly.

"Not a word I've ever cared for, but I'll make it mean something different."

"I know you will." It was a strange thing, since Brady wasn't this infant's father, but Gage's news and words crystalized what Brady had to do.

He'd grown up in the Sons. Thanks to his oldest brother's belief in right and good, Brady had come out believing in right and good, as well. Jamison had sacrificed a lot to get Brady and Gage out of the Sons together. He'd given them the gift of hope, and the gift of each other.

So, Brady believed in laws and rules—the following of them, the enforcing them. Believed in good. In doing the right thing. Always. Because of Jamison's example. Because of Grandma Pauline and the privilege he'd had to escape from the Sons and grow up in a real home, with real love.

But if he truly believed in Jamison's example, it couldn't be just about upholding the law. It had to be about keeping this innocent life out of the Sons. Which meant accepting that he'd bend some rules to do it.

"Gage. I've been keeping a secret," Brady announced.

Gage's eyebrows went up. "What kind?"

"The Sons kind," Brady said grimly.

CECILIA WAS BEING WATCHED. She could feel it, and see the signs of it. Still, she went about her workday. Answering calls. Patrolling the rez. She kept her body on alert, ready to fight off whatever was watching.

But she didn't stop doing what she loved to do. Being a tribal police officer was everything to Cecilia, and even being watched wouldn't stop her from handling her responsibilities.

She didn't remember her early years here with her mother. Vaguely, in a misty kind of way, she remembered her mother. Mostly, she thought, because Aunt Eva had made sure of it.

But Aunt Eva had moved Cecilia off the rez and onto the Knight ranch after Mom had died. Cecilia had been loved, she'd had sisters, and the kind of stability her mother had never been able to give her. Aunt Eva had died a few years later, and that had been hard, but she'd had Duke and her sisters.

Still, she'd missed this feeling of community and belonging, of having a tie to her history. Maybe she spent an awful lot of time seeing the bad parts of the rez as a police officer, but she'd needed to figure herself out as an adult there. Right there.

She liked to think she had figured herself out, but this situation with Layla and Mak was testing everything she'd learned since joining the tribal police seven years ago.

No doubt she was being watched because Elijah knew she'd taken Mak. Which meant there was no hope of sneaking off to Brady's tonight and visiting him.

She'd be able to call, though. Elijah wouldn't be able to intercept that. So, she'd call and make sure Mak was okay and it would have to be enough for now.

It didn't feel okay. She'd left that sweet little boy with a stranger, and no matter how she knew that stranger was one of the best men on earth, Mak didn't.

Cecilia walked down the road toward her house. She waved at her elderly neighbor who liked to tell her stories about her mother. Cecilia wasn't sure they were true, but she liked listening to them nonetheless.

But when she saw her front door open behind the screen door, Cecilia didn't have time for neighborly chats. She hurried inside through the screen door, heart pounding in panic, hand on the butt of her weapon.

But it was no intruder. Cecilia's hands fell to her sides. "Rach?"

Rachel was in the kitchen, puttering around with making tea. She flashed a smile. "Hi. You're home early."

"What are you doing here?" It wasn't unusual for her cousin to visit, or to spend nights with her. Rachel was a teacher on the rez, and she split her time between here and the Knight ranch so she could keep an eye on her father when she wasn't teaching.

Normally, Cecilia loved having Rachel underfoot. She liked having company in this house. She loved her cousin, who'd been like a sister growing up.

But Rachel had been visually impaired since she was a toddler. Normally Cecilia didn't even think of it. Rachel knew how to get around. She'd dealt with the impairment since she was a child, and now she was an adult who could take care of herself.

Today, with someone watching Cecilia's every step, the last thing she wanted was Rachel here. She'd be vulnerable to whatever Cecilia had gotten herself wrapped up in, and more so because she wouldn't necessarily see an attack coming.

"Rach. I…" Rachel was Aunt Eva and Uncle Duke's only biological daughter. In some ways, Rachel and Cecilia had a closer connection because of that biology—cousins. Not because they didn't think of Eva and Duke's foster daughters as their sisters, but because the foster girls had always felt a certain kind of jealousy toward the biological relations.

It had never impacted their friendship, their love for one another. Cecilia would lay down her life for any of them, just as she knew they'd do the same for her. The four other Knight girls were her *sisters*. Luckily adulthood had smoothed over a lot if not all of those old resentments, but it didn't erase the special bond she had with Rachel.

Rachel was like her baby sister. She wanted to protect her. "You shouldn't be here today."

"Why not?"

Cecilia couldn't tell Rachel, no matter how much she wanted to. She'd already involved Gage, Felicity and Brady. Adding more people would be dangerous. For them.

The Wyatts and Knights had been through enough danger in the past few months.

And every time a Knight goes to a Wyatt man for help—what happens?

She shook that thought away. Liza had asked for Jamison's help, yes, and they were getting married and raising Liza's half sister. But they'd been together as teenagers.

Which was the same as Cody and Nina, who'd already eloped and were living in Bonesteel with their daughter after a teenage romance that had been broken up by the Sons, then rekindled again.

As for Felicity and Gage, well, that was a bit of a shock, and an odd pairing, but they made each other happy.

It was a parade of coincidences that had nothing to do with Cecilia and Brady.

"Cee, what's going on?" Rachel asked.

Cecilia forced herself to smile. "It's been a rough day." Rachel was already here, so sending her away wouldn't do any good.

"And you were hoping to be alone?"

"Yes. No. It's fine." Rachel was here. Whoever was watching Cecilia had seen her be dropped off and come inside. Cecilia just had to figure out a way to mitigate the situation.

She wanted to go to her room and cry. Or better yet, go home to the Knight ranch and hide from all of this.

But she wasn't weak—couldn't be, for Layla as much as for herself. She hadn't become a police officer because it was easy. She didn't want to help people only when it was comfortable.

Still, this was the biggest challenge of her career, of her *life.* Which meant doubts and fears and wanting to cry was normal. She just couldn't give in to those things. And she couldn't let on to Rachel that she felt them.

"You going to cook me dinner?" Cecilia asked, trying to infuse some levity into her tone.

"That's my lot in life," Rachel returned. "Cooking for a passel of helpless Knights."

"Helpless seems harsh. And not a word Sarah would appreciate." Sarah was the only one of the Knight girls who'd taken an interest in ranching, keeping her at home full-time. She was everything a ranching woman should be—tough, hardworking, and hardheaded.

"But it fits when she refuses to even learn how to make spaghetti. I won't be around forever."

A blip of panic bloomed in Cecilia's chest, but she kept her tone light. "Going somewhere?"

Rachel shrugged restlessly. "You got off the ranch. You have a life."

"You do too. You're here every summer and—"

"And driven by my daddy. Or my sister, which is fine. The rez isn't for me like it is for you. But maybe the ranch isn't either. Felicity is getting married and having a baby and I… Well, I'm never going to meet anyone the way my life currently is."

"Just get yourself into a life-threatening situation like Felicity did. Brady will follow in Gage's footsteps of falling for the damsel in distress and *bang.*"

Rachel wrinkled her nose. "Felicity was hardly a damsel. Besides, Brady is so…stuffy."

"He's not—" Cecilia clamped her mouth shut. Defending Brady's stuffiness was not what she needed to be doing right now. Luckily, a knock on the door made the subject easy to change. It was probably Mrs. Eldridge wanting to share another story. "Be right back," Cecilia said, heading for the front door.

She opened it, expecting her elderly neighbor's face and finding no one. She looked around. No kids giggling in the bushes playing ding-dong-ditch. Just…quiet.

She began to close the door before she noticed the small lump of fur on the porch. Cecilia stopped short as her stomach heaved.

There was an arrow sticking out of it, though the prairie dog clearly hadn't been killed by an arrow. Cecilia swallowed, forced herself to look, to pay attention.

Worse than the fact it was a tiny dead prairie dog, there was a note attached to the arrow with three simple words written on it in capital letters.

See you soon.

She stared at the scrawled words until her vision blurred. She was only shaken out of her frozen state by Rachel's voice.

"Who is it?" Rachel called.

"Just a prank," Cecilia replied, swallowing down the bile in her throat as her fingers closed over the butt of her holstered gun. "I'll be right back." She stepped outside, closing the door behind her. She scanned the area—houses, a quiet street, no one skulking around.

Anymore.

She let her hand fall off her weapon. She'd dispose of the dead animal, and then get Rachel the hell back to the Knight ranch.

Then she'd play Elijah's game, she decided grimly. It was the only way to keep him off Mak's trail.

Chapter Four

Brady was bleary-eyed the next day. Since Mak had slept so much before Felicity had left, he'd spent most of the night up and fussy. Brady and Gage had a list of instructions on baby care, but it had still taken three tries and watching a how-to video online to get the diaper on right. Making bottles and feeding them to the kid was pretty easy, and Mak was mostly a happy baby. Still, Brady was glad Gage was here with him. He wouldn't have survived the night without help—at least not with his sanity intact.

Brady had filled Gage in about Elijah…to an extent. There were things he hadn't told his brothers. The reasons he'd had for keeping Elijah a secret still existed, so keeping some parts of his story to himself made sense. Giving them the truth didn't mean giving them *all* the truths.

It bothered him that he hadn't heard from Cecilia. Not even a text. Shouldn't she want to check in on the baby? What was he supposed to do all day? Gage would go in to work, and Brady couldn't keep having visitors. If someone was watching or looking into him, the trail of people would be suspect.

Not as suspect as it might be at another time in his life. People had been traipsing in and out of his apartment to help out for too long now. Maybe it wouldn't send up any red flags, but there was no reason to chance it.

Gage had smuggled up a foldable, portable crib thing in his duffel bag. Mak was currently sleeping peacefully, and Brady knew he should try to catch a few hours too. Maybe even wake the baby up in an effort to keep him on a correct day/night schedule.

But he couldn't bring himself to wake up the boy when he looked so peaceful, and Brady's shoulder was currently throbbing too much to sleep through.

He went to the kitchen and made coffee, took some ibuprofen and the last of his antibiotics—praying they worked this time. He was tired of hospitals and doctors and being poked at and *hmm*ed over.

Gage came out of the spare bedroom dressed in his uniform. It was the last week he'd be putting that particular uniform on. He was transferring from Valiant County to Rapid City PD to be closer to Felicity's job at the National Park, and Brady still hadn't fully grasped the reality of not working with his twin brother anymore.

"I know you miss it," Gage said, either not understanding the pain Brady felt, or purposefully changing the topic to another painful one.

Brady gestured at his bum shoulder, tried to sound nonchalant. "Not much I can do with this."

"It's not permanent."

"No." It felt it, though. He was *supposed* to be back at work by now, not sidelined by an infection. He was *supposed* to go back to work knowing Gage would be there, but Gage only had three shifts left before his life changed.

He'd marry Felicity, have a kid, be a cop somewhere else.

If Brady looked too closely at all that, he might find the source of the low feelings he'd been having before he'd been shot.

So he decided not to look closely. "Coffee?"

"I'll just grab some at the station. I want to check on Felicity before my shift starts. She's feeling a little off in the mornings."

"It fits, you know, you two. I wouldn't have predicted it. But it works." Brady didn't know what possessed him to say it, but there it was.

Gage grinned. "Yeah, I know." His smile dimmed. "This Elijah…" Gage sighed. "What do I tell the others?"

Brady loved all of his brothers—would fight next to, protect and die for every single one of them. But he and Gage had escaped the Sons together, thanks to Jamison. They'd been together from the very beginning, and no matter how old they got, there was a deeper bond or connection between them. They were twins.

The fact Gage was willing to keep part of the story a secret from their brothers only made Brady feel guilty that there were still things Gage didn't know.

Brady didn't like to deal in guilt—he refused to wallow in it. If a man was guilty, he needed to change his actions to not feel guilty anymore. Maybe there'd been reasons to keep Elijah a secret, but the reasons had lost their weight.

"I think I should tell them. Everything. Together. I don't think Mak and I should stay here. I think we should hide. I just have to figure out how I can get him somewhere without being seen—and making sure Cecilia is okay."

"Heard from her?"

Brady shook his head.

"I don't like it. I know she can take care of herself, but I don't like it."

"Same, but I also know there's no getting through to that hardheaded woman." Brady didn't know why she had to be contrary for the sake of being contrary, but he knew she would be. No matter what he said.

"Let's set up a family dinner. Cecilia comes and you come. We find a way to hide Mak. If everyone descends on the ranch and there's no baby—it'll throw anyone off the sent."

"But how do we completely hide the presence of a six-month-old?"

Brady looked down at the baby in the portable crib. Mak was still fast asleep, little fist bunched and tucked under his chin, knees bent but spread wide-open. Felicity had brought some clothes so he was wearing dinosaur footie pajamas.

Though he didn't say anything, Brady could tell Gage was thinking about his future as a father.

"I hate to bring anyone else into it..."

Gage fixed him with a stern look. "I think you know everyone else would be more than happy to help keep that or any child out of the Sons' clutches."

Brady nodded. He knew it was true, but it was still against that moral compass he'd always listened to. Don't bring more people than necessary into Sons danger. Especially innocent ones.

"Gigi has that doll she carries around. She was even pushing it around in a stroller last time she was at the ranch." Brady shrugged away the guilt that was already poking at him. Gigi was four, and though she'd spent most of those four years in the Sons' camps before Liza and Jamison had saved her, she didn't deserve to be dragged back into it.

"Mak's a bit bigger than a doll, but it's not the worst plan," Gage said thoughtfully. "Especially if it's just between apartment door and truck. I bet Cody could find us a truck with tinted windows." Gage rubbed a hand over his jaw. "I'll make the arrangements."

"I can—"

"You got a baby to take care of. You take care of him. I'll take care of getting him to the ranch."

Brady looked at Mak's sleeping form. Completely and utterly defenseless. Brady might want to protect him all on his own, but this child deserved everyone he had in his arsenal.

"Let's do it as soon as possible."

THE NICE THING about Rachel staying with her was that Cecilia was so worried about Rachel, she didn't have much worry left for herself. She spent a sleepless night checking and rechecking the doors and windows in her house to make sure they were locked.

Bleary-eyed the next morning, she subsisted off coffee—which she normally didn't drink—and as much sugar as one human could possibly stand. She did a quick walk around the house looking for any more dead animals or threatening notes.

As she stepped back inside, Rachel was shuffling into the kitchen with a big, loud yawn. Rach had never been a morning person. Cecilia didn't know why she'd taken a teaching job that required her to do most of her work in the morning, but she could only assume Rachel loved it.

When Rachel stayed with her, she usually walked to and from the school with her probing cane. Cecilia would feel better if she had a support dog, but Rachel had lost hers last year to old age and hadn't had the heart to go through the process of trying to get a new one.

"I'm going to drive you in today."

Rachel frowned as she deftly poured herself some coffee. "Why would you do that?"

Cecilia had prepared for that question, and still she winced. She hated to lie to Rachel. So she didn't lie… exactly. "There's been some stuff going on. Pranks most likely, but the kind that can escalate if given the opportunity."

Rachel's frown deepened. "That's vague."

"It's a vague kind of thing. You'd probably be fine walking, but it'd make me feel better if I drove you."

Rachel sighed a little, and Cecilia half expected her to press the matter.

"It's too early to argue," she said around another yawn. "But I'm walking back after my classes are done."

Cecilia tried not to snap that it wasn't an option. Compromise was the best bet when talking to a stubborn Knight woman—she should know. "Can you walk with someone? Maybe one of your older students?"

"If you really think it's necessary."

"I do."

Rachel shrugged and sipped her coffee. "I'll be ready in about twenty."

While she waited, Cecilia rechecked the house to make sure it was all locked up. She called in on her radio to start her shift, and drove Rachel to the school.

The morning was warm but with a hint of a chill. Fall was starting its slow unfurling, usually Cecilia's favorite time of year.

It wouldn't be this year with Layla in the hospital and trying to keep Mak from Elijah and the state.

Cecilia pulled to a stop in front of the school, tried to bite her tongue and failed. "Don't forget to have someone walk with you back to the house. Someone you trust," she said as Rachel got out of the car.

Rachel paused. "You're going to have to tell me what this is all about."

"When I've got more information, I will," Cecilia lied.

Rachel made a disbelieving sound, then closed the car door and walked toward the school. Cecilia watched until she disappeared inside.

Once she was sure Rachel was inside, she did her normal rounds. It didn't appear she was being followed today, which was only a minor relief. Someone could start at any moment.

After her first call of the day, a minor vandalism situation that had been solved by involving the mother of the teenage perpetrator, she almost felt relaxed.

Of course, that was when she noticed her tail. She tried to act nonchalant, to keep doing her job, but every hour it was harder to pretend to be unaffected. If they were watching her, was Rachel safe? If they were following *her*, would Rachel be left alone?

If they were following her in particular, what would they do if they found her isolated and alone?

Nothing, because you're a trained police officer carrying many weapons with which to defend yourself.

She wanted to believe that voice in her head, to feel

sure of it, but she also knew she was *one* police officer. She didn't know how many people were following her.

She got another call, this time a disturbance, and had to put her stalkers out of her mind while she tried to make peace between two neighbors fighting about property lines. It was an annoying, pointless screaming match—but it was her job to smooth it over.

It took a full hour, and her head pounded by the time she was walking back to her patrol car. People who couldn't—wouldn't—compromise always gave her a headache.

She glanced at her watch. Rachel would have walked to the house by now. Maybe Cecilia could drive by the house, just check in on her. Pretend like she'd forgotten her lunch and was grabbing a sandwich so Rachel didn't get unduly worried.

The pounding in her head stopped, as did her breath and perhaps even her heart when she saw a piece of paper tucked under her windshield wiper. It fluttered in the breeze.

It could be anything, but Cecilia knew what it would be. Another note—sans dead animal this time.

Or so she thought, until she stepped closer to her patrol car. Under the wheel was a dead raccoon. As if she'd run it over.

But she hadn't.

No, it was another sign. Another warning.

Steeling herself for another threatening note, Cecilia pulled a rubber glove out of the glove pouch on her gun belt. She picked up the note and read it.

She's pretty.

Cecilia didn't let herself react outwardly. Inside she was ice, her heart a shivering mass of fear and panic. But outside, her hands were steady and her gaze was cool. She slid into the patrol car and set the note carefully on the passenger seat, pulling off the glove as she did so.

She turned the ignition, calmly eased on the gas. Keeping her attention evenly split between phone and road, she clicked Rachel's name on her phone screen and called.

The phone rang. And rang.

"Pick up," Cecilia muttered, swearing when it went to voice mail.

She was tempted to increase her speed, fly through the rez to her house on the eastern edge.

The only *she* the note could refer to was Rachel. It was a threat against Rachel, and Rachel was alone. Cecilia should have predicted this. Should have insisted Rachel…

What? Not teach her class? Hide away? It wouldn't have been a fair demand, but Cecilia still knew she should have done *something.*

Cecilia drove within the speed limit, watching her surroundings in case it was a trap. An ambush. Because threatening Rachel was only about getting to her. Rachel didn't know anything.

Or would Elijah think she did?

Cecilia swore again, increasing her speed, though not enough to draw attention. She came to a screeching halt in front of her house. If anyone was watching or following, she'd broken her calm facade.

Since she already had, she raced inside, hand on the butt of her weapon. But Rachel was safe as could be, curled up on the couch, earbuds in.

She pulled one out and looked at Cecilia's form with raised eyebrows. "Everything okay?"

Cecilia let out a ragged breath. This couldn't go on. She knew Elijah was purposefully trying to scare her, and giving in to threats and scare tactics would give him what he wanted, but…

She couldn't risk Rachel.

"I have to take you back to the ranch."

"Cee, you're being super weird this week." Rachel's expression wasn't confused so much as concerned. "You're going to have to tell me what's going on."

"I know. I know. Look… I'll explain everything when we're home. With everyone." She had to fill everyone in on what was happening. It was the only way to keep Rachel and Mak safe. To make sure none of them were brought unwittingly into this.

Because Elijah was clearly ready and willing to threaten everything she loved. She didn't have to live with threats. She should act.

"Let's get to the ranch," Cecilia said. "I just have to call someone to take the last two hours of my shift."

"I can have Dad—"

"No. No, I'm taking you."

"This is really bad, isn't it?" Rachel asked, twisting her fingers together.

Cecilia didn't mind lying to the people she loved if it saved them from worry, but she wasn't sure she had that luxury anymore. "It could be, if I'm not very careful."

Rachel slid off the couch, crossed the room and took Cecilia's hands in hers and gave them a squeeze. "Then let's be very, very careful."

Chapter Five

Brady had faced unhinged people with guns, big men so high on drugs nothing short of severe use of force would subdue them, and a slew of other scary, life-threatening situations in his tenure as a police officer and EMT.

He had been shot trying to save Felicity from her father, had hiked the Badlands trying to find his brother before Ace killed him. At eleven, he and Gage had almost been caught escaping the Sons.

Yet none of those instances had ever made him as bone-deep *afraid* as the one he found himself in right now. Even in the moment he and Gage had been found by a member of the Sons. Brady had been sure they'd be dead, but instead the man had let them go.

He'd been murdered days later.

Why this was more terrifying, Brady had no idea. Liza was buckling Mak into the doll stroller Gigi had happily pushed into his apartment. Gigi was now holding the doll, making funny faces at Mak in an effort to make him laugh.

Brady couldn't say he'd been particularly welcoming when Liza had shown back up in their lives a few months ago. As the oldest brother, Jamison had gotten all of them out of the Sons before he'd saved himself.

When he'd saved himself, he'd brought Liza with him. The Knights had taken her in and Brady had always assumed Jamison and Liza would live happily-ever-after.

He'd had to believe it was possible. Then Liza had left, gone back to the Sons, breaking Jamison's heart. Brady had never let on how much that had affected him. He secretly wondered if they weren't a little cursed by the Wyatt name.

It hadn't helped when Cody's girlfriend Nina, another Knight foster, had also taken off. Not to the Sons but to no one knew where.

A few months ago, Liza had reappeared, needing Jamison's help to save Gigi, her half sister, from the Sons. A while after that, Nina had shown up, gunshot wound and all, needing Cody's help to keep their daughter safe.

And somehow, they were all back together and happy with it. Like the time in between didn't matter.

As an adult, Brady didn't know what to make of it. How to reconcile the things he'd begun to think were impossible, with what was in front of him. Possible and growing.

"It'll be fine," Liza reassured him, likely misreading the course of his thoughts. "Gigi will be gentle."

Brady had no doubt Gigi would handle this with the utmost care. Even at four, she'd dealt with more than most kids should ever handle. "He could make a noise."

"He could," Liza agreed, crouching to give Mak's belly a tickle. The baby gurgled appreciatively. "But Gigi and I will be chatting loud enough to cover any baby sounds."

Brady looked dubiously at Mak. He'd heard the boy scream pretty effectively for all manner of reasons, but he was freshly fed, changed, napped and seemed happy enough.

"I didn't want to drag you and Gigi into this."

Liza stood slowly, and she fixed Brady with a look. "I don't know why it's so hard for you hardheaded Wyatts to realize we were there too. Even Gigi knows what it's like in there. We'd always be part of helping someone stay far away from the Sons. No matter the risk. Because it's always worth the risk to get out."

Brady looked down at Gigi, who looked up at him solemnly. She was wearing a pink T-shirt that said *Girl Power* in sequins.

She knew too much for a girl of almost five. Brady knew, from his own experience, that escaping at eleven had given him a determination to *help*. And even as young as Gigi was, he saw that in her expression.

"All right. Let's go."

GIGI WAS GIVEN the stroller. Liza pulled the hood down so that it obscured all but Mak's feet.

Gigi took her job as pusher very seriously, slowly and carefully pushing it forward. Mak babbled in baby talk, but Liza started talking over it. She asked Gigi about some TV show Gigi liked and Gigi began a monologue on the merits of each character.

God bless her.

He and Liza worked to carry the stroller down the stairs, Gigi admonishing them to be careful with her baby.

They reached the tinted truck they'd borrowed for the occasion. Brady tried to search the perimeter without giving away that's what he was doing. He didn't spot anyone, but that didn't mean they weren't being watched.

"Now, you go on and get in your car seat," Liza said to Gigi, helping her into the back seat.

"Make sure you buckle my baby in," Gigi ordered sternly. She was an excellent actress, though she did give Brady a little wink as she scrambled across the back seat.

Liza sighed as if it were a silly request. "Dolls can't get hurt, sissy. It's a little silly to—"

"You *have* to buckle her in. Just like me," Gigi insisted.

Liza rolled her eyes and nodded and bent down to pick up Mak. He made a little squealing sound, but Liza had angled her body so that it would be almost impossible for any watcher to see what was supposed to be a doll actually wiggle.

Gigi started singing the ABCs at full volume, clearly obscuring Mak's noises.

Brady could only watch in awe as these two people managed to enact his plan even better than he'd imagined, and without a hitch.

"Hop in the passenger seat, cowboy," Liza said as she closed the back door.

"I can drive."

"No, you can't."

Brady scowled at Liza. "I've been cleared to drive." His shoulder was feeling moderately better. He hadn't even wanted to cut it off when he woke up this morning. It was possible the last round of antibiotics had worked.

Liza snorted. "My truck. I drive. Those are the rules, bud. Now, you can stay here, or you can come out to the ranch for some of Grandma Pauline's potato casserole."

She was still playacting, and continuing the argument would make it seem more important than it was.

So he had to suck up his control issues and go to the passenger side.

If he grumbled to himself a little bit while he did it, no one had to know. He slid into the seat and closed the door and then let out a long breath. They'd gotten through one hard part successfully, he thought. Mostly because of the precocious little girl in the back seat.

Brady twisted in his seat, though it hurt his shoulder, and gave Gigi a big grin. "Gigi, you're a star."

She beamed at him. "I like pretending. And I like Mak. We're going to keep him away from the bad men."

"Yes, we are." He turned back to face forward. From inside the truck he could do a better scan. Still no one. He blew out a breath, warning himself not to relax. There was a lot that could go wrong yet.

But one hurdle had been jumped.

Gigi entertained Mak in the back seat by talking and making faces. Mak happily gurgled and drooled back. Brady let himself watch that, reminding himself that he wasn't so much bringing Liza and Gigi into danger as letting them help an innocent child escape it.

They'd both crossed Ace, in a way, and so they were already living under that specter—no matter how many high-security prisons the man was put in.

Brady scanned the highway in front of them, then glanced in the rearview mirror. There was a lone Chevy truck. Something about it didn't sit right with Brady.

"Speed up," he ordered.

Liza raised an eyebrow, not taking her eyes off the road. "Tone, Brady."

Brady didn't have the patience to sweet-talk Liza. "Not crazy speed. Just enough so I can tell if this Chevy is pacing us."

This time she didn't make a snarky comment, she did as he asked. When the Chevy kept pace, Brady inwardly swore. He kept that emotion out of his voice when he spoke. "We have a tail."

"That doesn't mean he knows we have Mak," Liza said calmly, reaching across the console and resting her hand on his arm. "In fact, if we can convince him we *don't*, all the better."

Brady flicked a glance at Mak in the car seat. Gigi had reached across the space between their car seats and was holding his squirming baby hand in hers.

"Then I guess that's what we have to do."

CECILIA DROVE OFF the reservation, watching her rearview mirror. She hadn't spotted a tail yet, but that didn't mean there wouldn't be one. Surely Elijah or his "buddies" hadn't simply stopped following her because she'd left the rez.

But she made it miles and miles down the mostly empty highway. If she saw a car, it usually passed her or was headed in the opposite direction. Cecilia knew she should relax as mile by mile they continued without being followed.

But she couldn't seem to let her guard down. Elijah wouldn't give up that easily, which meant he had something else up his sleeve.

If they made it home, she'd have help. Support. She didn't want to bring her family into this, but her family was already in danger. She might have felt guilty for getting involved in the first place, but all she could think of was Layla lost in the dark cloud that had become her life.

She'd begged for help. Begged for a chance to be a mother to her child.

There was no way Cecilia could have turned away from that, even to protect her family. And she knew, because of how her family was made up, because of what they'd been through, there was no way her family would have wanted her to turn away from Layla.

They'd *want* to be part of the fight too. So many of them had been impacted by the Sons. The Knights were not the kind to turn away from the dangerous just to save their own skin. The Wyatts even less so.

Thinking of it made Cecilia feel a little teary, so she focused on the road. On getting home.

When they weren't too far away from the turn off the highway to head toward home, both her and Rachel's phones chimed in unison.

Rachel sighed as she dug her phone out of her purse. "I really hate simultaneous texts. They're never good." She hit the button for her phone to read her text to her.

From: Gage Wyatt
Knight-Wyatt dinner at Grandma Pauline's. Everyone mandatory.

"Do they have to be so bossy?" Cecilia muttered. Then she frowned. "Brady can't go." How was he going to get out of "everyone mandatory"? Or would he try to bring Mak to the ranch? Surely not.

"Why can't Brady go and why do you know that?"

Cecilia didn't want to explain the whole thing yet. She only wanted to go through it once, hear all the disapproval once. And there was going to be some *serious* disapproval. "We'll get to that. Just text him that we're already on our way."

Rachel used her voice-to-text to send the reply.

Cecilia signaled the turn onto the gravel road that would lead them to the Reaves Ranch, Grandma Pauline's spread.

Instead of making an easy turn, Cecilia heard a faint pop, then the car rumbled and the steering wheel jerked. Cecilia almost lost her grip, but managed to tighten her hold at the last second. She braked a little too hard, fishtailing and tipping precariously into the gravel.

She managed to wrestle the truck to a stop, and quickly braked. She wasn't sure what had happened, but that pop she'd heard had sounded like a gunshot to her.

"Stay put," Cecilia ordered, heart hammering in her chest. Still, her voice was calm and authoritative.

She slid out of the driver's side, pulling the gun out of its holster but holding it behind her as she eyed the area. A big truck slowed to a stop on the highway a few yards away from where she stood.

She kept the gun out of sight as the driver leaned out of the window. "Need some help?" The man offered a pleasant enough smile. Cecilia was also certain she'd seen this same exact man come out of Layla's house with Elijah. It had been a long time ago, probably a year or two, but Cecilia rarely forgot a face. Especially one that ugly.

She fixed a grateful smile on her lips. "Oh, wow. That would be so great! I've got a spare in the back, but changing a tire can be such a pain."

The man smirked and shoved his truck into Park. It looked like there was potentially another passenger in the vehicle, but hiding. Cecilia pretended like she didn't notice. He slid out of the truck and there was a gun in his hand as a sleazy grin spread across his face.

Cecilia didn't pause, didn't hesitate. She kicked

straight out, landing the blow on the gun itself and knocking it out of the man's hands. She pivoted quickly, landing an elbow against his jaw. A nasty cracking sound whipped through the air and blood spattered.

Cecilia didn't have time to wince, she had to duck the returning blow. She didn't duck low enough and it clipped her head. Which probably hurt his hand more than her skull, all in all. But the satisfaction of missing most of that blow knocked her off-balance for the next, which hit her right in the cheekbone.

Pain flashed behind her eyes, but she could hear someone approaching. She didn't have time to even suck in a breath. She landed a knee to the man's groin and he let out a wheezing breath as he fumbled. She whirled to face the man, gun at the ready.

He had his own, so she shot, aiming for the arm so he'd drop the gun, ideally before getting off his own shot. She wanted both of them alive. They might have useful information after all, but if either of them went for Rachel, she'd shoot to kill.

The man howled and dropped his gun as the bullet hit him in the forearm. Blood gushed and he grabbed his arm and screamed.

The other man was crawling toward the dropped gun, still wheezing, but Cecilia quickly scooped it up off the ground. She held one gun on each man and eyed them with disgust.

"Elijah sent you."

"He'll keep sending more," the man she'd cracked in the jaw replied with a bloody smile.

"And I'll keep kicking their asses," Cecilia replied with a shrug. "Rach?"

"I already called Gage," Rachel said. Apparently she'd

gotten out of the truck during the fight, but Cecilia had been concentrating too hard on the men to notice. “He’s not on duty, but he called dispatch for us.”

The faint sound of sirens wailed in the distance, a sign that help was on its way. “Guess you boys are headed to jail,” Cecilia said with a smile. “Anything you want to tell me about your buddy?”

The one she’d shot had stopped screaming, but he looked at her with cold eyes as he gripped his bleeding arm. “He’s going to get you. He’s going to make you pay. He’ll only kill you if you’re lucky.”

A cold shiver went through Cecilia, but she didn’t let it show outwardly. “He’s going to try all those things, and he’s going to fail. Just like you.”

She tried to believe her own words, but the cold chill remained as she waited for backup.

Chapter Six

Brady paced the living room at Grandma Pauline's, Mak snuggled into his good arm. The boy cried if he tried to put him anywhere else or give him to anyone else. As it was, he wasn't sleeping. He was simply looking up at Brady with big brown eyes, a serious expression on his little face.

Brady didn't know what to do with *that*, or Gage currently coordinating officers to arrest the men who'd attacked Cecilia.

Brady didn't know if it was the same men who'd tailed him and Liza yet, but his tail hadn't approached them. They'd kept driving when Liza had turned off onto the gravel road to Grandma Pauline's.

Gage strode into the room, and Brady didn't even let him speak before he was peppering him with questions.

"Make and model?"

Gage's expression was grave. "Same as yours. They must have backtracked and waited for Cecilia and Rach."

Brady swore.

"It might not be such a bad thing."

At Brady's glare, Gage held up his hands. "You—the guy with the baby they're looking for—were deemed not as important. That means they don't know where Mak is."

"I don't think Cecilia and Rach being a target is a *good* thing."

"I didn't say that. I said it's not such a *bad thing*, because it means they don't know where the baby is. Based on the condition of the two men that tried to ambush Cecilia, I don't think we need to worry too much about her safety."

Brady grunted. He knew Cecilia could take care of herself. She was a fine cop, even if he didn't always agree with her methods. But it only took one second to be taken down. Since he was currently the one with a gunshot wound that wouldn't heal, he thought he had some perspective on the matter.

But it wouldn't do to argue with Gage over it.

"You want me to take him for a bit?"

Brady gave a shrug. "Seems to be happy here. Where are Cecilia and Rachel?"

"Should be any minute. Just finishing up giving their statements." As if on cue, they heard a commotion in the kitchen. Both men moved toward it.

Mak began to squirm in Brady's arms as he registered Cecilia's voice. Still, Brady stopped cold when he saw her.

Grandma Pauline was bustling around her while Duke Knight demanded to know what was going on. Sarah and Liza helped Grandma gather ice and towels, Tuck led Rachel to the table where Dev was already sitting with Felicity. Wyatt boys and Knight girls—men and women now—always working together to help each other.

"Well. Have that seat, right there." Grandma Pauline motioned to Cecilia, pulling an empty chair out from the table.

"I'm fine," Cecilia said, but she was already moving for the chair because God knew you didn't argue with Grandma Pauline.

Her eye was swollen. Blood was spattered across her shirt, but it didn't look like it was hers. When Gage had told him there'd been an incident, but Cecilia had taken care of it, Brady didn't realize "incident" meant fight and "taken care of it" meant gotten hurt in the process.

Something dark and vicious twisted inside of him. Brady couldn't say he fully understood it. He'd felt similar when seeing what his father or the Sons had done to his brothers—but this had a sharper edge to it. Not just anger. Not just revenge. Something closer to vengeance than he'd ever felt.

"You hand that baby over now," Grandma Pauline ordered Brady, already settling a bag of frozen peas over Cecilia's eye. "Nothing better for a few bumps and bruises than holding a sweet little boy."

It took everyone in the kitchen turning to stare at him to be able to move, to relax some of the fury on his face. To just…breathe. He met Cecilia's confused gaze past the bag of peas Grandma Pauline held under her one eye.

He had a flash of that ill-fated New Year's Eve kiss. Where she'd been laughing at him, poking at him. She'd kissed him out of some kind of…dare inside of herself, he'd always been sure.

But something had changed when she'd pressed her lips to his. A seismic shift inside him. An opening up of something he'd wanted closed. Maybe *that* was the moment everything had started to unravel for him.

It was all her fault, he was sure of that. If only he

could be sure of what was winding through him, tying him into knots.

Mak squirmed, started babbling somewhat intensely, breaking Brady from the moment. He looked down at the baby, then remembered what Grandma Pauline had told him to do. He moved to Cecilia's chair and had to kneel down so he could shift Mak into Cecilia's waiting arms. It required getting close, smelling her shampoo, brushing her arm.

Cecilia still looked at him, as if she could see into his thoughts. As if it shook her as deeply as it shook him.

He stepped away, shoved his hands into his pockets. He was losing it. Hallucinating due to lack of sleep. That was all.

That was *all*.

"I guess some of you need an introduction," Cecilia said softly, looking down at Mak. She took a deep breath, gazing down at him. "I had wanted to wait for..."

The door open and Jamison walked in with Cody and Nina and their daughter, Brianna.

"...the Bonesteel contingent," Cecilia finished.

If Brady wasn't totally mistaken, she seemed a little deflated everyone had shown up so quickly. But there was no more putting it off.

"You explain your end, then I'll explain mine," Brady said. Maybe it came out more like an order, but he wasn't feeling particularly genial or accommodating at the moment.

"Yours?" Cecilia asked, just enough acid in her tone to get his back up.

Brady'd kept one secret from his family, from Gage in particular, in his entire life. And it was this. Everything culminating with Cecilia needing his help.

Would he have ever told if she hadn't? If her problem hadn't connected to Elijah through this innocent child?

Would-haves didn't matter, because this—what was in front of him—was all he had. "Yes, my thing. My connection to Elijah, and why I think we need to disappear."

THE ENTIRE KITCHEN seemed to go supersonic. A cacophony of noises and arguments on top of arguments. Cecilia winced against the noise, then against the pain in her cheek.

Cecilia wouldn't admit it out loud, but a few of the jerk's blows had landed and left her feeling sore and achy. At least she'd taken the two guys out all on her own.

She had to admit, Grandma Pauline was close to being right. Mak in her arms didn't take away the pain, but it certainly shifted the pain to something bearable under a curtain of calm.

Mak was safe. No matter what happened today, no matter what would happen after today, Mak was safe. Maybe she should have brought him to both families in the first place, but she wouldn't beat herself up for what could have been.

He was here now, a large group of people ready and willing to fight for him.

Tucker had said, from his standpoint as detective, he thought the men she'd beaten up had followed Brady and Liza first. They'd given up on them and switched their gears for Cecilia and Rachel.

Which meant they didn't know Mak had been in the car with Brady the whole time.

She couldn't relax completely of course. Elijah would keep coming for her, and she was *here* now, which meant he or his men would be soon enough. But Cody had all sorts of security on the Reaves Ranch.

This was the safest place.

And Brady wanted to disappear? No way.

A piercing whistle stopped the competing voices. Grandma Pauline scowled at all of them. “Now. How are we ever going to know what to be mad about if we don’t let them explain themselves? Boy—”

“Cecilia needs to go first,” Brady said.

Usually it amused Cecilia that Grandma Pauline still called any of the Wyatt brothers *boys*, when they hadn’t been that for a very long time. Even more amused that they answered to it without complaint.

But Cecilia couldn’t find the means to be amused right now. Mak was in her lap, happily squirming and talking to her in his own language. His dark eyes were wide, trusting.

And she knew without a shadow of a doubt she’d have to leave him again.

But first she had to explain Mak and her dilemma to all the Wyatts and all the Knights. *Then* she’d have to figure out how to disappear…and lead Elijah away.

Which was going to be quite the challenge with *all* these voices in her ears.

“Let’s start with the simple question,” Grandma Pauline said. “Who’s the boy?”

Cecilia explained who Mak was, and how she’d taken him to Brady because she thought he’d be protected there. “He was protected too. Elijah knows I took him, but he hasn’t figured out where. So, that’s our priority. Keep Mak a secret.”

“We’re all here. How much of a secret could it be?” Brady demanded.

There was a dark, edgy look in his demeanor that was so…not Brady. Brady was the even-keeled one who never lost his temper. When Dev or Cody raged, when Jamison got too high-handed, when Gage didn't take things seriously enough and Tucker was too quiet, there was always Brady ready and willing to bring the disparate parts together to create a unit. There wasn't a dark side to Brady.

She'd never thought.

But this was…uncomfortable. Like realizing you hadn't known someone at all. He was fierce, angry, and just barely tethering his temper…all completely visible in his expression and his demeanor. It was like he'd become someone else altogether.

"I needed to let everyone in on what's going on so Rachel isn't caught in the crosshairs—"

Rachel made a noise as if to interrupt, but Cecilia kept right on talking, not giving her a chance to object. "There was a vague threat at the rez. She wasn't safe there, and no matter who drove her here or picked her up, they were going to get a target too. Elijah knows I took Mak, and he might not know where, but everyone I care about is going to be suspect. So everyone needs to know what's going on, but I need to go back to the rez and my job. If Elijah wants to follow me there, he can go right ahead."

"No," Brady said, as if he had *any* say in the matter.

"I think I'll make my own dec—"

"No," Brady repeated.

Cecilia couldn't physically react what with holding a baby and Grandma Pauline holding the bag of frozen peas to her face. So, she could only do her best to come off as dismissive and haughty.

"And you have some big, bad reason for telling *me* no as if you have any right?"

Still, none of that darkness clicked off. There was no calm, blank demeanor like she expected. Brady Wyatt was visibly, unrelentingly *angry*.

Cecilia found that amazing fact undercut her own anger at his high-handedness. Had she ever seen Brady react to anything with this edgy fury? What was causing it? Why did it make her heart flutter?

"Elijah Jones is a sociopath," Brady ground out. "And a murderer, though I've never been able to prove it. He's Ace's protégé in every way, and he's spent the past eight years screwing with me, in particular, because I had the misfortune of being the first Wyatt to arrest him. My first arrest."

"You know this Elijah," Jamison said, his voice deceptively calm. Cecilia didn't believe that calm for one second. "A Sons member, who idolizes our father, targeted you. And this is the first we're hearing about it? Some eight years later?"

Brady was quiet for a long while, some of his normal stoicism clicking into place as he stood there. But his hand was still clenched in a fist at his side. "I think he would have settled for any Wyatt," Brady said after a while, purposefully ignoring Jamison's question. "I got lucky."

"How?" Jamison demanded.

"Pranks, mostly. Threats, sometimes. Nothing concrete and nothing dangerous. It was just like being taunted. It's why I didn't tell you. It was nothing. Just annoying."

"Why?" Tucker asked quietly. "What's the motivation? Ace is in jail. There's no need to win his favor by screwing with one of his sons."

No matter who asked the question, Cecilia couldn't seem to tear her gaze away from Brady.

"I couldn't say. If I understood it, I would have already dealt with it, or told you all about it," Brady said. With every word he was locking down those pieces of his usual calm. The fire in his eyes banked, the tension in his arms released. He was still intense, but the anger had disappeared. Or he'd hidden it.

"He hasn't visited Ace," Jamison said. "If he's some kind of protégé there hasn't been a connection since Ace has been in jail."

Cecilia sighed. "He's not looking to *be* Ace. He's looking to *replace* Ace. He wants to lead the Sons." She let her finger trace Mak's cheek. "If he's targeting a Wyatt, it's not for Ace so much as Wyatts are the Sons' enemy. You guys are the biggest threat to the Sons right now. You took down Ace and Tony. They've been scrambling."

"Eight years," Jamison said gravely. "That hasn't been true for the eight years he's been harassing Brady."

"True. Maybe there's something more to it. I can't speak to that. I didn't know he'd been harassing Brady either. What I do know is that Elijah wants to take over the Sons. It's why he started recruiting on the rez. The more people he enlists, the more power he has in the group itself."

"Why didn't he start his own?" Dev demanded.

"Why start your own when you can take over one of the biggest, most dangerous gangs in the country? I'm not saying it's always been his plan. I'm just saying things changed when Ace was arrested. Elijah's been different the past few months—around the rez, with Mak's mom. He's already got his own little group. It's not enough for him. He wants the Sons." Cecilia looked down at Mak in her arms. He'd started to doze there, immune to the tension around him. "But first, he'll want *his* son."

Which was why she had to leave. Any security could be breached if there was a constant, determined effort to get through. If Cecilia stayed, Elijah would only work on it until he breached it—which wouldn't just put Mak in danger, but Grandma Pauline, her sons, the Knights and any of the little ones.

Cecilia couldn't stick around. And she couldn't let anyone know she was getting out and leading Elijah away. They wouldn't let her.

But the sooner she disappeared, the better off everyone would be.

So, she let the Wyatts and the Knights argue it out, and she kept her gaze and her attention on Mak in her arms. If it was going to be the last time she saw him, held him, she was going to soak it all up.

"So, it's settled then," Jamison said, always the de facto leader. "Everyone stays put until we have a better read on what Elijah Jones is planning, or even better, until we can find a reason to arrest him."

Cecilia tore her gaze from Mak and found Brady's. The anger was back, but he didn't argue with Jamison. He just stared right back at her as if he knew what she was planning.

But he couldn't, and even if he did, he wouldn't stop her.

No one would.

Chapter Seven

"She's going to bolt." Brady found himself pacing. He'd already not felt like himself for months now, but these past few days had taken away all his usual coping mechanisms. All the filters and layers he put over his true feelings so he wasn't…

Well, his father.

This morning was worse. Everyone seemed content to just hang around Grandma Pauline's, pay extra attention to Cody's security measures, and wait.

They couldn't just *wait*. Cecilia would do something stupid. She was too rash. Too…her. She was going to try to lead Elijah away and Brady seemed to be the only one who realized it.

"Cecilia knows better," Tucker insisted, shoveling eggs into his mouth. He was sitting at Grandma Pauline's kitchen table dressed for his work as a detective. Slacks and a button-up shirt. Though he didn't live at the ranch, he would be staying close just like everyone else while they tried to protect Mak from Elijah.

"She most certainly does not," Brady returned. "Are you even listening to yourself?"

"She's a cop."

"She's a…" Brady didn't say "loose cannon" out loud

because it sounded like a bad line from some '80s action movie, but she was.

She always had been.

"I think you're underestimating her," Tucker said, with just enough condescension Brady ground his teeth together.

Still, he bit back the words he wanted to say. Because *no, you are* was childish, even if it was true.

If no one would listen to him, he'd have to take matters into his own hands. He gave half a thought to trying to lure Elijah away himself, but Brady didn't think Elijah would go for it. Cecilia had been the one to take Mak. Cecilia would be his target. Elijah was too smart to think Brady was doing anything except setting a trap.

Which meant Brady had to get Cecilia and Mak away from here—without Elijah being any the wiser.

"How's the shoulder?" Tuck asked around another mouthful of eggs.

"Fine," Brady replied without thinking about it. He gave it a little shrug. He had to admit, it hadn't been paining him as much lately. Maybe the third round of antibiotics had actually done what they were supposed to.

"When's your next doctor's appointment?"

Brady gave Tucker a puzzled frown over his sudden interest in doctor appointments. "Next week."

Tuck nodded. "Then I'd make sure you don't miss it," Tucker said blandly, moving away from the table. He took his plate to the sink and rinsed it, and left the kitchen without another word.

Brady frowned after him. It had been a subtle *don't go anywhere.* As if by being subtle, Brady wouldn't read the subtext and be irritated his younger brother was trying to tell him what to do.

Grandma Pauline breezed in, a basket of eggs hooked to one arm. She gave Brady a critical look. "You're not so peaked looking."

High praise, Brady figured. "I'm doing better."

"Good," she said firmly. "Now, when are you going?"

"Going?"

"Don't think I can't see through you, boy. And that hardheaded woman. You've both got it in your head to hightail it out of here. Neither of you can let the other do it alone. So. When do you sneak out?"

"I..." He could lie to his grandmother. He'd done it before. It just so rarely worked, and she seemed approving. "I was just going to stop her when she did, then convince her the three of us should—"

"No, you'll leave the boy here," Grandma interrupted matter-of-factly.

"But—"

"The safest place for that boy is here, especially if both you and Cecilia take off. Just like when we had Brianna while Cody and Nina were off."

"Only because they got ambushed on their way back from the jail, Grandma. They wouldn't have left Brianna by choice." When Ace had sent men to threaten Nina and Brianna, Nina had come to Cody for help. They'd been separated from their daughter and trying to survive Ace's men, but not because they'd chosen to be.

"They would have left her with me, and would still, if it was the best way to keep her safe," Grandma returned, as if that was just fact, not her opinion. "And Brianna was older. She could hide and be quiet. This little one can't do that. And you can't move fast enough carrying formula and diapers and a crib. Not if you're going to catch her."

"Catch her?"

Grandma Pauline rolled her eyes. "You don't think that girl is already making plans? She's not going to wait to skulk away under the dark of night. She would have done that last night, if so. My guess is she's going to come up with an excuse to run to town, make sure no one goes with her, and hightail it from there."

Brady stared dumbfounded for a moment, because of course that was exactly what Cecilia was going to do. He'd expected more subterfuge, but she hardly needed it when she was an adult woman who would need to do some things without supervision.

"Packed you a bag."

Brady blinked at his grandmother. "Why didn't you kick up a fuss last night? Tell them that their plan was wrong?"

"What's the point in arguing with all you fools? You're going to do whatever you want anyway. You take that truck Liza borrowed. Bag is packed with supplies. Don't you let that girl out of your sight. You can each take care of yourself, there ain't no doubt about that. But this is dangerous, which means you need to take care of each other. And trust us to take care of the little one."

It was hardly the first time in his life his grandmother had helped him, or seen through him or the rest of them. It was hardly the first time she'd known exactly what to say, and when to say it. He'd been blessed to have her for these twenty years he'd been free of the Sons.

Brady pressed a kiss to his grandmother's cheek. "I know you don't like to hear it, but we would have been lost without you. Lost. Separate. Maybe like him."

Grandma only grunted and shooed him away. "Not

one of you has got it in you to be like him, not truly. Be better off if you believe that. Now go."

Timing was everything when a person was planning their unapproved escape.

Okay, escape was maybe an exaggeration. Cecilia wasn't being held *prisoner.* She was just trying to avoid her family's arguments.

So, that morning, Cecilia waited until Duke and Sarah were out with the cattle. Cody, Nina and Brianna had stayed at the Knight ranch last night to put up some extra security measures, but Nina and Brianna had gone over to the Wyatts' this morning so Gigi and Brianna could have their homeschool lessons. Cody was currently installing something on the entrance gate. All Cecilia had to do was wait to hear Rachel turn on the water to the shower, and she could slip out.

They'd decided it safest if Mak stayed at the Wyatt ranch, since they already had a crib and a few baby supplies that Brady had brought in with his backpack. There wasn't anything at the Knights', so it would have required bringing baby things in and out—which could have been detected by anyone who might be watching.

Cecilia could have spent the night at the Wyatts', but she'd decided to say her goodbyes last night. That way she could get a handle on her emotions for today. Today required strength of spirit, not doubts born of the selfish need to be with Mak.

A quick note, a careful route across the property to the back exit—avoiding the pastures Duke and Sarah were in today—and she was home free.

Her gut twisted at the idea of causing her family worry, but worry was better than harm. No amount of words or arguments would allow them to accept Elijah's prime target was *her*, which meant she needed to be far away.

So, as she'd learned to do as a teenager, instead of fighting the brick wall of a united Wyatt-Knight front, she'd sneak away and do the thing she knew was right.

She *knew* it was right. If only she was in danger, maybe she'd agree with her family. Teamwork was better than going off on your own.

But it wasn't about her. It was about Mak.

So, Cecilia wrote her letter. She decided not to leave it in the kitchen, just because it would set the alarm too quickly. She needed a head start so they didn't think they could come after her.

Mailbox. Perfect. She'd slip it in on her way out. Duke or Sarah didn't usually head out that way until the end of the day. Plenty of time.

Satisfied with her plan, she slung her bag over her shoulder and slid the letter into her pocket. If she happened to get caught, she'd just pretend she was taking some stuff for Mak over to the Wyatt ranch. Then she'd try again tomorrow.

She heard the groan of pipes as Rachel started the shower. She took a deep breath and reminded herself she knew she was right. This was the right thing for Mak and that was all that mattered.

She slid out the door as quietly as she could. Keeping her eyes on the horizon on the off chance Sarah or Duke would unexpectedly come back to the house before lunch. Or one of Dev's dogs—he'd insisted Sarah start keeping them with her—might start barking.

Nothing. She moved quickly and stealthily to the

other side of the house where her truck was parked—purposefully away from views of the doors or windows.

But she stopped short when she turned the corner and spotted Brady leaning negligently against the hood of her truck.

He tipped down his sunglasses, clearly made a mental note of her bag, and then smiled. "Going somewhere?"

For a few full seconds all Cecilia could do was gape. Surely…this was a coincidence. He wasn't sitting there because he knew what she was up to.

She kept walking toward her truck, trying to keep the suspicion out of her tone. "Just gotta run some errands. I left in kind of a hurry yesterday," she said, trying to sound casual.

Brady gestured to the tinted out truck Liza had driven to the ranch. He'd parked it behind hers so she couldn't back out. "I'll drive you."

She frowned, clutching the strap of her bag. "Why would you do that?"

"You can't get very far on that doughnut tire, and I'm assuming you want to go a little farther than the rez."

He laid that accusation so casually, she almost agreed. She caught herself in time, harnessing her indignation that he'd clearly seen through her. "I don't know what you're talking about."

"Sure," he agreed easily. "But I'll drive you all the same."

"I don't need a chauffeur, Brady. Go back to the ranch and rest up that bum shoulder of yours."

He rolled the shoulder in question, then shrugged. "Feels plenty rested to me. Think I kicked that infection this time around. Isn't that handy?" He gestured at her. "Might be kind of hard to see around that swollen eye. Probably be better if I drive."

She didn't know what to do with…whatever he was doing. The way he was acting. "Did you and Gage switch bodies or something? Is that why Felicity jumped ship so quick?"

"Careful," he warned, and his tone had an edge to it that reminded her of last night when he'd been so *angry*.

His expression was calm, though. And she felt two inches tall for making a comment about Felicity's old crush on Brady, when it was clear to anyone who paid half a second of attention she genuinely loved Gage.

"Go away, Brady," Cecilia said, her control slipping. This was hard enough without having to fight him. "I've got stuff to do, and it's got nothing to do with you."

"That'd be easy, wouldn't it? But we both know it isn't true."

"Whatever," she muttered. She wasn't going to argue with him. She was going to get in her truck and leave.

She stalked toward the door. Brady stepped in front of it. Her temper snapped and she gave him a shove.

He didn't budge.

"I'm not afraid to hurt you, Brady," she seethed through gritted teeth.

"Try me."

The arrogance in his tone had her lashing out without thinking the move through. He dodged the elbow she almost landed on his gut, then grabbed her arm and moved it behind her back like he was getting ready to cuff her.

Her temper didn't just snap now, it ignited. She kicked out, landed a blow to his shin, which weakened his grip. She wrenched her arm away and swung.

He blocked the blow, feinted left well enough she fell

for it. Then he had both her wrists in his grasp and held them against the truck behind her so she was trapped.

They both breathed heavily and Cecilia didn't fight the hold. She could get out of it, but as much as she didn't have any qualms about sparring with Brady, she didn't feel right about actually hurting him—which she would have to do to escape his grip.

She took a deep breath, tried to turn the fire of fury inside of her into ice. She angled her chin toward his wounded shoulder. "I could get out of this in five seconds flat if I fought dirty." Even if he was finally healing, one well-placed strike to his wound would have him on his knees.

He didn't even blink or wince. "Not if I fought dirty right back."

"You?" She snorted, even though his hands were curled around her wrists and his body was way, way, *way* too close to hers. She could feel his body heat, and he didn't have to be touching her anywhere but her wrists to get the sense of just how big and strong he was.

And this was really not to the time to wonder what it would feel like if he *was* touching her anywhere else.

Except, then that's exactly what he did. Inch by inch, he pinned his body to hers—her back against the metal door of her truck, her front against…him. And she wasn't sure which was a harder, less giving surface.

It was meant to be threatening, maybe. A show of power, and that he was bigger and stronger than she was. But she didn't think it had any of the desired effects, because what she really wanted to do was press right back. Even with his hands tight around her wrists.

Brady's face was too close, and he had that fierceness from last night that, God help her, it really did something for her. She liked he had some secret edge. That he wasn't perfect or so easily contained.

Which was not at all what she should be thinking about. She should be fighting dirty. Getting out of his hold, even if it meant hurting him. But she couldn't bring herself to.

"He knows you took Mak," Brady said, his voice a razor's edge against the quiet morning. "I get it. He's not going to stop until he figures out what you did with him. But his men also followed me and Liza. Maybe they gave up, but Elijah has some unknown beef with me too. We're in the same boat. Stay, we lead him to Mak. It can't happen. But if we leave? We lead Elijah away."

Cecilia had to swallow to speak, to focus on his words instead of the heat spreading through her. The throbbing deep inside of her. "Just what are you suggesting?" she managed to demand. Or squeak. She wasn't sure which sound actually came out of her mouth.

"That we do this together, Cecilia. Lead Elijah away, and take him on. While having each other's back."

Chapter Eight

There was a faint buzzing in Brady's head, and he was having a hard time not letting it take over. If it won, this wouldn't be about Elijah or danger or anything else. It would be about *them.*

But today wasn't about the surprisingly soft woman he was currently pressing against a truck. Today was about keeping Mak safe. Keeping Cecilia safe.

Seriously, *why* had he pushed her against the truck? To prove some point that he was physically stronger? He was well aware Cecilia could hold her own if she was giving it a full 100 percent. She had gone easy on him in their little tussle because of his shoulder, just like he'd gone easy on her because neither of them wanted to actually *hurt* each other.

So, why was he crowding her against the truck as his body rioted with…reaction? A heat that *should* have warned him of danger. He shouldn't want to lean into it, explore it.

Relish it.

He realized belatedly he was leaning in, getting closer. He could smell her, feel her. What would it matter if he—

That just could not happen. He was *not* this person.

He released her abruptly. Which wasn't his best move. It showed her way more than he wanted to admit. He stopped himself from scraping his hands over his face. Stopped himself from gulping for air like he wanted to. He tried to picture himself encased in ice so any and all further reactions were frozen deep inside of him.

What was wrong with him? He felt like there was some rogue part of himself sprouting up and refusing to be caged away like it usually was.

He wasn't attracted to Cecilia. She irritated him. She challenged him. That *infuriated* him—it didn't make him want her. This was simply an aberration. A…hallucination.

Something real and enticing for the first time in a long time.

Which didn't matter. Not now. What mattered was outwitting Elijah.

"Get in the truck, Cecilia," he managed to say, without sounding like he felt. Raked over coals. Shaken until his brain was mush. "Or we'll be found out before we leave the ranch."

Cecilia stood there, still pressed to the truck like she was afraid to move. Which was ridiculous. Cecilia was never afraid. Certainly not of him. She'd fought right back when he'd tried to stop her from getting in her truck.

But he could see her pulse rioting in her neck. She breathed unevenly, lips slightly parted. And she didn't move.

Everything inside of him *ached* with something he refused to acknowledge or name.

"No one else knows?" she finally asked, her voice

more or less a whisper. Infused with suspicion, but a whisper nonetheless.

Brady forced his body to level out. When he spoke, it was controlled. Even. "Grandma Pauline. She's the one who convinced me to go with you, not stop you." And not go on his own. But Cecilia didn't need to know he'd had the same plan as she did. "She said we should leave Mak."

Cecilia visibly swallowed as if that hurt, but she nodded. "He'll be safer here. Away from me."

He could *see* the way that pained her, just like he could feel an echoing of that same pain inside of him. There was something about taking care of Mak that had crawled inside of him, lodged somewhere near his heart.

"He'll be safer away from us," Brady corrected, because he needed the verbal reminder himself. "It might not connect, but I'm Elijah's target too."

Cecilia nodded, as if agreeing. Then she pushed herself off the truck and went to the one with tinted windows that he'd been driving. They both climbed inside in silence, buckled in that same heavy absence of noise.

Brady spared Cecilia a glance as he turned the key. She had her hands clasped in her lap and she looked straight ahead. Long strands of black hair that had slipped out of her braid framed her face. He'd known her since he'd come to Grandma Pauline's. She was as familiar to him as his brothers, more or less.

But he found himself staring, when he had no business staring. When he had no business being…affected by said staring.

"It'd earn him respect," Cecilia said abruptly. "Elijah. For him to screw with one of those Wyatt brothers who left, who went into law enforcement and thumbed their nose at their father, at the Sons—"

Brady jumped on this thread he could follow without getting as lost as he felt when he was staring at her. "Who got Ace thrown in jail. There are plenty of men in that place who like Ace. Hell, worship Ace. He's the best leader they've ever had. If Elijah takes a chunk out of us, my bet is he gets the respect of those who follow Ace even now." Brady nudged the truck forward, watching the surroundings to make sure they weren't spotted.

"But us leaving together… Doesn't that prove Mak is here? That we left him here?"

"Depends. I think we can make it look like anything, if he doesn't know where Mak is right now. We can make it look like we have him. We can make it look like we've taken him somewhere else. We can even make it look like we split up, so he won't know which thread to follow. He'll have to split resources thinking we're apart, but we'll be together the whole time."

"We," Cecilia echoed. She squeezed her hands together. If it were someone else, he might have attributed that gesture to fear.

"We," Brady said firmly, because at least in that he was sure. "Whatever his reasons, Elijah's targeting us both right now. He followed us both. So it's a we. I want to keep Mak safe as much as you do."

"Is it that bad?" She squeezed her eyes shut and shook her head. "I don't know why I even asked that. Of course growing up in a gang is *that bad.*"

"I wouldn't know it was that bad if I hadn't gotten out. I knew it was… Wrong isn't the right word, because when you have nothing else it's not wrong. It didn't fit, though. It didn't seem right. And Jamison, well, he could remember living with Mom at Grandma Pauline's. He'd had that glimpse of different. He made us all believe in it. Believe we deserved it. Mak wouldn't have that."

Cecilia inhaled sharply. "Would it have been different? If you didn't have Jamison?"

She'd never know how often he'd asked himself that. How often he'd wondered if Jamison was the reason he'd followed the straight and narrow against the bad that must be inside him. How often he'd hoped it was something deeper, something good inside of *him*.

But he could never be sure. "I'll never know," he said, pulling out onto the gravel road on the back of the Knight property. It would lead them to the highway. And then…

"Where are we going?" She sounded more like herself again. In control and ready to fight whatever came their way.

"That's an excellent question. Got any ideas?"

CECILIA GAPED AT BRADY. "I'm sorry…you don't have a plan?"

He gestured her way, though he kept his gaze on the road. "This is the plan."

"This isn't a plan. It's not even half a plan. It's the teeny tiny beginning of a plan." She forced herself to take a breath so she didn't start sounding panicked, even though that was the exact feeling gripping her throat. "*I* had a plan. You come in and ruin my plan and then… I can't believe you of all people would do something without thinking it through."

"I've thought it through. We find someplace to hunker down. We contact Elijah and see if he'll come after us. Then we work together to arrest him."

"*Someplace* is not a plan. *See if* is not a plan!"

Brady rolled his eyes. "We'll work it out. Do you think my apartment is far enough away?"

"No. Besides, too many innocent bystanders in an apartment building. Same with my place. Too close to neighbors he could use."

"And where were *you* going to go?" Brady asked loftily.

"Motels. Crisscross around. Make it look like I'm running, trying to lose him." She threw Brady a condescending glance that he didn't see since his eyes were on the road. "You can't contact him. That's too obvious."

Brady shrugged negligently. "I think Elijah runs toward the obvious."

"Maybe. But he doesn't think *we* will. He reacts to fear." Cecilia looked out of the windshield at the highway flying by, the rolling hills, patches of brown from the fading summer heat against the green, slowly morphing into the landscape of the Badlands. Rock outcroppings in the distance that would take over the whole horizon. She thought of the dead prairie dog, the dead raccoon, the simple notes. "He wants me afraid. If we act like we're running, he'll take the bait. Though I wouldn't mind leaving a few dead animals for *him* to find, I think acting like we're on the losing side is what we should do."

"He left you dead animals?" Brady asked, and for a second she was fooled by the deadly calm in his voice, so she simply shrugged.

"That's serial killer behavior."

She turned at the cold edge of fury in his voice. It was mesmerizing, seeing anger on Brady. She knew he'd been angry before. It wasn't that she'd ever been truly fooled by the careful armor he placed over himself. It was just she couldn't understand why it had broken down *now*. The Wyatts had been through some bad things the past few months.

Maybe it was the gunshot wound, and the infections. Just frustration bubbling over. Maybe it had nothing to do with this.

With you.

Uncomfortable with that thought, she pushed it away and focused on what he'd said rather than how he'd said it. "Like you pointed out last night, he's a sociopath. Though I don't fully understand how so many sociopaths can congregate in one group, follow one leader. How do people like Elijah and Ace get whole swaths of men following them? Willing to kill for them?"

"They normalize each other's behavior and lack of feelings. That's how groups like the Sons form. People with all sorts of mental problems normalized by each other, exacerbated by each other. They're told the outside is the enemy. If they're miserable, if they're poor, if they've been hurt—the outside is the reason for it. The outside is the reason they're miserable, and if they strike out enough they'll finally be safe and happy."

It made a sad kind of sense.

"But make no mistake, Cecilia, people like Ace and Elijah are worse. They know what they're doing. They know how to manipulate people. Maybe they have their own warped view that the world has harmed them, so they have to harm the world, but there's nothing to feel sorry for."

"Did you mistake me for someone with sympathy?"

He flicked a glance her way. "You aren't without sympathy."

"You know how it is. You're a cop long enough, it starts to eat away at you. Hard to watch people make bad decisions over and over for no good reason and not develop a certain kind of cynicism." She wasn't sure why she said that. She wasn't in a habit of admitting her cynicism—though she knew Brady would understand, would have to. He'd been a cop a few years longer than she had, and he didn't have the same connection to the people he served as she did.

"I think everything you did for your friend, and for Mak, proves that whatever you might feel on a bad day isn't who you actually are. That's not a criticism. If you lose all your humanity, badge or no, you're no different than Ace or Elijah."

The way he said it had her stomach twisting painfully. "Do you worry about that?"

He stared hard at the road, his grip on the steering wheel tightening before she watched him carefully relax it. "Sometimes."

"You shouldn't. I don't know a better man than you, Brady."

"Duke," he replied automatically, trying to defer the attention to someone else, it was clear.

"Duke's a great man," Cecilia agreed. She didn't like feeling soft, didn't like this need to soothe. But Brady brought it out in her, because she knew a lot of men and Brady *was* the best. Whether he wanted to believe that or not. "He's a wonderful father or father figure. But he's a crusty cowboy with a chip on his shoulder who still hasn't quite accepted his daughters are grown women. Jamison is like that too—he looks at all of you, and all of us like we're still kids. It doesn't make them bad people, it just… Well, you don't do that."

He shifted uncomfortably, like he didn't know what to do with the praise. She doubted any of the Wyatt men were particularly used to having nice things being said to their faces. Grandma Pauline was amazing—but she wasn't *complimentary*.

"I guess that's just being the middle child. One foot in each door. Understanding the oldest side and the younger sides." He slid her a look. "Or maybe not, since technically you're in the middle and you still treat Rachel and Sarah like babies who need protecting."

Cecilia frowned. "I do not."

"Okay."

She stared at him in shock. He was *patronizing* her. "Don't *okay* me. I do not treat them like babies!" She was being *nice*, and he was turning on her. The jerk.

"You're right," he added, with almost enough contrition to mollify her. "You treat them, and Felicity, come to think of it, more like toddlers than babies."

Her mouth dropped in outrage. She couldn't believe Brady was criticizing her. And over how she treated her sisters. Which was not any of his business, and certainly not an area he was an expert on. "I was being *nice* to you."

"Yeah, and I'm telling you the truth," he replied, still so casual as if they weren't arguing at all. "Which you know is the truth or you wouldn't be pissed off." He nodded toward the road sign for the next three towns. "You have a motel in mind?"

Cecilia crossed her arms over her chest, tried not to feel petulant. She did *not* treat her sisters like toddlers. She was just protective of them, because she knew all the awful that was out in the world. Who cared if Brady understood that or not? They had far bigger problems at hand. "The Mockingbird in Dyner."

Brady winced, but nodded. "All right. Hope you brought your hazmat suit."

Chapter Nine

Brady drove toward the scummy motel Cecilia had named. It wouldn't have been his choice, but he understood Cecilia's thinking. They had to look like they were trying to evade notice. A cash-only, by-the-hour motel room would be just the place. He'd have to put his comfort aside.

The trick was going to be to get Elijah himself to come after them. He likely had a never-ending supply of men who'd take orders under the right incentives or threats. Brady figured they could fight off attacks, as long as Elijah didn't know where Mak was, but that would be the constant, overwhelming worry.

Brady slowed the truck about a block away from the Mockingbird. He turned to Cecilia, who was still pouting by his estimation. He didn't know why that *amused* him. It should be irritating or frustrating or *nothing*, but something about tough, extreme Cecilia pouting over being called overprotective made him want to laugh.

This was very much not the time or place for that, so he focused on the task at hand. "I think you should go in there alone. We should try to make it look like you're running away by yourself. We're more likely to lure him out that way."

Cecilia blinked at him. "That's what *I* was going to say."

"Then we're on the same page."

She turned in her seat to face him, to study him as though she were somehow confused by their agreement. "You're not going to pull the macho you-need-a-man-to-protect-you card?"

"No, in part because you don't need a man—you just need a partner. But also in part because, if Elijah is anything like Ace, he thinks less of women. Which means you being on your own is going to be impossible for him to resist. It won't occur to him he could be beaten by a woman. He's more likely to go after you, most especially if he thinks you're alone."

She nodded grimly. "True enough. So, I'll walk the last block, and you'll stay here. Can you do that?"

He nodded, though the idea of her walking that last block on her own made him edgy. "You'll have to watch for anyone who might be following you. Have your phone and your gun and—"

She rolled her eyes. "*Duh*, Brady."

"Duh. Really?"

She shook her head, digging through her backpack to pull out a holster. She slid her gun inside. "I'll walk over and check in. I'm thinking you should stay here till dark so no one at the hotel sees you."

Brady glanced at the clock. No, that'd be too much time. "You'll text me the room number and leave the rest up to me."

"We want everyone to think I'm alone so no hotel employees can give us away if Elijah or his men come sniffing around. You're hardly inconspicuous."

"What does that mean?"

"You're—" she waved a hand at him, from his head to his foot on the brake "—big."

He raised an eyebrow.

"Come on. You're all Wyatt. Tall and broad and it isn't going to take a genius to put it together. There's no mistaking a Wyatt."

He didn't like it, but she was probably right. Much as he'd rather not admit it, he and his brothers all looked like Ace. Whoever Elijah sent would be able to put it together pretty easily even if they'd never seen Brady.

"He's after both of us. Maybe we both—"

"Don't start second-guessing just because you want to protect me, Brady. You were right the first time. If he thinks I'm alone we're more likely to get Elijah."

"It's not about wanting to protect." He wasn't sure what it *was* about, but surely he was more evolved than that.

"My butt." She slid out of the truck. "Wait until dark," Cecilia insisted before quietly closing the door.

He did not like being told what to do, and liked even less the high-handed way she'd ended any more discussion on the matter. They were supposed to be partners, working together.

Even if he'd all but forced her into that. Still, she'd *agreed*. Which meant they had to agree on the next courses of action. Teams *agreed* on what they were doing.

He could have gotten out of the truck and followed her. He could have driven over to the parking lot. There were a great many things he *could* do—she wasn't in charge of him.

But they'd come up with this plan, and he knew it was the best one. Even if it bothered him, on a deep, cellular, not-intellectual level that she was walking by herself, getting a room by herself. He wouldn't even know if she'd been intercepted.

He tightened his grip on the steering wheel and tried to talk himself out of all the worst-case scenarios. But worst-case scenarios existed because sometimes the worst case did.

He didn't have to blow their plan to bits to try and mitigate some potential worst cases. He'd parked on the curb of a pretty deserted street. Empty storefronts, a few with broken windows on the higher stories. There were two cars parked on the street—one in front of him, and one behind. Both were rusted severely, and one had a flat tire, so they likely hadn't moved in a while.

If he backtracked, there was a narrow alley. He could fit the truck back there, and as long as he made sure the buildings on either side were empty, and it looked like the alley was unused, he could park there without being noticed.

Then he could sneak up to the motel behind the building. Check things out and see if Cecilia had anyone watching her. He hadn't spotted a tail on the drive over, so he was pretty sure they hadn't been found yet.

Satisfied with his plan, he took a circular route to the alley—still no tail, and there weren't many places for one to hide in this deserted part of Dyner. He parked the truck, searched the alley for signs of use, and when he found none, settled his bag on his shoulder and started walking toward the motel.

It was easy to go around back and avoid the parking lot. The motel was a small, old, bedraggled building. It was squat but long, and separated into two sides of rooms with the main office at the end. The back of the buildings abutted a small copse of scraggly-looking trees.

Brady used the trees as cover as he moved toward the motel. From the back it was just a slab of concrete with the tiniest of squares in each unit that were bleary windows that didn't look like they'd been cleaned in decades.

The two sections of rooms were split by a breezeway in the middle. Brady stopped and watched the narrow space. It would have taken Cecilia some time to not just walk up to the motel office, but also check in. If Brady stayed put and watched the breezeway and Cecilia passed, he'd know her room was on the east side. If she didn't pass after a certain amount of time, she was likely on the west side.

Unless she'd already gone to her room. But just as he was considering that possibility, Cecilia walked briskly past the breezeway.

He moved out of the woods, careful and alert to the potential of being watched. He moved through the breezeway, looked out just in time to see Cecilia step into the last unit.

He retraced his steps to the back of the building, moved down the length of the east side until he reached the end. He sent her a text telling her to unlock the door.

Her response was about what he expected.

I told you to stay put.

So he repeated his previous text: Unlock the door.

She didn't reply to that one. He moved around the corner, watching the entire area around him for someone who might be watching the door Cecilia had gone into. She hadn't just left it unlocked, she'd left it ajar.

He slid inside.

She closed and locked the door behind him, and while her stance was calm, her eyes were fury personified.

"I told you to wait."

"It was too long to wait. I could have just as easily been spotted in that truck. I haven't seen any tails or any signs of being watched. Have you?"

She frowned. "No."

"They haven't figured us out yet."

"That only means they're hanging around the ranches. I don't like that."

"Neither do I, but you yourself said we can't contact Elijah and lure him out. He has to think we're on the run." Brady looked around the room. It smelled like stale cigarette smoke and mildew. He was sure the bedding hadn't been updated since 1990, at best. Everything had a vague layer of grime over it.

"I gave a fake name at the desk," Cecilia said, pacing the small patch of threadbare carpet. "They didn't ask for my ID."

"He'll be looking for someone with your description, not your name."

"I know." She hugged her arms around herself. "I just hate that while we wait for him to find us, he's going to be harassing our families."

"Cody will have that covered."

She didn't say anything to that, but he could read her doubts. There was no way to assuage them. He had doubts of his own. No matter that Cody had trained with the CIA and been part of a secret group who's purpose was to take down the Sons, no amount of security could protect everyone 100 percent. Not long-term.

So, they had to focus on the short term. "Tomorrow, we'll head east. I'll check in at the next motel and you'll hang out in the truck till the coast is clear. We'll switch off like that—in different directions, buying two or three days in the motels and only staying one. I think he'll follow you, but if he sends some men after me, it'll split his resources."

"You're not in charge here, Brady. You can't just stomp in and order me around."

"I wasn't ordering, and I most definitely wasn't stomping."

She crossed her arms over her chest and lifted her chin. "Weren't you?"

"Is there a problem with my plan?"

She made a face—pursed lips, wrinkled nose, frustration personified. "No," she ground out, clearly irritated.

"Well, then."

"You're infuriating," she said disgustedly.

"I don't see how."

"You're a Wyatt. You wouldn't." She plopped herself on the edge of the bed. She sat there like that, looking irritable and pouty. After a few moments it changed. She looked around the room, then narrowed her eyes at him.

After a few more seconds, she smiled, and boy did he not trust that smile.

THERE WAS NO way to fight Brady when he was right. No one was onto them yet, so it made sense he'd come into the room. Moving to another motel tomorrow and doing the same thing, only with Brady being the one to check in made sense too.

It would work better if they split up, but that would leave them both in danger. It made more sense to be partners in this.

But if he was going to irritate her, she had the right to irritate him right back. So, she smiled. "Guess we're gonna share a bed tonight." Because if there was one way to *really* make Brady uncomfortable it was to acknowledge that little spark of heat between them.

"No."

"Afraid I'm going to take advantage of you?" she asked sweetly.

His eyes darkened, and it was probably warped, but she shivered a little. She could picture it just a little too easily. Especially now that he'd pinned her to the truck and she'd felt his body against hers.

What she knew now, that she hadn't known or fully believed back on New Year's Eve, was that he felt it too. That undercurrent of attraction. She wasn't sure she'd ever felt a buzz quite that potent. She'd always assumed she was immune to that—something about being a cop, being tougher and harder than most of her past boyfriends. They'd all liked the *idea* of her, but in practice it had never worked.

No man wanted a superior. At best they wanted an equal.

Brady is definitely equal.

"We shouldn't both sleep at the same time, Cecilia. That's just common sense."

Oh, she hated that *reasonable, condescending* tone. More annoying, the fact he was right when she was just trying to get under his skin. There really *was* something wrong with her thinking he was so attractive when he was equally as obnoxious.

There was something really pathetic about the urge to needle him when she should let it go. So, he hadn't listened and stayed in the truck. She had no doubt he'd evaded any kind of detection. Everything was as fine as it could be under the circumstances.

But she wanted to poke at him until he exploded—until she saw some of that reaction she'd seen last night when he'd been angry and incapable of controlling it.

Apparently he was having the same kind of thoughts.

"Would calling the ranch and checking in make you feel better? Check in on your babies—I mean sisters?"

He asked it so blandly she might have missed the direct dig. She might have even let it go if it didn't make her think she was having the same effect on him that he was having on her. That edginess that left each other incapable of acting reasonably.

When they *had* to act reasonably. They had to focus on the danger they were in, and first and foremost, keeping Mak safe. "I do not treat them like they're babies, but maybe I should treat you like you're one. Or just a cranky five-year-old in need of a nap."

"It was just a joke, Cecilia," he said in a bored tone. "Let it go."

Which of course meant she couldn't. "I will not let it go. I do not treat them that way. If I'm a little protective, it's because *I'm* a cop."

He rolled his eyes. *Rolled. His. Eyes.* "Okay."

She jumped up. "You don't understand because you Wyatts are all cops. So you don't have to worry about any of you being naive." She winced a little. "Or were cops." A reference to Dev whose injuries had ended his police career after just a few months on the job.

"What does it matter if I think you treat your sisters like toddlers?"

It didn't. Not at all. But he was purposefully goading her. And she had to be the bigger person. She had to let it go. "It doesn't matter. At all, in fact."

"There you go." Then he reached out and patted her on the head.

Patted her. On the head.

She poked him square in the chest, which was quite the feat when what she really wanted to do was deck him. "Don't *pat* me on the head, you pompous jerk."

"Don't *poke* me," he returned, taking her wrist and pulling her hand away from his chest. But each finger that wrapped around her narrow wrist was like fire.

It was ridiculous and so over-the-top potent, this thing between them. And it was just going to keep happening. Trying to lure Elijah toward them while working together—spending nights in the same room together—the fights would get old, and they would all end in this. Attraction was going to keep leaping up until they dealt with it head-on. One way or another.

She met his gaze. "We can't pretend this away, Brady."

He dropped her wrist, his armor clicking into place clear as day. "Watch me."

Chapter Ten

Pretend. Brady didn't have to pretend anything away, because this…thing between them was nothing more than weird timing and circumstance. It was just an illusion made up of frustration and fear and danger.

If there was some teeny tiny ember of attraction, it could be easily stomped out.

Once she stopped poking at him.

Why he'd expect her to do that was beyond him. Cecilia was not someone who stepped back from any kind of challenge. She met them head-on. She said things like *we can't pretend this away.*

But clearly she had no clue who she was talking to, because there were a great many things he could pretend away. This included. *This* was at the top of the list.

He pulled his phone out of his pocket and dialed Cody. "Need to check in," he muttered to Cecilia without looking her way.

He didn't watch for her response, so if she had one, it wasn't verbal. When Cody answered, Brady kept his greeting short.

"What's the status?"

"You can't be serious."

"Why not?"

Cody sighed. "You just took off. You and Cecilia. We agreed—"

"We didn't agree on anything. Have you had any incidents?"

Cody muttered something Brady couldn't make out, which was probably for the best. "We've definitely had some people poking around, but it's all been pretty weak. I think they know you guys aren't here, and don't suspect you left Mak. Unless they're biding their time."

"Any word on Elijah himself?"

"No. He's laying low as far as we've been able to figure—without digging too deeply so he might realize we're looking into him. Where are you?"

"Best if you don't know."

"I've been in this exact position," Cody said, his tone serious and grave. "Working together, all of us, was—"

"Something that worked for *your* situation, and it might in the future work for this one. But right now, we have to keep Elijah away from Mak any way we can. This is the best way."

Before Cody could respond, the phone was plucked out of his grasp. He turned to scowl at Cecilia.

She had his phone to her ear and a *screw you* expression on her face. "Cody? Yeah. Listen. Stay away from Elijah. Your priority is Mak. All of you out there—your priority is Mak. You let me and Brady deal with Elijah."

Whatever Cody said in response must not have met with her approval because she clicked the end button and then tossed his cell on the disgusting bed.

"Mature, Cecilia."

"I don't need to be mature, and I don't need your baby brother's approval." She crossed her arms over her chest. "We need Elijah to follow us. That's it."

"Did it occur to you I wasn't seeking approval so much as diplomatically trying to get everyone on the same side without barking out orders?"

She waved a dismissive hand. "We do not have time for every Wyatt and every Knight to get on board. Not right now."

"And if they go after Elijah themselves? You're not the only one who does something just because someone tells them not to."

"They won't," she said, as if she actually believed it. "Not only is it not in anyone's best interest—if they start reaching out to Elijah, it puts us in more danger. He'll build his forces for a Wyatt showdown. If he thinks we're working on our own, we have a better chance. Every one of your brothers will come to that conclusion before they try to take something upon themselves, especially with Mak there to remind them."

She wasn't wrong. His brothers might not approve of the plan, but they wouldn't try to interrupt it unless they could guarantee it didn't put more danger on him and Cecilia. Knowing the Wyatts were involved would no doubt increase the danger, so no matter how they complained about it, they wouldn't interfere unless they had a safe way of doing it.

"You can admit I'm right at any time." She smiled at him, all smug satisfaction. Then she moved closer, a saunter if he had to characterize it. With that same look in her eyes she'd had on New Year's Eve.

She did the same thing too. Moved right up to him and placed her hands on his shoulders like they belonged there.

This time though, he knew. She wasn't drunk. She wasn't joking. She was...probably projecting. Better to irritate him, to come on to him and make him angry, than think about the reality of her life.

Which almost made him feel sorry for her. Almost.

If her hands felt good there, if his system screamed in anticipation, he didn't have to—and in fact wouldn't—react.

But she didn't just leave her hands on his shoulders, she slid them up his neck, locking her fingers behind it. She molded her body to his, and it was that same blazing heat as when he'd backed her up against the truck.

Why did all this make his body tighten when he knew better. *Knew* better. "It's just attraction." He had to say it out loud. He had to hear the words himself. Because there was only one tiny little thread of reason holding him back.

She widened her eyes, all fake innocence. "Gee. I thought it was chaste, attraction-less, pure-hearted happily-ever-after."

He puffed out a breath and reached behind him to pull her arms from around his neck.

She didn't let herself be pulled. In fact, she sort of rolled against him and for a second he was frozen, holding her arms, pressed to her, blood roaring in his head.

What would be the harm?

"It doesn't have to mean anything, Brady," she said, her voice soft. "Consider it a distraction under stress. You're not exactly *unmoved*."

That at least poked holes in the haze of attraction and want, because it was a lie. Because he heard a hint of desperation she was trying so hard to hide. "You think it'd be that easy?" He laughed, though it wasn't a particularly nice laugh. "How naive are you?"

She looked a bit like he'd slapped her, and while that

gave him a stab of pain, she had to understand what she was saying. And he had to be kind of a jerk so she'd stop…doing this. "Did you forget about that kiss at New Year's Eve, Cecilia?"

"No."

"It didn't mean anything, so it never occurred to you to think about it again?"

"Brady, I—"

"You kissed me and any attraction that prompted it evaporated. You didn't want to anymore." He gestured to the small space between them. Derisively. "Clearly. It all went away."

She blinked at him, some of that sexy certainty slipping off her face. "That was just a kiss."

"And what you're suggesting is just sex." He unwound her arms from around his neck and she finally released him. "If a kiss lingered, what would sex do?"

"It doesn't have to be like that," she said stubbornly.

"Doesn't it? You've actually slept with someone and all feelings and attraction immediately disappeared?"

Her eyebrows drew together like she was trying to make sense of a foreign language. "Of course."

"Of course? Cecilia, you must have had some spectacularly bad sex." Which was not an easy thing to think when she was still so close. Clearly…missing out.

She bristled. "You have no idea what kind of sex life I've had."

"No. And I don't want to." Not in a million years did he want to imagine what kind of morons she'd been with. "But sex changes things. It's nakedness and intimacy, and that's fine if you're casual friends or you pick someone up at a bar. It's fine if you think you're going to date and see if you're compatible. It's not fine if you're practically family."

"Because you decreed the laws and rules of what's fine and what's not?"

She was the most frustrating woman in the world. He had no idea why that made him want to put his hands on her face, to show her—long, slow, and thoroughly—what a real kiss would do.

Luckily he was distracted from the impulse by the alarm going off on his phone. "I need to change my bandage," he said stiffly, and grabbed his bag and walked into the bathroom, hoping he could leave all *that* behind him.

CECILIA DIDN'T PARTICULARLY enjoy being chastised, or other people being right, but there was something about the way Brady had handled her that made her feel both—chastised and very, very wrong.

She wanted to pout over it, but the predominant feeling—nearly eclipsing the ever-present worry that she couldn't keep Mak safe—was a heavy sadness.

She sat down on the bed and rested her chin in her hands. He wasn't wrong exactly. It was nice to throw herself at him, argue with him, because it didn't leave much room for worry. She could turn that off, and *God* she was desperate to turn that constant, exhausting anxiety off.

There were other ways to argue with Brady. Not such easy ones, but she didn't have to throw herself at him. Especially when he so easily countered all her moves.

You must have had some spectacularly bad sex.

She scowled. What did Brady know? He was uptight and repressed. Sure, he was hot. And that brief moment he'd returned the New Year's Eve kiss had been something like electric, but there was no way Brady wasn't just stern vanilla.

Then I think you're attracted to stern vanilla.

She heard a muttered swear from the bathroom and leaned sideways to see through the crack in the door.

Brady was clearly struggling with removing and bandaging his wound himself. Stubborn mule.

She got to her feet and marched for the tiny bathroom. She inched the door the rest of the way open. "Oh, for heaven's sake. Let me help you."

He scowled at her in the mirror over the sink. "I can do it on my own."

"Not well." She stalked over to him and tugged the alcohol wipe out of his hand. She set to tending the wound, ignoring the fact he was shirtless. She was mad at him, and she wasn't going to soak in the sight of pure *muscle* on display. She was above that. "It looks better." She coughed. "Your wound."

"Antibiotics must have worked this time," he said in that robotic Brady voice that made her want to scream.

Instead she finished disinfecting the area. "That's good."

"It is."

She rolled her eyes at the inane conversation. She pulled the new bandages out of the box on the rusty sink, then pointed to the bed. "Oh, go sit down."

He grunted, but did as he was told. She followed, noting that the beautifully muscled torso and arms both had their share of scars. "Where'd you get all those?" she asked, positioning herself in between his legs so she could get close enough to adhere the bandage on both the front of his shoulder and the back.

He didn't answer her, merely shrugged as she

smoothed the bandage over the slow-to-heal gunshot wound. His skin was surprisingly soft there, her hand looking particularly dark against the expanse of pale skin that rarely saw the sun.

Brady wasn't a shirtless guy, so his shoulder was all white marble, aside from the bandage she'd adhered herself.

She was standing between his legs and something… took over. It wasn't wanting to poke at him; it wasn't even that flare of attraction. This was something softer and different than she was used to and she didn't know how to fight off the urge to run her fingers through his hair.

He looked up at her, something flickering in his stoic gaze. It wasn't anger like usual. Or even annoyance at her. There was something deeper there. Her heart twisted and she suddenly wanted…

She wasn't sure. Not to throw herself at him or annoy him or try to start a fight. She didn't even want to act on that flare of attraction. She wanted…she didn't know. Just that it was deeper. Like he'd be some kind of salve to a wound.

"I get it. This is scary. You're scared for Mak," he said, his voice grave. Weighted, like he really did understand. "You're worried about your friend. It'd be nice to just chuck it all out the window for an hour or so. But it would change things. Things we can't afford to let change. It *would* mean something, whether either of us wanted it to."

She stared at him. He was right. It was terrible and true, and so completely right. And there was this part of her she didn't recognize that, for one second, wanted that change.

"Cecilia."

"Shh."

She cupped his face with her hands, and she ignored…everything she usually listened to. She did something without purpose, without certainty. She pressed her mouth to his, and it was almost timid. Not like she had on New Year's Eve—bold and a little drunk and mostly just *determined.* This was born of something else altogether. Seeking out that solace, or an understanding, that had always evaded her.

No one understood her. Not really. Not her family, not her friends, certainly not any ex-boyfriends. They thought she was tough and fearless.

But Brady had said she was scared for Mak, and she'd be damned if that wasn't the truth.

So, she kissed him with a softness she'd never found inside of herself.

He kissed her back. Not in that second of shock and reaction, but actual response. As if it was her gentleness that unlocked all his concerns and denials. And though she was standing, holding his face, there was no doubt that he took control of the kiss.

Kept it soft, kept it warm. Kept it like a connection, like a comfort.

She felt vulnerable, like her heart was soft. Like he wasn't just right, but had only scratched the surface when he'd said things would change.

It was fine enough to be attracted to Brady, to think sleeping with him would just solve that. It was something else for her to feel…*this* big thing.

She dropped her hands from his face and took two big steps back and away. "You're right. This is a bad idea.

I'll stop." She had to gulp in some air to calm her shaky limbs, her even shakier heart.

He looked at her and the gaze was inscrutable. His words had no inflection whatsoever. "Well. Good, then."

The stoic way he delivered those words stung, even if they shouldn't. She was reeling—turned inside out, and he was a robot. "Fantastic."

And it was. She wasn't going to get *involved* with Brady Wyatt. After that kiss…she was willing to finally admit that if they acted on anything, involved was just what they'd be.

There was no way that was ever going to work. Not knowing that she'd sacrifice everything to keep Mak away from Elijah.

No, she had to listen to Brady for once and let this whole thing go. Because sliding in headfirst was a disaster waiting to happen.

Chapter Eleven

Even when it was his turn to sleep, Brady didn't do a very good job of it. Between the musty smell of the bed, the slightly sticky feel of the sheets, and the whirr of the pitiful air conditioner, there just wasn't much in the way of comfort.

Then there was his own…state. After Cecilia had kissed him on New Year's Eve, and even after yesterday morning with the truck, he'd been able to redirect the pang of attraction into indignant anger. A righteous certainty that she was wrong and he was in the right.

After last night's kiss, full of gentleness and something bigger than even he'd imagined, he didn't have that anger. Didn't have much of anything except confusion. And a baffling sense of loss.

Which didn't make any sense whatsoever, so he pushed the feeling and the nagging ache away and focused on the task at hand. It was always how he got through life. Why should this be any different?

They moved to the next motel on the west side of the county with limited conversation and absolutely no interference. Another night in another crappy motel with no one finding them passed in the same uncomfortable, grimy way. Another check-in with the Wyatt and Knight ranches to find nothing had really happened.

"I don't like it," Cecilia muttered, driving the truck north to another seedy motel in the neighboring county. They'd agreed she would drive when it was her turn to check into the motel and vice versa. "It shouldn't take this long to peg one of us. And the fact they're not going after the ranches… Something isn't right."

"If he's really been watching Ace, taking hints from Ace, he knows patience is Ace's greatest strength. Regardless, if they're not poking at the ranch, Mak is safe."

Cecilia slid him a look before returning her gaze to the road. "What do you know about Elijah that you haven't told me?"

"Nothing." If only because *know* was a tricky word when it came to Elijah Jones. He kept his expression carefully blank, ignored the need to shift in discomfort.

"I don't think that's true."

Brady shrugged and didn't elaborate. Cecilia kept driving.

The tension between them wasn't gone, but it had certainly shifted. Before it had been almost antagonistic and definitely argumentative. This was flat and…almost timid. Like they were suddenly tiptoeing around a bomb that might detonate.

He supposed, in a way, they were.

When Cecilia reached Frisco, a tiny town north of Valiant County, she did what they'd been doing this whole time. Found a deserted place to park the truck a block or so from the motel. In this case it was a roadside park surrounded by trees.

But she didn't immediately slide out of the truck to

start her trek to the motel. She turned in the seat to face him, her expression grave.

"I need you to tell me whatever you know or think you might know. You keeping secrets about Elijah doesn't do anyone any good."

"I don't know anything, Cecilia. Anything I could say would be…supposition. Inference. Not fact."

Her eyebrows drew together. "I want those things from you. I think we need it all out in the open. I've told you everything I know about his relationship with Layla. Every time I've had an interaction with him on the rez or heard someone else relate one. You know my side. You're here, and I don't know your side. Just that you arrested him a long time ago and he's 'poked' at you ever since."

She wasn't wrong, much as he hated to admit it. Fact of the matter was, when Elijah was poking at him but never bothering his brothers, it didn't matter. But that wasn't going to last, and if he'd kept this secret…

He didn't want it out in the open. Was always waiting for his worst fears to be disproven. But maybe he had played into Ace's hands the whole time.

He could ease into it. Lead Cecilia to her own conclusions, but because it was Cecilia, he knew he could just…blurt it out. She'd take it, work through it, and make her own opinion. He didn't have to lead her anywhere.

Still, the words stuck in his throat. He'd never vocalized his worst thoughts. Never wanted to. But he needed to do it—to keep Mak, and Cecilia, safe as he could.

She reached forward, rested her hand on his knee. Everything about her was earnest and almost…pleading. Which wasn't Cecilia at all.

The words tumbled out. "I think Ace might be Elijah's father."

"What?" Cecilia screeched. "How? Why? When? What?"

"Which of those questions do you actually want me to answer?" he replied dryly.

"Brady. Holy… Oh my God. Why do you think that?"

"I don't know," he returned, frustrated with things he couldn't fully name. "There's something about…" She was right, he reminded himself again. Knowing everything gave them ammunition. It gave them armor. Ace had made a habit of keeping secrets and using them against people.

Brady wouldn't be like his father. Wouldn't let this potential secret, no matter how far-fetched, be the thing that felled him or Cecilia.

That didn't make it easy to explain the gut feeling he had. "Maybe he's not. But there's more to their relationship than a random Sons member taking a shine to our psycho in chief. Elijah would say things, when he'd goad me into arresting him. 'We're more alike than you think.' Lots of pointed remarks about my brothers. It just started to make me think…there's more there. Maybe it's not a father-son relationship, but there's more there. I can't imagine a man like Ace was faithful to my mother, especially toward the end when she was just getting pregnant to keep him from killing her."

"Did he kill her?" Cecilia asked, and her tone was simple. Straightforward. There wasn't that layer of pity he was so used to.

Which made it impossible to avoid, even if he hated this line of conversation. "Can't prove it."

"But you think he did," she insisted in that same even tone.

Brady shrugged jerkily. "Thinking it doesn't matter. Not when it comes to Ace and the Sons. Elijah being one of Ace's. We need fact."

Cecilia was quiet for a few humming moments. "I don't know about that," she said after a while. "If Elijah was Ace's son, don't you think we'd know?"

"Why would we?"

"Elijah wouldn't keep that a secret. He'd want everyone to know he was the president's son. He would have already taken over, I'd think."

"Unless Ace wanted him to keep it a secret." Brady shifted in his seat, wishing he'd kept his big mouth shut. "Like I said, Ace's best weapon is his ability to be patient. If he wanted to use Elijah when it would do the most damage… I'm just saying, there's a reason to keep it quiet. And it makes sense why he only ever hinted at the truth with me—why he focused on me. If he'd messed with all my brothers, wouldn't we put it together? But just one of us he could goad without the clues lining up."

"He's lived on the rez as long as I can remember."

It was suddenly too much. This was why he'd never brought it up with his brothers. It didn't matter when there was no way to know for sure. When it probably *wasn't* true. "I don't want to argue the validity, Cecilia. I'm just saying, that's my theory. One I don't even fully believe but you convinced me to tell you."

"You don't have to get touchy." She frowned out the windshield in front of them. "I'm trying to work it out. He's always lived on the rez, but he bounces from house to house. I don't know who his parents are. Not even his mother. I always figured they were both dead."

"And they very well might be."

"But your theory is based on eight years of watching this guy, right? Eight years of him toying with you. Eight years of you not telling anybody someone was harassing you." She blinked, looking up at him. "That's why you didn't tell your brothers."

He refused to meet her gaze. "I didn't tell them for lots of reasons."

"You didn't want them to have to think there were more Wyatts out in the world. Ones who didn't get out."

"Look. We're here." He pointed in the direction of where the motel would be. "Go check in and—"

"You could never be like them, Brady," she said quietly, but with a vehemence that had him looking over at her. "Jamison or no," she said, dark eyes straightforward and fierce. "Grandma Pauline or no. You could never be like them."

Something inside of him cracked, because it was the lie he'd always wanted to believe. But how could he? "We don't know that. I don't need to know that. Because I'm *not* like Ace or Elijah. But Ace and Elijah are the constant threats in my life, and I'm tired. I want this over. So, why don't you go check in, huh?"

She pursed her lips, but nodded eventually. "All right," she said, and slid out of the driver's side, leaving him in the truck alone with his thoughts.

Not a place he really wanted to be.

CECILIA'S MIND REELED as she walked toward the motel. Elijah as Ace's secret son. It made a creepy kind of sense. An awful kind of sense.

No matter how she tried to reason and rationalize it away, she kept coming back to the simple fact it was *possible.* Maybe even *probable.*

It put Mak in even more danger, especially with the Wyatts. Hell, it made Mak part Wyatt.

If it were true. She understood Brady's hesitation to believe it. There wasn't evidence and it didn't make sense why Ace would have kept it a secret. It also opened the horrible Pandora's box that Ace might have more children. Children who hadn't been saved like the Wyatt brothers had been.

And if Ace had kept them all a hidden secret—or even just Elijah—the reasons could only be bad. Really, really bad.

Cecilia stepped into the motel's cramped front office.

"Got a room available?" she asked the woman behind the counter, remembering belatedly to smile casually rather than frown over the problem in her head.

The woman looked her up and down.

"You a cop?"

Cecilia managed a laugh even as she inwardly chastised herself for walking in here with her cop face on. "No. I really look like one of those nosy bastards?"

The woman wasn't amused. "Got any ID?" she demanded with narrowed eyes.

"Oh, sure," Cecilia said casually even though her heartbeat was starting to pick up. The woman's careful inspection might just be the sign of a conscientious business owner.

But Cecilia doubted it.

She patted down her pockets. "Must have forgotten it in my car."

"Then I suggest you go get it, if you're really wanting to stay here."

Cecilia rolled her eyes. "My money ain't good enough for you, that's fine." She tried to sound flippant rather than irritated.

The woman behind the counter didn't say anything, just crossed her arms over her chest. Which Cecilia took as a clear sign that she would *not* be handing over any keys, regardless of money, without ID.

A little prickle of unease moved up the back of Cecilia's neck. She couldn't help but wonder if Elijah, or his men, had already been here and warned the woman off letting Cecilia get a room. She hadn't run into any motel owner this discerning yet.

Or maybe they'd been asking questions and that had simply made the woman nervous enough to take precautions.

The woman hadn't seemed afraid, though. Suspicious, distrusting and a little rude, yeah. But not afraid.

Cecilia moved back out of the office into the early-afternoon sun. She immediately picked out two men pretending to be otherwise occupied, but she knew they weren't. She didn't recognize them on a personal level, but she'd bet money they were Elijah's messengers.

She could take two. Unfortunately she had the sneaking suspicion there were more. Surely Elijah realized that she had no problem fighting off two of his pea-brained followers.

Still, she walked through the parking lot as if she didn't have a care in the world. She didn't have to look behind her to know the two were following her. Carefully and at a distance, but the farther she got from the hotel, the closer they got—to each other, and to her.

She'd made it maybe half a block, the park still not in view, when a man stepped out from behind a building in front of her.

Two behind. One in front. Not great odds, but if these three were as dim-witted as the two who'd knocked her off the road with Rachel, she could do it. Probably get a little banged up in the process, but she could do it.

She reached into her pocket and palmed her phone. She'd made a deal with Brady that if she didn't text within twenty minutes, he could come barreling after her. It hadn't been more than ten. Maybe she could get off a quick text and—

"Wouldn't do that if I were you." A fourth one popped out right next to her. Unlike the other three, who were likely armed but had their guns hidden, this one had his out and pointed at her. She froze with her hand still in her pocket.

As a police officer, Cecilia had learned how to defuse situations. How to talk men out of doing stupid things. Her goal, always, was to remain calm and use her words first.

As a woman in the world, she knew the opposite to be true. So, she didn't use her words, or wait.

She fought. Her immediate goal was disarming the man closest to her. She managed to get the gun out of his hand, but the others were quickly circling her.

She couldn't pay much attention to them when the one she'd disarmed was coming at her with a big, solid fist, but the fact no gunshots rang out meant they were supposed to keep her alive.

She had to hope.

She dodged the fist, landed a knee and her attacker dropped. She whirled to the ones she could feel closing in on her. They stood in a triangle around her. One had rope, one had a knife, and the other was just big as a Mack truck.

Crap.

Chapter Twelve

Brady surveyed the White River in the distance. It was narrow, the banks a grassy green where most of the landscape around him had gone brown under the heat of late summer. But here, near the river with a constant supply of life-giving water, things were green.

He tried to focus on that, on the landscape of his home state, on anything except the ticking seconds.

He'd promised Cecilia he wouldn't come barreling in like he had last time, though he did not characterize his previous actions as *barreling*. Still, there was no need today. They had their routine down pat and they'd found a compromise with her texting an okay after twenty minutes.

Still, the seconds seemed to tick especially slowly as he waited for a text message.

Brady got out of the truck. Not to *barrel* after her. Simply to stretch his legs. To walk off a little of his anxiety over the situation. Just in the little park.

He checked his watch. Twelve minutes down.

Now, *technically*, if it was twenty minutes from when they'd *stopped*, there'd only be three minutes left. And it would take him those three minutes to walk to the motel, so really he could head that way and not be breaking their deal.

She'd argue, but he had a…thin, shaky argument. Still, it *was* an argument.

She'd probably call it sexist, but he considered it just two different temperaments. She apparently couldn't fathom every possible worst-case scenario while she'd waited for him yesterday.

It was *all* Brady could think about while waiting for her. It wasn't a gender thing. It was a personality thing.

He'd start walking, but he'd do it slowly. Eke out the minutes but at least get the motel in his sights. Scout out a back way to get to the room without being detected.

Nothing wrong with that.

He locked the truck and started out. He stopped and frowned at a strange, faint noise. Something like a shout. Probably his imagination.

But maybe it wasn't, and he was a cop, trained to investigate that which didn't add up.

He moved stealthily up the street, hand already resting on his weapon with the holster unsnapped. He heard the noise again, closer this time, in the direct path between the park and the motel.

He forced away all those worst-case scenarios and focused on the task at hand. He approached the corner where he'd have to turn to continue the route to the motel. He took one calming breath, readied his body and his nerves, and then moved carefully to get a view of what was happening.

Immediately he could tell there was a fight. Four men—one on the ground crawling away from three men who seemed huddled around something. Maybe another person, it was hard to tell from this vantage point.

Brady inched forward, gun pointed in the direction of the scuffle. If he announced himself, they'd no doubt scatter and he wanted to get an idea of what was going on and descriptions of who he was dealing with before he decided which one to target.

The crawler wasn't going to be hard to pin down, but Brady noticed he was moving toward a small pistol. If he ran, he could beat the injured man to it, but judging by the fact he was hurt, the guy might just as well be a victim in the whole thing.

Brady glanced back at the trio. One let out a howl of pain and bent over, giving Brady a glimpse of what the three were huddled around.

He froze for less than a second, then immediately pointed his gun at the man crawling. No one had seen him yet, and shooting would put all four men on alert, but Brady couldn't let the crawling man get the gun. Not with Cecilia in the middle of that pack of jackals.

Brady shot, aiming for the arm that was reaching for the gun. The crawling man rolled onto his back, grabbing at his arm as he screamed. The three men around Cecilia jumped. They looked toward the crawling man, then wildly around until they found Brady.

Cecilia struggled to her feet, a piece of rope dangling from one arm, blood trickling down her face in a disturbing number of places.

Despite the fact she was clearly severely hurt, she didn't even pause. She kicked out, landing a blow to one's back. He stumbled forward, then whirled on Cecilia.

Brady charged forward as one man brandished a knife. Brady found it odd none of these three seemed to have guns, but he didn't have time to question it.

He ducked the first jab, pivoted and landed an uppercut so the man went pitching backward. Someone behind him landed a nasty kidney punch, but Brady only sucked in a breath and flung a fist backward. He connected with something that let out a sickening crunch followed by a wail of pain.

The knife flashed into his vision, and an ungainly leap backward allowed him to duck away from the sharp blade's descent with only a centimeter to spare. As the knife missed and momentum brought the assailant downward, Brady used his elbow as hard as he could.

A loud, echoing crack and the sound of a gurgling scream as the man stumbled onto his hands and knees. Brady kicked him with enough force to have the man falling onto his back. Brady stepped on his wrist—eliciting another gurgling scream from the man, but he let go of the knife.

Brady kicked it away and turned to find Cecilia. She'd taken one of the other men out, but the third man was trying to drag her by a rope he'd apparently tied around one of her arms.

"No, I don't think so," Brady said, reaching out and grabbing the taut rope. He ripped it out of the other man's grip with one forceful tug. He aimed his gun at the man's chest. "You want me to kill you, or you want me to let Elijah do it, nice and painful?"

The man sneered. "One of these days, every last high-and-mighty Wyatt's going to be wiped off this earth."

"I wouldn't count on it." Brady decided not to shoot—with the men unarmed he could call up the sheriff's department and have these four rounded up once he got Cecilia to safety. So, instead, Brady leapt forward and used the butt of the weapon to deliver a punishing blow to the head.

The man crumpled immediately and fell to the ground.

Brady whirled to Cecilia. She was kneeling next to the two men on the ground and had used the rope that had been tied around her wrist to tie them together.

"Want to add him?" she asked, her voice raspy. She was shaking, but she'd managed decent knots.

"He'll be unconscious for a while."

She struggled to get to her feet. There was blood just…everywhere. Parts of her shirt were torn and her hair had come completely undone so it was a wild tangle of midnight around her face.

"Almost had 'em," she managed to say before she swayed a little.

Brady scooped her up before she fell over. He didn't think he could stand to listen to her tell a bad joke in that ragged voice.

She wriggled slightly in his grasp as he started walking purposefully back to the truck. They weren't staying here. Not in this town or at that motel. He needed somewhere clean and sanitary to check out her wounds.

"I can walk."

"I can't say I care what you *can* do right now, Cecilia." He walked toward the crawling man who'd apparently gotten over the initial shock of his gunshot wound and was dragging himself toward the gun again.

"Don't know when to stop, do you?" Brady adjusted Cecilia's weight in his arms and then kicked the gun as hard as he could into the grassy field. If the injured man found the gun before Brady managed to call for backup, Brady'd consider him a magician.

He walked briskly back to the truck. With care, he placed Cecilia on her feet, though he kept one arm around her and supported almost all her weight.

"I'm fine," she muttered as he dug his keys out of his pocket. He ignored her and unlocked the truck, opened the door, then lifted her into her seat over her protestations. He even buckled the seat belt for her, though she weakly tried to bat his hands away. Then he looked her right in the eyes. "Don't you dare move," he ordered.

He was more than a little concerned that she listened.

CECILIA ONLY HALF listened as Brady drove and made a phone call. First she knew he was talking to the police. He was giving descriptions and accounts and locations of the fight that had transpired.

Cecilia closed her eyes against a wave of nausea. Four against one wasn't such great odds and as much as she'd held her own she was pretty banged up. She'd never admit it to Brady because he'd fuss, but she wasn't sure when she'd ever had such a bad beating.

But all four men would wind up in jail, and she would heal. So. There was that.

Brady made another call, driving too fast down deserted highways. She couldn't watch or she'd throw up. At first she'd figured he was calling his brothers, or worse, a hospital. But then he'd said something about cabins and fishing and her brain was a little fuzzy.

It was hard to focus and think over the bright fire of pain in various parts of her body. Harder still not to whimper every time the truck hit a bump. But if she showed any outward signs of pain Brady was going to baby her even worse than carrying her around.

It had been kind of nice to be carried but it was certainly not behavior she wanted to encourage. Maybe it was the worst beating she'd ever gotten, but she'd been in her share of fights. Breaking them up, having big men take swings at her. She wasn't some helpless stranger to a few punches.

Of course, she'd never been stabbed before, and she wasn't quite sure how she was going to hide that from Brady. Surely she could find some Band-Aids and take care of it.

She winced a little, knowing it was probably too deep to be handled by a Band-Aid. It was fine, though. She'd figure it out. Brady would whisk her away to a hospital if he knew and that just couldn't happen. Not now when they'd delivered a blow to Elijah.

God, he'd be pissed she'd taken on *four* of his men. It almost made her smile to think of.

She wasn't sure if she'd fallen asleep or lost consciousness or what, but suddenly the truck was stopped and Brady was already standing outside. She tried to push herself up a little in her seat, but it nearly caused her to moan in pain.

She bit it back last minute as Brady was opening the passenger door.

"Where are we?" she demanded. She looked around, but nothing was familiar. They were on a little gravel lot and there was a scrubby little yard in front of a tiny, *tiny* cabin on a small swell of land.

Beyond the cabin was pure beauty. A sparkling lake stretching out far and wide, bracketed in by rolling rock. If she had to guess, they were closer to the Badlands than they'd been out in Valiant County.

It distracted her enough that Brady had her unbuckled and back in his arms before she had a chance to protest.

"I can walk, Brady."

"But you're not going to. Not until I check you out." He started walking, as if she weighed next to nothing and his shoulder hadn't been hurt for months. He took the little stone stairs up to the cabin without even an extra huff of breath.

"Buddy of mine's," he offered conversationally, even though his expression was completely… She didn't have a word for it. Tense, determined, fierce. "Well, more Gage's buddy. Pretended like I was Gage. Haven't done that since middle school, and it was never me. Gage was always the one pretending."

"He couldn't have fooled anyone who actually knew you two."

"You'd be surprised." He set her down, with the kind of gentle care one might use with a one-hundred-year-old woman. Then he futzed around with a planter in the shape of a bass. Something wilted and brown was growing out of the fish's mouth, but Brady pulled a key out from underneath.

He unlocked the door, pushed it open, then turned to her.

She held up her hands to ward him off. "If you pick me up again, I'm going to deck you."

With quick efficiency, he moved her hands away and swept her into his arms again. Why did her stomach have to do flips every time he did that? And why couldn't she muster up the energy to actually punch him?

"Guess you're going to have to deck me."

She was so outraged she couldn't do anything but squeak as he marched her to the back of the cabin in maybe ten strides. He went straight into the bathroom and gently placed her on the floor again.

"Take off your clothes."

For a full ten seconds she could only stare at him. "I most certainly will *not*."

"You're bleeding God knows where. We need to get you cleaned up and patched up. Now. Shirt and pants off. You can leave your underwear on if you want to be weird about it, but I've got to see what kind of injuries we're dealing with."

"Weird ab—" She could feel fury and frustration somewhere deep underneath the pulsating pain of her body, but she couldn't seem to change any of that irritation into action. She leaned against the wall, trying to make it look like she was being casual, not needing something to prop her up. "Not the time to try to talk me into bed, Brady."

"Don't mess with me right now. Take off the clothes. I'm an EMT. I've seen plenty of naked women and manage to control myself each and every time. I have to see what kind of injuries you have so I know how to patch you up. Lose the clothes, Mills."

"How about you listen to the woman with the injuries. I'm fine. Just a bit banged up. I'll take a shower—alone, thank you very much. If I need a bandage, I'll ask for your expert services."

It didn't have the desired effect—which was to get him to back off. She figured it might at least hurt his pride a little if she took a shot at the EMT side of his profession. She knew Brady took the paramedic stuff very seriously, that he'd once wanted to be a doctor. Acting like all he did was slap on bandages should offend him.

But he merely narrowed his eyes at her. "What are you trying to hide?"

She bristled, her tone going up an octave. "Nothing."

"Bull," he returned. "You want to be difficult? Fine. I'll do it myself."

He moved toward her, and if she'd been 100 percent she would have fought him off. She would have done whatever it took to keep his hands off her.

But she was beaten up pretty good. There wasn't any fight left in her, there was only fear, and she was very afraid she'd cry if she let him take her shirt off her.

So, she whipped it off herself. It wasn't about being shirtless in front of him. Her sports bra was hardly different than a swimsuit or what she'd wear to the gym. But she knew his reaction to her wounds was going to… hurt somehow.

He swore, already leaping for the little cabinet under the sink. In possibly five seconds flat he had a washcloth pressed to the stab wound. She hadn't dared look at it herself, but maybe she should have, judging by the utter fury in his gaze.

"What the hell were you thinking?"

"It's not that bad," she said weakly. Maybe it was bad enough to have mentioned it. She'd only wanted to handle it herself. She didn't need him manhandling her and…

She blinked, desperately holding on to the tears that threatened. She didn't want to break down in front of him ever again. That one time in his apartment over Mak was bad enough. This would be worse.

Because she wasn't sad or upset. It was the adrenaline of the fight wearing off. It was the need for release. She didn't want to be petted or taken care of.

She wanted to be alone. To handle it herself. To build all her defenses back without someone here…taking care of her. Because if he took care of her, he'd see all the marks of how she'd failed to take care of herself.

What kind of cop was she, then?

She looked up at the ceiling, didn't answer his questions and definitely didn't dare look at him. She blinked and blinked and focused on staving off the tide of tears.

But then he did the damnedest thing. He rested his forehead on her shoulder and let out a shuddering breath. Something deep inside of her softened, warmed, fluttered. Without fully thinking through the move, she lifted her arm that didn't hurt too much and rested her hand on his head.

"I'm okay. Really," she managed to say without sounding as shaky as she felt. "Just a little flesh wound."

The sound he made was some mix of a groan of frustration and a laugh.

"You've fixed worse on people," she reminded him. "Your own brothers in fact."

He shook his head, but lifted it from her shoulder. He didn't look at her, his gaze was on the washcloth he was pressing to the wound. "All right." He blew out another shaky breath, but the inhale was steadier. He seemed to shrug off the moment. When his eyes finally met hers, they were clear, steady and calm. "Let's get you really cleaned up, and I'll see what I can do for the stab wound."

Chapter Thirteen

Brady instructed Cecilia to hold the towel firm against her wound. Even the brief glimpse he'd gotten told him she needed stitches. He was no stranger to stitching up his brothers, but mostly as a paramedic that skill was left to doctors at the hospital.

He started the shower and tried to focus on the practicalities. She didn't just have the stab wound. She had bruises and he'd need to make sure she hadn't broken anything. He'd also need to check for a head wound because she'd dozed off in the truck—whether exhaustion as the adrenaline wore off or loss of consciousness he couldn't be sure until he examined her.

But first and foremost she had to get the grime and blood off of her. She could stand and she was lucid, so a quick shower was the best option.

The fact she hadn't even acted like she was in that much pain just about did him in. Why had she hidden it? To what purpose?

He couldn't focus on that. He'd nearly fallen apart when she'd finally taken off her shirt and he'd seen that deep, bloody gash.

It hadn't even occurred to him she was *that* hurt. She'd been acting so…flippant. At least when he'd worked on his brothers it had always been pretty visible how bad off they were up front. And when he dealt with them he'd have privacy after to rebuild his defenses.

There wasn't going to be any privacy here until the Elijah threat was taken care of.

Still, he was a trained EMT. He should have a better handle on his reactions and he would. He would.

"Do you think you can handle a shower?"

"No. Why don't you sponge bathe me, Brady? Of course I can handle a *shower.* You know, if you give me some privacy."

"Sorry. I'm not going anywhere until we know you didn't suffer a head injury."

"I didn't."

"How do you know?"

"Wouldn't I know if I got knocked in the head?"

He didn't look at her, even to give her a raised-eyebrow look. "Does your head hurt?"

She was stubbornly silent, which was as clear a *yes* as an immediate denial would have been.

"I'll keep my eyes closed." He moved away from the shower that was going, nice and hot, enough to make the room a little hazy.

"You don't have to be *that* much of a gentleman. I don't think a glimpse of nipple is going to send you into a crazed sex haze."

Still, Brady kept his back to her and the shower. "Use soap," he instructed, trying to pretend like she was a child who needed to be told what to do. Not someone some warped part of his brain wanted to see naked.

Which could *not* be considered, so he focused on the next. He had a first aid kit in his pack. It had the appropriate disinfectant. He didn't have anything strong enough to numb the area where she'd need to get stitches. That was going to be a problem, because while he was in no doubt she'd handle it, he wasn't so sure *he* could handle giving her that much pain.

"Probably gonna need a little help with the sports bra," she said after a few seconds. "It clasps in the back, but..."

She didn't come out and say one of her arms hurt, but that was clearly the implication. She couldn't get them both behind her back, which was a bad sign. "You have to be in a lot of pain," he said flatly, turning to face her.

She still held the cloth to the gash on her side. "I'm alive, Brady. Managed to hold off four guys, one with a knife and one with a gun. I'll take the pain, thanks." She frowned. "What pack of four morons only brings one gun to kidnap someone?"

"The kind that aren't allowed to kill you," Brady said wryly, motioning for her to turn around so he could unclasp her bra for her. "Elijah will want to hurt you himself. Trust me. It's why my brothers and I are still alive." He focused on that, not the smooth expanse of her back.

She shivered—he was sure because of what he was saying, not because his fingers brushed her bare back to unclasp the bra.

"So, why doesn't he come after us?"

Brady forced himself to drop his hands and turn around again. "That I haven't quite figured out. Do you need help with anything else?"

"No. I think I can manage."

Brady focused on finding a towel rather than the sound of her taking off her pants or stepping into the shower. He breathed in the heavy, steamy air and refused to think about showers or nakedness, because the naked woman was hurt and bleeding with a potential head injury. He wouldn't even be able to determine if she had breaks or fractures. He wasn't a doctor. He didn't have the right equipment.

He should take her to a hospital. It left them with less control of the situation, but she'd get checked out. Fully checked out. It had to be worth the risk.

The water stopped and Brady heard the clang of the curtain rings moving against the shower curtain rod.

He held out the towel, keeping his gaze and body angled away from her.

The towel was tugged from his hands. "God, do you have to be so noble?" she demanded irritably as if it were some flaw.

"I don't know how to respond to that."

"Of course not. I managed to stay upright in the shower. Are you going to let me walk on my own or do I get the princess treatment again?"

"Put pressure on that gash," he instructed, rather than answer her question. "We should—"

"If you mention the word *hospital* I won't be responsible for my reaction, Brady. You're a trained, licensed EMT. You can check me out."

"You need stitches."

"I'm fine."

"You're not. I can tell without even a full examination that it's deep, long and in a bad spot. We bend and move our sides far more than we know. If you don't get stitches, not only is it going to scar, but we're going to have to watch out for too much blood loss. Infection is a near certainty, and just plain not healing is an even bigger one."

"He says, from experience," she replied sarcastically.

She didn't know the half of it. "I know my way around a knife wound personally and medically, Cecilia."

"Get in a lot of knife fights?"

He ignored the question. Just closed that whole part of him off, encased it in ice. Had to or he'd never get through this.

"Oh, turn around for Pete's sake," she muttered. "I've got the towel on."

"A hospital would be a better bet," he insisted. Though he did turn around and face her, he kept his gaze on her eyes. Refused to dip to even her nose. Didn't check the towel placement or if she was putting pressure on her side where the gash was.

"Surely it's not that bad."

He tried not to let his irritation, and all the other feelings clawing inside his chest, get the best of him. "It's not that good."

"Right, but you've patched up worse," she insisted.

"Yeah. Usually with help or better supplies. I had an actual medical doctor talk me through fixing up Cody after his car accident, and that was only until he could get to the hospital. I don't have what I'd need to stitch you up, and you need more than a temporary solution."

"I'll be fine with a temporary solution." She waved a careless hand. "Just do what you can."

It was that carelessness, the utter refusal to listen to him that had his temper snapping. Every time his brothers came to him and said the same thing. Years of that, the past few months especially. Everyone was so sure they were *invincible* simply because he knew some basic emergency medical treatment.

He sucked it up and did his best, knowing it might not be good enough. What else was there to do?

But she didn't seem to get it. She was *seriously* hurt, and he wasn't a damn magician. "Did it occur to you—any of you ever—that you might not be fine? That I'm *not* a doctor. That I can't just magically *fix* you all when you come to me bloody and broken because of Ace Wyatt."

She stood very still, regarding him with a kind of blankness in her expression he recognized because it was the same face he put on when dealing with someone not quite stable.

"This doesn't have to do with Ace," she said, softly, almost sympathetically.

Which pissed him off even more. "It all has to do with Ace. Always. And forever. Now I need to find someplace to examine you, so stay put."

CECILIA WAS ALMOST tempted to do as Brady ordered as he stormed out of the small bathroom. There'd been something painful about his little outburst. A little too much truth in his frustration. If she stayed put, he'd compartmentalize it away and they could focus on the real problems in front of them.

But the fact he had all of that… Insecurity wasn't the right word. She was certain Brady understood his abilities, and knew he was an excellent EMT. The thing none of them had ever really thought about was the fact that doctors and EMTs weren't supposed to work on their families. That's when emotions came into play, and that put undue stress on the people doing the work.

The past few months, Brady had been tasked with working on some of the people he loved most in the world. They'd all asked it of him without a second thought—because it had been necessary. But no one seemed to think about the emotional toll it might put on the one cleaning up everyone else's injuries.

Especially while he was still trying to heal from his own complicated injury.

Cecilia inhaled. She didn't need to feel sorry for Brady. She was the one standing here wet, naked under a towel, bleeding and bruised. *She* was the one people should feel sorry for.

Trying to keep that in mind, she finally forced herself to move out of the bathroom and into the rest of the cabin. There was a kitchen/dining/living room all in the center, but right next door to the bathroom was another door.

It was open, and Brady was inside the bedroom fussing with the bedding. He'd already set out a line of first-aid stuff on one side of the bed. He didn't even look up, though clearly he knew she was standing there.

"Lay down. Once I've made sure everything aside from the stab wound is fine, you can get dressed and we'll decide what to do from there."

"No broken bones, Brady. No head wound. I've had both, I'd know what they'd feel like. I've got one nasty cut there, and a much less nasty one on my back. The rest are scratches that don't need any attention and bruises that could use some ibuprofen or some ice or a heating pad."

"Lay down, please."

She groaned at his overly solicitous tone, but she slid into the bed, still holding the towel around her. Once she was settled, Brady pulled the blanket up to her waist, then carefully rolled the towel up to reveal her abdomen without showing off anything interesting. Didn't even try.

Seriously, would it kill the guy to try to cop a feel or something?

He'd put on rubber gloves and immediately began inspecting the stab wound on her side. He sighed and shook his head as he inspected it. "I know what happens to a wound this deep that doesn't get stitches, Cecilia. We need to get to a hospital."

"Let's say we don't—"

"Ce—"

"Hear me out. Let's say we give it another couple days. You wash it out, bandage it up, and we try to get a few answers on Elijah's whereabouts or plan. *Then* I go to the hospital and get it stitched up. What's the risk of a few days?"

"Infection," he said, so seriously as if that was going to scare her off.

"Last time I checked, they have meds for that. Which you should be well acquainted with."

"I'm also well acquainted with what happens when you try to let a wound like this heal on its own but don't actually take it easy."

"How?"

"How what?" he muttered irritably. He grabbed some disinfectant from his lineup of first aid and Cecilia immediately tensed, waiting for the pain.

"How are you well acquainted with what happens when you don't care of a wound like this?" she asked through gritted teeth, waiting for the sting.

He stared at her for a full five seconds like she'd spoken in tongues, holding the cotton swab in one hand. "I...have a dangerous job." He focused back on her wound. "This is going to hurt."

She snorted. "Look, I'm a cop too. I know we get into

dangerous situations and we get hurt. I'm sure we've both got a few scars from *work*. But getting stabbed isn't exactly a day at the office." She hissed the last word out as the disinfectant stung like fire. "I think I would have heard about your stab wounds."

After a few humming breaths as she tried not to outwardly react to the sting, Brady spoke. His words were quiet and measured, but there was something lingering inside of him that was neither. "What do you think happens when you're a kid in a gang, Cecilia? Someone bakes you brownies?"

She blinked. *Oh.* Well, of course. Being hurt and not getting medical attention was probably life in the Sons of the Badlands. She just so often forgot he'd actually… spent years there. Innocent, vulnerable years. He was so good. So strong. She couldn't even picture it knowing what he'd looked like as a boy—reserved and gangly. It *hurt* trying to imagine. "Who stabbed you? Other kids?"

He was silent, but he was unwrapping butterfly bandages from their plastic wrapper, which meant she was getting out of a mandatory hospital visit for now.

"Brady."

He paid very careful attention to the wound on her side as he attached the bandages, one by one, along the line of sliced skin. "Ace had a game, is all. A nice little game just for me. Usually he missed."

Cecilia's blood went cold, but she knew if she let that seep into her voice he'd shut down and shut her out. She breathed, steadied her voice. "Usually?"

He shrugged, attached another bandage.

Then it dawned on her. She'd seen him with his shirt off that first night. She'd been somewhat surprised he'd been so marked up, but it hadn't occurred to her to wonder *why.* “All those scars. They’re from not-misses. He stabbed you.”

“He threw knives,” Brady corrected, as if that were better instead of somehow worse. “Gotta learn to expect the unexpected. Though he was always pulling them out to toss my way, so I’m not sure how it was unexpected, but here I am trying to rationalize a madman’s thinking.”

“He threw knives at you,” Cecilia said, because she *couldn’t* picture that. Not just because it caused her pain, because it was nonsensical. It was *insane.*

Brady lifted his gaze to hers over the bandages. She realized she’d let emotion, horror mostly, seep into her tone.

“I’m alive, Cecilia. I survived. But I’d rather not take a trip down memory lane if you don’t mind. Can you sit up?”

She blinked. It was her turn to feel like a foreign language was being spoken. After a few seconds she managed to sit up. He put a pad of gauze over the butterfly bandages, then used a wrap bandage around her waist to keep it in place.

“This is stupid. You need stitches. The chance of infection, of losing too much blood, of this not healing, are extraordinarily large.”

She heard the exhaustion in his tone. The worry. And maybe even the ghost of a little boy whose father had thrown knives at him. She hadn’t had that rough of a childhood. She’d thought it had been the worst, but it really hadn’t been. Being poor and neglected and then moved into a loving house at the age of six had nothing on Brady’s experience.

But she thought they needed the same thing in the face of those old ghosts. The only thing that had ever helped her had been to face down the current ones. And win. "Elijah's not coming for us, Brady. We have to go to him."

She thought he might pretend to misunderstand her, but his words were stark. "We don't know where he is."

"I know where he'll be. I know you do too."

Brady inhaled. "I promised myself a long time ago that I'd never go back there, Cecilia." He met her gaze. "Never."

She was closer to crying than she'd even been in the bathroom, but she didn't look away. "We need to."

Chapter Fourteen

Brady didn't precisely agree with Cecilia, but in the end he didn't argue with her. He'd patched her up best that he could, got her some clothes from her pack, ibuprofen for the pain, and ice for the particularly nasty bump under her eye—because apparently she'd gotten hit in the same exact spot as a few nights ago.

He ignored his own aches and pains as he ran through a shower. They'd agreed to spend the night at the cabin and get a fresh start in the morning. A fresh start doing *what* was still up in the air.

Go to the Sons camp? He'd promised himself he'd never do that, with one simple caveat: only if his brothers ever needed him to.

Cecilia wasn't his brother. Mak wasn't his brother. But wasn't it all the same? You went back if you had to protect the people you…cared about.

Brady dried off from the shower, examined his own injuries. His gunshot wound continued to heal, and that was something to be thankful for. He had a riot of bruises rising across his chest and arms, but that was to be expected after the fight they'd had. He was in a lot better shape than Cecilia.

He'd brought in a change of clothes but forgotten to

grab his own stash of bandages. They were going to run out at the rate they were going.

He took a moment to look at himself in the foggy mirror. He wasn't sure what he'd expected when he'd started down this path. He hadn't really *planned*—he'd only wanted to protect.

He'd been somewhat…disapproving of his brothers rushing in to face what they'd all left behind. He'd understood Jamison's need to help Liza save her young half sister from the human trafficking ring the Sons had been starting. A person, especially Jamison, couldn't turn his back on that. And yes, Cody obviously had to save his ex and his secret daughter from Ace's threats. And when Gage helped investigate the murder Felicity had been framed for, of course it ended up connecting to the Sons.

Everything did.

He'd known going in Elijah had ties to the Sons and his father, so going back to Sons territory seemed inevitable.

Still, he recoiled from it.

He scrubbed his hands over his face. A good night's sleep and surely he'd have a better handle on everything roiling around inside of him. He'd be able to compartmentalize and function as he normally did.

But there was something about *this* situation that made it harder. He'd patched up Cody's horrendous injuries. He'd helped Gage after he'd been basically tortured by Ace. Granted, those were after-the-fact situations. Mopping up a mess, not wading into one while worrying about the woman wading into it with him.

He didn't understand it, though. He trusted Cecilia, as much as any one of his brothers, to take care of herself. He didn't understand why this felt harder. Maybe it was his own weakness. A mental softening from all his time off.

He stepped out of the bathroom, determined to shove it all away again.

She was sitting up in the bed, though he'd told her to be as still as possible. Her hair was damp and leaving spots of wet on her T-shirt. She had an impressive bruise forming on her cheek.

She was not a weak woman, or even a soft one. She was all angles and muscle with a smart mouth and a sharp mind, who could take care of herself and save herself, no questions asked. He did not understand his desperate desire to wrap her up and keep her far from harm.

He wanted to protect his brothers, no doubt, and same for the Knight girls. He'd quickly and easily thrown himself in the way of harm to protect them, save them.

But this was different. This *thing* he felt toward Cecilia was different, and not liking it and pushing it away didn't seem to change anything.

When she glanced his way, she threw the covers off and started to move. "Oh my God, Brady. Look at you."

"Don't you dare get out of that bed. You are supposed to keep that cut immobile." He looked down at himself and frowned. "What?"

"You're *covered* in bruises," she said, outrage tingeing her words, though she had stopped herself from getting out of bed. "You didn't say you'd been hurt."

"I'm not hurt. Like you said, I know what serious injuries feel like. Just a little bruising."

"These aren't little. And there are quite a few."

"You really want to have this argument when I can still load you up in that truck and take you to a hospital?"

He stalked over to his pack and pulled out the bandage and disinfectant he needed for his shoulder.

"You really *don't* want to have this argument when you gave me hell for not telling you right away I'd been stabbed?"

"Stabbed. A stab wound that needs stitches and I—"

"You're insufferable." She held out a hand toward him when he sat down on the opposite side of the bed. "Give it to me."

"You need to be still."

"Give me the damn bandage, and scoot over here if you don't want me to move."

He grumbled and did as he was told. She smoothed the bandage on the back side, then he turned so she could do the front as well.

She touched his most pronounced scar, which was in a similar spot as her wound. The injuries were in fact quite similar, though he'd been ten when he'd gotten his. She sighed. "I don't know how you survived this and still became you, Brady. I really don't."

He shrugged, trying to ignore the effect her touch had on him. "You just do." He reached for his shirt, but something about her touching his scar kept him from his full range of motion.

"*You* do. You did. I know you don't want to go back there." She looked up at him, though her fingers lingered on his scar. "I don't want you to have to go back there."

"If you're about to suggest you go alone, you can—"

"No. No, I know better than that, believe it or not. We have to do this together. Have each other's backs. At some point that might mean splitting up, but not yet."

"Not ever."

She studied his face, as if looking for something. An

answer. A clue. A truth. She reached out and cupped his cheek with her hand, the other hand still pressed to his scar.

He held himself very still, trying to think back to all the arguments he'd had against this when she'd been throwing herself at him to irritate him.

But this wasn't that. Even he knew this wasn't that.

"Brady, I really thought I was going to die. Maybe not out there, but if they'd gotten me, taken me to Elijah, I knew it was over."

Fury spurted through him. "He won't—"

"Shh," she said lightly, her thumb brushing against his cheekbone. "I'd do it. I don't *want* to, but if it would keep Mak safe, I'd die for him. I think we all feel that about our families, but I've never actually been put in a position where I had to specifically accept it would be at someone's hands. Elijah's hands."

Maybe she wouldn't let him say it, but he'd do everything in *his* power to make sure that never, *ever* happened.

"I don't want him to take anything from me. I will fight tooth and nail to make sure you and Mak *and* I come out of this in one piece. I'm not being fatalistic here, I'm just telling you…"

She cupped his other cheek, moved so they were knee to knee. He would have admonished her for moving, but her body brushed his—lightning and need.

"I know it would change everything, but maybe everything needs to change. Maybe it's already changed."

He had to clear his throat to speak. "It wouldn't just change us. Our families. Duke isn't exactly thrilled with my brothers for similar happenings."

Her smile was soft, her touch on his face even softer.

"Duke doesn't approve of anything I've done. Becoming a cop. Living on the rez. Et cetera. He loves me anyway." She trailed her fingers over his cheeks. "You didn't have to do any of this. I brought you into this. I plopped Mak in your arms and—"

"Elijah already—"

"Shut up and *listen*, Brady. I came to you and convinced myself it was because you were the one who had the time, but it was because you were the one I trusted. I could have gone to Jamison or Cody—they have experience keeping children away from the Sons' reach. I could have gone to Tucker, he's a detective for heaven's sake. They all would have helped me. I came to you."

He didn't know how to react to that, or how to sift through the assault of emotions. Hope too big among them.

But then he didn't have to, because she kissed him. It was soft and gentle. He didn't think either of them had much of that in their lives. Maybe it was why they needed to show it to each other.

Maybe all this time he'd avoided her and that New Year's Eve kiss because he hadn't wanted to allow himself that. It certainly didn't feel right to take it now, except she needed it too.

And how could he resist giving her what she needed?

CECILIA WASN'T SURE what had changed inside of her. Only that something had opened up or eased. Something had shifted to make room for this, and once it had, she couldn't hide it away again.

She'd kissed Brady on New Year's Eve because he made her feel something she couldn't name, and for a long time she hadn't wanted to. Still, it hadn't gone away so she'd convinced herself it was merely attraction and backed off when Brady made her understand it couldn't be only that.

Now, just a little while later, she was the one kissing him. Saying things had already changed.

His hands were gentle, his kiss was *dreamy*, and it was as if those tiny pieces inside of her that had still felt so out of place clicked together and made sense.

If it hadn't been for this afternoon, fear of change would have continued to win—continued to keep her hands off when it came to Brady. But fear of death—and the possibility of that death being very much right in her face—made the fear of change weaker. Change was hard, but regret was too steep a price to pay.

What would be the point of this life she'd been given if she didn't accept all the emotions inside of her? She wasn't perfect. She wasn't even good half the time, but the things she felt for Brady were real. They were here.

Why had she been avoiding that? To not be embarrassed? To not be hurt? It seemed so *silly* in the face of what could have been her last day on earth. Maybe that was dramatic, but it had led her here.

No one had ever kissed her like she was both fragile and elemental all at the same time. But it was more than just the kiss.

No man, including Duke—the only man in her life she'd let herself truly love as both uncle and father figure—had ever made her feel understood. No one in her whole life had made it seem like the strong parts of her and the weaker parts of her were one complex package…one that someone could still want and care for. She was either fully strong or fully weak to others, but inside she was both.

She didn't want to be protected, but sometimes she wanted to be soothed. She didn't need anyone to fight her fights, but sometimes she needed someone to dress her wounds. Literally. Figuratively.

Brady was that. Just...by being him.

His fingers tightened in her hair, and the kiss that had begun as soft and lazy heated, sharpened. Something ignited deep inside of her, a hunger she hadn't really thought *could* exist inside of her. It had certainly never leapt to life before.

But now...now she wanted to sink into that heat and that unfurling desperation. It was new and it was heady and it was better than all that had come before.

But she could feel Brady pulling back. "You're hurt," Brady murmured against her mouth, as if he wanted to break the kiss but couldn't quite bring himself to.

She was vaguely aware of her sore body, but mostly those aches and pains were buried underneath the sparkling warmth of lust. She didn't just want a kiss, she wanted Brady's body on hers. She wanted to get lost for a few minutes in something other than pain and fear.

Some part of her she didn't fully understand wanted the hope of more with Brady when this was all over. Change seemed better than standing in the same place feeling alone. Feeling as though no one understood her or loved her as a whole, complex human being.

She sank into another kiss, desperate for him to forget her injuries. Forget where they were and what they had to do and finish *this*.

"I'll live," she insisted. "I want this, Brady. I want you."

He undressed her, and she *knew* he was being mindful of her injuries, but she didn't *feel* it. She felt worshipped and surrounded by something bigger than she could describe. A light, a warmth, a renewal of who she was.

Made somehow more awe-inspiring by the fact the man currently kissing her scrapes and caressing her many bruises was…gorgeous. He was all muscle and control. In another world he might have been a movie star, if he wasn't so raw and real. So… Brady. Good and noble and making her body hum with a desperate need she was sure, so *sure*, he could take care of.

And he did, entering her, moving with her, a gentle, heated tangle of all those things she'd been afraid of: change, need, hope.

Why had those been fears? When they were this *good*. This comforting and *right*.

He said her name and it echoed inside of her. It felt like a hushed *finally*. Like they'd been waiting all their years to do this, when she didn't think they had. Certainly not consciously.

But it was here now, and she knew this was just… it. Him. Them.

She slid her fingers through his hair, focused on pleasure over the pain of her injuries, and gave herself over in a way she'd never done before. Because she trusted Brady. Wholeheartedly. He was the person she went to when she was in the most trouble, and he was the person she wanted to be with in this dangerous, desperate situation.

Always.

The crest of release washed over her, a slow roll of pleasure and hope and relaxation. A *finally* whispered through her body as Brady followed her into oblivion.

She sighed into his neck, snuggled in when he carefully tucked her against his body, and slept.

Chapter Fifteen

When Brady's phone trilled, waking him from a deep, restful sleep, he jerked, then immediately relaxed his body so he didn't jostle Cecilia, still curled up against him. Naked.

He hadn't meant to fall asleep. Then again he hadn't meant to sleep with Cecilia. But both had happened and left him feeling…settled. Instead of the scatterbrained panic, hopping from one problem to another, he felt clearheaded.

Guilt could seep in if he let it. That this was the wrong time and the wrong place and it was not precisely…*right.*

But it had felt right. Righter than most of the choices he'd made in the past year or so.

He had spent a lot of years in his life convincing himself that no one could understand him like his brothers did. They'd shared a kind of tragedy, something other people couldn't imagine. Based on the way Cecilia had reacted to his explanation of his scars, she couldn't imagine it either.

But she treated him like something other than the boy who'd spent his formative years in that gang. More than a piece of the Wyatt whole.

He yawned when his phone trilled again. He'd almost forgotten that's what had woken him up in the first place. A repeated phone call when the world was still dark could mean nothing good. He grabbed his phone and saw Cody's name on the screen.

He only got half of his brother's name out before Cody was talking over him. "There's been a fire at Duke's. Everyone's safe and fine, but it was set purposefully and in the middle of the night like this. It was meant to scare us."

Any good feelings or relaxation seeped out of him. He tensed and disentangled himself from Cecilia, pushing into a seated position on the bed. "You're sure everyone's all right?"

"Thank God for Dev making the dogs stay with us at the Knights'. Cash was barking before I think the thing was even lit. I thought for sure it was a ploy to get us out, but nothing else happened. We're all over at Grandma's and we haven't been able to find anyone on the property."

"What is it?" Cecilia hissed from behind him.

He waved her off. "It's got to be Elijah, though."

"Seems the only option. Everyone is fine, so I'm not sure what his purpose was. They got around my security measures, but didn't actually hurt anyone or take Mak? All these near misses seem…unlikely."

"Yeah. Yeah, they do. Listen, I've got to explain it to Cecilia. Then we'll go from there. Keep watch, though. Be careful. Anything else happens, keep us updated."

"Same," Cody said before Brady ended the call.

"What is it?" Cecilia demanded, before he'd fully pressed End. "Mak? Is it—"

He took her hands in his, trying to find his own calm and reason before he attempted to give her any. "Mak is fine. Everyone is fine. There's been a fire at Duke's house. Luckily, Dev had been making Sarah take care of his dogs and they—"

She immediately threw the sheets off and began to pick up her clothes. He could tell she regretted the sudden movements by the hiss of her breath, but she kept going. "We have to go. We have to go to them."

"No. No, I don't think so." He got out of bed himself, slid his own boxers and shorts back on before crossing to her side of the bed where she was now fully dressed and looking at him furiously. "Sit down. Don't hurt yourself. Listen."

"Listen? Listen!" She waved her arms wildly, then winced. "They burn down Duke's house—his *house*—at night which means even if they're okay Duke and Sarah and oh, God, Brianna and Nina were staying there and Rachel, she—"

Brady stood in front of her and took her hands in his again. It was the only thing to keep her still, and when she tugged he squeezed hard enough to have her taking a sharp breath. "Another one," he ordered. "Deep breath in, and then out."

He didn't expect her to listen, but she did. Still, when her gaze met his it was determined. Haunted. "We have to go. Now."

"Cecilia, no. We can't do that. This is what he wants from you. From us. Think."

She wrenched her hands out of his, groaning out loud this time. "I don't give a flying leap what he wants from me. He burns down my family's home and thinks I'm going to what? What would you have me do, Brady? Sit here? No. I refuse. I don't care what Elijah's plans are."

"You need to," he said sharply. He didn't like being sharp with her, not right now, so he softened his words by cupping her face with his hands. "*We* need to. Remember you're not alone. Mak's not alone. So, we have to work through that fear and not let it lead us. That's what he wants. It's what they always want. When fear wins, so do they." He couldn't let Elijah win *ever*, but now it seemed even more imperative to find an end. For all of them. So Cecilia could heal, so Duke could rebuild, so they could live…normally, if that was ever possible.

She rested her hands over his on her face. "But I *am* afraid, Brady," she said in little more than a whisper.

He knew that was a great big hard admission for her, so he made his own. "I know. So am I. Fear is normal. We just can't let it make the decisions. When you got Mak, you didn't panic. You didn't run right to me. You made plans. You were careful, and so far Mak is safe and sound. So that's what we have to do."

She sucked in a breath and nodded with it. "Okay, okay. Maybe you're right. I knew… I knew I couldn't just run with him or he'd be hurt. I had to think. I had to plan. So, yeah. That's what we have to do. So… He set a fire—"

"That didn't hurt anyone. It's important to remember that. Everyone is fine. He set a fire to lure us home. To *scare* us home. I believe that. Don't you?"

She didn't answer right away. He could tell she gave herself the time and space to really think it over. "Yeah. He's tired of sending his goons after us and failing. He's setting a trap."

"We can't fall for it. We need to do the opposite of what he'll expect. I think…" He sighed heavily. This changed things. There was no escaping what he'd hoped to avoid. "You were right. We need to go into Sons territory. He doesn't think we will, which means we'll have the element of surprise. We need to take him off guard. It's the only way we win."

She searched his face, as if looking for doubt or that earlier reticence. She didn't find it. He wouldn't let her.

She nodded once. "All right. Let's pack."

BRADY EXPLAINED TO her where the fishing cabin was located, and that it wasn't that far from the Sons' current camp on the east side of the Badlands. They were going to have to be strategic about where and how they entered the area, but getting there wouldn't be too long of a haul.

They'd both gotten a couple hours sleep, and that would have to tide them over for a while. She wanted to be in Sons territory by sunrise, but they'd have to hurry.

She didn't let herself think about Mak, or her childhood home being on fire. She didn't think of poor Nina and Cody having to get Brianna out, or what the confusion might have done to Rachel in worse circumstances. She couldn't even begin to let herself think about what would have happened if the dogs hadn't been there.

Her brain wanted to go in *all* those directions, but she couldn't let it. She had to focus on Elijah. How to take him off guard. How to take him down before he did another thing to hurt or scare her family.

"I found a backpack," Cecilia offered, coming into the bedroom where Brady was carefully counting first aid items and foodstuffs and the few camping supplies Grandma Pauline had thought to pack them. "We can both carry a pack now," Cecilia said.

"You better fill yours with bandages and anything that can be used as bandages," Brady muttered.

"I think we've got a lot bigger fish to fry than fussing over a few..." She trailed off at the look he gave her. It was a warning and a censure and yeah, a little hot. Since they didn't have time for a repeat earlier performance she held up her hand. "Okay, the injuries are dangerous and we have to take them seriously."

"You shouldn't be hiking, camping or fighting off biker gang members at all. Nothing is going to heal. *Something* will get infected, and I promise you it's not the picnic you seem to think."

"I suppose not, but once we do all those things, and get Elijah arrested, you can lock me up and nurse me back to health in whatever ways you see fit."

He snorted. "You wouldn't agree to that in a million years." He surveyed the items he'd spread out. "Your pack needs to be lighter. I don't want you arguing over that. It's because of the extent of your injuries, not because you *can't*. Got it?"

She wanted to argue, just out of spite or pride, but both had to be left behind. Elijah had started a fire at Duke's house, and even if he hadn't hurt people, he'd made it clear he could.

That couldn't continue.

She put the pack she'd found on the bed next to Brady's, then let him divvy up the supplies as he saw fit. She didn't let herself watch, because she would have argued.

"We'll get as close as we can to Flynn in the truck. It'll be a hike to get to the main camp."

"Yeah, but I don't think he'll expect us here. Even if we never show up at the ranches, he won't think we've come for him. He'll think we've only run farther away. He won't expect a direct attack. I don't think he could."

"No, I don't think he could," Brady agreed. "But, we have to be prepared if he does." Brady stood back and examined both packs, now full. He scratched a hand through his hair. "This could easily be a suicide mission. Even if the Sons are weaker than they were, the fact they're still inhabiting Flynn and not moving on to a new, smaller camp means they're not falling apart, or even factioning off from what we can tell."

"The camp wasn't at Flynn when you were a kid."

"No. Flynn is Ace's origin story. It's where he was abandoned. It's his mecca, and it's where he tried to make us all into Wyatt men." Brady rolled his shoulders as if to physically move past those old, awful memories. "He built camp there this year to make his final stand… or something. Didn't quite go as planned for him."

"And if Elijah is Ace's son, he might be the cohesive reason they're not splitting off."

Brady nodded grimly. "Exactly."

He was being stoic. Planning and trying to figure the situation out, but the weight of what he would be facing hung over him. "I know this is hard for you."

Brady shrugged that away. "Jamison did it. To save Gigi. I can do it."

"The ability to do something and the toll it takes to do something aren't the same."

His gaze met hers over the bed. "If you're trying to talk me out of something, you don't know me very well."

"Situation reversed, you'd do the same thing, only you'd tell me you were trying to protect me."

"Is that what you're trying to do?"

She shrugged much like he had. "Maybe." It felt a little uncomfortable. After all, Brady was bigger, stronger and more versed in what the Sons could do than she was. It seemed kind of ludicrous, even with her law enforcement background, that she *could* protect him.

But the more she learned about his horrifying childhood, the more she wanted to at least shelter him from that.

"It won't affect my ability to get this done."

Cecilia frowned. Were all men this dense or only Wyatt men? "Maybe I was worried about something else."

"Like what?"

"Like your *feelings*, Brady."

His eyebrows drew together like he didn't understand how that could possibly be a concern.

Which irritated her enough to say something she'd planned to keep to herself. "When you care about someone, you care a little if they have to relive their childhood trauma."

He stared at her for a minute before skirting the bed. She wanted to run away. To forget they'd ever had a conversation about anything. There were far bigger problems than *feelings*.

But he came right up to her and touched her cheek. "I'd relive a hundred childhood traumas for that innocent baby. For my brothers. For the Knights. For a lot of people."

Outrage and hurt chased around inside of her chest, leaving her unable to speak or move. He'd do it for *anyone*. Fine and dandy.

"It would be my duty, no question. But I'm doing this not just as a duty, Cecilia. Not just because you'd do it without me or because God knows you need someone making sure you take as much care of those injuries as possible."

His fingers traced her jaw, causing a shiver to snake through her even as she tried to stand tall and unmoved.

He had just told her he'd do this for *anyone*, as if that wasn't some kind of warped slap in the face.

"I love my brothers with everything I am, but because of how we grew up there…we have to protect each other. Have to. I'm sure we've all felt a certain level of protectiveness for you girls, but it's not the same. Early on I had to accept I can't save or protect everyone."

"What is your *point*, Brady?" she muttered, wishing she had the wherewithal to pull away from his hand gently caressing her cheek.

"The point is there's no obligation here. Not really. I could convince myself I don't need to help you but that would be denial. Because in the end, for whatever reason, I want to be by your side for your fights, and I want you by my side for mine. Not blood, not obligation, not shared crappy history, but because you're the person I need. Because there's something here. I wouldn't say I would have chosen that, but there's no turning back now."

Cecilia didn't often find herself speechless, but that just about did it. Words were not her forte, more so, she didn't think they were particularly Brady's forte. But he'd laid it all out. Honesty complete with uncertainty of how or why, but a certainty it existed.

And he was still touching her face, watching her like there was anything she *could* say.

She cleared her throat. "When this is over…" She didn't know what she was trying to say. Or maybe she did and just didn't want to admit it to herself. The words stuck in her scratchy throat anyway.

Brady pressed a kiss to her forehead, briefly rested his cheek on the top of her head. "Let's get it over, first."

Which somehow wasn't the answer she wanted. Or

the reassurance. "Just know, if you take it all back, I'll kick your butt to Antarctica *and* tell your family you're a turd."

A smile tugged at his lips despite the pressing, dangerous circumstances. "Deal."

Chapter Sixteen

Brady did best with a specific goal in mind. The goal was to get to Elijah before they were expected. If he focused on that goal, he didn't think about how close he was to stepping into his own personal hellscape, or that Cecilia was seriously compromised by her injuries.

It was still dark when they reached as close to the Sons camp as he dared go by truck. The sky to the east hinted at the faint glow of dawn, but the stars still shone brilliantly above the inky dark of the shadowy Badlands.

It was beautiful and stark and it had Brady's chest tightening in a vise. His father had believed this land had anointed him some kind of god, and so Brady had never had any deep, abiding love for it.

But he remained, didn't he? He could have moved. He could have left South Dakota altogether, but he still lived just a quick drive from the place where all his nightmares had been born.

He wasn't sure what that said about him, and knew he didn't have time to figure it out now.

"Jamison and Liza did their best to give me an idea of the different areas of camp. Liza wasn't familiar with Elijah—not as a member, or a high-ranking official."

"What about as Ace's potential son?" Cecilia asked.

Brady shook his head. "I didn't bring it up, but she would have told Jamison if she'd heard anything like that."

"And you think Jamison would tell you?"

"Maybe not before, but knowing Elijah is after Mak and we're after Elijah? Yeah. He would. He'd have to."

"So, we have an idea of how the camp is laid out. Any idea where we find Elijah in it?"

"Depends. What Liza described to me isn't all that different than the camps when I was a kid. Different location, but same basic tenants. There were a few more permanent residences than the Sons are used to, but those were blown up a few months ago by North Star."

Cody had been part of North Star, a secretive group working to take down the Sons of the Badlands, and had delivered the first devastating blow to the Sons by taking out some of their higher-ranking members and arresting Ace, but still the Sons continued to exist, and cause harm.

Brady considered what he knew about the gang both from growing up within its confines, his work as a police officer, and what Liza had told him during their phone call.

"My guess is they constricted. Got closer together. That'll help. But I don't know where Elijah fits in the hierarchy. Ace was still in charge when Liza was there."

"He has men he can send after us. Doesn't that put him high up?"

"I think so. The guy with the gun yesterday—I recognized him. Not by name, but I remember that face. He's not just Elijah's man, he's been a Sons member for a while. Elijah has to be some kind of leader to have veteran members doing his bidding."

"Unless it's a coup. Maybe he's trying to overthrow Ace? He's recruited men in the Sons like he recruited some kids from the rez?"

"Could be. One thing we know is that with Ace in jail, the foundations of the Sons have been shaky. Cody overheard them talking about power vacuums a few months ago."

"Maybe Elijah filled it."

"Maybe." Brady took a deep breath. "It's the hypothesis I'm going to work off of, and it just so happens I know where the powerful men of the Sons congregate."

She shifted in the seat. They were sitting in the dark so he couldn't see her face, but he didn't really want to. He didn't like to be reminded of his father's former standing in the Sons. He didn't imagine other people found it very comfortable either.

"You know, I don't know anything about my father. He could be the leader of some gang somewhere. He could be a murderer. He could be a million terrible things."

"The difference is I do know. I appreciate you trying to comfort me, but I know exactly what my father is and what he's done." Probably not everything, but certainly enough to be haunted by it.

"And I know exactly who you are and what you'll do." Her hand found his in the dark of the truck.

He squeezed it. They needed to get going, put some distance in before the sun rose. He kept her hand in his. "I need you to promise me that you'll be honest with me about the state of your injuries. If things hurt. If there's bleeding—or bleeding through bandages. You have to let me know when we need to stop and take care of those issues. I need you to promise."

She was quiet for a few humming seconds, and he waited for the lie or the argument.

"All right," she said gravely, with enough weight and time between his words and hers for him to believe her. "I promise."

He gave her hand a squeeze. "Then let's get going."

They both got out of the truck, loaded their packs on their backs, and set out into the rocky landscape before them.

Brady had his cell phone on silent, though the service out here would be patchy at best. He had a mental idea of the area that hadn't changed all that much since he'd been tasked with survival out here as a child. He had the pack on his back and he had an injured Cecilia hiking beside him in the dark.

Not exactly where he'd planned to be a few weeks ago, or months ago, or certainly after New Year's Eve.

He'd had some disdain for the way Gage and Felicity had gotten together. Brady could admit it now, in the privacy of his own thoughts. He'd understood Liza and Jamison, Nina and Cody—they'd had a history before going through their ordeals. But Felicity had been harboring a crush on Brady for he wasn't sure how long. Brady hadn't understood how dangerous situations gave way to honest, deep feelings.

No matter that he could see Gage and Felicity now and knew they were happy, he'd been skeptical.

But now he understood that danger and running stripped away the walls and the safety exits you built for yourself without fully realizing it. He'd been able to lecture Cecilia about kissing him on New Year's Eve because his life had been intact and he'd been able to use that as an excuse to wedge between them.

But danger—life or death danger. Worry—keeping a baby safe worry. These were the things that stripped you to nothing but who and what you were.

It was a lot harder to fight feelings here.

Brady took a deep breath of the canyon air. He didn't love the Badlands, and he didn't love the act of hiking—both brought back ugly memories of an unpleasant childhood. He preferred the rolling hills of the ranch or the sturdy, square grids of town.

Because in the dark, in the unusual shapes of the Badlands built by rivers and wind, Brady knew the only thing they were really going to find was danger.

DAWN BROKE, PINK and pearly. A gentle easing of sun over dark. It felt like some kind of promise. Peace.

Cecilia knew Brady was keeping the hiking pace slow for her. Normally she would have chastised him for it, but everything hurt. Her feet, her body, her injuries—especially the stab wound. Her head pounded and even though he made her stop every so often and drink water, her mouth was miserably dry.

She was both hungry and nauseous and utterly, completely miserable. She walked on anyway, because Elijah or his men had set a fire at her childhood home with the people she loved most in the world inside.

She glanced at the man in front of her, bathed in the golden light of sunrise.

Love was a very strange, complicated word. She adjusted her pack, happy to focus on how heavy the light load felt rather than anything like *love*.

"Need a break?"

"No. No. Rather get this over with than break."

"I think we're close enough if we can get high enough,

we can see the camp. I want to climb up here and try," Brady said, pointing to a large, steep rock outcropping. "You can stay put, be the lookout."

Cecilia shaded her eyes with her hand. The climb looked difficult even if she were in perfect health. Still, she didn't want to be down here caught off guard if someone came upon her, or vice versa. "Let's see what I can do."

"Favor that side," he instructed. Clearly he didn't want her to make the climb, but didn't want to leave her alone either. They started the climb, and Brady basically hovered over her trying to mitigate any effort to her side.

She wanted to be irritated, but she wouldn't have made it without his help. Even *with* his help, she felt more than a little battered when they reached the top. But she could almost put that aside when she looked out below.

This wasn't strictly national park land, but the Badlands still stretched out, all canyons and valleys with only the occasional patch of flat and grass. In the lowest valley, some distance off, there was clearly a camp of some kind

And while they were alone in *this* moment, it was clear people used the flat area of this rock outcropping. There was a lockbox dug into the ground, rocks pushed together to form a kind of bench. Signs of footprints.

"Lookouts," Cecilia muttered, toeing the locked box.

"Might have caught them during the dawn changing of the guard," Brady said, looking out over the valley below. "But they don't keep lookouts all the time. With their diminishing numbers they probably only do it when there's a threat."

"What would be considered a threat?"

"Cops or federal agents mostly. A few months before Jamison got Cody out, there was a big ATF investigation. Nerves were high. Always a lookout then."

She couldn't help but watch him when he offered little pieces of his childhood like that. It was purposeful. He'd never once spoken about his time in the Sons to her before, and so doing it now had to be because…

Well, because he'd decided to trust her. Or care about her. Or something.

He pointed to the camp below. "If Elijah has an actual position of importance, and I'm thinking he does, that's his compound right there to the north. He might not have the main tent, but he'd have a tent in that area."

"So we climb back down and hike around to the north side?"

"Not to the north, no. The main compound is more guarded than the rest. They'll have guards positioned all along the north perimeter to make sure no one tries anything. I think especially with all the factions and power issues, you're going to have a lot of presence there."

"We can't exactly cut through the camp."

"No. I'm too recognizable, and you may be too at this point. It's going out on a limb, but I don't think he'd be here right now. He's either at the rez, or close to the ranches. He's going to be somewhere he thinks we're going. So, our goal is to cut him off before he gets to the camp when he realizes we're not rushing home."

Brady pointed again, this time to the southern portion of the camp. "That's the main entrance. See how they've got it set up? You've got tire tracks coming in right there—and I don't see any other vehicle points of access. So, that's the road in."

"He's not going to be alone."

"No. And we can't just ambush him. All that does is land us in another fight, and it doesn't give us any grounds to arrest him."

"So, what are you proposing then?"

Brady finally took his gaze off the camp below. "Do you know how Jamison created a big enough distraction for me and Gage to escape?"

Cecilia wasn't sure she wanted to know. Every time he told her some awful story about his childhood she wanted to wrap him in a hug. Which wasn't exactly a comfortable reaction for her, even if she was coming around to the idea of…well, whatever she felt for Brady.

"He'd gotten Cody out almost two years before us. A few months before us, he'd gotten Tuck out. Obviously, the suspicion was that Jamison had orchestrated it, but no matter how Ace tried, he couldn't figure out how. He beat Jamison, he beat Gage, he beat Dev. He threatened, raged, demanded answers from the people around us, but he never could find actual evidence that Jamison was behind the escapes."

"Why didn't he beat you?" Cecilia asked.

Brady blinked. Then he turned away from the camp, made a move to climb down.

"Brady. I asked you a question."

"He believed me when I said I didn't know since he said I couldn't lie to save my life. It wasn't worth the energy to beat me." He held out his hand to help her down the first steep descent. She knew she should just take his hand, not react to that…horror.

But it was so *complex* in its horror, and the more she got a glimpse into what he'd endured the more in awe of him she was. No *wonder* he could be a little stuffy and standoffish. No *wonder* the rules meant so much to him.

Why on earth had he slept with *her*?

Which wasn't a question they had any time for.

"The point of the story is that Jamison created a distraction," Brady continued, waiting for her to take his hand. "He ambushed someone he knew had been working with the cops, called a Sons meeting and told Ace this was the man he'd been looking for."

Cecilia nearly stumbled as Brady helped her down. "Jamison threw someone under the bus?" She couldn't begin to imagine. He'd be right to. He and his brothers stuck in hell, she wouldn't blame Jamison a bit. Still, it surprised her.

"Not exactly. The guy *had* been working with the cops, but he'd gotten pissed off and killed one of them. So, while Jamison had set this meeting in motion, he'd also managed to send evidence to the local police department that this man was the culprit. So, the distraction was twofold—finally finding the perpetrator, and the cops coming to the compound."

"That sounds complicated."

"It was. I don't know how many weeks he spent working it all out, getting the timing right. And he did it all on his own. Well, I think Liza helped him. We still almost got caught. All that and we still almost got caught." Brady shook his head as if he could shake away old, bad memories with it. "Anyway, point is we need that kind of distraction. Something to keep Elijah focused and busy on one hand, while we're working to arrest him on the other."

Cecilia looked around the vast landscape. The camp was now hidden behind the rocks to their backs. "How on earth are we going to do that?"

Brady paused. “Well, he wants both of us for different reasons. If he had one of us...”

Brady trailed off.

“You don’t honestly think one of us could be a distraction?”

“It makes sense. One to distract, and one to observe the arrestable offense. And then move forward with the arresting.”

“And let me guess—you think *you* should be the distraction?”

“Actually, no. I think it should be you.”

Chapter Seventeen

Cecilia stared at him, mouth actually hanging open. She'd stopped her forward progress down the steep incline, but she still held on to his hand.

Brady couldn't say he *liked* his idea, but unfortunately it was the most sensible. He thought she would have seen that herself, but apparently not.

"Unfortunately it makes sense. You're hurt, which means it's going to be harder for you to be stealthy. It'd make more sense for you to pretend to be caught. I can move around easier, observe with more ease and care, *and* arrest with more force. Plus, your jurisdiction is limited to the rez. While we're outside Valiant County lines, I've got more of a legal standing than you. In a court of law."

She blinked, mouth still hanging open. When she finally spoke, it was only to echo his own words. "Court of law."

"It has to be legal, Cecilia."

She blinked again, multiple times, as if that would somehow change anything. "You're going to let me be a sacrificial human diversion. You said we'd never split up and you want to do just that."

"Let's not use the word *sacrificial*. All the elements

have to come together right. Including making sure we've isolated Elijah before we allow you to be any kind of diversion. Then, it has to be absolutely certain I'll be able to follow, observe and arrest. Not split up, give the illusion of splitting up."

She finally started moving forward again, letting him take some of her weight on the way down. When they reached more even ground and a tuft of grass amidst the rocky terrain around them, he started leading her toward the best positioning for their purposes.

"We'll want to keep ourselves by the road, a ways away from camp. The biggest challenge right now is to figure out a way to block Elijah from getting to camp—and keeping him separate from camp if we do let him catch you."

"Let him catch me. You're going to *let* Elijah catch me."

"No, *I'm* not going to let him, Cecilia. You're going to either make the decision to be the diversion or not. If you don't want to do it, we'll devise a new plan." And part of him really wanted her to refuse, even though he knew she wouldn't. Even though this was the only way.

"We can't do this alone. It's just not possible with only the two of us. Not this close to literally *hundreds* of people who'd help him."

"What about three of us?"

At the sound of a third voice, Brady whirled, gun in hand. He hadn't heard a sound, even a potential for someone sneaking up on them. He was ready to shoot first and ask questions later, but the voice was too familiar.

Brady stared at his brother for a full twenty seconds,

gun still pointed at him. "Tucker. How… Wh… What on earth are you doing here?"

Tucker's smile was easy, but it hid something that made Brady fully uneasy. "I'm a detective. I'm detectiving."

That didn't make any sense. Brady could only frown at Tucker. "This isn't your jurisdiction."

Tuck shrugged. "I needed to do some looking myself and get a grasp on what I'll need local law enforcement to do when we're ready to move. It's a pretty complicated case. Lots of departments and moving parts."

None of that made any sense, least of all Tucker having some case that tied to the Sons that none of them knew about.

"And you just *happened* to come across us here in the middle of nowhere?" Cecilia demanded, not even trying to hide her suspicion.

Brady didn't know how to be suspicious of his own brother, even when none of this felt right.

"It's not exactly the middle of nowhere," Tucker replied, unoffended. "It's the Sons lookout that gives the whole camp's layout." Tucker waved an arm as if to encompass the camp behind the large outcropping they'd just climbed down. "And now I can help you guys."

"How did you find us?" Brady returned.

"I'm not here for you, Brady. I mean, I can help. I want to. But it isn't why I was here. I was here for my job. I heard you guys and came closer. By the way, I listened to your plan and it kind of sucks without backup."

"I wouldn't call one more person backup," Cecilia replied, her demeanor still suspicious.

Brady could only feel conflicted. His gut was telling him that something was off, but this was Tucker. Tucker was... Probably the most well-adjusted out of all of them. He was good like Jamison, without Jamison's penchant for taking on too much responsibility. He worked hard like Brady without letting it make him too uptight. He had Gage's good humor without using it as a shield.

But none of this made sense, and Brady didn't like the fact Tucker was clearly lying to them. To *him*. When had Tucker ever lied?

"Elijah was camped out near the ranches. Had a small group with him. Only two other men that we could tell. The group or person who started the fire is gone, so he's traveling light. So if we can somehow take out his communication, three against three isn't such bad odds."

Brady opened his mouth to tell Tucker Cecilia was hurt and didn't count as a full person, but he found something so off-putting about all of this, he just closed it right back up. He couldn't put Cecilia at risk until this felt less...wrong.

"You can't be serious," Cecilia said. "You can't honestly think we buy any of this."

Some of the forced cheerfulness melted off Tucker's face. "But if you buy it, I can help." He turned his attention from Cecilia to Brady. "Surely you trust me to help."

Brady had never once questioned his brother's honesty or loyalty. Even as kids. Tucker was honest to a fault. On more than one occasion the Wyatt brothers had ganged up on Tuck for telling Grandma Pauline something she would have been better off not knowing.

Nothing about this felt right or honest, but it was *Tucker*. "Of course we do."

"Speak for yourself," Cecilia interjected. "You're acting fishy as hell. I don't trust that for a minute."

"Cecilia," Brady muttered.

"No, it's all right. She doesn't have to trust me." Tuck smiled. "But you trust me, Brady. Right?"

Never in his life had he hesitated to trust one of his brothers. It was alarming to hesitate now. But something wasn't right—and he didn't know how to figure out what.

CECILIA FELT A little bit like crying. Tucker Wyatt wasn't some Sons spy. She knew that in her gut, in her heart.

But her mind was telling her he was sure acting like one.

It didn't take anyone with some great understanding of Brady to see that the hesitation cost him. Hurt him. Hence the tears, because the idea of Brady being laid low by his brother's potential betrayal just ate her up inside.

But how could they trust Tucker with their lives when he very clearly wasn't telling the truth?

"I trust you, Tuck. How could I not?" Brady said, very gravely, very carefully as if every word was picked for greatest effect. "You've never given me a reason not to."

Cecilia kept her mouth shut, even though *shady appearance out of nowhere* was at the top of her list for not trusting him.

"My theory is they'll head back to camp this afternoon. They won't wait around at the ranches *too* long for you to show up, because if you're not going to rush back, you're probably not coming, right?"

"Were you there when Cody called me to tell me about the fire?" Brady asked, frown still in place.

"In the room? No. Dev and I were out searching for signs of Elijah's men."

"But you were home at the ranch when the fire started?"

"Well, yeah, we've all been taking turns keeping

close. If we're all there it looks suspicious, so Jamison and Liza were back in Bonesteel with Gigi. Cody is having some guys work on his house so it looks like he and Nina and Brianna are staying with the Knights during renovations. And I come and go like I usually do, though I try to stick around a little extra time without being too conspicuous. That's what we planned from the beginning, isn't it?"

It all sounded good, and Tucker seemed at ease with the questioning and with his answers. Cecilia shouldn't have that gut feeling that something was all wrong.

But she did.

"We've got a few hours to set up some kind of… booby trap, for lack of a better word. Something that will stop Elijah from getting close to the Sons camp. Of course, our main problem is he could easily message for backup—and backup would come ASAP."

Brady helped her over a particularly unsteady part of the rock where she was struggling to get her footing. He didn't say anything, so she did the same. Tucker followed, as if happy to walk in utter silence with no feedback on his plan.

"We put out a few things that take his tires out. Then a little ways down the road we do some kind of…ambush? Trap? Something they can't get past. The only problem we're up against is their phones."

"Won't they immediately call for help if they blow out a tire? Before they even get out of the car?" Brady returned.

Tucker shrugged, continuing to follow them down closer to that makeshift road. "Depends on how in a hurry they are. Out here blowing a tire wouldn't be that uncommon. Probably used to it. No reason to get extra people when they'll have the ability to make a quick change themselves."

Cecilia studied Brady. He seemed to be considering Tucker's ludicrous argument. Brotherly love or not, Cecilia would not walk them into an ambush like that.

"That's ridiculous," Cecilia said forcefully. "Elijah wouldn't sit around waiting for the tire to be changed. Especially if he's trying to figure out why we didn't come chasing after him like he hoped. He'd call for another ride, or he'd walk it. He's not going to sit around and change a tire or wait for his men to."

Tucker didn't argue, but he didn't pipe up to agree with her assessment either. So, she kept talking. "It can't be something they need to be rescued from or can be helped out. It has to be their idea to get out of the car, without raising any red flags that might make them call ahead to the camp."

Tucker and Brady mulled this as they walked. When she hissed out a breath from landing too hard on her already aching leg, that sent a jolt of pain through her stab wounds, Brady held out a hand to help her again.

She noticed Tucker watched the exchange carefully, and it dawned on her that Brady hadn't mentioned her injuries to Tucker. It was pertinent information, especially as they made plans. But he'd avoided the topic.

Maybe he didn't fully trust Tucker either. Her heart twisted because she knew that had to be eating him up alive. To question one of his brothers. And if Cecilia was right in her gut feeling? If Tucker was up to something wrong?

The whole Wyatt clan would be...wrecked. There was no other word for it.

They walked farther in silence. Cecilia kept her eye

on Tucker. Something was up with him. She didn't want to think it was nefarious, but what else could it be? If it was anything *good*, he'd tell them.

They were coming up on the path that worked as entrance into the camp now. "If I'm going to be the prisoner anyway, why not use me as a diversion here?" Cecilia pointed to the road a ways off.

"He might think something's fishy about stumbling upon you," Brady returned.

They all stopped and Brady passed her a water bottle, which earned another careful look from Tucker. Cecilia met his considering gaze and raised an eyebrow. Tucker only turned away.

Something was *really* not right here.

"We'd have to set it up. Make it look like I'm trying to get to camp, trying to not be seen, only we have to make sure he sees me. And doesn't see either of you."

Brady studied the area around them. "It's too open. Why would you be hiking through here when you could be in the rock formations?"

Cecilia considered Tucker. Her best idea was to milk her injuries, pretend like she was struggling to hike and needed the even ground. But Brady hadn't mentioned her injuries, and that had to be purposeful. So she flashed a fake smile at Tucker. "You mind giving us a few minutes?"

Tucker's eyebrows drew together. "Huh?"

"I want to talk to your brother in private. Without you listening. Can you go over there?" She pointed to some rocks in the distance.

"You can't be serious," Tucker replied, and his outrage didn't seem fake. That felt very real. The first real reaction he'd given since they'd "bumped" into him up on the lookout point.

It was good to see *something* could elicit a real response out of him. "I'm very serious. What I have to say to Brady is private. So..." She made a shooing motion.

Tucker turned his indignant gaze to Brady.

Brady sighed. "Just give us a few, Tuck. This isn't about you anyway."

Tucker's mouth firmed, but he walked toward the pile of rocks Cecilia had motioned to. And boy, did he not seem pleased about it.

Which, in fairness, could be his reaction whether he was trying to help or sabotage. The younger Wyatt brothers were never very good at being dismissed. Which was why she'd always gone out of her way to find ways to dismiss them.

She glanced up at the Wyatt brother still with her. He'd always handled it the best. With just enough disdain to irritate her right back. None of the carrying-on or male bluster, just a calm nonchalance that always had her losing her temper first.

That warm feeling was spreading through her chest again, but she had to shove it away and focus on the problem at hand. "I didn't want to say it in front of him, but if I overact my injuries, it might be a plausible enough reason for Elijah to believe I was taking the easy route in."

"Maybe, but only if it was dark. I don't think he'd believe you doing it midday. There'd be no reason."

Cecilia frowned. True enough, but if Elijah was coming back this afternoon, they didn't have time for that.

"Why'd you send him over there for that?" Brady asked.

"Why didn't you tell him I'm hurt?"

Brady scrubbed a hand over his face. "I...don't know."

"I know why, Brady. You didn't tell him because we can't actually trust him. Something isn't right about all this."

Brady's forehead lined and he stared at Tucker bent over the rock. "Maybe it's not right, but… I can't let myself not trust my own brother. Not Tuck. He wouldn't… He just wouldn't. Whatever is off is something he can't tell us, but that doesn't mean it's wrong or bad."

Cecilia frowned at him even as her heart pinched. She understood his loyalty, the need for it.

But she absolutely could not be caught in the cross fire of his misplaced loyalty.

Chapter Eighteen

Brady felt as though he was being pulled in two very correct directions. This was not black-and-white. There was no one clear, right answer.

He had to trust his brother. His younger *brother*. Tuck, who had always been good and dedicated to his law enforcement career, to taking down Ace and the Sons. Brady absolutely had to trust Tucker—it was the right thing to do.

Brady had also made a successful law enforcement career through listening to his gut, and the facts. Both the facts and his gut pointed to this being all wrong. Those things told him not to trust Tucker.

Then there was Cecilia. He'd made her sit down because she looked too pale. She was all but staring daggers at Tucker who was moving back over to join them.

"I have an idea," Tucker said grimly. "You probably won't like it."

"You're finally catching on," Cecilia muttered.

Tuck pretended not to notice. "The thing is, he expected you both to run back to the Knights after the fire. He expects you to be mad, right? Probably doesn't expect you to run to the Sons camp, but it wouldn't be out of the question for either of you to come after him directly. He wouldn't necessarily find it out of character if one of you were waiting here for a standoff."

"That'd be suicide," Brady replied.

"Would it though? I don't have any evidence Elijah has ever killed anyone. Do you?"

"We could say the same about Ace," Brady replied, resisting the need to rub his chest where that truth always lodged like a weight.

Tucker shook his head. "We know better. And sure, Elijah could use his goons as mercenaries to keep his hands clean. Ace did enough of that. But Elijah isn't Ace. He's not the leader of the Sons. He's trying, sure. Maybe he's even getting there. But he's lived his life outside the camp. No matter how involved he's gotten."

"He thinks we're dumb, Brady," Cecilia offered. "He thinks he's smarter than us. And I think he'd want to have a face-off. He'd want to talk. He wouldn't shoot first."

"But he could," Brady insisted. "We could let Cecilia stand out there in the middle of the road, ready for a showdown, and he could just flat-out kill her in two seconds. Not happening."

"*I* took Mak. *I* know where Mak is, and his goons didn't try to kill me. They tried to take me."

"Which is exactly why you wouldn't be stupid enough to go after him. He might underestimate us, but I don't think he's going to be fooled by a standoff with you."

"Not her," Tucker agreed. "Mak or no, I think the potential for Elijah killing her is certainly higher than not. He'd want to torture her a bit, but if she was antagonizing him, he'd be fine with just taking her out. You, on the other hand, are a Wyatt. Ace Wyatt's son. Ace might be in jail, but we both know he still has some power here.

You're worth more alive than dead as a power move. Even if you were threatening him, if he could bring you into camp, make some kind of example out of you in front of the group members—"

"Yeah, no," Cecilia said firmly, pushing up from the rock with a wince. "We picked me to be the distraction for a reason."

"But it's not just you two anymore," Tucker said evenly. "You have me."

"If I'm not standing there facing Elijah, neither is he. End of story."

"You two seem really worried about each other."

"So what if we are, Tuck? Got a problem with wanting people to stay alive?" Cecilia returned, and clearly wasn't thinking of her injuries when she stepped toward Tucker threateningly, like she was ready to fight him.

Tucker didn't react except to move his gaze from Cecilia to Brady. "Would you do it?"

Cecilia whirled, her eyes all flashing fury. "Think very carefully about how you answer that question, Wyatt."

Which gave him some pause. He didn't care for being ordered about in that high-handed tone, but the reason behind it was, well, care. She cared about him. Didn't want to see him taking unnecessary chances any more than he wanted to see her taking them.

The more they talked about variables, adjusted plans, the more he realized…he couldn't let any of them get caught by Elijah. It was too much risk.

"He'd expect some kind of ambush if we were the aggressors," Brady said, carefully avoiding Tucker's direct question. "No matter how stupid or emotional he thinks we are, he'll suspect there are more of us waiting."

Tucker's expression was inscrutable, and the awful *don't trust this guy* feeling burrowed deeper. Tucker was never inscrutable, except at work. He had said this was work. But it was also life.

All three of them turned toward the sound of an engine. It was far off, carrying over the wide-open landscape around them.

"We don't have enough time for a plan. Just hide."

Tucker swore. "Where?" he muttered, whirling around. "You two, there," he said, pointing to the small pile of rocks. "Three of us can't fit, but I can run over to those."

Tucker didn't wait to see if Brady would agree. He started to run and Brady couldn't argue with him. They didn't have time. He grabbed Cecilia's hand and they ran for the pile of rocks.

"If we're here they shouldn't see us unless they look back, which they'd have no reason to. You get situated in the most comfortable position. I'll get in around you."

"Just get out of sight, moron," she returned, settling herself behind the rock. He sat beside her. He'd need to sink lower.

"You need to be in a comfortable position that isn't putting too much pressure on that stab wound."

She muttered irritably under her breath, readjusted her position lying behind the rock, then he pretzeled his body to fit around her so they were hidden by the rock. Someone would really have to be looking for them to see them.

God, he hoped.

The engine was getting closer, though it was hard to tell how close the way noise moved and echoed in the vast valley. He could only keep his body as still as possible, focus on keeping his breathing even, and not crushing Cecilia.

Seconds ticked by, stretching long and taut, but he had been trained to deal with these kinds of situations. He couldn't think of what-ifs. He couldn't let his brain zoom ahead. He had to breathe. Steady himself and believe the car would pass. Everything would be fine.

He could tell the engine was getting closer, but how close was impossible to discern. He wouldn't be able to believe it was past them until he didn't hear it at all. So he focused on the even whir of the engine carrying on the air. Once it was gone, it would be safe.

A car door slammed above the low buzz of the engine. Both he and Cecilia jerked, almost imperceptibly. Training could keep them tamping down normal reactions, but it couldn't eradicate reflexes completely.

Cecilia's hand found his arm and she squeezed. Their breathing had increased its pace, but he could feel them both working together to slow it. In then out. Slow. Easy.

He couldn't hear over the pounding in his ears, or maybe there was nothing happening. Maybe the car door was miles away. Maybe they were overreacting.

"I saw something."

The voice was clear, close, and most definitely Elijah.

Brady listened as footsteps thudded. It sounded like the men Elijah was speaking to split up and went in different directions, but he couldn't be sure. He was tempted to risk a look, but Cecilia was still squeezing his arm as if to say *don't*.

Silence was intermittently interrupted by footsteps, the faint murmur of voices, or a scuttling sound that Brady eventually figured was rocks being kicked.

Then suddenly the sounds of a scuffle, maybe even a punch and a grunt. Then a voice Brady didn't recognize.

"Found a Wyatt."

More footsteps—farther away from Brady. The sounds seemed to fade away, but he could just make out Elijah's words. "Well. This is an interesting development."

Cecilia's nails dug into his arm, as if she could keep him here. And it should. Brady should stay put. So, he held on to the fact that Tucker could take care of himself. He was smart. A detective. And a Wyatt, so like he'd said—more valuable alive than dead.

Elijah seemed surprised to have found him. Which meant whatever odd reason Tucker had for being here, chalking it up to coincidence, didn't have to do with the Sons.

Or does it just not have to do with Elijah?

"Not the Wyatt I expected, I have to say," Elijah's voice echoed through the midday heat. "Of course, where there's one, there's usually more."

"Yeah. Probably," Tucker replied, sounding almost cheerful. "Home sweet home, you know?"

Cecilia's intake of breath was sharp and audible. Brady shook his head just a bit, even though he doubted she'd see or feel it.

Tucker wasn't ratting them out. He was bluffing to Elijah so Elijah didn't go looking for them.

"Hurt him till he talks," Elijah ordered crisply. The order was immediately followed by a thud and a whoosh of breath.

Brady had to close his eyes, even though he couldn't see from behind the rock anyway. Tucker could take it. He could handle it.

Brady needed to stay put. Protect Cecilia. Tucker could take care of himself. This wasn't all that far off from what they'd been planning. Let him be taken, carefully follow. Arrest.

Tucker could handle it. Brady repeated that fact to himself as he heard the thud of blows, the grunts of pain. This was still better than sending an injured Cecilia to do the job.

He opened his eyes as the sound of fighting increased.

Brady couldn't stand it. He simply couldn't listen as Tucker got beaten by three men. Even if they kept him alive, they could do anything to Tucker, and Brady couldn't live with himself if he just…stayed put. He tried to move, but Cecilia's fingernails dug into his arm.

"Let him get captured, Brady," she hissed as quietly as possible. "It's half our plan anyway. We'll save him after. We'll—"

Brady shook his head, taking her hand off his arm. He quietly got to his feet and quickly shook off his pack. Gently and as silently as possible, he knelt and set it next to her. He looked her in the eye. "I can't. I'm sorry. I just can't do it." He pressed a quick kiss to her mouth. "If it were you like we planned, I wouldn't have been able to do it either. I'm sorry."

Then he left her. She had weapons and a cell phone and the chance to escape. Tucker didn't, and Brady couldn't let him go down alone.

CECILIA WAS SHOCKED into stillness for probably more than a minute. All their talk and debating about plans, and it had just gone up in smoke. Brady walked away, all grim determination.

I wouldn't have been able to do it either.

That echoed inside of her. He'd planned to let her get caught, but he would have never been able to go through with that plan. She wanted to be angry, furious. She wanted to march after him and drag him back behind this rock and their little bubble of pretend safety.

But she understood too well what he'd meant. She was half-convinced Tucker was on the wrong side of things, even now, and it was still hard to listen to someone she'd grown up with and cared about get beaten up.

If it was one of her sisters? She wouldn't have lasted even as long as Brady. Still, this was…suicide. Surely. Maybe Brady and Tucker could *fight* three men off, but Elijah's men had to have weapons. Maybe Brady and Tucker were somewhat protected by their Wyatt name, but if they fought back hard enough, would Elijah really care to keep them around to use them as examples to the other Sons.

And what could she do? There was no cell service out here. She could shoot, but that made her a target too, and if she was a target, how would they get out of this mess? Someone needed to be safe to find the option to *get* help.

She heard the sounds of fighting and closed her eyes, taking a steadying breath. She had to think clearly, without emotion clouding her judgment. Emotion would get all three of them killed. And probably only after Elijah tortured them.

Torture. Would Brady give under torture? Tell Elijah exactly where Mak was? She didn't think so. She thought he'd die first.

But Tucker? Once she would have put her utter faith into him, but not today. Not with his weirdness.

She couldn't let them get captured, or at least not for very long. But in order to figure out what she was going to do, she had to look. She had to know what was going on to make an informed decision.

Maybe it'd be easy to get a shot off, to pick all three men off and end this here and now. It was possible, but she wouldn't know it unless she risked being seen.

She unholstered her weapon, and took another slow breath, calming her heart rate, trying to keep her limbs from shaking. Slowly, she peeked over the rock.

Tucker and Brady were holding their own in the fight. Brady was a little worse for the wear, probably since he'd already been beaten up the day before. But he and Tucker worked together like a team to take on the other two men, who fought like individuals. Elijah's men landed blows on Brady and Tucker, but they didn't make any headway on actually taking Brady or Tucker down.

Both of Elijah's men had guns strapped to their legs, but they didn't use them. Why not even use them as a threat? Brady was living proof you could shoot a man and have him survive. Why wouldn't they use the strongest weapons they had at their disposal?

"Why does none of this make sense?" Cecilia muttered to herself. She lifted her gun, trying to test if she could make two successive shots and take down both men before they returned fire.

There was too much struggle, though. She'd be just as likely to hit Brady or Tucker with the way they were all moving and stumbling and swinging at each other. And she wasn't guaranteed to make a glancing blow either. What if she missed altogether?

Wait. Two against two. Why were there only two men? Where was Elijah?

She looked toward the car Elijah and his men had left in the middle of the path to camp. It was still running, but she didn't see anyone. Had Elijah walked on to camp, leaving his lackeys to handle the Wyatt brothers? No. He wouldn't have done that.

There was a crack of sound behind her, like a gun being cocked, then the cold press of metal against the back of her head. She froze.

"Well hello, Cecilia," Elijah's voice said softly in her ear. "Didn't see this coming, did you?"

He peeled the gun out of her hand, and she had to let him. Because she had no doubt Elijah would pull that trigger if she provoked him.

"Now. On your feet. We have so much to talk about."

Chapter Nineteen

Brady took another ham-fisted punch to the kidney and nearly lost his balance, but Tucker was there, backing him up, blocking the next blow and landing one of his own.

All of them were breathing heavily, not doing much more than landing punches that hurt but didn't take anyone out or down. Brady's gun had been knocked out of his hand before he'd been able to get a clear shot, and Tucker had lost his long before Brady had come to help.

It felt…pointless, Brady realized, ducking another punch with enough ease dread skittered up his spine. "Something isn't right," he muttered to his brother.

Tucker dodged a blow, landed a decent fist to one of the men attacking them.

One of the *two* guys. There were only two.

"Where'd Elijah go?"

Tucker swore, and not half a second later landed an elbow to one guy's temple that had him crumpling. In a fluid, easy move and with absolutely no help from Brady, he managed to get the other in a choke hold.

Had Tucker been…holding back?

No time to think about that. He let Tucker deal with

handcuffing the two debilitated aggressors and searched the area around them for Elijah. Nothing.

He looked over to the rocks where Cecilia should be out of sight. Instead, past the rocks, he saw two figures. They were far away so he couldn't make them out well enough to be certain it was Elijah and Cecilia, but who else would it be?

"Go ahead," Tucker said. "Follow. I'll be right behind you. We can't have these guys coming behind us, and we have to see where he takes her. Go."

"No, Tuck. You don't follow me. You go get help. We can't do this alone. We need backup. You have to go get backup." His brother hadn't been acting normal. His actions didn't make sense, but Brady had to be able to trust Tucker. "Promise me."

Tucker was kneeling, tying the men's feet together with rope Brady had no idea how he'd gotten. "You could both get killed in the time it'll take me to get help. You don't even have a gun," he returned, not meeting Brady's gaze.

"We'll take our chances." Brady was already walking away from Tucker, toward Cecilia. He didn't have time to search for the one that had been knocked out of his hand or he'd lose sight of Cecilia. "We don't have *any* if we both go in there. But we do if you get help. We can arrest him. He's taken Cecilia against her will. We have arrestable grounds. All we need is enough law enforcement to make it happen."

He was running by the time he was done talking. Cecilia and Elijah had disappeared behind a large rock formation. Brady headed for the rock first, thinking to grab the pack quickly on his way.

But there was a fire. Small and it wouldn't spread

thanks to the rocky landscape, but both his and Cecilia's packs were in the middle of the blaze. There was no chance of saving anything or finding a weapon.

Brady didn't stop to think about the implications, and while he considered the fact that Elijah could just shoot him dead in the middle of the Badlands, it didn't really matter.

If he'd wanted him dead, Brady could have been dead multiple times. He had to bank on the fact that either Ace's shadow, or potential family loyalty, or *something* was keeping Elijah from taking him out.

Maybe that wouldn't extend past an attack, or an attempt to get Cecilia back, but it was a risk Brady was willing to take.

And if Tucker doesn't get help?

Brady slowed his pace. It was an irrational fear. His brother had taken down those two men, fought beside him. Tucker would go get help.

He could have ended that fight a lot quicker.

Whatever it meant, whatever weird thing was going on with Tuck, it didn't mean he was helping Elijah or the Sons. Brady had to stop letting stupid doubts plague him.

Even with Cecilia's life at stake?

It was too difficult a choice. Trust his brother over all else? Risk Cecilia over it? There was too much at stake to make an error.

He could only focus on himself. On what he could do.

He'd laid out a plan where Cecilia was captured, and even though he wouldn't have been able to *let* it happen, it was currently happening. And he was following, just like he'd planned. With or without backup, he could arrest Elijah. He had grounds.

All he had to do was catch up, somehow get Elijah

away from Cecilia without her getting hurt and arrest him…with no weapon, no handcuffs and no help whatsoever.

He'd eased into a brisk walk instead of an all-out run. With the dust and rocky debris, there was a decent enough trail to follow as long as the wind didn't pick up and Elijah didn't realize Cecilia was digging her heels in and making enough of a track for him to follow.

Occasionally, he paused to listen to try and figure out how close he was, but he never got close enough to hear actual footsteps or the struggle Cecilia must be putting up.

She wouldn't go easily. Even if Elijah had a weapon. She wouldn't just docilely be marched along. Which meant, surely, Elijah had no plans to kill her either.

Brady wasn't sure how long he'd walked, following a trail, and not getting close enough to hear a scuffle before the landscape started to feel…more familiar. Too familiar. Bad familiar.

Brady stopped short. He knew this area too well. Old memories tried to surface, but he couldn't give them space. Couldn't give them power.

Couldn't allow himself to picture Ace on that rock above, throwing knives. Leaving him out here, seven years old and all alone.

Brady looked at the towering rock around him, preparing his body for that searing pain out of nowhere, as if he expected Ace to jump out and do what he'd always done. Brady wouldn't put it past Ace to share with Elijah how he'd tortured his children.

Ace had tortured them each in different ways, and they'd each kept that a secret from each other, thinking it was an individual personal shame. After Gage's ordeal, he'd told Brady about the ways Ace had tortured him.

Gage's admission had prompted them all to share their secrets. Which Ace wouldn't know. He'd think those secrets were ammunition, and wouldn't it make sense for Elijah to have been given all the ammunition to hurt Brady and his brothers?

Maybe Ace was in jail, but that didn't mean Elijah couldn't put men up there, armed with knives and Brady's nightmares.

The trail led right through the narrow chasm of rocks where Ace had often left Brady, only to torture him later. Where Brady had been forced away from his brothers to survive. On his own. As a child.

When he had nightmares, they all took place here, no matter how incomprehensible his dreams might be. Following that trail would be walking into his own personal hell.

I'll never go back there. Not for any reason. That's a promise I'm making to myself and I won't ever break it. No matter what.

He could hear his own words, spoken to his brothers, to his grandmother, to anyone who'd listen during that first year they'd all been out and with Grandma and *living* a real life.

Brady could stop here. He could go back. He could wait for help. He didn't have to brave his own personal hell.

Except Cecilia was at the end of this trail, and no matter what that twelve-year-old had told himself, there were reasons you broke promises to yourself. Reasons you did the things that scared you the most.

And that reason boiled down to one thing, always.

A thing Ace didn't understand, and Elijah probably didn't either.

Love.

EVERYTHING IN CECILIA'S body hurt. Which wasn't new, it was just worse when there was a gun to her head and she knew Brady would come after her and they could both end up dead.

She tried not to let herself think like that. Fatalism *could* be fatal in her current situation. She needed to believe in Brady, and Tucker and even herself, that they could find a way to survive this.

No matter what hurt, no matter how impossible it seemed, she had to believe or she'd never find a way to survive this.

"Ah, here we are," Elijah said as if he were a waiter showing someone to their reserved table. Instead it was a tower of rock interrupted by a small crevice.

Without warning, he shoved her into that opening hard enough she stumbled and fell to her hands and knees. Which would have been his mistake if her body was cooperating. She would have immediately jumped up and disarmed him.

But her arms gave out on her so she fell onto her side, unfortunately her bad one, which hurt so badly she had to fight back tears and an encroaching blackness that wanted to take her away.

But she fought both away, breathing through the pain and the frustration. At first she'd thought he'd pushed her into a cave, but above her was bright blue sky. The air was hotter here, like the rocks were trapping it between them or radiating heat. She desperately wished she had her pack and could drink some water.

Though if she were wishing things, she supposed she should be wishing she wasn't here at all. Or that she'd shot Elijah before he'd snuck up on her.

"On your feet now."

Cecilia grimaced, but did as she was told. If it came down to it, she'd fight and run, but for now it seemed in her best interest to listen to him.

"You're bleeding," Elijah offered, with a slight frown. He almost sounded concerned, but that tone was belied by the fact he was aiming a gun point-blank at her forehead as he moved closer to her, studying the red stain that had seeped through her gray T-shirt.

He stepped closer, reaching out. Cecilia braced herself for pain, for *something.* But all Elijah did was carefully lift her shirt and look at the stab wound.

Cecilia tried to control her breathing, tried to keep a handle on her revulsion. She failed. Miserably. No matter that it was preferable to say, being shot, it was creepy. It made her skin crawl as he kept her shirt lifted and studied the wound.

"You really should have gotten some medical attention for that. No stitches?" He tsked, lifting his gaze to meet hers. "What *were* you thinking."

She didn't answer him. Why would she? Still, she kept his gaze rather than stare at the gun that was so close to her forehead she could hardly think about anything else.

"You know, Layla quite liked being hurt," he said mildly. "Maybe you two have that in common."

"And maybe I puke all over your shoes."

Elijah lifted a shoulder as if it were of no concern of his. "I don't mind a little force, a little hurt, but you would invariably do something stupid, and as much as you fancy yourself the center of this, I'm not here for you."

She tried not to show her confusion, but Elijah's smile told her she'd failed.

"Don't worry. Brady will appear soon enough, ready to swoop in and save the day." He tapped his wrist. "I'm surprised it's taken two Wyatts this long, though. I wonder why it *did* take so long. Seems odd. Two strong, perfectly able-bodied men working together. Almost as if they, or one of them, wasn't trying to take the men out."

Cecilia's blood went cold. She refused to take anything Elijah said at face value, but could that mean Tucker was working for Elijah?

Please God, no.

She didn't speak until she knew she could do it and sound steady. Strong. "Brady will come with backup, and then where will you be?"

"He won't come with backup." Elijah let out a snort. "He'll run after you immediately. Especially since you're hurt. Wyatts and their noble pride are endlessly predictable."

"And yet alive. All six of them. And not incarcerated, unlike a certain Wyatt." Still, Elijah's words created some doubt. Surely Brady wouldn't come after her without backup… Except, wasn't that what he'd done with Tucker? Taken off to help without thinking about how he'd get himself out of it.

No. He'd expected *her* to get them out of it. So, she had to. Somehow.

"You know, Cecilia, you're making a grave mistake if you think I'm like Ace or your average thug. Killing leads to jail time. You don't always need to *kill* someone to get what you want."

She eyed the gun. If he wasn't going to kill her…

His smile was slow and self-satisfied. "Now, don't get too excited. Killing is often an excellent plan when it certainly can't be traced back to you. Which is why we'll wait for Brady's grand entrance."

"We know you're Ace's son." It was a gamble. Maybe it would make him more inclined to kill her. But maybe it would set him off-balance enough to give her a chance to best him.

Instead, Elijah laughed. If they were in a different situation, she would have believed it an honest, cheerful, good-humored laugh. "You know I'm Ace's son. You *know* that, huh?"

"Yes, I do."

He leaned in close, so their noses almost touched and the steel of the gun touched her forehead.

"You know *nothing*, Cecilia. And you're smart enough to know that, deep down. You're in over your head. Completely lost and completely expendable. You think I care about a *baby* when I'm building an *empire*?"

Cecilia didn't know how to parse that. He wasn't after Mak? Then what was the point of the fire? Of threatening her at the rez? Why on Earth were they *here* if not for Mak?

Whatever the reason, he wasn't lying when he said she was expendable. Which meant she had to tread very, very carefully.

Brady would have gone to get backup. He wouldn't have followed her half-cocked. Tucker wouldn't let him. He'd been impulsive when Tucker was getting beaten up so he'd waded in, but he would think before coming to her rescue. Or Tucker would.

If Tucker wasn't on the wrong side of things.

She had to close her eyes against the wave of debilitating fear, because God knew none of what she told herself was true.

Chapter Twenty

The heat was excruciating. Dehydration was likely, if not a foregone conclusion. Brady was surrounded by his own personal nightmare and he had lost Cecilia and Elijah's trail.

Brady stood in the middle of the vast Badlands and wondered where the hell he'd gone so wrong in his life. He'd tried to be good and do the right thing. He'd been *shot* helping Gage save Felicity. He was a good man.

Why did he have to be a failure?

Failure or no, he couldn't give up. Not while there was a chance Cecilia was still alive. He couldn't have fully lost the trail. He'd made a wrong turn was all.

He backtracked, wiping the sweat off his face with his shoulder. He went back to the last place he saw the trail. It didn't end abruptly so much as got fainter and fainter. Perhaps a breeze had blown through and made the track lighter.

He stopped where he absolutely couldn't be certain it went on, then stood still and studied the land around him. All rock. All gradients of brown, red and tan broken up by the occasional tuft of grass. But there was a familiarity here, like there'd been in that corridor of rock earlier.

He was somewhere near…something he recognized. He couldn't place it yet, but he would.

Then he heard a thud. The lowest, quietest murmur of voices. It would be hard to tell where it was coming from the way sound moved in the Badlands, but he used the direction of the trail and his own instincts to propel him forward.

Then, as landmarks became clearer, he realized he didn't need to use either. He knew this place again. He knew where Elijah would have taken her.

There was no way Elijah wasn't Ace's son if he knew all Ace's spots. All Ace's ways of torture. They had to be linked *somehow.*

Brady took a moment to pause, to send up a silent prayer that Tuck would get backup and manage to find them in time, then moved quietly toward the entrance of the circle of rock.

But Elijah poked his head out of the small entrance between the rocks. "Welcome," he greeted sunnily. "Come on inside. Have a chat." Elijah cocked his head. "Unless you want her brain matter splattered across the rocks. Can't say *I* do, but I'll oblige if necessary."

Brady stepped into the wall of rocks. It was where he and Gage had hidden during their escape. It was where Andy Jay, a random member of the Sons, had taken pity on them and lied to their father, allowing them to continue on to Grandma Pauline's.

Brady had no doubt it was where Andy Jay had died at his father's hand, as punishment for letting them go. Andy's son hadn't forgiven the Wyatt brothers for their role in his father's death. He'd tried to take down Cody not that long ago and failed.

Brady couldn't think about that. His sole purpose was not letting Cecilia die here too.

He didn't do more than give a quick glance to make sure she was all right before he turned his attention to Elijah. Brady positioned his body between the gun Elijah was pointing and Cecilia.

Elijah rolled his eyes. "Do you really have to be so noble? It's boring and predictable. I can shoot her regardless of what you do, so take a seat next to her like a good little soldier and we'll keep her brain intact."

Brady considered rushing him. They were in a small enclosed space, and Cecilia would back him up, even injured.

But if he could keep Elijah talking, he might get more information to use against Ace. To keep Elijah in jail longer, and to bide time until Tuck got back with reinforcements.

If Tuck comes back with reinforcements.

Brady took a careful seat next to Cecilia on the rock. She looked pale. He noted the splotch of blood on her shirt. She was bleeding through her bandages, surely dehydrated, and nothing about the situation they were in was good for that.

"If you don't think I've figured out you're Ace's son, you're not as smart as you think you are."

Elijah laughed, enough to make Brady…uncomfortable. He was certain it was true, but Elijah's laugh was…off.

"I'm not Ace's son," Elijah replied, keeping the gun trained on Cecilia's head.

"Is that what he makes you say? I wonder why it's gotta be such a secret."

Elijah shook his head. "See, I was chosen, Brady. I

wasn't just born. Ace picked me. He saw something in me. He didn't knock up some dim-witted gang groupie and have some warped sense of loyalty because of *blood*. I was chosen because I'm better. Smarter. I can see things people like you never will."

"You mean you were his brand of crazy and you listened to what he said?"

Elijah's humor was quickly sliding away. His eyes went icy, his grip on the gun tightened, and his smile turned into a sneer.

"You're his weakness. The lot of you. You aren't the reason he's in jail. His delusion that one of his blood-born children would take over the Sons is what got him there. Blood. As if that matters. I will take over the Sons." Elijah tapped his chest. "I'll leave Ace behind if I need to. I'm the next in line because he saw something in me, and I'm the best prospect to take over."

"I'm not part of the Sons. What do I care if you're better? It'll always be my job to take down the illegal activity in my jurisdiction."

"You're a part of Ace, which means that you're currency, Brady. Not important, but usable. Taking you out was an option, but it doesn't send the message I want. I don't want blood and destruction like Ace. No, I want the Sons to be a real machine. Murder leads to anger and revenge and all that nonsense with Andy Jay and his son coming after you. I don't want that. I want consensus. I want loyalty."

"What about Mak?" Brady asked, to draw out the conversation but also because he didn't understand what any of this had to do with Cecilia.

"I don't care about that kid. I don't care about *blood*. Being chosen is what matters." Elijah took a deep breath as if to calm himself. "But I don't appreciate being *stolen* from. Sometimes you have to make a statement. Besides, I've studied you. I know your weakness." The gun pointed at Cecilia. "Damsels in distress. Long as I have a gun to her head, you'll do what I say."

"But I won't," Cecilia returned.

"You will. Because he wants you to."

"This is a really terrible plan, even for you," Brady muttered. Cecilia gave him a look as if to say *back off*, but Brady knew this kind of delusional behavior. He'd grown up under its highs and lows.

Anger would create an unstable environment, and Elijah might lash out, but he'd also lose sight of his plan.

"We've got two against one here. I've got more help on the way. You'll never win." Brady shifted, trying to get his feet beneath him in a better position so he could lunge at Elijah.

He could take him out before he could shoot Cecilia. If he got a shot off, he'd hit Brady. Surely it could give her enough time to finish the job. He glanced at Cecilia. She was still too pale, and looked a little shaky, but she gave him a nod as if she knew what he was thinking.

Elijah lifted the gun and pointed it at Brady. His hand shook, color was rising in his face. "You're very lucky killing you isn't part of my plan."

Brady was pushing too far. He should stop, but his own anger was swelling up inside of him. That this continued to be his life. Tormented by power-hungry men, invested in being smarter and more important than everyone else.

Even when Ace was in maximum-security prison, Brady was fighting back the things Ace wrought, and he was tired of it.

"Face it, Elijah. You're a crappy leader. Your son will grow up knowing you were right about one thing, though. Blood doesn't matter."

"Crappy leader? I will rule the Sons, and they will reach more glory than they've ever known. He *chose* me."

Brady shrugged, ready to strike. "Ace chose wrong."

Brady leapt, but in that same second, Elijah's gun went off.

THE SOUND OF the gun echoed in the chasm they were in, followed by a howl of pain. Both men were on the ground, grappling, but Cecilia wasn't sure which was moaning in pain, or if they both were.

She couldn't see the gun either. Just a tangle of limbs rolling across the rocky ground.

The rocks. Cecilia lunged for the biggest one she could hold. She'd just need one clear second and she could bash Elijah over the head.

But there was no opportunity. There were only grunts and groans of pain. She saw blood, but couldn't tell who it came from. Her stomach turned, but she had to focus on getting Elijah's gun.

Screw the rock and her own injuries. She had to get in there and do what she could. When Elijah was on top, she grabbed his hair and pulled. He reached back with the hand holding the gun, and she grabbed it by the barrel, trying to point it anywhere but at her and Brady.

Out of the corner of her eye she saw Brady scoot out from under Elijah. Elijah had one hand still wrapped around Brady's leg, but Brady kicked it until he shook off Elijah's grasp.

The blood was Brady's. It was already soaking

through his pants leg, but Cecilia couldn't focus on that when she was grappling over the one gun in this god-forsaken place.

She tried to rip the gun out of Elijah's grasp, but he held firm. With his other hand free, he swung up and landed a blow right on her stab wound.

The pain knocked her to her knees, but she kept her grip locked on the gun. She couldn't give in. She wouldn't give in.

Elijah was trying to scramble to his feet, pulling the gun with him, but she held fast. She used her whole body weight to keep the barrel pointed down rather than at her.

"You're going to die," Elijah said as he huffed and puffed and wrestled over the gun. "I'm going to make sure of it."

Pain screamed through her, but this was life or death. She had to try to shut out the pain and focus on getting the gun away from the man who would most definitely kill her, and then probably Brady too. If he hadn't already.

She couldn't let it happen. There had to be a way to survive.

She saw out of the corner of her eye Brady try to get to his feet, only to fall to his knees. She couldn't let the fear he'd been irreparably hurt weaken her limbs or her resolve. She needed to get the gun so she could get help for Brady.

It's a lot of blood.

She adjusted her footing, still pulling down on the barrel of the gun, as Elijah readjusted his grip. She kicked out, managing to land a decent blow. Elijah didn't go down quite the way she'd hoped, but she got a better handle on the gun. With one more yank she could—

Brady grabbed her, pulling her off Elijah, which wrenched the gun from her grasp. She wanted to protest, but it was lost as he pushed her out of the opening at the same time something exploded.

Reflexively, she ducked and covered her ears. Rock rained down on them and Brady tried to cover her body with his. She shoved ineffectively at him. *He'd* been shot. She should be covering him.

From…an explosion? She finally managed to dislodge Brady from on top of her and looked at where she'd been not a minute ago.

The rocks had exploded. There was little more than rubble on two sides.

How… How?

She looked around the rest of the area, stopping short at the figure standing a few yards opposite the explosion site.

Tucker.

She blinked at him. Was she hallucinating?

"What on earth just happened?" Her ears rang, so her words sounded muted and far away. She looked at Brady. He was sitting on the ground, leaning against a wall of rock, injured leg out in front of him.

There was so much blood. So much…

Tucker handed her a strip of fabric. He must have torn it off his own shirt. She took it and wrapped it around Brady's leg.

"Let me guess, you need a hospital," Tucker said grimly, looking down at Brady's seated form and bloody leg with a certain amount of detachment. The rubble behind them seemed to be of no consequence to him.

The words were still heard through a muffled filter, but Cecilia *could* make them out.

"Wouldn't hurt," Brady returned, his voice strained as Cecilia pressed the cloth Tucker had handed her to his wound.

"Ambulance is getting as close as it can. Paramedics will take the rest by foot and will be here any minute." Tucker's gaze moved from Brady to Cecilia. "You'll both be transported. Depending on Elijah's status, he might need to go first. And I'm not putting the three of you in the same ambulance."

"Shouldn't you..." Cecilia trailed off because she realized there were two people moving the rubble. Where had they come from?

Cecilia looked at Brady. His complexion was gray, but his eyes were open and alert.

"Elijah didn't think you'd get backup."

His mouth tugged upward ever so slightly. "I'm stupid, but not that stupid. Sent Tuck."

Cecilia looked back up at Tucker. She really thought he'd been against them, but here he was with backup.

Apparently the kind of backup who could explode rocks. She frowned. "How did you..."

Tucker shook his head. "Keep the pressure on that. You seem in better shape. I'm going to go help the paramedics find us."

He walked off and Cecilia looked at Brady. He was so gray and so still. "I hope you're not entertaining any grand plans of dying, because that's not going to work for me."

His mouth tugged up at one corner. "Nah. Surviving close range gunshot wounds is my specialty. You know what they say. Getting shot twice in a year is lucky."

"No one says that, Brady."

"Well, unlucky would be dead, and I am not that."

The word *dead* gave her a full body shudder, so she rested her forehead against his, still keeping the pressure on his wound. She let out a shuddered breath, and said what she never thought she'd say to a man. A near-death experience changed a girl, though. "I love you."

He let out his own shaky breath, and she just couldn't stand it. This. His hurt. Her hurt. God knew what had happened to Elijah, but here they were. Alive. Bleeding, but alive.

"So. You know, you better feel the same way or I'm going to kick your butt."

He chuckled, winced, made a half-hearted attempt to raise an arm that just fell by his side.

"And you can't die."

"Not going to die," he said, though he seemed incredibly weak. "Gage is never going to let me live this down after the hard time I gave him about Felicity." This time he seemed to focus all his energy and lifted his hand to briefly touch her cheek. "If I'm a little out of it here for a few minutes, it's just the shock. I'm not going to die. Got it?"

She swallowed down the lump in her throat and nodded.

"But you can be sure that I love you too. Because God knows I'd be a lot more pissed about getting shot again if it wasn't with you."

"That doesn't make any sense," she muttered, losing her battle with tears as one slipped over.

Brady opened his mouth to say something else, but one of the men by the rubble spoke first.

"He's alive."

Chapter Twenty-One

Brady had been shot before, and not that long ago. There was less fear this time. More irritable acceptance.

Cecilia was sitting next to him. A paramedic had done a quick patch job, but they were currently working on getting Elijah out of the rubble and onto a stretcher.

Brady had heard them mutter that if there was any hope of saving Elijah, he'd have to be transported ASAP. Brady's and Cecilia's injuries were serious, but they'd have to wait for a second transport.

"Why are they prioritizing saving him? He would have killed us," Cecilia muttered in Tucker's direction.

"Elijah might have some information that would… help my investigation."

Brady frowned at his brother. It was news to him he had any current investigation that connected to Elijah.

But there was something about this whole thing that made him keep his questions to himself.

The paramedics strapped Elijah to the stretcher, which would stabilize his body and keep him from being able to fight any of the paramedics, nurses or doctors who would deal with him on the way to the hospital.

His head was turned toward them as the paramedics walked by.

"There's so much worse coming for you Wyatts. So much worse," Elijah rasped. His face was bloody and torn up, but the hate in his eyes was clear and fierce.

"I think we'll handle it," Cecilia returned.

"Just like we've handled the rest," Brady added. If Ace kept coming, in whatever form, they'd keep fighting. Because they'd built real lives—with love and loss and right and wrong and hope. Real, life-changing hope.

Everything Elijah and Ace had was a delusion. It made them dangerous, sure, but it didn't have to rule their lives. If every time Wyatts and Knights came together they fought for right and good, well, that was life.

As long as they built one.

"Do you think..." Cecilia leaned close to his ear, eyeing the men who were still going through the rubble. "Do you think Tucker's part of Cody's old group and that's why he's being so weird?"

"It seems possible. We can't say anything, though. They kicked Cody out once other people knew he was part of the group. If Tucker is working with them, we have to keep quiet."

Cecilia nodded once, then rested her head against his shoulder. "We're okay," she murmured, as if she had to say it out loud to believe it.

It was odd. He was in an unreasonable amount of pain, bleeding profusely, and she wasn't doing much better. Bloody and banged up, sitting in the middle of the Badlands with the afternoon sun beating down.

But he felt...right. Like the things that had been all wrong for the past few months, all that gray and frustration and anxiety had lifted.

The Sons still existed, Ace and Elijah were both alive—if in jail. But even in the face of that, Jamison and Cody had reunited with their first loves. Cody had a daughter, Jamison had Liza's young half sister looking up to him like a father figure, and Gage and Felicity were getting married and starting a family.

And Brady Wyatt had at some point fallen in love with Cecilia. Who didn't care so much about right or wrong, but did what she had to do. Who fought, tooth and nail, for the people she loved.

What wasn't to love about that? "I love you," he murmured into her dusty hair.

"Sure you're not dying?" she joked. Or half joked. He could feel the anxiety radiating off her.

But he was going to be just fine.

Epilogue

Two weeks later

Cecilia sat in Grandma Pauline's kitchen. It was a full house these days. Sarah and Rachel were staying here while the Knight house was repaired from the fire. Duke had insisted on staying on the property, and no one could get through to Duke when he had an idea in his head.

Cecilia had been forced to stay at Grandma Pauline's once she'd been released from the hospital, and so had Brady. Everyone had been surprised when Cecilia insisted they share a room, but people seemed to be getting used to their new normal.

Well, not Brady, who was back to being surly as he recovered. The gunshot wound to his leg had been serious, and though it hadn't shattered any bone it had done some damage that would take considerable time to heal.

Having to accept help to get around did *not* make for a happy Wyatt, but he was the one who'd come up with their current plan. If she hadn't already been in love with him, she would have fallen for him when he'd suggested it.

The door opened, and Jamison stepped inside, gesturing Layla to follow him. She looked nervous, but better than she'd been in the hospital.

Cecilia immediately got up and went to gather Layla into a hug. Layla squeezed back, sniffling into Cecilia's shoulder. "I wasn't sure I wanted to come, but I knew you'd come get me if I didn't. And you need your rest." Layla pulled away. "Where is he?"

Cecilia nodded thanks at Jamison who slipped away. "I can't hold him yet because of my injuries, so he's upstairs being spoiled. Jamison will go get him, but I wanted to talk to you about something first."

"I know. I can't have him back. I… I feel better, but I can't—"

Cecilia kept her hands on her friend's arms. "I think you can. But you don't have to, Layla. You've got to do what's right for you, first and foremost."

"The state can't take him, Cecilia. And when Elijah gets out of jail—"

Cecilia led Layla to the table and made her sit down. "We're going to protect you and Mak from Elijah. Always. Never worry about that."

"I lost my job. My therapist said I'm doing better, but—"

"But it's hard. You've been through *a lot*." Cecilia took her friend's hands in hers. "You should be around your son. You should have work that allows you to do that. And you should feel safe."

"I don't—"

"I'm going to offer something, and I want you to understand it was the Wyatts' idea. I didn't have anything to do with it, so don't feel like you have to take it because you owe me."

"I owe you my life. I owe everyone…"

"Layla."

She sucked in a deep breath and nodded. "I know. You're my best friend and I would have done the same for you. I'm just…fragile, Cecilia. I don't feel strong enough for anything." She winced. "My therapist says it's good to tell people that, but it feels awful."

"Which is why we want you to move in here. We've got two people recovering from major injuries. The Wyatt brothers come and go with their families in tow. Grandma Pauline is…well, let's just say everything she has to do for this big house and ranch is a lot for a woman her age." Cecilia prayed to God Pauline didn't hear that one. "She could use help. Live-in help. You'd work for her, be part of taking care of your son, and those of us hobbling around until we're better. It can be temporary until you feel well enough to look for a new job, and live on your own. Or it can be permanent."

"But…" Layla blinked, tears filling her eyes. "That's too good to be true."

Cecilia smiled, squeezing Layla's hands. "The Wyatts are a little too good to be true sometimes. It's easier if you just accept it, not question if you deserve it. So, what do you think?"

Layla hesitated. "What about when you and Brady are better and go back to your real lives? Will Pauline really need my help? Will Mak have…stability, you know?"

Cecilia blinked. She hadn't been thinking about when she and Brady were better. At all. She cleared her throat, trying to hide her uncertainty from Layla. "Well, Pauline will still need help. And Brady and I come out here all the time. We wouldn't just abandon Mak."

Layla's eyebrows drew together. "His own mother did."

"No. His own mother got sick, and now she's doing better. And she has a whole village who wants to take care of her and her son. Mak's very lucky."

"I..." She sucked in a deep breath. "I can't say no, can I? It would be...it'd be stupid to say no." Layla abruptly got to her feet. Cecilia turned in her chair. Pauline had brought in Mak and Layla was crying over him.

Cecilia smiled at Grandma Pauline, but Layla's words were rattling around in her head. *What about when you and Brady are better?*

"Why don't you take him into the living room, sweetheart. Let me show you," Grandma Pauline said, ushering a crying Layla holding a babbling Mak into the living room. "We'll give you a few minutes of privacy, huh?"

Layla sniffled and nodded and disappeared into the room. Cecilia stood alone in the kitchen.

What about when you and Brady are better?

No, she wouldn't sit around worrying over that question. She went to her and Brady's makeshift room and found him lying on the bed, reading a book.

"What about when we're better?" she demanded with no preamble. She didn't know why she felt so...angry. So shaky. But they hadn't discussed this. Why hadn't it even come up?

Brady looked up from his book. "Huh?"

"What's going to happen when we're better?"

He blinked then, shifted in the bed. "Well..." He cleared his throat. "I'm not sure what you're asking me, Cecilia."

"Where are we going to go? Are you going back to your apartment and I'm going back to the rez? Does this continue?" She gestured between them. "What are we *doing*?"

He set the book aside. "I'm not going to have this conversation with you standing there, acting like you're accusing me of something. Come sit down."

"Oh, don't use that high-handed tone to boss me around."

He raised an eyebrow. He had a tendency to do that and make her feel like an idiot for wanting to stomp her foot and yell.

She plopped herself on the bed next to him because she *was* reasonable, even if it felt like one simple sentence had sent her a little off the deep end. Then he wrapped his arm around her, pulling her close until she rested her head on his shoulder.

"Once you're back to work, you'll want to stay on the rez," he said rationally.

"I guess so."

"I don't have to live in the county, and it's not like it's too far to drive every day."

She sat up straight, something like panic beating through her. "Are you suggesting you move in with me?"

"Isn't that what *you're* getting at?"

"No… Well, sort of. I mean, we're basically living together now. Just with a grandma hovering around."

"Exactly."

"I…"

"Alternatively, we could stay here and both commute when we're reinstated. Or I could just stay here, and you could live on the rez. Commute will suck, but I'm not going to be able to deal with those stairs at my apartment for a long while yet. Hell, I'm half convinced to just give up my badge."

She pulled out of his grasp, outraged. "You can't do that."

"Why not? I've been out for months. I'll be out for longer now. Why go back?"

She shook her head. She knew he was tired of being hurt. Tired of not working, but he couldn't honestly be thinking about quitting. "Because you love it."

He was quiet for a while. "I guess I do." He squeezed her close. "I think the point, Cecilia, is that we'll work out whatever we do next together."

She tipped her head up to look at him. Life was funny. She'd always looked up to Brady. Always been in a certain amount of awe of him, even when he was irritating her to death. She wouldn't have admitted it. Even at New Year's Eve, kissing him, she hadn't admitted she had *this* inside of her.

It had taken fear. Struggle. Now, she wouldn't stop admitting it. Her pride wasn't as important as being honest with him.

"You're a pretty good guy, Wyatt."

"Yeah, yeah. What did Layla say?"

"She's going to do it."

"Good. You know, it wouldn't be so bad. Staying here. Helping Grandma and Dev out. Keeping close to Mak. I wouldn't mind it so much."

Cecilia settled back against his chest. "No, I wouldn't mind it either."

This was not ever what she'd planned for her life. A guy like Brady. Living this close to home. Having her best friend and her best friend's baby under one roof. It wasn't a normal family by any stretch, but she'd never had *normal*.

What she'd had was love, and now she had more of it.

She settled into Brady and sighed. "I love you," she murmured. Because no matter what happened, love was always the reason you gutted through, fought for what you had to, and most of all, survived.

* * * * *

HUNTING THE COLTON FUGITIVE

COLLEEN THOMPSON

To the fellow authors I've met along the way,
thank you for all you do to offer inspiration,
encouragement and a pathway through
the darkest thickets.

Chapter One

Sitting at the built-in computer nook of a bunker hidden in the secluded foothills surrounding Mustang Valley, Ace Colton had long since lost track of whether it was day or night. With little access to natural light and zero human contact, he'd spent much of the past weeks obsessively sifting through news reports while considering the evidence against him. Trying to make sense of the so-called *witness* to his confession, the planted weapon and the way the solid and successful life he'd so long taken for granted had fallen to pieces since January.

No, *fallen* was the wrong word. That implied something that had simply happened on its own, for no rhyme or reason. It was obvious by this point that his life as Payne Colton's eldest son, the hardworking and successful CEO of a billion-dollar corporation, Colton Oil, had been deliberately blown to pieces. *Stolen* from him by whomever had sent out that email telling every other member of the board, his family, that he was, in fact, no real Colton, but an imposter foisted off on them at birth.

Then, before the sickening shock of it, the sense of isolation and displacement, could begin to settle, his job was ripped away, too, though he'd done absolutely nothing wrong—known nothing of any scheme involving his being switched at birth.

He would never forget the searing pain of hearing his father, the man he loved and trusted, tell him that only a real Colton was fit to lead the company. Afterward, harsh words had flown between them, words Ace would regret forever. For as understandable as his hurt and fury might have been, he'd been overheard, making him the prime suspect later when his father had been found lying on his office floor, barely breathing, with two bullets in him.

Is he breathing still? When Ace had fled after a so-called *witness* had implicated him, and a gun linked to the shooting was found beneath a floorboard inside Ace's own condo, the man he would always think of as his real father had still been in a coma, in critical condition. As badly as Payne had hurt Ace by acting as if, without a genetic link, none of his business acumen, hard work, or the relationships he'd spent a lifetime building made one damned bit of difference, he couldn't hang around his condo waiting to be arrested, even though he knew he'd let down the people who cared for him by going into hiding.

But neither could he actually leave the area, not without doing whatever he could to track down the real shooter, protect his family from further harm, and find some way to get his life back on track, even if he had to do it using his laptop to connect to the untraceable virtual private network that was his sole link to the outside world. He thanked his lucky stars that he'd purchased this plot of land several years ago from the cash-strapped, out-of-state nieces of a former owner. Only after the property's closing had Ace learned of the existence of a survival bunker from some old receipts and a set of long-forgotten plans found among a packet of yellowed paperwork he'd been given.

That long-ago investment, based on his vague instinct that the land, with its scenic views of the valley below, might someday prove a good place to build vacation rental cabins, had paid off in spades, a gift from his younger self to the desperate fugitive Ace had become. A gift he'd carefully retrofitted and provisioned as best he could in the weeks before it became apparent that he would soon be taken into custody.

Within the tomblike confines of the bunker, he searched his online sources for any relevant local updates from the Mustang Valley area, from the obituary he dreaded to the longed-for news that his name had been cleared. Finding neither, he began skimming other headlines, only to nearly jump out of his skin when an alarm wailed over speakers placed throughout the bunker.

Whoop! Whoop! Whoop!

The security cameras he had installed above-ground set off a siren that echoed throughout the confined space, alerting him to the presence of an intruder.

Heart thrashing against his rib cage, Ace leaped to his feet before typing in the code to access the hidden cameras. As his screen divided into six sections, a glimpse of swift movement and a clearly human outline on the lower right panel, near the entrance hatch, made his gut clench, though the lighting was too dim to make out any details.

There was a bright flash of light and then a muffled boom. Carefully hung tools fell from the walls of the bunker as Ace's panic spiraled.

Was it the police, detonating the hatch and coming to arrest him? Surely not, he thought, reasoning that law enforcement, if they found him, would arrive en masse rather than what had appeared to be a solitary presence. His instincts told him it was far more likely that this was the same person who'd made the attempt on his father's life and set him up to take the fall. Had the perpetrator come to bring him in—or to shoot him down, too?

Sweating bullets, Ace went for the handgun he'd procured before going into hiding and wondered if he had it in him to pull the trigger. With only one way in and out of the bunker, there was no avenue to flee, and locking the inner submarine-style door would only give his unwanted guest time to gather reinforcements—or trigger yet another blast.

Something clattered from the hatchway. Ace tensed, his stomach going icy cold.

Reaching above his head, he flicked off the LED lights that would expose him when the interior door opened. After weeks of solitude in the confined space, he knew the bunker's every twist and turn by heart—the only real advantage he had against a well-prepared intruder.

Pushing himself back into the alcove adjacent to the opening, he waited in pitch darkness, feeling more like a trapped feral animal, teeth bared and claws ready, than the polished, urbane and occasionally ruthless corporate warrior he'd been for so long.

Against the shallow scrape of his own breath, he heard the turning of the door's mechanism, followed by the *whoosh* of its hydraulics. Dim light flickered; then came a shadow, followed by a puff of air cooler than the scrubbed bunker atmosphere he had been breathing. Smelling of leaves and needles, earth and fresh greenery, it spoke of the foothills, nighttime—and an imminent threat to his freedom or his life.

With a wordless shout that echoed through the bunker, he jumped out and wrapped his arms around what he swiftly realized was a smaller person, twisting his body to slam his unwelcome guest headfirst into the bulkhead. There was a thud and a cry of alarm—higher pitched than he expected. An instant later the intruder twisted free, the silky sweep of long hair brushing across his face and filling his nostrils with a clean, light scent that triggered a memory of one of his sisters' shampoos.

"Ainsley?" He drew back reflexively, wonder vying with relief to imagine his attorney sibling tracking him here somehow. Guilt came next as he recalled how he'd thanked her for her efforts to help him by disappearing on her, and horror at how hard he'd slammed her into the bunker's unyielding steel framing. "Ainsley, are you all right? I'm so sorry if I hurt—"

Out of the darkness, something came at him like a guided missile, a blow that struck his temple hard enough to knock him off his feet.

Head swirling on a raft of nausea, he found himself on his hands and knees a moment later, feeling for the pistol, which had gone flying from his hands. A second click preceded the flashlight's beam, and the whole bunker was once more flooded with bright light.

Before his eyes could adjust, the intruder sent his gun spinning out of reach with a kick. A no-nonsense yet decidedly feminine voice ordered, "On your feet, right now. Keep your hands where I can see them."

The speaker was not his little sister but a small and slender woman, maybe early thirties, whom he had never seen in his life. With her wavy, red-blond hair pushed back behind squared shoulders, she was aiming an intense green-eyed gaze, along with the business end of her 9mm automatic, directly at him.

"I said, on your feet—*now*," she repeated, her face as softly feminine as her voice was firm. "That is, if you aren't still seeing stars from that left cross."

"That was *you* that hit me?" He staggered a little as dizziness washed over him when he rose. "With your actual fist?"

Sure, he'd dropped his guard when he'd mistakenly imagined he had body-slammed his little sister, but this woman, who couldn't be more than five-four and maybe one-fifteen soaking wet, had damned near knocked him out with a single blow. "Tell me you clocked me with that gun or something. Leave a man a little pride, at least."

"Come to think of it—" eyeing him critically, she waved the weapon to direct him farther inside the tube-shaped bunker "—maybe you ought to sit down. That punch to the head has you talking nonsense."

As he moved in the direction she indicated, she bent to sweep up his pistol with her free hand before dropping it into a side pocket of her dark gray tactical pants, her movement so deft and assured that he knew immediately he was dealing with a well-trained professional.

There goes my last chance at freedom, he realized, his heart sinking. Unless he started talking fast.

"Who the hell are you," he demanded, "and what do you want with me?"

"Relax and take a load off," she suggested, gesturing toward a built-in leather sofa across the narrow corridor.

With little choice, he complied, while his captor stood across from him, her back pressed against the command center's chair behind her.

"Nice little hideaway you've got down here," she said, waving to indicate the pristine white walls and birch shelving, lined with boxed supplies that could easily stretch to last him for another six months. "Lucky thing for me your former real estate agent is the talkative sort. Very eager to chat about how understanding you were over the irregularities with the paperwork—including this little unpermitted building project that you could've thrown a fit over since it had never been inspected."

"I couldn't see much point of causing those two young women any grief over some old mothballed bunker I never had any intention of using," Ace said, shaking his head. "And you actually looked up my real estate agent?"

She smiled. "In my experience, it's a rare runner who strays too far from his home turf. Especially one with the kind of family ties that you have…and properties to spare."

"In your experience as what?" he asked, more certain than ever than the armed intruder who'd packed such a wallop wasn't law enforcement, since she hadn't identified herself as such. "The woman who's come here to kill me?"

She shook her head and made a scoffing sound. "I'm not here to kill you, Colton. I've come to escort you to the Mustang Valley PD so I can collect the bounty I've been promised."

SIERRA MADDEN TENSED as Ace Colton leaned toward her, a lump rising where she'd slugged him and his dark brown eyes boring uncomfortably into hers.

"Start explaining, right now," he ordered, looking better than he had any right to, considering his month-long confinement.

The neatly groomed light brown hair in his corporate headshots had given way to a somewhat longer, more unruly look. In place of the expensive suit and silk tie, he now wore a tight black T-shirt with worn jeans molded to a trim, athletic body. Though the bulge of his biceps made her suspect he'd been working off some of his frustrations with free weights, he was a good deal leaner than he'd been in photos from his CEO days. A spiky layer of stubble, frosted with a hint of silver at his jawline, gave him an edgy look of the sort that she'd always been drawn to…sometimes to her detriment.

Some men dressed up nicely, she knew, but leave it to her to come up with one whose appearance had been improved by life on the lam. *Not that it matters. Ace Colton's nothing to me but the fat paycheck I need to buy my way out of big trouble.*

"First off, I need to know exactly who you are," he added, "and who it was that put you on my trail."

She chuffed a laugh. "You know, you're awfully demanding for a guy with a goose egg on his head and a gun pointed at him. Or is arrogance just an occupational hazard for you CEO types?"

"*Ex*-CEO," he said, sounding irritated, "as if you haven't made it crystal clear already you've done your homework on my background. Which gives you a distinct advantage over me."

"I happen to *like* advantages. But then again, who doesn't?"

"Come on. A name, at least? What's that going to cost you?"

She shrugged. "Fine, then. I'm Sierra Madden."

"And you must be a bounty hunter, right? But how can that be? I haven't been arrested, so there's no bail bond for me to have skipped out on. What authority do you even have to—"

"The way I figure it, I'm aiming all the authority I need at you right now." She jerked her gun a smidgeon higher. "But you're right. This isn't usually the way I work. And in your case, there's no need to think of me as the enemy. I'm here to help you, Asa."

"It's *Ace*," he corrected—unnecessarily, since she knew full well from her research that no one ever called him by his given name. "And I don't know which part of that story is the most convincing, the part where you break in here aiming a gun at me or maybe it's when you said you were about to turn me in to the police to be arrested."

Frowning, Sierra reminded herself that Ace Colton was, for her, a means to an end. She didn't have to *like* him—plus, he was wanted for attempted murder. "I've been hired by a member of your family interested in bringing you home so the best possible defense can be arranged for the pending charges."

"I've been through all that with my sister." He grimaced as if the memory pained him. "I know Ainsley means well, but with someone intent on setting me up to take the fall for our father's shooting—"

"Ainsley?" Sierra shook her head. "It wasn't her who sent me, or any of your siblings. It was your stepmother."

"My *stepmother*? You can't mean Genevieve? Why would she, when she thinks I've shot her husband?"

"No, not your father's current wife. The other one. Selina Barnes Colton was the woman who—"

"*Selina?* Are you out of your mind?" Ace erupted, rocketing to his feet so quickly that Sierra shrank back, abruptly reassessing her earlier assumptions about the soft, rich man she'd thought to find here, a previously pampered forty-year-old heir who'd been unable to accept the abruptness of his change in status. "That woman doesn't want to help me. She's never wanted anything except to feather her own nest and— Hell, for all I know, *she's* the one who shot my father and tried to pin it on me in the first place."

"Sit down right now," Sierra ordered, pointing the gun squarely at his chest. "Or so help me, I will make your stepmother very sorry that she didn't specify that I had to return you in one piece to collect the bounty."

"She'd throw you a party if you shot me. Believe me, from the moment she weaseled her way into the family, that woman has never, for a single moment, had anyone's best interests but her own in mind." Ace shook his head, his eyes darkening with fury. "Marrying my dad after my mother died and playing our stepmother for a hot five minutes was only a means to an end for her and nothing more."

"So she was never the maternal type? That's what you're saying?"

Ace scoffed and waved the question off, bitterness twisting his expression. "She might've had my father fooled at one time—and for all I know, she still has something on him, considering how she's managed to hold on to her job at Colton Oil and the nice house he built for her on ranch property—but believe me, she's not fooling anybody else."

Sierra caught her breath, recalling her own suspicions. The rational, rehearsed-sounding explanations the polished businesswoman had given, along with the outsized bounty Selina had offered, hadn't jibed with the raw avarice gleaming in the cool depths of her eyes.

Ordinarily, Sierra would have asked more questions. Or even trusted her instincts and walked away from the highly irregular agreement. But the truth was, she'd been desperate, more than desperate, and the deal, coming when it had, had seemed like a miracle from heaven. Or from whatever Great Beyond accepted broken-down gambling addicts like her father.

"She's never given a damn about any of my father's children," Ace said. "For her, it's always been about getting her hooks into the family fortune. And I promise you, whatever she's paying you to do is part of the next round in her game plan, because she has to know that we'll toss her off the property in a minute if my father—if he—"

He stopped himself abruptly, his forehead creasing with worry. Sinking back down to the sofa, he asked quietly, "Tell me I haven't missed something while I've been stuck here, that my father hasn't—that he isn't worse. Or even— I keep checking online when I'm able, but I know that sometimes, in cases like these, the hospitals and police withhold information."

"As far as I know," she said, "there's been no change in his condition."

He sighed, some of the tension draining from his face. "Thank God for that."

"I suppose you're sorry then, about what happened," she said, reminded of how many times she'd heard such sentiments from killers in the past. Maybe, she supposed, they even meant what they were saying. But in her world decent people didn't shoot or stab or strangle the people they loved when they got angry. They didn't leave them grievously wounded while they fled like cowards from the consequence of their actions.

"Of course I'm sorry someone did this to him. Did

this to all of us," Ace blurted, his deep voice shaking with emotion. "I didn't hurt my father. I never…no matter how upset we both were—you have to believe me."

She shrugged a shoulder. "No offense, Ace, but I'm not really the person you need to waste your breath convincing. You'll get an attorney, I imagine a first-rate one with all your money, and he or she will—"

"I love my dad," he insisted, his dark gaze never wavering. "I always will, and he'll always be the man I think of, the ideal I'd want to emulate, should I ever get the chance to be a father."

Though she was well aware that Payne Colton wasn't Ace's biological father, it struck her that Ace's words still resonated in a way that his stepmother's hadn't. But Sierra had run across plenty of people who were perfectly capable of harming a family member and then pretending—even to themselves—that it had never happened. Or praying that the victim would pull through so the charges they themselves faced would be limited to assault rather than murder.

"You'll get your chance later to explain all this," she assured him, eager to move things along. Yet, she couldn't stop thinking of how he'd said, *should I ever get the chance to be a father.* Her conscience prickled but didn't stop her from reminding him, "I still have to take you in now."

He shook his head. "You can't. Don't you understand? Selina only wants me dragged in to take the heat off her. Or she's setting me up somehow. Probably planning some *accident* to take me out before I ever go to trial."

"If that's really the case," Sierra assured him, "you're better off in jail. I'll see you get there safely."

"I'm safer *here*, where I can keep working on finding the real shooter and figuring out exactly who's behind all this."

"I hate to break it to you, but that ship has sailed." Sierra lifted her chin. "Even if I wanted to pretend I'd never seen you, when I take on a contract, I deliver."

"If it's professional pride," Ace said, "what pride could there be in doing the bidding of a conniving schemer like Selina?"

"Listen, Colton, I've just met you. And even you have to admit, you've got a lot of very compelling reasons to lie your head off at this point."

"Then pick up a damned phone. Ask anybody in the family. They'll all tell you the same thing about that woman. She's clearly up to something. And she means to destroy me, or maybe the whole family, to get it."

Not my circus, not my monkeys, Sierra told herself, recalling one of her father's favorite proverbs. No matter how compelling a case Ace Colton made, or how ridiculously hot he looked doing it, it didn't change that fact.

But there was something in his expression—or maybe it was guilt over the secret she'd learned before coming to look for him, the secret she was keeping from him—that had her explaining, "It's nothing personal, but you're not the only one with father issues. And mine are about to get a whole lot messier if I don't deliver you and collect the bounty Selina promised me tonight."

"What could possibly be messier than having a framed man—or maybe even a dead one—on your conscience?"

She scowled, her stomach souring at the reminder of her most pressing problem.

"Losing a leg to my father's loan shark," she said bluntly, "all because he's hell-bent on making an example out of me."

As tough a customer as the bounty hunter holding him at gunpoint appeared to be, Ace couldn't miss the flicker of fear in the depths of her green eyes warring with her apparent need to appear strong.

Yet, he sensed an opening, too, like a hairline fault in a rock face that would allow a skilled climber a toehold.

Praying that he wouldn't plummet, he tried, "Your *father's* loan shark? How's that work?"

She tensed visibly, bristling at the question. "I don't owe you some longwinded explanation. It's enough that I tell you we're going to—"

"You're right." He shrugged. "I don't *need* a damned thing. But it looks to me like you could use to tell it. And why not to me? After all, who am I but some attempted murder suspect with a bounty on his head?"

Having said his piece, he fell silent, giving her the space to work it out for herself. If he failed, he had lost nothing. But if she opened up to him, he figured he might find some avenue to somehow talk his way out of this mess.

"You know, you're not the only one who loves your

old man," she said accusingly before her voice went husky with emotion. "I loved mine, too, still do, God rest his stubborn soul. He taught me everything I know about the bounty hunting business, most of what I know about men. And everything I've learned about picking up on human weakness. The problem was, he was stone blind to his own."

"We've all got our blind spots," Ace said. He'd erupted in anger after his world had crumbled instead of using his head and working harder to figure out whatever angle the woman who'd apparently switched him at birth had been playing.

"Part of it was Vegas," she continued, "that whole world where I grew up, and the cash, the flash and the high rollers he was always drawn to, especially after my mom left us. By the time I realized he was keeping everything afloat, even feeding the two of us, on borrowed money, he owed a small fortune. I did my best to help out, worked my tail off in the family business to pay down the debt, got him into a gambling rehab program, but it only got worse and worse until..."

Sighing heavily, she reached up to pinch the bridge of her nose, the gun drooping a little in her right hand. Ace wondered if she might eventually drop her guard enough for him to turn the tables.

"For a while," she continued, "it really seemed like things might work out. He was doing better. *We* were—until the cancer got bad."

"I'm sorry," he said reflexively, unable to keep his mind from going back, however briefly, to the hell of losing his mother when he and his siblings were just kids. Though Sierra was a woman grown, it sounded as if she had no other family, no one else at all, to lean on.

She nodded in reply. "The worse the news from his doctors, the more he needed an outlet for his stress—and the more convinced he became that he was on the brink of scoring that one big win that would finally turn everything around. It was so infuriating, listening to him claiming he was doing it for me when he was only making things worse."

Ace told himself he'd been alone for too damned long, getting sucked into her story this way. "I totally get that. Ainsley and our siblings could never understand our father's addiction to Selina. His refusal to banish her from our lives, no matter what she did."

"By the time my father died," Sierra continued, her gaze so distant that it made him wonder if she'd even heard him, "he owed doctors, the hospital—but the worst was the hundreds of thousands, with interest compounding daily, he had on the books of the most cutthroat loan shark in Nevada."

"But those debts were your father's," Ace said, trying not to let her catch him watching her gun hand droop a little farther, "not yours."

"Try telling Ice Veins that."

"Ice Veins?" Ace shook his head. "You're kidding. The name sounds like something out of some old gangster movie. With cases of machine guns and crates of bootleg whiskey."

Sierra shrugged. "You don't get a reputation like his by being subtle. Or reasonable, either. You would think he'd like to keep me in one piece just to keep his payments coming, but he took offense last month—*extreme offense*—when I refused to turn loose a bail jumper named Eddie Harris who happened to be his favorite nephew."

"Maybe under the circumstances you should've considered—"

She shook her head, a hard, emerald fire sparking in her eyes as the gun twitched back to its full, upright position. "My dad might've owed the guy, but that doesn't mean that Ice Veins *owns* me. And I'm not letting a homicide suspect, no matter who he is, walk for anybody. Especially not someone like Eddie, who's been accused of other killings in the past."

Ace's heart fell. Because that was all he would ever be to the beautiful Sierra Madden. Another scumbag suspect to be handed over. *Why would you even care what this woman thinks?*

"Immediately after that," she said, "Ice Veins called in the rest of my note, said I needed to pay off the final chunk by two days ago, or he was going to personally see to it that I came up a leg short."

"A leg? He threatened to cut off your *leg*?"

"Smash it, sever it, shoot it… I didn't ask for the specifics. All I know is I won't be working, or making further payments, without two good legs to stand on. Which means I'm a dead woman if I can't come up with the twenty-five thousand dollars that Selina promised me for bringing you back to your family."

Twenty-five thousand dollars? Selina clearly wanted him back—and no doubt, locked up—in a big way, if she was willing to cough up that kind of cash. And it was crystal clear that the bounty hunter wasn't about to—and couldn't—set him free with her own health, possibly her life, hanging in the balance.

"So what if I told you," he said, weighing the possibilities, "*I'd* be willing to pay you that same twenty-five grand. Get this gangster off your back forever, if you'll only—"

"You have the money here?" she asked, the skin crinkling around her nose. "Just lying around this bunker?"

"Well, no," he claimed. A knee-jerk reaction, when the truth was more complicated. And far too dangerous to share with a woman with a gun and such a pressing need. "Not exactly, but—"

"But nothing. I haven't been in this business for a dozen years without having desperate fugitives try to buy me off before. I suppose you think I'm dumb enough to take a personal check?"

He made a scoffing sound, thinking quickly about how would be the best way to do this without guaranteeing that he turned his bunker hideaway into his tomb. Because he might feel for Sierra's predicament, might even find her sexy, with those big green eyes and that tight little body that could so handily knock him on his ass, but he'd be a fool to trust the woman with his life.

"You can handle an online transfer, can't you?" he asked. "I can't access my accounts from here. We'll need to get well away so I can use my cell without leading the authorities straight here."

He'd been fantasizing for weeks about returning to the surface. Feeling the wind whispering against his skin, smelling the fresh scents of the underbrush and seeing the outlines of the foothills, along with the variegated greens of the foliage at this elevation. But he knew that the moment he powered it up again, his phone would ping the nearest cell towers. And surely the police would be working with his telecom provider, waiting to spring into action the moment they could get a bead on his location.

She looked doubtful. "I don't know, Ace. If I'm seen anywhere with you and I don't turn you in like I agreed to—"

"It's not like I can afford to take that kind of a chance, either," he said. "That's why I took the precaution of stocking this place with some things I might need in case I had to disguise myself."

"You sure you're only a first-time fugitive?" Amusement quirked the corners of her mouth. "Because you've really done a first-rate job on your prepping."

He snorted and shrugged. "It's the CEO in me. I've always been a big believer in the value of insurance. Let's see if I have anything here in my bag of tricks that might work as a disguise for you, too."

Pulling a duffel from one of the boxes on the shelves, he reached to unzip it.

"Not so fast," she warned. "Push that over to me first, will you? Slowly."

Looking up at her, he said, "Listen, I can assure you that you're holding the only gun I had with me in the bunker."

Red-blond brows, a shade darker than her hair, rose. "Forgive me if I need to make sure you haven't planted a little *insurance* elsewhere."

As she squatted down and checked through the bag's contents, he said, "If I give you the money for this loan shark, I'll need your promise you won't lead the police to my bunker's entrance."

Sierra pulled out a cowboy hat, followed by an oversize snap-buttoned shirt and a pair of Western boots. "And you're willing to take me at my word on that?"

He offered a half smile. "If you won't sell out your honor for a man like Ice Veins, I have some hope, maybe this much—" he pinched his fingers about a half inch apart "—that you won't do a woman like Selina such a favor."

"I'll tell you what," Sierra offered. "You drop that money into my account, and I'll make myself scarce. I promise. I'll take off for Vegas before sunup. And I won't volunteer any help to the police with their investigation."

"But if you're brought in and questioned?"

She huffed out her disbelief. "You aren't seriously asking me to outright lie to the cops for you? Come on, Colton. I've already told you what I *will* do. What I *can* do if I want to keep my license."

He stared a challenge at her, certain that all he'd have to do was wait before his silence and the lure of desperately needed money would convince her to give up even more. It was a tactic that had worked for him more often than not during business negotiations.

But it was clear from Sierra's expression that she wasn't falling for it. Clear enough that he dropped the idea of sweetening the deal with an additional sum of money almost as quickly as it occurred.

"You've heard my terms." She rose from her seat, the gun held firmly in her hand. "So are we still dealing? Or do we make the drive to the police station instead?"

He sighed, realizing that trusting in this deal—and whatever luck the universe might have on offer—remained his best shot to steer clear of whatever his *loving stepmother* was plotting. It was his best chance, too, to buy himself the time to figure out whether Selina might be somehow linked to the woman who had apparently switched him with the real Colton heir—or his father's shooter.

"All right, then," he agreed. "Let's do this disguise thing."

"Just don't make any quick moves or do anything you haven't vetted with me first," Sierra warned him, "or your particular get-up may involve an eye patch and extra bandaging..."

Chapter Two

Having altered her appearance on many previous occasions, Sierra was quick to improvise. While he turned his back to make his own choices, she stripped off her gray fleece top, then pulled an oversize navy men's work shirt from Ace's bag of tricks over her tee.

After shoving the rolled sleeves up to her elbows, she tackled her long hair, twisting it into a long ponytail, which she tucked up beneath another duffel find, a tweed newsboy cap. Also large for her, the hat slanted jauntily, its short brim resting atop a pair of chunky, horn-rimmed glasses. To that, she added a distinctly teenage male slouch and the bored and sullen sneer that had made any number of jittery bail jumpers miss her among crowds before.

"Wow," Ace said when he turned around a couple of minutes later. "If I didn't know there was a good-looking woman underneath that..."

"And for a diamond cufflinks, silver-spoon type, you make a half-convincing cowboy," she said, honestly assessing his new look, thanks to the black Stetson, Western shirt and boots and the red bandanna he'd tied around his neck. But then again, she reminded herself, he wasn't biologically a Colton, so maybe this version was closer to the truth than either one of them imagined.

"I've got a fake beard and some spirit gum if you think that'll help."

Making a face, she shook her head. "Just keep your collar high and your hat low because if anybody gets close enough to look at either one of us too hard, this is gonna be a real short trip."

Sierra couldn't help noticing how nervous Ace looked as they emerged from the hatch that her charge had blown open earlier into a darkness brightened by the glow of a full moon. As he peered into the deepest shadows, he jerked his head toward the sound of an owl hooting and a soft wind rustling through the treetops.

"Relax, Ace," she urged him, more concerned about his frame of mind than she was about running across anyone else on this isolated hillside. "I had every reason to make sure I wasn't followed coming up here. We're all alone, not a soul for miles. My car's hidden just a couple hundred yards below."

"Sure," he said, his voice hoarse as he used some fallen branches in an attempt to disguise the now vulnerable entrance from other prying eyes, an entrance she'd had a devil of a time finding earlier, in spite of the rough map the real estate agent had sketched for her. But as he rose and walked beside her, their feet crunching on dried twigs and grasses, she could easily spot the tension in his movements, as if every muscle lay coiled, waiting to spring into action at the slightest sign of trouble…

Or was he waiting for his chance to get the drop on her?

Increasingly concerned that he might try something that would end up getting one or both of them hurt—or cost her her crucial payout—she began to wonder if sticking with Selina's deal would prove the safer bet.

"Maybe this offer of yours isn't such a good idea," she suggested as he lifted a pine bough and held it to let her duck under. "Twenty-five grand's a lot of money just to delay a problem you're going to have to deal with sooner or later anyway. And besides, if you really were right about your stepmother plotting something—"

"I'm willing to take my chances," he said, his breath catching for a moment as he caught his first glimpse of the lights of town, many miles in the distance.

"I'd be just as happy solving my problem with her money as yours," she admitted, reaching up to adjust her cap, which had slid down to obscure her vision. "Besides, you could hire a really good lawyer with that kind of—"

Returning his attention to her, he waved off her concern. "*Lawyers and money* I've got," he said bitterly. "Money I've saved my whole life for the family I never took the time away from work to start. And now, for all I know, I'll never get the chance to..."

"Ace..." Her heart twisted at the thought of the latest news from Mustang Valley. A personal matter and a secret that a complete stranger like her had no business sharing with the fugitive.

She weighed her options, struggling to balance the knowledge of the heinous crime this man stood accused of against the possibility that just maybe, telling him would ground him, giving him some reason to be careful. A reason that might help ensure her future, keeping her alive, as well…

HER GAZE CONNECTED with his. A real connection that Ace felt running through him like a strong electric current. And in that moment he sensed, with a clarity unlike anything he'd experienced in his entire life, that there was something that she meant to tell him. Something that would fracture the plane of his life into two distinct parts: *before* and *after.*

"There's no easy way to say this except to come right out and tell you," she began, her voice vibrating with emotion. "You have a daughter. A daughter of your own who's waiting patiently to meet you."

"*What?* What the hell?" Adrenaline spilled through the floodgates, unleashing a throbbing in his chest, a burning tightness stretching over his skin. Followed by absolute fury that she would mess with him like this. "Why on earth would you tell a lie like that when you know damned well I've just lost any claim to all the family I ever had?"

"Whoa, whoa, cowboy," she said, a glint of moonlight off the handgun's metallic surface giving away the fact that she had raised it. And making him realize he'd advanced on her in a way she clearly found threatening. "Pipe down for a minute and just *listen* to me, would you? I've seen a picture of Nova myself, thanks to Selina, and heard that your brothers and sisters introduced her as your *daughter*. A daughter by blood, Ace. There's already been a DNA test."

"But that's...impossible," he said. "I don't have a little girl—I couldn't possibly."

"She's in Mustang Valley," Sierra told him. "And she's a young woman, not a child. Not only that, but she's—"

Stiffening, Sierra cut herself off to glance back over her shoulder.

It was the only warning Ace had before a dark bulk separated itself from the deeper shadow. A loud crackling sound preceded her cry of pain and alarm as she buckled forward.

Before Ace understood what was happening, she'd collapsed completely. He spotted a large man hunched over her and pressing a stun gun to the side of her neck, which was sparking and snapping with the rattling sound of a transformer arcing.

"Hold it right there," a deep voice growled as a second man grabbed Ace's shoulder from behind and pressed something hard and unyielding—*stun gun*, it had to be—against the sore spot at his temple. "Move another muscle and you're dead when you don't hafta be. Our beef's not with you. It's this little deadbeat we got business with."

"Stop it now! Stop shocking her before you kill her!" Ace shouted, sickened by the popping noises, the helpless jerking of her body beside the shaved-head ox squatting beside her, his mouth stretched into a leer of pure cruelty. Sierra Madden might be Ace's captor, but this sickened him—and had him wanting to turn their weapons on the two thugs that had jumped them. Thugs that gave credence to the story she had told him about the loan shark who went by the name Ice Veins.

When the crackling ceased abruptly, the man holding the gun on him, a heavily muscled specimen with a dark chinstrap beard, told his partner, "Careful frisking her for weapons. My buddies from down the boxing gym tell me she's won her last two matches by knockout, and half the guys are scared to spar with her."

No wonder she took me down, Ace realized. Not that it made him feel one bit better to hear the bald guy laugh or watch him pin her down with one meaty hand splayed across her chest while she whimpered, struggling to regain control of her still-twitching limbs. "Bitch won't be punching nobody for a while. Nice try with the disguise, Miss Madden."

With that, he tossed aside the fake glasses and pulled her hair free of its makeshift updo.

"N-no," she protested. "G-get your—h-hands off me."

Ace surged forward in response, only to grunt with pain when the bearded goon holding him sharply cracked the gun against his brow and cheekbone. Vision graying out, Ace dropped to his knees.

By the time he could see again, the bald thug was pocketing both Sierra's weapon and the one she'd taken earlier from Ace inside the bunker. Rising with a grunt, the huge man took a step back, aiming a revolver so long that it practically qualified as a hand cannon above the bounty hunter's breast.

"I didn't come across any wad of cash that felt like

my boss's twenty-five thousand dollars in those pockets," he told her, a satisfied sneer spreading across his broad face. "So which leg do you want blown off? The right one or the left?"

NAUSEATED FROM THE threat as she felt uncoordinated from the jolting, Sierra pleaded, "You can't do this—"

"If you'll be patient just a minute—" though dark streamers of blood were running down his face, Ace Colton spoke with the forced cheer of a determined salesman "—I'll be happy to take care of Ms. Madden's bill here."

Both men's heads snapped in his direction. Along with Sierra's surprised gaze. Why would he volunteer his assistance, now that she was both unarmed and helpless? Did he think they'd kill him otherwise, eliminating him as a witness to their violence?

"All of it?" the bald man asked him, his pale eyes narrowed with suspicion. "Because we've got strict instructions not to leave Mustang Valley without either the money or a photo of the mangled leg she owes my boss."

"And personally," his bearded cohort chuckled, "we kinda figured that ole Ice Veins would just as soon have us blast her leg off, on account of the way she jammed up his favorite nephew."

"Every penny," Ace insisted, "if you don't mind waiting for me to head down to where I can get a decent cell phone signal so I can transfer the funds to—"

The bearded man nearest to him snorted. "You think

we take electronic transfers? I imagine you want us to print you out a nice, neat receipt, too?"

The men's coarse laughter had panic bubbling up into Sierra's throat.

"This is a strictly cash operation, mister," the larger bald man told him, his voice dropping to a more menacing pitch as he straightened to tower over her. "But it's your lucky day, and we're giving you one chance right now. Walk away and forget you ever saw or heard us, and you don't have to be a part of this. Otherwise... I've got some extra ammo in this gun."

When Ace glanced toward her, Sierra felt truly lost, as alone as she had ever felt in her life. For Ice Veins's men were offering him the escape he craved and needed.

Certainly, he didn't owe her, Sierra knew as she steeled herself, her gaze connecting with the fugitive's for a fraction of a second. Nice for Colton to try; he surely wouldn't risk his own skin for the woman who'd burst into his lair and decked him with a left cross, the woman who meant nothing to him other than a threat.

"What if I told you I could get it all in cash," Ace blurted, looking from one of the loan shark's men to the other, "by tomorrow morning? And what if I sweetened the deal with, let's say, five grand each for the two of you? You know, to reward you for your patience if you'll only wait?"

Sierra's heart skipped a beat, her lungs refilling with the sweet, fresh breath of hope. Though she couldn't imagine how Ace could actually come up with so much currency so quickly, his gambit flooded her with the energy she needed to reach down and carefully begin lifting up her pant leg, reaching for the boot that her captor hadn't checked nearly as carefully as he should have.

"I don't know," the bald man told Ace. "We do have somewhere else we're supposed to be."

"And besides," the bearded one said, "if Ice Veins figures we're trying to run some kind of side deal on him—let's just say he's not the most forgiving of bosses."

"Who's to say he has to know?" Ace asked. "Or that it even has to be five thousand? What if I made it eight apiece?"

"Or how 'bout ten for each of us, big spender?" The bearded man laughed. "Is this bitch worth it to you?"

"You may not be an ATM, but I'm not your piggybank, either," Ace said, abruptly shifting from affable salesman to tough negotiator. "So take it or leave it. It's no skin off my teeth. I'm just trying to save us all some fuss and bother."

"You'll be no bother to anybody when you're dead, Slick," said the bald man, spinning his bulk toward Ace so quickly that Sierra knew for certain that he meant to shoot him.

It forced her to spring into action, grasping the little pepper spray gun from her boot holster. With its palm-size orange safety tip—designed to let police know it was not a lethal weapon—it might not look like much, but the toy-like plastic backup sent a stream of noxious fluid straight into the big man's face.

Yelping and choking, he dropped to his knees, clawing at his streaming nose and eyes while blindly squeezing off a round from his huge gun.

Rising, Sierra whirled around, hoping to spray the bearded man's face, too. But she saw that Ace was grappling with him, the two of them fighting to control the gun still in the thug's right hand.

Get out of here, her instincts screamed. *Get to the car before the other creep manages to shoot you!*

But there was no way she could leave Ace, not when she was responsible for dragging him into this mess. So instead she looked around desperately until she found a fallen tree limb. Snatching up the thick branch, she whacked the bearded man so hard across the back that the breath exploded from his lungs.

The force of the blow sent him lurching into Ace. Yet another shot, a deafening *crack*, echoed through the darkness.

For a moment she held her breath, listening for something, anything, beyond the coughing and the cursing of the pepper-sprayed bald thug, to let her know what had happened.

Then she heard the unmistakable crash of a man's body thudding to the ground.

Chapter Three

Ace's breath roared in his ears as the two of them pounded downhill, Sierra hauling him by the hand. One of the loan shark's goons roared threats as the moans of the bearded man, who'd been shot in the struggle, faded behind them.

"Hurry. Car's this way." Panting out the words, she spoke urgently into Ace's ear, "And whatever you do, keep your head low. The big guy's still got his gun!"

Ace wasn't sure how ducking was supposed to stop a bullet, but he instinctively heeded her advice as he scrambled after her. Practically blinded by the darkness and the blood streaming into his right eye, he was repeatedly whipped and scraped by branches.

But regardless of the outcome, he'd cast his lot with this woman. And now he had no choice except to trust her to get them both out of this situation.

Even so, when she drew up short and peered around a few minutes later, doubt flooded in. With his injured face throbbing in time with the pounding of his heartbeat, he asked, "You've lost the car, haven't you? Maybe if we crouch down and hide, they'll pass us by."

"There! It's over there." Her sigh was audible as she let go of him and led him to a small depression partly shrouded by thick undergrowth. "The door's unlocked, so—"

Needing no more invitation, he clambered over and climbed into a dark-colored sedan. Seconds later she was in the driver's seat and snapping on a seat belt before cranking up the engine.

The car lurched backward and swung clear of the brush before she dropped it into Drive.

From outside there was a pop, followed by a splintering sound as, just behind Ace's head, the rear passenger window shattered. "Go, go, go!" he shouted.

The tail end of the car careening, the tires suddenly gained purchase. As the headlights came on to illuminate the path ahead, Ace shouted an unnecessary warning. Sierra was already swerving around tree trunks thicker than his legs.

Belting himself in in an effort to remain upright, Ace said, "Dirt road's to your left. There! We're clear now, or I think we are—unless he's got wheels nearby, too."

She darted a glance into the rearview mirror, her eyes wide and her face frozen in a grimace. His admiration rose another notch as she visibly pulled herself together, slowing her gasping breaths and mastering her body's shaking.

"Half blind as he's gotta be and with his partner shot, we're sure to lose him." Sierra flicked a look in his direction as she pulled onto an old logging road and mashed down on the accelerator. "Are you—your face?"

Wiping away blood, he said, "I'll be okay, I think. What about you? Are you hurt?"

She gave a hoot of laughter. "Ask me once the adrenaline wears off, why don't you?"

Ace suspected the same might be true in his case, with the thundering in his chest, the crazed buzz of adrenaline drowning out everything except the immediate need to get clear of the two men who would surely kill them, given half a chance.

It didn't sink it for another mile or two down the dark and tree-lined road that the wound he had inflicted on the bearded man during their struggle might very well prove fatal.

"I've never shot a man before," he said, sounding as numb as he felt. *Let alone maybe killed one, despite what half of Mustang Valley and the police seemed to think.*

Sierra slid another look his way. In the faint glow of the dashboard lights, he saw her narrow-eyed skepticism give way to a nod. "If it makes you feel any better," she said, "he wouldn't have any qualms about putting a bullet in you before he plugged me."

"I know there wasn't any choice. It's just… I'm not—I don't know how to deal with any of this."

"I get that, Ace, and I appreciate it," she said. "Just the same way I appreciate that you didn't turn your back on me when they gave you the chance to walk away."

This time it was Ace's turn to laugh, a humorless sound like the scraping of dry tree limbs in the wind. "I've been on the wrong end of enough business dealings to know when I'm flat-out being lied to. Those guys never meant to let me go. They would have sooner shot me in the back the moment I turned around than trust me to leave and keep my mouth shut."

"You have good instincts," she allowed. "In their line of business, witnesses are liabilities. But thanks anyway. It means a lot. Without your help, I'd've definitely..."

"You're welcome, I suppose," he said when it became apparent that she didn't care to finish the thought. "But where to now? If they do catch up with us, I doubt they're going to be in the mood to stop with your leg."

She slowed before turning left onto a hard-packed caliche road. "That's my problem, not yours. I'm taking you back to the police station, where you'll be safe from my issues and will be free to start getting your life back in order."

"Free?" he fired back. "We both know the first thing they're going to do is lock me up so I don't disappear again."

"Haven't you been in a cage all this time anyway?" she asked. "I don't see what the difference is, except for this time your family has some high-priced lawyer working on your issue."

"Oh, there's a difference, all right. Come on, Sierra. Can't you see? We're in this together now. You've already said you owe me."

"I owe you more than getting you killed over what just happened. Which means putting space between us."

"Or better yet, making sure they don't find either of us. And I think I know a place where we can hole up, at least for the rest of the night. A little mom-and-pop motel outside of town, well off any of the main drags, where we can get a room in cash—I've got enough on me to give you some to register so they won't see me—and lay low for the rest of the night."

She glanced his way. "You mean a *no-tell motel* where you rich boys take your mistresses?"

"Don't look at me." He shrugged. "I'm an unrepentant bachelor with my own private condo in town and a home on the Triple R. But I've heard about this place… and I'm willing to bet that those two haven't. They're from Las Vegas, aren't they?"

"They are, but—" She gasped and braked hard as a tan blur whisked before their headlights. The tires grabbed the gravel, but not fast enough to avoid the large deer that had come out of nowhere.

As the car shuddered to a halt, the buck thudded down across the hood, its head bent backward and one point of its antler at the center of a fist-size spider's web in the middle of the windshield.

With her face pale and her hands clenching the steering wheel, she stared openmouthed, tears pouring down her face. "The poor thing—I didn't—I never saw it coming—Oh, no—I'm sorry, deer. I'm really *sorry.*"

"It's all right," Ace said, struggling to still the shaking in his own voice. And oddly touched to see this experienced bounty hunter, who apparently dealt knockout punches as a boxer, so affected by the animal's accidental death. "It happened so fast. I can't imagine he felt anything. Here, let me get out and try to move it. We have to—we need to leave as fast as we can, before those guys catch up with us."

Bailing out of the car, he tugged and hauled at the heavy carcass and, with a grunt of exertion, rolled it to the ground. After checking out the car, he went around and opened the driver's side door.

"Move over, Sierra. I'm taking the wheel from here."

She blinked up at him, her eyes huge and unfocused. "Wha—"

"Car looks drivable," he told her, "but I need you to move over. Switch seats with me right now. You've got to trust that I'm the best person to get us both clear of this in one piece."

PULSE RACING WILDLY, Sierra stared up at him, weighing the risks against the realities—and her lifelong inclination to fight any man attempting to control her.

Swallowing back reluctance, she told herself that accepting Ace Colton's help was the smartest, surest way to get them both to safety. For one thing, he knew where they were going. For another, she was shaking so hard her teeth were chattering and she thought she might be sick.

Still in overdrive from the adrenaline the stun gun attack had sent coursing through her, she'd had nothing in reserve—nothing at all—to handle this unexpected accident. And no choice now except to do what she had to in order to survive.

"Okay," she said, ignoring the hand he offered to climb out unassisted. On the way to the passenger side, she turned to look behind them and breathed a little easier to see no sign of pursuit yet. She also noted, with a chagrined glance, her Camry's dented steel-gray hood and damaged grill.

The moment her seat belt clicked, the car leaped forward, a few ticks and rattles hinting at some body damage but nothing that seemed to give Ace trouble. As the dark road straightened, he switched off the headlights before explaining, "If anybody's following, let's make their job a little harder. I know these back roads well enough to—"

"Just please, be careful," she said drily as they bumped along. "I'd hate to lose my safe driver discount with my insurance company."

Over the next twenty minutes Ace proved himself a skilled and confident driver, especially for a man who hadn't been above ground, let alone behind the wheel, in some time. As they descended from the hills, he turned the headlights back on, and she made out the darkened outlines of low-slung ranch houses and outbuildings with parked vehicles or cattle trailers nearby, along a narrow rural road lined with fence posts. Since it was after 1 a.m., only the occasional security light stood against the inky darkness of the Arizona night.

One such outpost marked an old beige stucco building that squatted before a rocky bluff. The Cactus Flower, read a spot-lit sign beside a once-grand but now tilted and half-dead saguaro—possibly a victim of the moderate earthquake that had struck the area recently. More modest rows of solar lights marked out a rock pathway—cracked across the middle, but otherwise intact—leading to an office with an old-school pink neon sign reading Vacancy.

"What do you think?" Ace asked, the sound of his deep voice startling her out of her thoughts.

"It'll do," she said, taking in the bar shape of the apparently undamaged double-sided building, which couldn't have more than twenty rooms, tops. On this side of the motel, she made out only two parked vehicles, and there were plenty of empty spots, which would allow them to leave the vehicle some distance from whichever room they ended up in—a precaution she preferred.

As Ace peeled off several twenties to go and check in, he said, "I'm not trying to be stingy, but the clerk's going to find it strange if you try to rent two separate rooms for us."

His obvious concern for her feelings made her stomach do a funny little slip-slide. Considering their circumstances, they both had a lot bigger worries than anything as old-fashioned as the notion of her honor as a single woman.

"You don't really think I'm letting you out of my sight, do you?" In spite of her fatigue, she felt a smile pulling at the corner of her mouth. "Besides, we have a lot to talk about before either one of us gets any shut-eye."

"Starting with what you said about this—this alleged daughter of mine, if you were really serious about that."

"I may have my moments, bluffing in front of fugitives, but I would never lie about a thing like that," she insisted. "Never."

He hesitated, clearly weighing her claim before asking, "You said her name was Nova, right?"

Sierra nodded, seeing in his face how hard the possibility that he had a child had hit him, even if he wasn't certain he could take her at her word. "Nova Ellis Colton, yes. That's how I'm told your siblings introduced her. Just wait here in the car, but if you don't mind… I'll need to take my keys."

Anger gleamed in his eyes, like sparks flying off a struck flint. "I thought we were way past that, Sierra, that you'd decided you could trust me. You really think I'd drive off, when you're my only source of information on a young woman who's going around pretending to be my last known biological connection on the planet?"

"They're not treating her as a pretender, not with that DNA test. *And* she's not the last. But I'll tell you more when I come back out. *With* those car keys in my pocket." Sierra held her hand out.

Glowering at her, he demanded, "Are you kidding? After a tease like that one? Why on earth would I take off now?"

With a derisive snort, she popped the wide brim of the hat he was still wearing. "I can think of twenty-five thousand bucks' worth of motivation, cowboy. Which happens to be exactly the same number of reasons I can't afford to let you go."

As he sat waiting, keyless, in the car, Ace tried not to take it personally. Of course Sierra didn't trust him. He told himself he wouldn't risk it, either, if he were counting on the twenty-five thousand dollars she needed to repay a criminal with a name like Ice Veins and save her leg, if not her life.

Still, her distrust rankled, after what the two of them had been through, the way they'd worked together to overcome the armed thugs. And even more than that, he'd thought, back in the bunker, they'd truly been communicating on a deeper level than fugitive to captor.

You've been locked underground like a mushroom too damned long if you think for one moment that bounty hunter sees you as anything but another scum-sucking criminal to be hauled in for a reward. Reminding himself of the way she'd not only decked him but also come back from her tasing to pepper spray her assailant, he realized he had never met a woman half as hard-core…or any less likely to be persuaded by the Colton name, money and position that had drawn so many other women to him in the past.

Well, you can kiss all that goodbye now, he thought. Even if he cleared up the murder accusation, that suspicion would likely taint him for other companies looking for new executives, just as it would for the type of women he'd so long squired to charity events and social gatherings. Though the career part left him troubled—his role as the face of Colton Oil had always been more a matter of personal satisfaction than money to him—the thought of leaving behind those glittering social gatherings and the polished beauties who lived to dress up for them came as a relief. After all he and his family had recently been through, the thought of suffering through another season of superficial conversations about who was wearing what designer, driving which new luxury car, or vacationing at what exclusive beach or ski resort tempted him to head back to the bunker and hide himself away again.

He began to realize how much the past few months had changed him into someone else. Or maybe he had never been the man he'd liked to imagine in the first place. Maybe the real Ace Colton, the man whose life he'd inadvertently stolen, was meant to be that person and he was someone else entirely.

The wild thought chased its tail around his throbbing head until Sierra returned from checking them in, a small plastic grocery sack and a large, flat box in her hand.

"What do you have there?" he asked once she'd climbed in. "That smells almost like—is that *pepperoni*?"

"Hot and greasy," she said, her tone light with amusement. "The night clerk's maybe eighteen, and he'd just pulled a couple of those French bread pizzas out of this toaster oven they keep in there. Luckily, he hadn't trashed the box."

"You talked a teenage night clerk into parting with hot pizza?"

"Don't be too impressed. The kid had another box in the freezer, and it still cost me twenty bucks. But he did throw in a couple sodas." She added a shrug. "I figured we could use a little fuel."

Ace's stomach gave an unexpected growl, and he admitted, "I could eat," much to his own surprise.

"Apparently." She chuckled as she directed him to park the car on the deserted rear side of the building.

Afterward, as they walked to the far end of the room block, Ace noticed she was weaving slightly.

When she stumbled, he reflexively caught her arm to keep her from falling forward. “You all right there?”

Sniffing indignantly, she pulled free and straightened the box with the pizza. “Don’t worry, Ace. Our midnight snack is safe with me.”

He let it go at that, following behind her. And filing away the fact that the stun gun attack had taken more out of her than she was willing to let on.

Once inside the room, he locked and chained the door behind them and turned to see her frowning at the cramped space and tired decor.

“Sorry they didn’t have anything with two beds.” She set down the pizza box and the bag on a small, round table and pulled out one of the mismatched wooden chairs. “Apparently, all their rooms are set up like this one.”

“It’s no big deal. I’ll take the sofa.” Making an effort to look and sound more at ease than he was feeling, he pulled off the cowboy hat and tossed it onto the lumpy gold tweed cushions. “Now, about this girl you mentioned, the one claiming to be my—”

Sierra frowned and shook her head. “Young woman, you mean,” she corrected, pulling a couple of cans of Coke and some paper napkins out of the bag. “But first, why don’t you go wash the blood off your face, bruiser?”

Wincing at the reminder of the crack he’d taken from the bearded thug’s gun to his face, Ace ducked into the small bathroom to clean up as best he could. A few minutes later he returned after stripping down to his black tee to rid himself of the now-stained Western shirt and bandanna and washing carefully so as not to reopen the split skin at his cheekbone.

Sierra looked up from the seat she'd taken at the table. "That looks better, though I can already see you'll have a shiner." She passed him one of the two Cokes. "How's it feeling?"

"It's stopped bleeding." As he popped the can's tab, he shrugged, not mentioning the halo of bright specks he'd seen around the bathroom's bare lights or the dull but steady throb in his head. "I'll take that as a win at this point. What about you? Seriously, you okay?"

"Nothing I can't handle," she insisted with a defiant gleam in her eyes that made him suspect her answer would be the same even if those thugs had lopped off her leg.

Once he'd claimed the chair across from her, each of them grabbed a pizza. Over the next few minutes they ate in silence, making short work of a meal that failed to satisfy but would at least help to energize their tired bodies.

But it wasn't enough to keep thoughts of their earlier conversation from crowding in on him before Sierra pushed away her last half-eaten bite as he washed down a final mouthful.

"So you're going to quit putting me off and tell me about this Nova person," he prompted as he set his soda down. "I need to hear all of it, now."

Blowing out a breath, Sierra wiped her hands and pulled out her cell phone. When she looked up again into his eyes, he once more felt the impact of their connection, reaching all the way down to his spine and crackling outward through the myriad nerve endings. He felt a buzz of anticipation, the unshakable sense that this tough, smart woman had come into his life to change its course forever.

Or maybe utterly destroy what little I have left...

"I'll do you one better, Ace," she told him. "I'll show you right now. You see, after Selina hired me, I realized I couldn't do the job without getting to know who's who in your family before I started interviewing them for clues regarding your whereabouts. I needed a system to document their names and faces since it's such a large clan, with so many siblings and half siblings."

"They're not really mine, though. Not anymore," he said, thinking of how not one of them was an actual blood relation. Of how he'd been cast adrift by that fateful email exposing him as an imposter.

"Well, they still think of *you* as family, your brothers and your sisters," she insisted.

The assertion sent relief zinging straight to his heart. Sure, his siblings had stuck by him at first, when Ace's body type hadn't matched that of the assailant seen in the grainy security footage from the office, nor from the failed sting operation. When another piece of evidence had turned up as well, an Arizona Sun Devils pin found beneath the boardroom air-conditioning unit in the wake of their father's shooting, that, too, had seemed to point in another direction, since like his father, Ace had never had much interest in collegiate sports.

But once that so-called *witness* had come forward, insisting that he'd confessed to shooting his father and hiding the gun inside his condo, Ace had lost hope that anyone would truly believe in him at all, much less still want to claim him as a brother.

"I got a picture of each of them from Selina and made notes as to how they were related." Sierra opened the photo section of her phone.

The rickety chair creaked as Ace leaned forward, straining to see familiar faces—faces that made his heart ache with nostalgia for simpler, happier times as she began to scroll. Would he ever again see them? Ever share another exchange not tainted by lies and weighted down by tragedy?

As his skin tightened and his pulse spiked, her voice took on an unearthly quality, seeming to echo in his ears. "That's your daughter, Nova Colton."

"Nova *Colton*..." His own words came out strained and parched as if he'd been trekking through an endless desert. Because this was impossible, some kind of tortured nightmare—or worse yet a flat-out lie, meant to disarm his defenses and lead him to his arrest as calmly as a lamb to slaughter.

As the panicked thought raced through his head, Ace stood so abruptly that the chair tipped to the floor behind him. "I *don't* have a daughter," he insisted, needing to let her know she damned well wasn't fooling him with this wild story. Or was he only trying to keep the ground from shifting out from underneath him, as it had so many times in these past months?

Coming to her feet as well, Sierra turned the cell to hold it against her chest. As she looked up at him, compassion eased the hard set of her jaw and softened her green eyes.

"You do, Ace. Yes, you do," she said. "And not only a daughter…" Flipping the phone around, she smiled, showing him a pretty young blonde woman, with an unmistakable bump at her midsection. "But a grandchild on the way."

Every atom of him shook, demanding that he turn away. Or curse her for the cruelty of this deception. Why hadn't he realized earlier she'd only been stringing him along?

He pictured himself storming out, vanishing into the dark desert night. If Sierra wanted to stop him, she'd have to knock him off his feet again or catch him in time to pepper spray his face as she had the bald thug's.

Except he didn't leave. Didn't even turn. He couldn't. Not with the wonder of her words still sinking in, of what he could see with his own two eyes on her phone's screen, igniting like a spark in a stack of drought-dry kindling.

"She—she's *pregnant*?" he found himself asking instead, as if what Sierra had said hadn't sunk in the first time. "But she's so young. What would you say?"

Sierra scrutinized the photos. "Twenty-two, maybe twenty-three, tops. Couldn't be much older. And you're, what is it? Forty now? Not that you really look it but—"

"Which would've made me— Hell, I must've only been about…" In the split second it took him to do the math, a buzz started inside his brain. A buzz that morphed into a swarm of tiny, bright dots as it hit him that Nova had her mother's jaw and forehead.

"Oh, hell," he said, groaning at the memory of a girl he'd scarcely thought about in decades. A memory that cracked the dam of disbelief.

"Maybe you ought to sit down before you fall down." Sierra's voice faded to a distant echo, worry threaded through it.

Swallowing hard, Ace righted the chair he'd toppled before sagging into the seat. But his mind was blazing with another face, with a name that struck like a bolt from the blue. *Allegra. Allegra.* "That girl. That summer… How could I have been so—" Face burning, he looked up at Sierra, miserable to think of what he'd done. And what he'd missed out on because of it. "Why wouldn't she have told me, given me a chance to— She never said a word. I don't understand this."

Sierra took a seat as well, saying nothing to absolve or encourage a confession. But the story spilled out of him anyway, too raw to keep inside.

"I was seventeen. We both were. I'm not even sure now," he admitted, "other than it was just a summer fling."

Ace caught the look she slid his way, read the disgust in it. Or maybe he was only seeing his own judgment of his teenage self reflected in her eyes.

"You're absolutely right," he said bitterly. "I was a jerk, a stupid kid who got caught up in the magic of summer and a few heady hours of freedom. What was the harm? I remember thinking. No one would ever find out."

Laughing bitterly, he added, "Joke was on me, I guess, since I never heard from her again."

"But you didn't reach out to her, either?"

Swallowing hard, he shook his head. "I never imagined there was any need to. I never suspected for a minute. But her—not a phone call, not even a postcard. If she had, I would have…"

He stopped short, knowing for a certainty how the man he was now, the person he'd grown into, would have responded to such a bombshell, especially after learning such a painful lesson about the real meaning of family. But back then, as a callow youth mostly wrapped up in his ambition and his pleasures, he couldn't say for certain—to his great shame—that he would have done right by the girl he'd barely known. Still… "Why didn't she at least give me the chance?"

"You can ask her daughter—*your* daughter—when you meet her," Sierra said, handing him her cell with the photo of the young blonde woman with eyes as green as Allegra's had been still on the screen. "It's why Nova came to Mustang Valley. To find *you*."

Swallowing hard, Ace nodded, feeling gutted. Emptied of the remnants of the man he'd left behind when he'd fled whomever was plotting to frame him for a crime he had not committed. Yet, along with the grief of that loss, he felt something more, as well. The dim glow of hope, a lone star emerging in the bleakest twilight.

"I might not've been the man I should've been back then, with her mother," he said, his throat tightening and his thumb caressing the image on the phone's screen. "But I swear to you, as long as there's any shot of my becoming a—a real father to this Nova and being there for her and her child, I'll do whatever it takes to make that happen."

Chapter Four

Though Sierra had met Ace only hours before, she believed him absolutely when he'd claimed he hadn't known. No way was he faking the roughness of his voice, the hint of dampness in his brown eyes. He'd been well and truly knocked out by the news she'd shared with him. News he had clearly accepted once he'd seen the photo.

Looking at the image of Nova, Sierra had some inkling as to why.

"Coloring's not the same," she said, "but I think your daughter looks like you quite a bit, too."

"The poor girl." Ace's laugh was as awkward as she might expect for a man who'd been under such a strain for months on end.

"Hey, I didn't say she'd inherited your three-days' growth," Sierra teased, barely stopping herself in time to keep from playfully reaching out to brush his jaw. "But the shape of the eyes, her cheekbones—believe me, she could do a lot worse. In person, you'll see she's even lovelier than this photo—"

"Yes, I *will* see," Ace said, capturing her hand in his

before she could move away. “Once we’ve proved my innocence so I can go home.”

“You need to let go of me right now,” she warned, her heart crowding into her throat and her body freezing. Except for her free hand, which reached down toward the boot holster…only to find it empty.

The breath deserted her lungs. She must have lost the little spray gun somewhere after nailing the bald creep in the face. Mind rifling through the equipment she’d had on her when she’d set out early this evening, she realized that the only resources that remained were the zip ties attached to her belt and her fighting skills. But with her muscles quivering with fatigue and her coordination off, she didn’t like her chances of subduing the far larger Ace in any kind of physical confrontation…

Raising his palms, he said, “You aren’t—you aren’t scared I’d hurt you, are you? Because I thought—aren’t we a team now, Sierra? Can’t we be? I’ll give you the money like I promised, to take care of your troubles and then we—”

She rose from the chair and took a step back to give herself more distance. Breathing space to remind herself why she’d come tonight. And what this man was to her. He was a means to an end: her own survival. No matter how drawn she was to him, or how sympathetic to his situation. “There can’t be any *we,*” she corrected, with a curt shake of her head. “After we finish our transaction, I drop you back off at your bunker and we forget we ever met. Then, if you’re very lucky, those guys will never connect the two of us. Never have any reason to think the cowboy who shot one of Ice Veins's thugs might be some missing Colton."

His gaze dialed in on her. "Do you really think *you're* going to be safe, Sierra? That this Ice Veins and his thugs are going to drop this after we get him his payoff?"

There he went again, using the word *we* even after she'd warned him off. Just as he'd gone on speaking of paying off Ice Veins even though Ace must surely know by now that she could no longer force him to honor the bargain they had struck. What was his angle in all this? Did he imagine if he solved her problem, she'd feel obligated to find a way to fix his?

"I don't know." Her anxiety ratcheted higher. Because what she'd said about forgetting they'd ever met—she already knew that part was a lie. She wasn't likely to forget him or what he was doing for her, whatever his reasons. "Since I crossed his nephew, Ice Veins has been looking for an excuse to make an example out of me. And now, with one of his enforcers shot? Odds are I'll never get clear of him, not even if I personally hand him over a stack of cash with a big fat bow around it. But there's no reason in the world for me to take you down with me."

Ace had troubles enough, but he also had a real shot at finding out who had set him up and hurt his father, and there were people in his life who still cared deeply about his welfare. Along with that, he had a daughter, and soon a grandchild, whom he deserved the chance to get to know.

"So what'll you do then, with the money?" Ace asked, worry lines etched into his handsome face.

"I'm not sure. Maybe try to call him, work things out directly. Or could be that going on the run's my better option," she said, wondering which, if either, was more likely to raise her life expectancy from hours or maybe days to years.

He moved in close again, so close that she feared he'd once more touch her. But only his gaze did, caressing her in a way that made her—heaven help her—long for more.

"Take it from someone who's been there," he said, his voice somber. "Once you start running, you'll always be looking over your shoulder. That's not the life you deserve."

"Ace," she said, her throat tightening as the hour, their situation and the insanity of the attraction she was feeling to a man she barely knew but couldn't deny rushed in on her from all sides. Or maybe it was the fact that he truly understood the secret she had been afraid to share with anyone—understood it as only a man currently locked in his own life-changing struggle could.

More likely, her judgment was impaired, too, along with her balance and coordination, for before she understood what she was doing, she pushed herself into his arms. But instead of feeling wrong or off, she felt nothing but relief, her body singing when his strong arms wrapped around her. He held her, cradling her protectively against him, as she hadn't been held in so very long.

"Why couldn't I have met you before?" he whispered, planting a chaste kiss atop her head. "Back when life was simple and I could've brought you home to the ranch?"

She chuckled. "Oh, yeah. I can just imagine your family's reaction to your slumming with a female bounty hunter who likes to punch people for sport. You should've seen Selina, side-eyeing my outfit and talking down to me as if I were the help. Which I suppose I kind of am, but still..."

He snorted. "Believe me, if Selina didn't like you, the rest of the family would have considered that a huge plus." Giving her one last squeeze, he continued, "But Sierra, as things stand, there's no way I can possibly—"

"Shh." Breath hitching, she jerked her gaze toward the window as a soft clunking sound carried on the nighttime stillness. "Was that a car door shutting?"

Ace was first to reach the blinds. Carefully lifting a slat, he cursed and warned her, "We need to get out now! Ice Veins's men've found your car—and it looks like they've brought reinforcements."

He grabbed her hand, pulling her toward the door.

"They must've gotten a GPS tracker on my car somehow," she said. "I should've known! I should've—"

"Never mind that right now," he urged. "Just move, before we end up boxed in! There are at least three of them out there."

But Sierra was still so wobbly, she knew there was no way she could escape—especially not with armed men in pursuit. No way she could do anything except get Ace caught, too.

So with her pounding heart in her throat, she told him, "Head off to the right now. Stick to the shadows."

When he tried to pull her, she jerked her hand away and pushed him forward, "Move! I'm just behind you!"

Except when she exited in his wake, Sierra made a sharp turn, heading to the left with her hands raised.

"HANDS UP AND on your knees, bounty hunter!"

The bellowed words, coming some forty yards behind him, stopped Ace dead in his tracks. As he stood panting in a deep band of shadow, he recognized that voice, that of the bald ox she had pepper sprayed earlier. Recognized, too, that the men must have been closer to the room than he'd imagined when he had emerged.

And that Sierra Madden had made the choice, before she'd pushed him out the door, to give herself up instead of running for it. That she'd made that decision to give him a shot at escape and a reunion with his family, knowing that, without his money to appease them, she had almost zero chance to avoid a gruesome injury—and that was if they didn't blow her brains out on the spot.

Stomach pitching as he overheard her assurances that she was unarmed and alone, he knew he couldn't let this happen. Couldn't leave such a beautiful, brave woman to a gruesome fate, no matter what it cost him.

Taking a deep breath, he pulled out his phone first, powered it on and prayed it would connect before they hauled her off somewhere to maim or kill her. His stomach pitched at the sight of Sierra kneeling with her fingers laced behind her neck as two men shouted down at her. Meanwhile, a smaller, slighter figure cried, "I'm sorry, miss! I'm sorry! I didn't want to tell them where your room was, but they barged into the office and stuck that big gun in my face!"

"Shut your mouth, you," warned the bald man before he began pistol-whipping the young clerk.

Bleating with pain, the kid raised his arms in an attempt to protect his head as Sierra called, "Please don't! He's just a boy. He doesn't know anything about this."

A blow to the side of the teen's head dropped him like a stone. If he was lucky, he might wake up with a headache. If he wasn't, they might pump him full of lead, too, leaving him unable to identify the men who'd been here.

Unable to risk being overheard making a voice call, Ace fumbled through the act of tapping out a text, his heart pounding like a war drum. Adding the motel's name and location, he hit *Send,* and prayed that Sergeant Spencer Colton would jump at this opportunity to bring him in. And that his relationship with his distant cousin, as strained as it was by this time, would ensure that the officer would arrive with the backup—sans sirens—that Ace had requested to deal with the *dangerous armed men on the scene.*

A smaller man wearing a calf-length coat with an extravagant fur collar, short-cropped hair and a full, but neatly trimmed red beard was gesturing angrily as he stood over and lectured Sierra. Ace could make out only a few words from this distance, chief among them *my money.* But a quiet menace carried on the chill breeze and something—perhaps a diamond—glinted coldly as a distant star at his ear.

The loan shark in the flesh, Ace thought. Just as he suspected, the notorious Ice Veins's personal involvement in this matter meant that Sierra and the clerk both might be long dead before Mustang Valley PD made it here.

"Please," he heard her saying, "don't do this. You know I've always made good on my dad's notes, and I'll *keep* paying. This is bad business, and I always thought you were a man who put his financial interests first."

Panic roared through Ace as the loan shark pulled out a thin knife, the blade's razor edge glinting in the yellow security light. Still on her knees, Sierra jerked her head back as he raised its point to hover above her face, an inch or so beneath her eye.

"Yeah, it is bad business," the loan shark said, "messing up such a pretty lady. Don't think I enjoy it. But you were warned, and I won't have it said that I'm a man who goes around making idle threats—especially after the way you did my favorite nephew."

"Your nephew—" Sierra's voice hardened into pure defiance "—is a piece of human garbage."

The loan shark said nothing in reply, but Ace saw the swift pivot of his body, the flash of steel as he drew back the weapon.

Ace shouted, "No!" emerging from the shadows.

Sierra, who'd clearly tracked the movement, too, threw herself to her side as the knife slashed the air an inch above her head.

"Stop!" Ace yelled, his shaking hands raised. "I've

got the money. I can pay you. Everything she owes. Every penny of it."

"Hold it! *You?*" The big, bald man spun around, the hand cannon's muzzle traveling in a swift arc to aim at Ace's chest.

"Don't shoot him," ordered Ice Veins. "At least not until I've heard him out."

Vibrating with fury, the human ox ground out through clenched jaws, "But he was the one who killed my partner!"

"In the business of enforcement—" Ice Veins shrugged "—these misunderstandings sometimes happen."

"But we're talkin' Choke here, boss. We worked together for nine, ten years, and this dude—"

Ice Veins's tone went glacial. "But when it comes to my final payment, which I've doubled to fifty thousand, I will tolerate no more misunderstandings—or any more delays."

Unlacing her hands to glare a challenge, Sierra shook her head. "You and I both know it's *twenty-five*, and I'm not about to pay a penny more."

The small man in the oversize coat, which Ace realized was a rich shade of deep purple, scowled down at her. "I'll *tell you* what the debt is…and the interest once you miss a payment *and* defy me."

Agile as a soccer pro, he landed a vicious kick against Sierra's side, one hard enough that Ace could hear the thud—and possibly a crack.

At her cry of pain, Ace yelled, "Stop!" boiling over

with a homicidal fury he never would have guessed that he possessed.

But as Sierra moaned, he was drawn up short by the bald thug's sneer as he sighted along the length of his gun barrel.

"Go on," the huge man taunted. "Give me an excuse to pull the trigger. Then my boss'll take your money and sit back and watch while I kick the legs off this little deadbeat so he won't have to dirty up his fancy boots."

Ignoring the oversize threat for the moment, Ace focused on Ice Veins—and on controlling his own desire to grab hold of that red beard and jerk the loan shark's sadistic head off his shoulders. Ace reminded himself he had to play this smart, to draw things out until help arrived. The help that was his only chance of saving both his and Sierra's lives. "Kill me, and you won't see a penny. I'm not a man who troubles with cash dealings—" jerking his chin toward Sierra, who was struggling to make it to her hands and knees, he added "—or a man who ever pays full price for damaged goods."

Shaking his head, Ice Veins spared him a perplexed look and pointed his knife in Ace's direction. "Just who the devil are you—and what do you want with the bounty hunter?"

"He's gotta be working with her," the bald goon said, "the way he took up for her before."

"The hell I am," Ace ventured, deciding to try an unexpected tack. One that might just appeal to the man's desire to avenge his family member, along with his avarice. "The truth is, she came to bring me in, just the way she did your nephew. She packs a hell of a punch, too." He gestured toward his swelling temple. "She'd just hammered me when your boys interrupted the proceedings—and I'm willing to pay to have a little private time with this lovely lady by myself. This lady…in my own lair, with my own weapons of choice."

"What?" Brows rising, Ice Veins shook his head and asked uneasily, "That makes no—what exactly are you wanted for?"

Ace caught Sierra's glance, a spark of comprehension in it, before she turned a seemingly desperate gaze back toward Ice Veins. One hand cradling her injured ribs, she begged, "Please don't take this monster's money. Let me zip-tie his hands and take him in, collect the reward and—then I promise you I'll pay you every penny. The twenty-five thousand can just be a down payment."

"Or we can do an electronic transfer," Ace said. "Have that money in your account in five, ten minutes, tops."

"No!" she cried. "Don't you get it? This man's a stone-cold killer. A sick sadist. Surely, you've read about his victims in the papers. The things this creep will do to me—" She threw in a shudder so convincing that Ace was almost disgusted with himself.

"They're lyin'," the bald ox insisted. "He shot Choke, I'm telling you."

"What's done is done," Ice Veins told him before Ace could offer up some explanation. "All I really care about is how fast you can drop that cash, all fifty thousand, into my account."

When the bald thug kept muttering under his breath, Ice Veins ordered him to pipe down. "And while you're at it, shut her up, too. You got a handkerchief for a gag, don't you? And tie her hands, too. I don't need her arguments while I'm trying to do business."

As the thug descended on her, Ace glimpsed Sierra's face go pale with terror in the moonlight. *Trust me*, he wanted more than anything to tell her, even as sickening fear crawled up the back of his throat.

With no choice but to play out his ruse, Ace turned his attention to the loan shark. "Just make sure my merchandise stays in good condition," he told Ice Veins as he pulled the cell phone from his pocket. "I've got big plans for her later."

Ice Veins frowned, discomfort playing over his pinched face, before chuckling and slapping Ace's shoulder. "Soon as that money hits my account, you can have yourself as big a night as you want. Bought and paid for."

"I'll need your account and routing numbers," Ace said as he opened up his banking app. As he began punching in digits, he kept wondering how long he could string this all out—and if he'd bet tragically wrong to rely on Spencer Colton's ability to gather reinforcements and make it here in time.

How could he be certain that Spencer had even gotten his text? Mentally, Ace kicked himself, wishing he had copied the message to Ainsley and maybe another of their siblings, too, asking them to call 911 immediately just to be certain.

"Where is it? Where's the money?" Ice Veins demanded, staring at his own phone. "Has it left your account yet? I'm not seeing it."

"Let me double-check," Ace said. "What was that routing number again?"

Clearly impatient, Ice Veins once more ran through the coding until finally, Ace had no choice but to show the man what he was doing and hit the send button, transferring a very real sum of money into the account of a lowlife loan shark.

But with his and Sierra's lives on the line, Ace told himself the money was the least of his issues.

Or so he thought until he clicked, and a new message splashed across his screen.

Accounts Frozen. Please Contact Customer Support.

His mouth going dry as ash at what he presumed to have been a law enforcement action, Ace turned the screen away, praying Ice Veins hadn't seen it.

"There it goes," he said, trying to disguise his rapidly escalating stress level. "It shouldn't take more than five, ten minutes, tops, depending on how fast your institution is at processing this sort of transfer, and—isn't it one of those weird bank holidays? So it could be a little slower than a normal—"

"Hand me over that phone," Ice Veins demanded, his small eyes glittering like the knife's edge. "I need to see where you sent it. And I need to see what you're playin' at right freakin' now."

Chapter Five

With the bald goon looming over her, holding a filthy-looking gag in his ham-size fist, Sierra managed to look past him, to cut a look in Ace's direction. In that moment she saw everything in his face. Regret. Sorrow. A wish that they had had more time to explore the astonishing but undeniable connection that had flared to life like a struck match between them. Or maybe it was the unspoken apology for what his roll of the dice was about to cost them both.

It was enough for her to take her own gamble that a distraction might save at least one of them. With a determined yell, she summoned every bit of strength she had to push upward off her bent legs and catapult her bowed head up and forward—

Spearing herself straight into Bald Thug's crotch.

Bellowing at the direct hit, he keeled over, reflexively squeezing off a round.

With the whine of a bullet passing her ear, Sierra rolled away and clumsily struggled to get her cramped legs underneath her and working once again. To her right, Ace and Ice Veins were both shouting at once—the two men blurs of motion.

"Freeze, police!" boomed a loud voice as a blinding spotlight forced her to raise an arm to shield her eyes.

An instant later the beam was eclipsed by the huge shape of the bald goon, coming at her with a roar. With no time to evade him and no doubt he was about to kill her, Sierra could only shriek before the *crack-crack* of gunfire brought him crashing down, bloody blooms erupting on his upper chest from the officers' bullets.

Still panting on the ground only inches away, her gaze glued to the fish-eyed dead man, Sierra heard an officer order, "Drop the weapon! Drop the weapon now!"

Ace yelped in pain, a sound followed by deep, aggressive barking moments before a police dog, a big chocolate Lab, charged past him, leaping toward the man in the long purple coat.

A vicious sneer on his face, Ice Veins raised the knife and swung it downward, clearly intent on stabbing the K-9. Instead, Ace, blood plastering his shirt to his chest, slammed into him with one broad shoulder, taking both to the ground.

Sierra struggled to get up, desperate to help Ace and find out how badly he'd been injured. But figures emerged from the darkness, uniformed and plainclothes, obscuring her view and shouting at her, "Stay down! Don't try to move and keep your hands in sight!"

THE NEXT FEW hours passed in a blur of pain, stress, and exhaustion as she and Ace were both transported to the hospital in separate ambulances. While he was whisked off to surgery to close his wound, she did her best to explain to Sergeant Spencer Colton what had happened—and convince him that the "evidence" against Ace deserved a second look.

Before she could make much headway, however, a technician rolled her from the exam room for X-rays. Eventually, she was released, and an officer drove her back to her lodging outside of town before asking her to remain available for follow-up interviews.

"I'll be happy to answer more questions," she told him, "but I can promise you my answers will make a lot more sense once I've had a chance to sleep off the pain meds they gave me in the ER."

Startled awake by her ringing cell phone late the following morning, Sierra jerked upright—or tried to—before crying out as pain arced around her injured rib cage.

Blinking in her room, where she'd come to catch a few hours' rest, she thought again of Ace's surgery. Though the police had placed him under guard, refusing to let anyone see him, she'd at least been able to reach his sister Ainsley by phone before collapsing into bed and had gotten Ace's sister to promise to let her know how he was doing...*and whether he's asking to see me.*

Okay. That last part was pure fantasy. Ridiculous, considering the hurdles he was facing. Dealing with a deep slash across his upper chest from Ice Veins's blade, what Sergeant Colton had indicated were looming criminal charges and a raft of complicated family issues, Ace surely had far more on his mind than the bounty hunter who'd dragged him from the relative safety of his hidden bunker to a near-death situation.

Before he could be transferred, she promised she would pull herself together and head back to the hospital, where she fully intended to plead her case to be allowed to see him.

Her phone's Caller ID showed the name Brie Stratford, a fellow boxer with whom Sierra sometimes worked out at the gym or grabbed the occasional lunch or coffee when their schedules weren't too hectic.

"Sorry, Brie. Can't spar today. I'm out of town on a job," Sierra told her, keeping the details to herself of how badly wrong the job had gone.

"So I've heard. At work." Brie was using her cop voice, a sure sign that she was calling in her capacity as a detective with the Organized Crime Bureau of the Las Vegas Metropolitan PD.

"Oh?" Sierra said. Though she'd known plenty of officers over the years, and for the most part got on with them well, Sierra was a firm believer in maintaining personal space. With cops, with friends, with anyone she sensed who might get close enough to eventually want more than she was willing to give. Or to take too big a chunk of her when they eventually walked out of her life forever, the way her mom had the day before her seventh birthday.

"Word is you took down Ice Veins Harris," Brie said flatly, "*and* two of his muscle."

"It wasn't me." Sierra felt fear twisting through her. Because that was the kind of rumor that could prove hazardous to her health with the loan shark's associates. "Ice Veins got tangled in his own feet, trying to slash his way out of a situation when the cops showed up. He ended up falling on his own knife."

Sierra could still hear the moans, the gurgling and choking from before he'd mercifully gone silent. She shuddered with the memory, thankful beyond measure that she, Ace Colton and the young motel clerk, who'd regained consciousness as he was being loaded into an ambulance, had all left that bloody scene alive.

"Considering the kind of grief he's caused so many people, that's practically poetic justice," Brie said of the loan shark.

"And the local cops took down his thug," Sierra quickly added, deliberately leaving out Ace's name out of the discussion. Because it was bad enough that her name was linked to the deaths. In custody and injured, Colton didn't need more trouble coming his way.

"Well, nobody in the department's taking up a collection to send flowers to any of the funerals for those three, I can tell you," Brie said drily, clearly referring to the second goon found dead in the brush, as well. "But are you all right? I've heard…some things."

Sierra sucked in a deep breath, triggering a flare of pain in her side. When she'd recovered, she quoted Brie's response after the last time Sierra had popped her too hard during sparring. "All right, *enough.*"

Because in the tough, male-dominated worlds where each of them operated, it mattered, being a woman who could take a hit and stay on her feet. And nobody wanted to hear them whine about it, either.

Brie gave an irritated snort. "I'm not asking as an

opponent, looking to find a weakness I can exploit the next time we're in the ring. I'm asking as a friend here. Why didn't you tell me you had trouble with that dirtbag, the kind of trouble that sends three men all the way to Mustang Valley, Arizona, of all places, looking for you?"

A cold chill had Sierra's skin erupting into gooseflesh. Swallowing came hard, her throat so tight it felt as if she were trying to choke down a fistful of poker chips.

"Sierra? You still there?" Brie pressed after the delay grew awkward.

"Where did you hear that?" Sierra blurted, her pulse popping.

"From one of my CIs first," Brie said, referring to the confidential informants used by the department. "And five minutes later from a colleague, who'd caught wind of it elsewhere. This is big news on the Strip, Sierra. Which leads me back to my question. Why didn't you tell me you were tied up with that loan shark?"

Sierra's tongue lay heavy in her mouth, the habit of her silence too powerful to break.

"I can't help if you won't tell me." As Brie spoke, Sierra could picture her friend, who fought a couple of weight classes above her, staring down at her, her expression a mixture of concern and exasperation. "And I can never be a real friend if the sharing only runs one way."

Sierra squeezed her eyes shut, knowing Brie was right. Whenever the two of them got together, the tall detective would blow off steam about her frustrations over what she saw as bureaucratic interference at work or her live-in boyfriend, Max, who imagined he could cook but always left her kitchen a disaster. Or she'd gripe about her mother, who wouldn't quit trying to set her up with higher-earning prospects—even when poor, hapless Max was in the same room. All the while Sierra, whose own mother had never once checked in after skipping town on her and her father, remained locked up as tight as Fort Knox, her own problems far too complex, too dangerous to share.

But she was terrified of losing one of the few friends who'd stuck by her since her father had fallen ill. Terrified enough that she finally forced herself to admit, "It was my dad, his problem. His gambling debt. Not mine to share."

"That's some inheritance he left you."

"Yeah…but Ice Veins wanted more from me than money. He wanted his nephew turned loose. You know that homicide where he—"

"I know the one. You brought him in. How that creep ever got bail in the first place…"

"I'm not sure what changed that caused Ice Veins to get mad enough to head down here in person, but—"

"Eddie Harris was stabbed," Brie said, naming the nephew. "Shanked over at the jail, either by one of Ice Veins's enemies or maybe just some fellow traveler who held a grudge over one of his past exploits."

"He still breathing?"

The detective murmured in the affirmative. "Breathing, talking—maybe even finding a way to get out the word that if a certain female bounty hunter turned up dead, there could be a substantial reward."

"What?" Waves of shock rolled over Sierra. "Eddie's ordered a hit on me?"

"I'm not telling you this officially, because we're still working to confirm the rumors, but as a concerned friend, yeah. That's exactly what I'm saying."

"He did this from the jail infirmary?"

"He had to be transferred for surgery, under guard, of course. But slip-ups can happen, sometimes bribes—or maybe the word was put out via another associate. You could try waiting for the official word, see if I could maybe scrape together enough funding for protection."

"You don't sound very confident."

"Because, speaking strictly off the record, I like your chances a whole lot better if you stay far away from home."

"But what about— I can't just— What about my Rocky?" Two years earlier, the battle-scarred gray tomcat had marched inside her townhouse and decided he was staying where the living was easy and the canned food plentiful. With his chewed ears and half-feral nature, Rocky Balboa would never be the most affectionate of cats, but Sierra had seen to the old reprobate's vetting and arranged for the retired schoolteacher down the block to care for him whenever she was out of town.

"Your cat's going to be fine. I headed off your neighbor this morning when I stopped by your townhouse, told her you'd asked me to take him back to my place. Took a little doing, but we got him rounded up, along with his worldly possessions."

"Thanks. That's really—"

"It's no big deal," Brie said, blowing off the favor as

if Rocky hadn't yowled and hissed and clawed in protest, as Sierra was certain that he must have. "And now I won't have to worry about your poor neighbor accidentally walking into who knows what."

"Thanks, but—but you think those guys know where I live?" Owing to her line of work, Sierra had always taken great care to keep her personal information private.

"You've never given *me* your home address, remember? And it took me all of ten minutes to track you down," Brie reminded her. "So let's assume they know already—and that walking through the door of your townhouse could be the last mistake you'd ever make."

"So where am I supposed to go?" Sierra asked, thinking of her damaged car, which had begun making some alarming noises when she'd driven it here from the hospital. "And how long do you think this might take to blow over?"

"Honestly," Brie told her, "it's probably better that you *don't* tell me where you're going. And as for how long…as someone who truly cares about your welfare, I'm thinking that a permanent relocation, and a change of profession to go with it, might offer you the best chance of surviving to a ripe old age."

STILL HALF OUT of it from the painkillers he'd been given following last night's surgery to close the slash wound to his upper chest, Ace cracked open his eyes to see Spencer escort Sierra into the hospital room. Sierra, who had featured so prominently in the disjointed dreams that kept punching through his drugged sleep, nightmares where Ice Veins sliced her beautiful face to bloody ribbons before ordering his bald thug into a black limo to run over her legs.

Anytime Ace had awakened, the new reality he'd encountered felt almost as horrific. He would never forget the sick feeling that had hit him when Spencer had read him his rights early this morning before informing him he was officially in custody for his father's shooting. Under arrest and forbidden from seeing anyone except his lawyer until after he was transferred to the jail.

But the knot inside Ace loosened at the sight of Sierra, looking healthy and far better rested. In the filtered late afternoon sunlight, slanting through the room's window, the red-blond waves of her hair were full and shiny, and she'd changed into jeans and a soft-looking, blue-green top that skimmed her slender curves.

Full of questions, he fumbled for the button to raise the head of his bed, only to be stopped short by the handcuffs connecting his right wrist to the frame. His heart sank at the reminder that he would soon be in the county lockup, the only place he would be permitted to see his family members—and meet his pregnant daughter for the first time, to his shame. How Sierra had wrangled an exception to get in here today, he had no idea, but seeing her was a balm for his battered soul.

Gesturing toward his shackled wrist, she swung an accusing look up at the sandy-haired sergeant. "Is that really necessary? Look at that black eye, and he's just out of surgery, for heaven's sake. He's not about to go dashing past the uniform you have posted at the door."

But Spencer only shook his head, proving once again

to Ace that despite his blue eyes and baby face, his distant cousin was one hundred percent serious when it came to police work. "This is for his safety as well as ours at this point."

"*His* safety?" she challenged. "Or are you more worried he'll embarrass you and the department by giving you the slip again?"

"Listen, Ms. Madden," Spencer warned, his gaze stern, "I only let you in here to talk to him for a few minutes as a professional courtesy to the Vegas Metro PD buddy who vouched for you. *Don't* make me regret it. Or ask you to leave right now."

Forcing his eyes farther open, Ace spoke up, his voice still raspy from the anesthesia. "Hey, you two. I'm right here. So there's no need to talk around me like I'm the furniture. What's happening?"

"About twenty stitches, the way I heard it," Spencer told him, "but I understand the knife wound wasn't as serious as it looked. Just nicked an artery, but once they got that closed off and gave you a unit of blood—"

"Thanks, but they told me all that in recovery," Ace said, the memory returning as he struggled to sit up. "Is—is my father in this hospital? Is he somewhere nearby? Could I—"

"Calm down," Spencer advised. "You'll open up your stitches."

"Ace, please," Sierra urged him.

Ace sagged back against the mattress, his mind still teeming with questions.

Before he could ask another, Spencer's cell buzzed in the pocket of his blue uniform.

Spencer frowned down at the screen. "Sorry, but I've got to call back my captain." With a warning look at Sierra, he added. "Fifteen minutes, twenty, tops, and remember my conditions."

An impudent smile made her green eyes sparkle. "Do I look like the kind of girl inclined to break the rules?"

Spencer frowned and left the room, muttering about this whole idea being against his better judgment.

Sierra snorted. "Your cop cousin doesn't much care for bounty hunters. Especially the kind who leave a mess like we did back at The Cactus Flower for his crowd to clean up."

"So what exactly happened back there?" Ace asked. "There were so many people and so much confusion."

"By the time I was able to check on you, you'd blacked out." She pinched the bridge of her nose. "When I saw all that blood, I thought for sure I'd gotten you killed, dragging you into an ambush with my enemies as if you don't have troubles enough of your own."

"It wasn't your fault. You couldn't have known they'd follow you across state lines," he said honestly.

"I *should* have, Ace. I should've guessed I'd made it personal with Ice Veins over bringing in his nephew when he was about to skip the country. What I didn't know, though, was that Eddie had gotten himself shanked at the county lockup."

"And Ice Veins blames you."

"Blamed, you mean. Because the man is definitely past tense, thanks to you."

"What do you mean?" Ace shook his head, struggling to remember.

"He was lunging for the K-9 when you slammed into him. Except somehow, the sergeant tells me, in that pileup with you, him and Boris—that's the dog's name—Ice Veins ended up with his own knife jutting from his throat."

Ace winced at the memory of that same blade slicing through his flesh like butter. "That had to hurt."

"Not for long." Sierra touched her side where she had been kicked. "And as far as I'm concerned, it couldn't've happened to a more deserving person."

"I'm with you on that," he said, his every movement pulling at his stitches, though the pain was muted by the anesthetic he'd been given. "How're the ribs, by the way?"

"Couple of hairline fractures, the ER doctors told me." She shrugged, her mouth set in a grim line. "I've had worse in the ring."

"You don't have to do that, you know," he said, reaching out to enfold her wrist with his free hand.

"Do what?" Her arm stiffened with his touch, but she didn't pull away. At least, not yet.

"Play the tough girl all the time, not around me."

"I'm not a girl. I'm a woman, and make no mistake, I *am* tough."

"From what little I know of you, I'm guessing that you've had to be. That for a long time now you've had no other choice, and no space at all to let your guard down." Though he, a man whose future and freedom hung in limbo, had no right to do so, he ran the pad of his thumb along her narrow wrist, feeling the velvety softness of her skin over the firm framework beneath it.

Her eyes slid closed, her sigh shaky. It was only then he knew for certain that she'd sensed what he had, that shuddering rush of air and ions between them, the way the sky seemed to gather itself in the high country with a big storm rushing in. The way he'd always felt waiting for the dark clouds to split open and the rains to bring a desert bloom.

"So your debt's cleared and your nightmare's over," he said. "And you can go back to your life without Ice Veins's threats hanging over you. You'll head home and be all right now." No matter what happened in his own life, he could content himself with that, with thinking of her from time to time, moving forward, happy.

She stepped away, turning her face from him, but not before he spotted her grimace and felt the tension rippling through her.

"What is it?" he asked.

"I'm worried about you. That's all." Her gaze shuttered when she looked his way once more. "Worried that I did the wrong thing, accepting your stepmother's offer and that bounty."

"I'd just as soon you didn't refer to that woman as my stepmother," he said, caring for more about that detail than the money. "Selina Barnes Colton is no family of mine."

Sierra nodded. "She did seem awfully pleased to hear you were in custody."

"So you've spoken to her?"

"As briefly as I could manage." Sierra wrinkled her nose in obvious distaste. "Especially when her reaction to learning that you had a knife wound was to ask me how I wanted the check made out for your capture."

"Capture?" If he'd ever harbored any illusions that Selina might have acted out of genuine concern for him, they certainly would have died there. The real question was: Why did it matter so much to her, seeing him imprisoned? Was she trying to hide her own involvement in his father's shooting, or did she need to keep the police from looking in her direction for some other reason?

"I almost told her where she could stick that check, and damn the paper cuts," Sierra said with a sly wink at that last part, "but then I decided I'd be better off pretending I'm not onto her, and using the money to pay you back for what you sent Ice Veins. Or a down payment on it, anyway."

"Never happened, so there's no need." Ace went on to explain that authorities had frozen his accounts, most likely in order to hinder his flight from justice. "So you go ahead and keep it."

She shook her head, her forehead crinkling. "But I don't feel right about—"

"I insist, Sierra," he said, thinking of how, since she'd been struggling to pay her father's debts, she must have little left to live on. And warmed by the fact that whatever happened to him, she would be okay now, safe from the danger that had followed her here. *"Keep it."*

She nodded, her eyes gleaming. "All right, then, but I mean to earn that money, from *you. Really* earn it, helping the police realize they've got the wrong man and getting you back to your family—and your daughter."

He stared at Sierra, his mouth going dry. "You believe me, then? Because that bank teller who came forward, who told the cops that I'd confessed to her that I'd hidden the murder weapon in my condo—was lying. That's where they found the gun, but I didn't put it there."

"You asked about your father right away, with me," Sierra said, looking directly into his eyes. "And with Spencer, too, here. You cared more about his well-being than you did about your own. That tells me everything I need to know about you."

Relieved as he was with her assessment, he couldn't stop himself from pressing. "Have you heard anything about him? Anything at all?"

She hesitated before nodding. "I spoke to Ainsley briefly last night. She told me he's alive. And here, somewhere, but don't even think of asking to see him."

"Alive," he echoed, gratitude pushing aside his pain. "Thank you. And it means everything that you believe me. Getting to know you, even for a few short hours— If things were different, Sierra… You're the first woman in a long, long time I can ever remember making me feel—"

He clenched his jaw, frustration surging through him. Because he had no right to be saying these things to her, no right to be feeling anything for her when his life was hell on earth. Only the most selfish of bastards would drag a woman that he cared for into this mess.

"I'm sorry," he said. "I shouldn't have said anything. I'm talking like a crazy man. You should probably leave now, go back home to Las Vegas."

She moved closer and leaned over him, brushing an

errant clump of hair from his eyes. “If you’ve lost your mind, Ace, I’m afraid I’ve taken the same wrong turn. Which means right now you’re stuck with me, for better or for worse.”

Chapter Six

Sierra brushed aside Ace's light brown hair and ducked her head, fully intending to drop a peck onto his care-lined forehead to seal the promise she had made to help him find his way to freedom. What she didn't count on was him fumbling for—and this time finding—the control to elevate the head of his bed. Or the feelings that cascaded through her when he raised his chin to press his lips to her mouth. Gently, tenderly, as if he sensed, just as she did, that if they didn't dare to take this stolen moment, they might never get another.

You should run from here now, her survival instincts warned as he reached up to gently run his fingertips along the side of her face. *Run from this before it traps you. Trade your dented car for some jalopy and drive across the southern border with Selina's money in your pocket.*

But she didn't move, could barely breathe, as within the span of that single kiss, so many possibilities unfolded. Of joyful days sharing each other's company, of nights spent coaxing each other's bodies to the peaks of pleasure. Of having someone she could finally trust enough to share the secrets weighing down her every step.

Thoughts like these, they're just mirages, she tried to warn herself as the kiss deepened, her hands reaching to frame his face, his drawing her nearer. *This close to the desert, they're beautiful, but cruel.*

Still, when she heard someone at the door, she could barely pull herself away. And when she spotted Spencer Colton frowning at the two of them, his disapproval was blurred by the unshed tears in her eyes.

Grasping her by the arm, the sergeant hustled her toward the door.

"Wait," she blurted, twisting to turn back. "We're not finished talking." She needed to ask Ace more about the evidence against him, evidence of a conspiracy she meant to unravel.

"What I just saw wasn't talking." The sergeant frowned at her. "And I specifically warned you earlier, no physical contact. Though I should have my head examined for trusting the kind of woman who's responsible for a shootout at a local motel and three dead Vegas wise guys in my jurisdiction."

"Please, Sergeant Colton, as Detective Stratford from the Las Vegas Metropolitan PD has already explained, I'm a legitimate professional with no ties to organized crime. It's just in my line of work, I sometimes end up crossing paths with—"

"You've had the time I promised, bounty hunter," he said firmly. "Now let's go."

Ace protested, "I needed to give her some information related to my case. Please, Spencer."

Sierra wondered if Ace's use of his first name was meant to remind the sergeant the two were somehow related and not just random strangers.

Scowling, Spencer proved he was a cop first, saying, "Tell it to your lawyer, Ace. You've forfeited your right to ask for any favors, or for any other visitors until you're processed into jail."

"You're seriously still doing this?" Ace demanded. "Come on, you know this is a setup, that it couldn't have been me in either of those videos."

"Then why'd you run, man? And how'd the weapon used in your father's shooting get inside your condo?"

"Why don't you ask your so-called *witness*? I'm sure that Destiny Jones—as if I'd go babbling secrets to some bank teller I barely know—" Ace's gaze flicked toward Sierra, connecting for a moment before returning to Spencer "—could lead you in the right direction."

Catching Ace's drift, Sierra nodded, reminded of the witness's name and her position.

"That's something else we're going to need to talk about," said Spencer, his frown deepening as his gaze bored into Ace's. "What's happened to Ms. Jones, because she hasn't been seen in weeks. And the one person who stood to profit from her disappearance took off and went into hiding right around the time of her last sighting..."

"You're not suggesting," Ace began, the color draining from his bruised face, "that I would—that I know anything about what might've happened to her? Because if that's the case, Sergeant, I'm going to need my attorney present before I say another word."

As Spencer escorted Sierra to the elevator, she said, "You can't honestly believe that Ace would harm this witness, do you? I've only known him for a couple of days, and it's obvious to me that he's no killer."

"And yet you've told me yourself he was involved in the death of that goon we found in the brush."

After waiting for a woman wearing a set of scrubs and a stethoscope to pass by, Sierra whispered furiously, "That happened during a struggle for a weapon. The man meant to kill us. And you should have seen how upset Ace was about it afterward, going on about how he'd never shot anyone before."

"And you believed him?"

"Pretty clearly, don't you think?" she asked, her cheeks burning at the thought of the eyeful she and Ace had given him when he'd first walked into the room.

Once they arrived at the elevator, Spencer reached for the down button but hesitated before looking at her, his serious expression giving gravity to his boyish face. "You need to understand something, Ms. Madden. I may be a shirttail relation from a poorer branch of the family, but that doesn't mean I'm looking to take down the former CEO of Colton Oil. I'm here to find the truth, that's all, as well as justice for any and all victims."

With a nod that indicated that he considered their conversation over, he firmly pushed the elevator button and gestured for her to step inside when the door to the empty car arrived.

Sierra pressed the button to hold the elevator without breaking eye contact. "All that's great, but *I'm* here to prove to you," she said, "that Ace Colton's not a perpetrator, just one more of those victims—and I plan to start by finding this so-called witness you seem to have misplaced."

SIERRA WALKED ALONG downtown's main drag the next morning, acknowledging that she had screwed up bigtime announcing her next move to the straight-arrow Sergeant Spencer Colton. Already, he had made it clear that he didn't believe that nice women ended up trailed by Las Vegas gangsters. Or maybe he was more annoyed by the way she'd broken his stupid no-contact directive before telling him she was hell-bent on undermining his case against Ace Colton.

Though she'd liked to imagine the sergeant had meant what he had told her about wanting to find the real truth, he'd clearly put the word out among his fellow cops that she wasn't to be trusted. Or at least, she couldn't get a thing out of the officers she'd attempted to chat up after *happening* upon them yesterday, one on his meal break at Bubba's Diner and two others making separate stops at a coffee house called Java Jane's.

She held out hope the bank might offer her an untainted source of information today. Stepping inside the lobby, she approached a matronly looking teller who walked her through the process of depositing Selina's cashier's check and even chatted a bit about the woman's plans for an upcoming vacation with her grown children.

"Speaking of family," Sierra ventured. "I happen to know that Destiny Jones's is very eager to have her home this Thanksgiving. Would you have heard anything from her lately? I promised I'd pass along whatever I—"

The friendliness in the teller's brown eyes was instantly extinguished, replaced by a look of glazed panic as she quickly shook her head. "I can't—I can't talk about that with you. Personnel matters here are...strictly confidential."

Her breathing quick and noisy, her gaze darted about as she looked to her fellow tellers for help.

Afraid that at any moment some nervous Nellie might hit the silent alarm, leaving her with a lot of explaining to do when the police came, Sierra raised her palms and peered at the woman's name tag. "It's all right, Ms.—Ms. Harding. Jane. I'm not trying to get anybody into trouble. I'd just like to help Destiny's family. They're very worried, and I thought that maybe you might've heard—"

"I said no," she repeated, this time loudly enough that the words echoed across the marble-floored lobby.

From his spot two stations over, a younger male teller scratched his nose and cut Sierra a meaningful look from his own station. But before she could do anything about it, the bank's manager clicked over in her high heels and escorted Sierra out with such firm insistence that she quickly found herself on the doorstep.

"Wowza," she murmured to herself of her brusque ejection. *Did Spencer somehow get to her, too, or is that woman hiding something instead? Something she doesn't want me to know about her bank and the missing Destiny Jones?*

Her instincts insisting it was the latter, Sierra headed

out to where she'd parked her car, pausing in front of a shop undergoing renovations, where she raised her eyebrows to see a photo in the window featuring the magnetic gaze of a middle-aged blonde woman. Below it hung a hand-lettered sign profusely thanking Micheline Anderson and the Affirmation Alliance Group for their help with earthquake recovery efforts.

"Hmm," Sierra murmured, wondering how such generosity fit in with the less savory rumors she'd heard about the center the woman had established outside of town.

With no time to ponder the question, she rounded the corner, she stopped abruptly at the sight of a slightly built female officer, a long, dark brown ponytail trailing down her back as she used a flashlight to peer inside the dented Camry's tinted windows. As Sierra stepped back out of sight, her stomach tightened as the cop drew her holstered weapon—as if she expected to find a clown car's worth of additional trouble out of Vegas. Or maybe, at the sergeant's direction, she was looking for some excuse to arrest Sierra, too.

It was enough to convince her to ditch the damaged Camry sooner rather than later, so after waiting until the ponytailed officer climbed into her patrol vehicle and drove away, Sierra headed for a small car lot she'd spotted when she'd first driven into Mustang Valley. In a rundown area not far past a biker joint called Joe's Bar, *Alonso & Sons* was marked by older model vehicles, sagging strings of tired-looking plastic flags, and hand-printed signs boasting E-Z Credit and Make Your Weekly Payment Here!

In less than an hour's time, she'd made a deal, trading the Camry, which was years newer than any of the beaters on the lot, for a low-mileage older Chevy with the Arizona plate attached and no nonsense about tax or registration, since she didn't haggle over the cash price. After she slipped a few hundred dollars extra his way, she had the salesman repeat the words, "I don't know the guy who bought it. It must've been my old man who sold him that car."

"Perfect." Climbing into the sun-faded blue Chevy, she checked some notes she'd made soon after her arrival in Mustang Valley, after conferring with Nikolas Slater, the PI Selina had originally hired to find Ace. Though Nikolas had seemed less than enthusiastic about Sierra's insistence that she meant to bring in Ace, he had been professional enough to give her a few helpful pieces of information he'd uncovered—including the address of the witness who'd reported the missing man's supposed confession.

Gratified to find the information quickly, Sierra verified the location on her phone before heading to check in with Destiny's neighbors over at her small apartment complex, tucked within a residential neighborhood only a few blocks from downtown. Here, too, evidence remained of the trembler that had struck the region, including one tumbled-down garage and a modest dwelling with a blue plastic tarp over a collapsed roof on an addition. For the most part, however, the area appeared to have moved on, thanks in large part, she'd heard, to the efforts of local volunteers.

Few of the second-floor residents answered Sierra's

knocks, and of those, none claimed to know the attractive blonde in her early thirties who'd vanished so abruptly. The only person willing to talk at all was a bony older man with jutting ears who used her introduction as the launchpad for a diatribe regarding the "troubles" with young women these days.

"They're out there takin' over every kind of man's job, and blowin' about as free as tumbleweeds instead of settlin' down to raise good families," he said over the sound of his whistling hearing aids, waving toward Sierra's bare left hand with a pucker of disapproval. "You ask me, we were better off back when a gal went from her daddy's house straight to her husband's, with no time for courtin' trouble in between."

"Yes, sir," Sierra said, raising her voice to be sure he heard her. "Appreciate the information, but you'll have to excuse me..." she added, already edging toward the staircase and the promise of escape.

"And another thing. Back then the women used to dress like ladies," he continued, his speckled scalp flushing beneath the thin, white strands combed across it as he scowled over her jeans and dusty boots, along with the form-fitting tactical charcoal jacket she found so useful for stowing gear and hiding weapons. "Put on some pretty lipstick or maybe some nice earrings before their man came home to dinner on the table."

"Thank you, sir, but I really have to go and find Ms. Jones now," Sierra repeated, frustrated. So often it seemed the only people who ever wanted to talk when she was on the job were the type who had, not useful information, but a lifetime of opinions they couldn't wait to unload.

As she turned to flee, the clump-slide of his rapid steps echoed on the landing just behind her.

"Wait!" he called.

She froze, eyes closing, before turning with a tight smile that she hoped disguised her grimace. *"Yes?"*

He lifted one hand from his walker to point down over the railing. "You maybe oughta ask that fella right there about my missing neighbor. I've seen him here a few times, comin' out of her apartment. My guess is that he's pickin' up some of her things before the landlord tosses 'em."

Sierra looked down toward the parking lot where a thick-necked man with a black soul patch, wearing a gray sweatshirt and a cap with the Arizona Cardinals logo, held a large cardboard box near the open rear gate of a beat-up dark red van. He stood frozen for a moment, his dark eyes flicking a wary look from the old man's outstretched hand to Sierra's face.

"Hi, neighbor. Just moving in?" she called down to him, offering what she hoped would appear a friendly wave as she took a couple of more steps toward the staircase.

"Didn't you hear what I just told you?" the old man put in, his words ringing off the concrete landing. "That's Destiny Jones's boyfriend, clearin' out her stuff."

In the lot below, the man in the ball cap cursed, shoving the box into his van and slamming down the hatch.

As he raced to jump inside, Sierra pounded down

the steel stairs, shouting after him, “I just have a few questions, that’s all! I swear I’m not a cop!”

But he was peeling off by the time she reached the lot, moving too fast for her to catch more than the first few digits on his license plate. Digging out her keys, she climbed into her new ride, cranked the engine and took off in pursuit. But the van’s head start enabled the driver to lose her in the tight maze of mainly residential streets.

Defeated, she pulled over in front of a small neighborhood park where she grabbed her cell, thinking of calling 911 and asking the dispatcher to have police put out a Be On the Lookout alert. But what could she say that would get anyone to listen to her?

Instead, she impulsively pressed to connect with Ainsley Colton’s number from her list of recent callers. On the second ring, Ace’s younger sister, an attorney for Colton Oil who’d seemed especially concerned about her brother’s welfare, picked up.

“Can you believe it?” she blurted, clearly upset, before Sierra could get a word out. “They’ve gone and transferred him to the jail infirmary first thing this morning—and they still aren’t letting me or anybody from the family see him. Poor Nova’s going crazy, knowing he’s this close and she still can’t meet him.”

“You need to listen to me, Ainsley,” Sierra said brusquely, though her heart twisted at the thought of Ace stuck behind bars on what she was now more certain than ever was a setup. “If you really want him walking free again, I need you to make a call for me now without wasting time with a lot of questions. Can you do that?"

"Of course I will," she said, pulling herself together with admirable efficiency. "Just tell me what you need."

Sierra ran it down for Ainsley, asking her to reach out to Spencer and tell him that she'd spotted Destiny Jones's alleged boyfriend fleeing her apartment. After rattling off a description of the man and vehicle, along with the partial plate number, Sierra added, "You need to see if he can have his patrol officers pick this guy up before he gets too far, because I'm certain he knows something—and Destiny's the key."

Once she ended the call, Sierra resumed driving, cruising the streets as she tried to plan out her next move. As she crossed over the main drag, she instead spotted something else of interest—the same slim, neatly dressed male teller who had tried to catch her attention before the bank manager asked her to leave.

Turning to follow him, she watched him head into Java Jane's, probably on his break, and decided to seize on the opportunity.

Finding no open parking spaces nearby, she quickly hung a right, intending to make the block. It was then she caught a glimpse, several cross streets ahead, of the deep red van she'd lost earlier.

"Finally, a little luck." Pumping the air with her fist, she abandoned the idea of trying to pry information from the teller and hurried off in pursuit.

Apparently confident he had lost her, the van's driver, recognizable in his Cardinals ball cap, proceeded at a normal rate of speed as he wended his way toward another residential neighborhood not far past the high school. If he so much as glanced at his rearview mirror, she didn't see it, since she stayed several car lengths back in the hope of avoiding detection.

She slowed, pulling to the roadside a few houses short when he swung into the gravel driveway of one bungalow, more rundown that most of its neighbors' with two dead palm trees in an overgrown front yard. After parking inside an even more dilapidated wooden garage, he quickly bailed out and pulled closed the barn-style double doors before heading toward what Sierra presumed to be a back door.

But Sierra wasn't the only person watching, she realized, a thrill zinging through her veins when she spotted the stirring of a curtain in one of the house's windows and caught a glimmer of sunlight off a platinum-blond head. That had to be the same pixie cut she'd seen in the missing teller's last social media postings, a look that made the petite woman's large, honey-brown eyes and plump, pink lips stand out in contrast. Attractive as the other woman was, Sierra dismissed the tiny twinge she felt when she wondered if Ace's confession had come on the heels of a passionate tryst. As far as Sierra was concerned, every word of Destiny's story stunk to high heaven.

Pulling out her phone, she placed a call directly to the police station and asked to be put through to Sergeant Colton.

Expecting to get his voice mail, she was surprised when Spencer picked up in person. And not at all shocked to hear how annoyed he sounded when she identified herself.

"What is this? You want me to put out another BOLO now, or do you have another wild goose chase you're hoping I can run down for you?"

"I take it you spoke with Ainsley, then. Good." Sierra made a huffing sound. "Now, if we're done with the small talk, I have the address where Destiny Jones has been hiding."

"You're sure about that?" he asked, his irritation seeming to fall away.

"I'd bet your goodwill on it," she said, just to yank the sergeant's chain. "I saw her at the window. Single residence at 2961 Saguaro Street, with a man I believe to be her boyfriend."

"Same white or Hispanic male in the red van from her apartment?" Spencer asked.

"Yeah. I spotted the guy and tailed him over here."

"Do not approach," the sergeant ordered. "I know that address—and that suspect. We're almost certain he's a drug dealer, very likely to be armed and dangerous—and I seriously doubt that he's alone… Ms. Madden?"

Dropping her phone as she heard a sound just behind her driver's side door, Sierra gasped and reached for her gun before remembering it hadn't yet been returned to her after its recovery following the motel shootout. Her split-second indecision gave the person who'd crept up behind her the time needed to fling open her door and bellow, "Freeze!" before she could hit the door lock or put the car in Drive.

Chapter Seven

The uniformed officer was no older than his midtwenties and clearly nervous, a flush in his fair cheeks and a slight tremor shaking the barrel of the weapon he'd trained on Sierra.

But his voice was firm, as was the look in his hazel eyes when he ordered, "Step out of the car, please, miss. That's it. Now turn around and put your hands against the car."

"Was all this really necessary?" Sierra grumbled as he frisked her, quickly but professionally, for any weapons—a search that turned up nothing more interesting that the zip ties she kept on her belt, which he decided to let her keep after she'd shown him both her bail bond agent ID card and Nevada driver's license. "If Destiny and her boyfriend didn't know we were here before, I'm sure they do by now."

"Look, I'm sorry if I startled you," said the cop, whose name tag read Ofc J. Donovan, "but my orders were to make sure we didn't end up having a civilian triggering another shoot-out like the one at the motel the other night."

"I'm not the one who started that," she reminded him. "Not that you would know it based on your department's persecution of one of the intended victims—not to mention the person who's gone ahead and tracked down not one but *two* missing persons for you in the short time I've been in town...not that I'm implying your department needs to step up its game in that arena."

Judging from his scowl, the look she'd slanted his way may have suggested otherwise. Could she help it if she had outspoken eyebrows?

"Don't get so cocky quite yet," he said. "We haven't determined Destiny Jones is inside that house, but as soon as my backup gets here..."

He turned his head as an unmarked car pulled up a few doors down the street and Sergeant Colton climbed out, along with what she assumed to be a plainclothes male officer, maybe a detective or someone pitching in from the administration since the department was a small one. Both were wearing vests, she saw, and Spencer quickly ordered Donovan to put his on, as well.

"And as for you," the sergeant told her, "we appreciate your call, but you need to stay in your car. And completely clear of this operation. Do you understand?"

"Fine by me," Sierra told him before cutting an annoyed look toward the younger cop who'd searched her. "I only hope they didn't slip out the back while Officer Obvious was alerting the whole neighborhood by frisking me right out on the street."

"And I hope you're not trying to back out of your earlier identification of Destiny Jones inside that house,"

Spencer told her. "Or sending my people into a dangerous situation on nothing but a fishing expedition."

"My best friend's a cop," she said, figuring that Brie counted as a best friend since she was really the only friend who'd made the effort to stand by her. Even if Sierra's desperation to pay off Ice Veins, along with her need for secrecy, had made it harder than ever for her to really be there for anyone just lately. "I'd never, ever do that—or anything I thought might come back on Ace."

Spencer's serious blue eyes studied her, but she didn't waver for a moment.

"All right, then, Ms. Madden," he said, giving her a subtle nod she took to indicate a truce between them... at least for the moment.

From inside her car, Sierra watched as the female officer with the darker ponytail, the same petite woman she'd spotted peering into her Camry earlier that morning, trotted up, her rifle pointed downward. All four convened before two of them, Donovan and the female officer split off and headed behind one of the neighbors' houses, probably to cover the rear of the targeted address.

Precisely two minutes later Spencer and the plainclothes officer both headed up the street to approach the front of the house, which Sierra couldn't see at all from her vantage inside the car. But no one had been assigned to watch her, and she felt that familiar tingle of anticipation, a fizzing itch in muscles eager to get out there and be part of the takedown. Her father's hunting instinct, as he'd liked to call it when he went out looking for the bail jumpers whose bounties fed them…and his gambling habit.

So she stepped out of the car—just to stretch her legs, of course, not to defy a direct police order. Once standing, she strained her neck and ears, catching the pounding at a front door, the deeply authoritative, "Police! Open up!"

Followed minutes later by a faint sound—one Sierra had only heard because she'd strolled to the end of a nearby walkway—of the female officer calling, "Sarge, the back door's open, but the red van's still in the— We've got a runner! White male, vaulting the rear fence! Donovan and I are in pursuit!"

Adrenaline pumping though her system, Sierra warned herself to get back to the car, stay clear of the situation, where she could end up, at worst, shot, or arrested for interfering with a police action. Sighing in frustration, she dutifully returned to her vehicle…

But Spencer hadn't said a thing about remaining *parked* there, so she decided, with that fizzing itch inside her growing, to circle the block, just to offer an extra set of eyes and ears well versed in tracking fleeing suspects. And to call in to dispatch anything she spotted that might constitute a threat to officers or lead to the escape of—

Right there, between a hedge of red-berried pyracantha and a stone retaining wall near the corner, Sierra caught sight of a movement, along with the waving of the shrub's canes, whose wickedly long thorns were notorious for piercing skin and catching clothing. *That has to be him. The runner the cops are after*, she decided as she parked along the curb as close as she dared and pulled out her phone.

Before she could dial, the runner broke cover—not the male in the Cardinals cap, as she'd expected, but Destiny herself, her platinum pixie cut partly hidden by a black watch cap and an oversize chambray work shirt serving to obscure her small, neat figure. She was cutting diagonally past Sierra's hood as she sprinted across the street.

Unwilling to let her get away, Sierra popped open the door, the surge of fresh adrenaline propelling her past the flare of pain in her ribs as she vaulted after the bank teller. Thanks to the bank teller's poor choice in footwear—a pair of sky-blue spike-heeled pumps—Sierra gained on her quickly, shouting, "Hold it right there! Freeze! Fugitive recovery!" just as the blonde wobbled to the opposite curb.

Whirling around with her honey-brown eyes flaring, Destiny turned to frown at Sierra before her painted nails dove for her rear pocket. Fearing she was reaching for a weapon, Sierra stepped in, twisting her body, and popping the blonde's midsection with an upper cut that knocked Destiny out of her heels and sent her tumbling to the ground.

Kneeling beside the gasping, sputtering woman, Sierra quickly confirmed that Destiny had been going for a cell phone rather than the gun that she'd imagined.

Thrashing in her attempts to rise, Destiny recovered breath enough to cry out, "H-help! Let me go! Police!"

"Just stay down, woman, or next time I won't pull my punch," Sierra said, pressing on her shoulder to keep Destiny from flailing about and injuring herself. Once she'd zip-tied her captive's wrists, she followed the direction of the teller's desperate gaze and sighed to see Sergeant Colton stalking her way, looking mad enough to arrest her, along with Destiny, on the spot.

Oh, snap.

"Didn't I tell you to stay inside your car?" he demanded. "This is a police action to recover a material witness, not time for an amateur to interfere with our operation."

"A simple *thank-you* would suffice," Sierra grumbled, wondering if the man imagined she routinely caught fugitives as some kind of *hobby.* "Or maybe you'd have preferred that I allowed her to keep right on running, wasting your officers' time and possibly putting them in harm's way, when she practically ran out in front of my car, trying to escape?"

Pushing herself into a sitting position, Destiny complained, "This woman *struck* me! Did you see her? I—I want her arrested for assault!"

Sergeant Colton swung an even harsher look in the teller's direction before saying, "Before you make any decisions about that, Ms. Jones, I think we need to have a long, hard talk about the company you've recently been keeping—"

"And I think you might want to check out, too," Sierra told the officer, "what she was up to at that bank where she was working. Because from the way her coworkers and her manager acted when I started asked questions earlier, I have to wonder exactly what an audit might turn up."

THE FOLLOWING AFTERNOON, two jailers escorted Ace from the infirmary, where he'd been stuck since the judge had denied his bail after the prosecutor had successfully argued that a wealthy man who'd already run once was the very definition of a flight risk.

It still hadn't sunk in that he would remain behind bars until his trial, that the only way he could hope to meet Nova and the grandchild she was carrying for the first time would be inside a jailhouse visiting room.

As the shame of it seeped through him, Ace realized that something was up, since neither guard had answered his question about where they were going. But the look the two men passed between themselves triggered a tightening in his gut. One that warned that he had more bad news coming.

"Is my lawyer here again?" he persisted, confused since Michael Seaver had told him yesterday he would be tied up in court this afternoon. "Or is this the family visit I've been promised?"

After weeks of separation, he was desperate to see a familiar face and hear the latest news firsthand—and to know that at least some among his family members were still speaking to him. Desperate enough that he was willing to swallow his pride and allow them to see the same man who'd once represented Colton Oil wearing expensive hand-tailored suits, designer silk ties and Italian leather shoes sporting the latest in bright orange jail garb and what was beginning to resemble a ragged beard. At least he was moving more freely now that the bulky dressing on his wound had been replaced with lighter bandaging.

"Didn't they tell you in the infirmary where they've been keepin' you all by your lonesome like some kind of rock star?" the younger of the two guards asked, his disapproval palpable over what he clearly considered special treatment. Even though at the present time, the county's small jail had no other prisoners in need of the infirmary. "It takes at least forty-eight hours for your visitors' list to be approved. *If* we can get to it."

Ace's heart sank, but he didn't respond to the taunting tone, the clear effort to get a rise out of him. Instead, he thought about the names he'd added to his list, including Sierra Madden's. Part of him hoped that none of them would show up, would see him humbled like this. Another part of him feared exactly that.

"I ever tell you," the taller of the pair, a scowling man, asked his partner, "how I was all set to start a job for Colton Oil once? Hard, dirty work, but honest, with good benefits and the kind of paycheck a man can be proud to take home to his family." His glittering, dark eyes were set deep beneath the shelf of a high forehead.

"Yeah, I think you did." His frog-faced younger cohort smirked in Ace's direction. "But why don't you go ahead and refresh my memory, Pete? I'm sure that Mister Bigtime CEO here would just *love* to hear that story."

Ace felt his stomach clutch, though nothing about the guard had struck him as familiar, no more than the name *Pete* rang any warning bells.

"I was all set to start in a few days," Pete said, scowl deepening. "They just needed me to come on in and fill out a little paperwork. And that was when the boss man—this same fine fella we have before us right here—puts a stop to things. Calls the Human Resources lady and tells her my rusted-out pickup is parked in the space marked off for his fancy imported sports car."

"If you're going to tell the story," Ace said, stopping to stare back a challenge as the incident came back to him, "maybe you ought to tell it right."

"You got something you want to say, prisoner?" the guard said, pulling his baton out of a holster as his small eyes glittered with menace. "Because I'm not your daddy, and you're not skulking around the office with a loaded gun."

Bruised and stitched up as he was already, Ace should have kept his mouth shut. And maybe he would've let the jackass tell his story his way had it not been for the crack about his father's shooting. And the fact that Ace had never had any patience when it came to lying bullies. "I was just going to say," he said, raining down the full weight of an authority he no longer had any claim to, "you left out the part about how Colton Oil security cameras caught you sideswiping my administrative assistant's car on your way in—the first brand-new car she'd ever bought in her life—*after* you'd stopped along the way for a few celebratory slugs from that flask you had on you."

Scowl deepening, the tall guard raised his baton high to strike, but instead of flinching, or turning a shoulder to block the inevitable blows, Ace stood there, saying, "Go ahead, man. Do what you want, if it makes you feel any better. Heaven only knows you can't make me feel much worse."

Lowering the stick, Pete sneered, "You'd like that,

wouldn't you? Seein' me lose this job, too, when we march you in to meet with the DA and your lawyer, and those others, all black-and-blue and bloody?"

"I'm meeting with the—" Dread coiled cold and oily in Ace's stomach. Were the charges against him about to be upgraded? Had any chance to make things right with the only father he had even known—or to get to know his daughter—passed him by forever?

"Don't get too cocky, though, Colton," the tall guard warned, "because the minute you're out of there, we're taking you straight to the general lockup—"

"*After* we've had a little talk with a few of our favorite troublemakers about the way you've been talkin' about how you don't want to be associated with broke-ass trash like them," his frog-faced younger colleague added. "And then we'll both get busy catchin' up on all that paperwork we've let pile up just lately. Maybe we'll even get around to seein' to your visitors' list—*if* there's anything left of you to visit."

As the two men shared a chuckle, Ace smothered a sigh, wondering if there was any chance that Sierra could possibly make good on her promise to free him from his nightmare—or any hope he could survive it long enough for the real truth to come to light.

ACE WAS STILL shaking two hours later when his attorney walked him out through the jail's rear sally port and into the bright spring sunshine.

"You all right? You should be walking on air now, what with all the charges against you being dismissed." A tall man in his late fifties, Michael Seaver led him toward a long, black Escalade with tinted windows in the rear of the parking lot. Dressed as usual in an expensive, slim-cut suit and designer glasses, he grinned as if he'd expected this outcome all along, even though they both knew that at their most recent meeting, the outlook had been far grimmer. "Instead, you look about ready to fall over. You feeling okay? Or are your injuries still—"

"I'm healing fine," said Ace, wearing an oversize sweatshirt with a pair of cheap, ill-fitting denim pants and canvas shoes he'd been issued for the unexpected release. "I'm in shock, that's all. I can't believe I'm walking out of here, a free man, and that—is that…?"

His attention was captured by Sierra, a sight for sore eyes in her silver hoop earrings and jacket over form-fitting jeans and soft, gray boots. A breeze stirred her long, red-gold hair as she raised her hand in a muted greeting from where she was standing near the Escalade.

When their eyes met, the warmth of her smile loosened the tightness inside his chest enough for him to breathe again.

She'd kept her word after all, he understood, earned her finder's fee and then some. And more than that, she'd elected to come here in person, to meet him at the gates of hell.

"You know this woman?" the attorney asked as she approached.

"Not as well as I'd like to," Ace admitted, his mouth going dry at the perfect combination of beauty and athleticism in her movement.

Seaver gave a snort of amusement. "I see your recent troubles haven't affected your good taste in ladies."

"Too bad they've made me the last man on the planet any sensible woman would want to get tangled up with."

"Never say die, man," the attorney fired back. "Never say die."

"You must be Ace's mouthpiece," Sierra said as she drew within earshot. "I'm a friend. Sierra Madden."

"Ah, the famous bounty hunter." Seaver scrutinized her with a look of frank admiration before he offered her his hand. "Yes, I understand you are a *very* good friend to the defense indeed."

A wicked smile lit her eyes over their brief handshake. "Don't let it get around. I'd hate to ruin my reputation as a heartless mercenary."

"Thanks, Michael," Ace said. "I'll be going with Ms. Madden now."

"You're sure?" The attorney's gaze flicked to his shiny black Escalade. "I did promise your sister I'd bring you straight to the family compound."

"You don't have to worry about that, Counselor," Sierra said with a nod toward Ace. "I've been in touch with Ainsley, and we've agreed we'll be meeting up at eight at Ace's condo in town."

"What about right now? I'm sure he'd love to get back home to the Triple R and his loving family."

"Don't you think Ace deserves a little time and space to get looking and feeling like himself again, eat a solid meal on neutral ground and shut his eyes without looking over his shoulder for a change?"

"Of course," Michael was quick to agree. But he

darted a questioning look at Ace nonetheless. “I just wanted to make sure this is all right by my client.”

“If it was any more all right,” he said, both relieved and touched by Sierra’s consideration of how ill prepared he’d been to dive into the emotional tumult of an immediate reunion, “I’d be kissing this woman on the mouth right here and now.”

Seaver grinned. “Just don’t be late or your sister will be blowing up my phone with calls and texts. And we both know what Ainsley’s like when she drops into full protective mode.”

Cracking a smile, Ace shook the man’s hand. “I won’t be late. I promise. I’ll even turn my phone back on—they returned it to me on the way out—once I’ve had the chance to charge it.” He wouldn’t promise to switch on the ringer, though. The thought of coping with what he suspected would be scores, or maybe hundreds, of notification tones from all the calls and messages he’d surely missed was enough to break him out in a cold sweat.

Once Seaver had climbed into his Escalade, Sierra showed Ace to a different car than the one she’d previously been driving, an older Chevy with Arizona tags. But Ace didn’t have it in him to ask what had happened to her damaged Camry, or where she was driving him as she turned away from both the ranch and his personal downtown condo.

All he could manage was, “I still don’t know what I’m doing here instead of getting my head caved in about now by a couple of choice inmates while the guards look the other way.”

She winced. "Sounds like a good time. But didn't they explain it to you inside? Why the charges were dropped?"

"Dropped for *now*, pending further evidence. I did catch that part. I'm afraid that after that, though," he admitted, "the rest was drowned out by the roaring in my ears and the pounding in my chest. So I have *no* idea how you pulled off this miracle."

"Don't give me too much credit," she said, using one hand to wave off his statement. "The whole thing was a team effort." She described her visit to Destiny's bank, along with how the manager had escorted her out after she'd started asking questions about the missing teller. "So after I found Destiny shacked up with her boyfriend, whom Spencer told me was a serious drug dealer, I suggested that the police start digging into her activities over at the bank."

"I did catch something about financial crimes," Ace recalled, noticing Sierra's frequent glances at her mirrors and how carefully she'd been checking every parked vehicle they passed. "But what's any of that got to do with Destiny's testimony against me?"

"I'm getting to all that," she said, slowing as a bell dinged, a red light flashed and a pair of rail crossing arms came down to block the road ahead for an approaching train. "Oh, great," she grumbled, her hands knotting on the wheel.

"Is everything okay?" Ace asked her. "You seem a little—"

"Sure, yeah," Sierra said dismissively. "Just eager

to get you away from here and back to the free world as fast as possible."

Shaking off the interruption, she went on to explain, "After Destiny's disappearance, her manager had discovered evidence that she'd been laundering money for her creepy boyfriend's drug operation—enough to send her to federal prison for at least a decade, with zero possibility of parole."

"Sounds like a solid dose of karma, considering all the lies she's told about me," Ace said, not giving a damn if it made him sound bitter.

"Except Destiny wasn't too keen on the idea," Sierra said as the engine passed, "so she cried and pleaded and finally offered to come clean about the so-called confession. All Spencer had to do was agree not to turn her over to the feds."

"So he made the deal?" Ace asked, absently watching as the rail cars, many of them marked with colorful graffiti, clattered along.

She nodded. "The feds would get the drug supplier, which was who they were really after, and Spencer wanted the truth. The truth about what really happened to your father. About what's really been happening with your family since that email arrived claiming you'd been switched for the real Ace Colton soon after birth."

His gut tightened, as it always did, at the thought that there was another version of him, his family's missing son and brother, out there somewhere. That he'd been the cuckoo's egg left in the nest. Though he'd been told there was a reason to believe he'd been the son of a long-missing nurse named Luella Smith, he had to wonder if anyone in his family had had any luck tracking her—or the prodigal firstborn Colton heir—down while he was gone.

But those questions, he'd known for the past month, would do nothing except drag him down a rabbit hole of misery, so he dragged his brain back to the conversation at hand.

"So what did Destiny tell him?" It must have been something pretty big, since he was sitting here with Sierra rather than killing time—or possibly dodging fists, thanks to his guard *friend*—behind bars.

"She said someone called out of the blue and offered her ten grand to plant the gun inside your condo when you'd be *otherwise engaged.* Then she was instructed to call the cops and give them the whole pillow talk story—"

"I've said it from the start. I never touched that woman."

"Even she admits that now," Sierra told him, startling as a poorly dressed, stooped man shuffled past them on the street, drinking from a longneck, partly wrapped up in a paper bag. If the suddenness of his appearance caught Ace off guard, the slip in the bounty hunter's normally cool demeanor surprised him even more.

"That old fellow's harmless enough. He's always around this neighborhood," Ace reassured her, now certain that something was amiss. "Definitely a local, if you're still worried about your friends from—"

"Ice Veins is in the morgue, so everything's okay now," Sierra said in the tone of someone who might be trying to convince herself of something. "Just taking note of my surroundings."

"Is that why you switched cars, too?" he asked, peering at her through narrowed eyes. "Or is this one just a loaner while yours is in for repairs?"

She hesitated before answering with one of her usual shrugs. "So I'm still a little keyed up. Who wouldn't be? Some habits are harder to get past than others."

"You're sure it's just a habit?"

She barked out a laugh. "Don't you have enough to worry over? For example, this story Destiny claims she was bribed to tell, saying that you'd confessed to the shooting of your father."

Ace scowled, quick to anger at the thought of all the damage the bank teller had done. "Why should anyone believe anything she says now—an admitted liar who launders money for drug dealers?"

"Maybe they wouldn't, except her story checks out from her phone records, though the caller couldn't be traced, to the timing of an anonymous initial payment to her bank account. And her prints were found inside your condo, underneath the flooring she lifted up to plant the gun."

"The real question is who paid her? Who was willing to buy her off to do it?" As Ace's overheated brain formed an image of his father's second wife, the same woman who'd coughed up an even larger chunk of money to bring him in, his shaking hands clenched and twisted the cheap fabric of his baggy jail garb. "Was it—was Selina involved in this? She seems to have a penchant for using her money to cause trouble for me."

"Or to *return you to the safety of your family,*" Sierra quoted, sounding as dubious as ever about the line the woman had initially fed her over the phone the day she'd first called to hire her to find Ace. "But be that as it may, Destiny swears she doesn't know who it was. She claims the caller blocked the number and the first half of the payment posted anonymously to her account. But the voice—"

"Was it a woman's?" he asked impatiently.

Sierra shook her head. "Male, she insisted, though she said it was rather high-pitched and younger-sounding. And now, get this. Destiny's furious that she went to so much trouble, brought all that scrutiny down on herself, and this dude stiffed her for the second payment."

"She knows more. She has to. Who would take a risk like that, sell those kind of lies for some strange young guy?"

"She might've looked and talked the part of the reliable witness, but Destiny Jones has got an expensive drug habit of her own that convinced her to take the risk in the first place," Sierra said as the final train car crossed before them. "But the longer things went on, the more nervous the whole deal made her."

"No wonder she took off, then, especially with her being involved in other crimes, too," Ace said. "So what's going to happen to her now?"

The railroad arms rose slowly, allowing Sierra to finally cross the tracks.

"They're holding her for the time being for possession, filing a false police report and whatever else they can come up with," she said. "There'll be additional charges, too, based on her breaking and entering your condo and planting the weapon."

"After everything she put me through, I ought to sue her, too," Ace said. "But it doesn't sound like she'd be worth the effort."

"I suspect you're right about that," Sierra said, "though at this point, no one could blame you for wanting to rain down some righteous retribution. Honestly, just thinking about the whole mess is enough to make me wish I'd slugged her harder."

"You punched her?"

"Yeah," Sierra said. "Right in front of Spencer, too, it turned out, who wasn't amused in the least, but I seriously thought the lying little hustler might've been reaching for a gun."

"I take it she wasn't."

"Oops. My bad," Sierra said, a smile in her voice.

In no mood for levity, Ace said, "When I find out who's really responsible for what she did, who gave her that gun to leave inside my condo, they'll have damned more than a *little* retribution coming their way, I can tell you."

Nodding, Sierra glanced his way. "Not to change the subject, but I need to make a quick stop." She nodded in the direction of a small Mexican cantina, a humble hole-in-the-wall strip center where Ace hadn't gone in years.

"Ah, I'm not really in the mood to eat," he said, unable to imagine facing the stares of other people who'd been reading about him in the paper or hearing about him on the evening news.

"I figured as much," she said, "which is why I phoned in an order for us right before you came out. Just hang tight. I'll be right back. Then I'll get you over to the lodge where I'm staying, where you can shave and shower and change into the clothes your brother Grayson brought over for me."

"You had—" Ace shook his head, surprised, since the two hadn't been especially close through the years. "*Grayson* knew you were planning to shanghai me, too?"

Pulling into the parking lot, Sierra nodded. "Actually, it was his idea in the first place. He understood how overwhelmed you might feel, and that you might need to prepare yourself before Ainsley and the others sprung your pregnant daughter on you. So he asked if maybe I could stick around a little while and help out. He seems like a good guy, and I could spare an extra day, so—"

"I'll be sure to thank him for that," Ace said, touched by his brother's thoughtfulness. "And thank you, too, for delaying your trip back to Vegas. I know you must be eager to get back to your life."

"I—ah—I'll be right out," said the bounty hunter, her green eyes avoiding his at the mention of her home city.

But not before he spotted the unease in them, the tell, as he'd learned to think of such things in the world of high-stakes business negotiations. It was yet another hint that Sierra Madden remained nervous. Though he imagined that anyone might suffer some level of fall-out—or even PTSD—considering the brutality she'd suffered at the hands of her father's loan shark and his henchman, he hoped like hell it wasn't more than that.

Chapter Eight

Just as Sierra had suspected, Ace must have been far hungrier than he had imagined. Though the chicken enchilada plates had cooled by the time he'd showered and changed into the clothing his brother had sent with her, he shoveled in forkfuls as if he hadn't truly tasted food in weeks. Which, she suspected from the loose fit of his storm-gray Henley shirt and jeans and the hollows of his freshly shaven cheeks, might well be the case.

"I don't understand," he said. "Why'd you bring me all the way out here instead of just heading for my condo?"

"Because if reporters catch wind that you've been released, I knew they'd be both there and at the entrance of the family ranch with camera crews. You know how those vultures are."

"All too well, unfortunately," he said, hating the thought of appearing in the media looking like a hunted animal. "Is that why you rented this place?" he asked, looking around the clean but rustic paneled room in the once-popular family lodge resort, with its faded drapes and dated cowboy-and-cactus decor and location miles from town.

She shook her head. "I've been staying out here all along. It's quiet, and it suits me."

"There are a lot more modern places with better amenities, closer to everything."

"I see more than enough generic chain motels in my line of work as it is," she told him. "And empty as this place is this time of year, it had a great deal on the rates."

He looked at her suspiciously, as if he sensed the half-truth of her statement. That rather than choosing this place for its old-time Western vibe and low off-season prices, she'd been more focused on finding the most out-of-the-way location possible—one with a room affording a view of the only road allowing access. She'd been grateful, too, to find the manager willing to accept a cash payment and not look too hard at the fake ID she'd presented upon check-in. But clearly, the older woman must have noticed, for when Sierra had turned down a room with a great view of the scenic foothills, asking instead for one that overlooked the road, the eyes behind the manager's half glasses had softened, and she'd quickly said, *Of course, dear. I understand completely*, before patting Sierra's hand with her own short, plump fingers.

As she closed the disposable container on her own half-eaten dinner, Sierra felt a twinge, suspecting the woman believed her to be fleeing an abusive spouse or lover—but if it helped to keep her safe from whomever Ice Veins's nephew, Eddie, may have sent gunning for her, she was willing to let the misperception stand.

"Seems like a lot of driving back and forth to save a few bucks," Ace pressed.

Irritated by the doubt in his voice, she snapped, "We weren't *all* born rich as your branch of the Coltons," before realizing what she'd just said.

Anger sparking in his eyes, he fired back, "You mean you haven't profited enough off my pain lately?"

She groaned, her face burned as if she'd been slapped. "I wasn't thinking about—about the real circumstances of your birth before I spoke. Forgive me."

Nodding, he blew out an audible breath. "Only if you'll accept my apology for being an ungrateful ass, too. Frankly, if you'd've taken twice that off Selina, I would've been fine with it. Or at least I would now, knowing she's getting nothing for her twenty-five thousand dollars—"

"Nothing but a whole lot of questions, I suspect," Sierra said, wondering if he really meant it. "I'm betting that Spencer will be looking hard at her as the potential source of that payoff to Destiny."

"But Destiny said the caller who hired her to lie and plant that gun was male, and younger."

"If that woman's a reliable source, I'm a Dallas debutante," Sierra said. "Besides, who's to say that your stepmother—I mean your father's second wife—couldn't have disguised her voice? A woman's voice and a young male's really aren't so far off, are they?"

"I suppose it's possible," Ace agreed. "Though why would Selina frame me, unless she'd shot my father herself? And why would she want to do that, since it would jeopardize whatever sweetheart deal she's had going to keep her job with the company and her home on ranch grounds all these years?"

Shaking her head, Sierra said, "We're not going to figure it out now. But there's an extra burrito inside the bag there. Want it? You look like you're still hungry."

"I'm good, but thanks. And thanks for thinking of it," he said. "I haven't had much in the way of an appetite this past month. Especially after I was taken into custody, not knowing the family was all convinced I'd— Did you know the ballistics came back as a match on that gun? The one found inside my condo? My attorney told me—"

She nodded. "Yes, I heard that. That's how they got the warrant for your arrest, I'm told."

"So all this time, my stepmother, Genevieve, the people I grew up thinking were my siblings—they had to have been convinced that that was why I'd taken off. That I'd really been the one to shoot him."

"They didn't all believe it," she tried to reassure him. But the haunted look on Ace's face, still marked with fading bruises, told her he didn't buy it. And that he was as nervous, in his own way, about his reunion with his family as she was about returning to her home in Las Vegas.

"Do you think they'll accept now," he asked, setting down his fork as he saw her noticing its shaking, "that Destiny was paid off to set me up? Or will they still figure I'm just a bastard who resents their birthright? Do you think they'll ever dare trust me again?"

Rising from her chair, she went to him. With the lightest of touches, she stroked the side of his face, running her hand over the barely discernible bump where she'd struck him that first night they had met. "They're waiting for you right now, Ace," she said quietly. "Waiting to welcome you back into the fold. Maybe not all of them—they don't want to overwhelm you—but it'll be a start. And don't forget, your daughter's there, too, with the man in her life. A daughter your siblings have already more than half-convinced to love you, sight unseen."

"*Love* me?" He shook his head. "How could—but she hasn't even met me, can't know anything about me except the fact I was a deadbeat father—"

"Not by choice, right? You didn't know, were never told—"

"I should've—"

"Cut yourself a little slack?" she asked. "After all, you *were* seventeen."

"And she's not so much older than that herself now, right? A young woman who's heard only that I'm some kind of jailbird. A man who fled arrest after shooting his own father following his firing."

Sierra shook her head and then dropped her hand to squeeze his shoulder. "A man who fled a frame-up to find justice. And something tells me there've been other stories, too. Stories about the man they all grew up with, the one who's stood by them through thick and thin. The man they'll always love as a brother—"

"But I'm not their brother, as you pointed out," he

said bitterly. "Just someone who happened to be around while we were all coming of age."

"What's family anyway?" she asked. "Is it somebody like my mom—or your own biological mother, whoever she might really be—who took off with no forwarding address and never looked back or made contact? Or is it the people who were there for us…like my dad, as flawed as he was, or the high school coach who steered me into a youth boxing program when he saw I was spiraling toward big trouble? Or what about the sister who hired you a lawyer and the brother who might not always know the right words but worried over picking you out the right clothes and grabbing your favorite boots to wear for your homecoming today? I can tell you which people I'd pick out, if I had the damned luxury of those kind of choices. If I had anyone at all left on the planet who cared half as much for me."

Coming to his feet, Ace caught the hand she'd touched him with in his, his gaze fierce as words had been as he drew her into his arms. "You must really be something in the ring, Sierra Madden. Because when it comes to speaking the truth, you certainly don't pull a lot of punches, do you?"

Her heartbeat quickened, her stomach swooping as he leaned toward her, hesitating long enough to lock in on her gaze, an unspoken question forming in the depths of his brown eyes. The downy hairs along her forearms and the back of her neck rose in answer, and a delicious rush of heat burned away every other thought but the imperative to close the space between them, to push her lips against his in a manner that removed all doubt of what she had no business wanting but ached for with a hunger that had caught her wholly by surprise.

ACE DIDN'T THINK. He couldn't, with his senses overwhelmed by the passion of the woman who kissed as fiercely as she tackled every other challenge. The woman who could have taken her money and hit the ground running but had instead gone straight to work to keep her vow to rescue him from hell.

Regardless of what she'd claimed about his freedom being the result of a group effort, he knew damned well it wouldn't have happened, perhaps not for weeks or months or even longer, if she hadn't put her mind to finding Destiny and unraveling her lies.

But as grateful as he felt, as exhilarated to be free of the immediate threat of custody, it was that eager little murmur of Sierra's, the way she wriggled closer as he pulled her tight body against his, that had him wondering what he'd ever been doing wasting his time, his life, pursuing the kind of women, the kind of life, that didn't count, when a human firecracker like *this* was waiting for him.

As he explored her mouth with his tongue, he ran his hands through her long hair, losing himself in the sensation of thick, silken sleekness tangling in his fingers. But he couldn't long be content, no more than she seemed to be rubbing circles along the back of his shirt. There were too many impediments between them, and way too many damned clothes. As a white heat blazed up between them, as undeniable as it was unmeasured, she led him to the queen-size bed where the fresh clothing he had so recently changed into very shortly hit the floor.

For all the eagerness she'd shown in helping him remove it, and every bit of appreciation that warmed her green eyes when she saw the effect she was having on his body, he couldn't help but notice how Sierra winced as she moved to pull her long-sleeve T-shirt over her head.

Remembering her ribs, he suggested, "How about you let me help you with that—if you aren't too sore?"

"If you don't get me naked fast," she promised, her face flushed and her swollen lips slightly parted, "I promise you, I'm not going to be the only one who's feeling pain."

Chuckling, he said, "Well, I wouldn't want to end up with another black eye, now, would I?" before peeling off her top—and stopping at the starburst of deep brown-and purple-centered bruising he saw along her left side, which sparked a memory of Ice Veins kicking her so brutally while she was down.

"Seeing that makes me want to kill that bastard all over again," Ace growled, his protective instincts once more roaring to life. "Makes me want to be sure he felt a hell of a lot more pain that second time around."

"Forget about that. It's okay now." She tried to cover the spot with the sheet, but he gently caught her hand.

"It'll never be okay, the things that happened to you that night. When I think about that Taser, and that bastard hauling off and booting you like a piece of—"

"Don't do that." Frustration digging a V between her red-blond brows, she shook her head at him as she stretched out, so strong and toned, yet softly female in all the right places, beside him on the bed. "Don't focus on the bad times, or the challenges to come. Not now, Ace. For one thing, you and I—we're a hell of a lot more than the sum of our wounds, our bumps and scars and bruises."

With a delicacy that took his breath away, her fingertips feathered along the edge of the light bandaging on his chest before drifting lower. "Or would you rather let the people who've hurt us, who have taken so much away from you and your family already, steal this joy from you, too?"

With that, she turned her head, leaning to devour his mouth with another kiss. As she did, she stroked the length of him, making him painfully, exquisitely hard and hot for more.

Part of him knew that this was crazy, that what he was feeling, what they were doing, was far more than the physical act of making love. That as he rolled her over, giving in to the need to worship every gorgeous inch of her with his hands, his mouth, and finally, the union of their bodies, that he was setting himself up big time.

That when the time came for her to leave him, as she surely would, this beautiful, brave woman would be taking half his heart.

A FEW HOURS later Sierra drove toward the industrial area of Mustang Valley—and Ace's condo. "Do you—do you like music?" she asked, darting an awkward look toward Ace. Since the sun had set hours earlier, the car's interior felt claustrophobic, a dim cocoon where she was trapped with her misgivings. Along with the low thrum of her sex-sated nerves, it made for an awkward combination.

"Um, music's fine. Whatever you like," he said, sounding just as uncomfortable as she felt. Probably far too nervous about seeing his family and meeting the daughter he had never seen, except in the photo she had shown him, to even wonder what the two of them had been playing at back inside her room.

She turned on the radio, scanning through the few stations she could find, including one playing a warbling old country crooner, another with an angry woman shouting about politics and a third an overpowered station broadcasting from south of the border blasting loud accordion music.

Switching it off, she said, "Turns out, I guess, that whatever I like best is silence."

"Good call," he murmured before adding, "except, Sierra, I don't want silence between us. Or any regrets, either. I—"

"You think I *regret* what happened? Or even that I didn't want it? Want *you*," she said. "I'm not going to pretend I didn't just happen to have that fresh, new pack of condoms on hand." She felt her face heating with the admission that she'd been thinking of the possibility—imagining how it might be, if they were allowed even the briefest window of time alone together—but she charged ahead nonetheless. "It's been…it's been a long time for me—a really long time, between my dad getting sick and everything that happened after, and I didn't want to be caught off guard…in case…in case something happened before I have to go."

It was those last few words that tightened her throat, making her eyes burn as her mistake sank in. The realization that, with a connection forged in the fires of survival, one mind-blowing round of sex, meant to take the edge off their raw attraction, could never be enough. Instead, the all-too-fleeting hours they'd shared had only served to underscore the darkness of the lonely years she'd endured.

Forget years, she realized as they passed an open bar and several closed stores outside the downtown area. She had *never* felt a connection like that or been touched in such a way by a man who clearly knew his way around a woman's body. Rather than glossing past what he had to deal with to gain his own pleasure, as her previous, on-and-off-again younger boyfriend had so often done, Ace had seemed to relish wringing every last gasp and cry of delight from her before he'd finally— It made Sierra dizzy just to think of the moment he had thrust inside her… She was even more moved, remembering how solicitous he'd been afterward, how concerned that he might have caused her injured ribs pain.

What ribs? she'd moaned, floating on a raft of pure bliss.

"You don't really have to go home, do you? Not right away, at any rate?" Ace asked her. "I know I have no right to ask, with my life such a mess now. I know there's nothing I can promise you, but—"

"It's not that. It's just—I have some things, some business back home I really need to deal with," she lied, not wanting to add her worries to the mountain he already had of his own.

"Some business..." he echoed. "And afterward?"

Words crowded into her throat, vows to call him when she could or maybe even come back for a visit. But she bit her lip against the pain, telling herself it was better to hurt him by remaining vague than by making promises she wouldn't be around—or possibly alive—to keep.

"I can't really say," she finally told him. "It all depends... I know you're going to have a lot on your plate coming up, too. Things you can't put off."

After taking a turn he pointed out, they passed the low, dark hulks of several warehouses, an area where the streetlights of downtown gave way to the more widely spaced and dimmer, golden, sodium-vapor security lighting that marked the area.

"Definitely. But that doesn't mean..." he said, before interrupting himself to point out a narrow opening between two storefronts. "Why don't you hang a right here, at this alleyway, and then take the second drive on the left? We'll see if we can get in through a rear entrance and avoid any photographers who might be lurking near the condo's main entrance."

"Will do," she said, checking her mirrors once again to reassure herself they didn't have company before making the turn.

"That doesn't mean," Ace continued, "that you're not near the top of my list of priorities. Which is why I'm warning you—"

"*Warning* me?" A chill of alarm ran through her.

Because she'd never gotten any sense that Ace Colton might be the possessive type. But maybe that was what came of falling head over heels for a fugitive she'd been sent to hunt down, a man she couldn't truly know, regardless of what the lies her heart had whispered.

"I'm warning you, Sierra, that I damned well *am* going to get justice for my father, figure out who I really am and make things as right as I possibly can with my family—and afterward I intend to cut a swath straight to Las Vegas to claim you."

She darted a glance his way. "*Claim* me?" Did the man think she was a diamond ring he'd left at a pawn shop?

"Claim you, woo you, throw myself at your feet," he said, sounding completely serious, "whatever it takes to make it clear that the only future I'm interested in building is one that includes getting to know you a whole lot better."

As narrow as the alley was, there was no place to pull over. So Sierra turned into the second drive as he'd instructed before stopping next to the warehouse-style garage where condo owners stored their vehicles to stare back at him, her mouth as dry as cotton and her blood rushing like a river in full flood stage in her ears.

"I know I'm coming on damned strong," Ace went on, "with all this crazy talk about a future when we've only known each other such a short time. But Sierra, if these past few months have taught me one thing, it's been that I've wasted a lifetime chasing the wrong dreams, the wrong women, the fancy cars and exotic vacations and all the things that it turns out can be whisked away and shattered with a single email—or a few lies to the wrong people. But in you, I've found something real. I know it. Please just say that you think there's a chance someday that you might. Or at least that I'm not scaring you half out of your mind."

She forced a smile to keep her tears back. "I've never been accused of scaring easy, cowboy. *Never.*" Leaning to her right, she pressed her lips to his, a kiss bittersweet with the knowledge that the future that he dreamed of was never going to happen, that there was no way to avoid endangering Ace Colton and the family that he cared for—except to break his heart.

Chapter Nine

Something was wrong with Sierra, Ace realized. If he hadn't been so distracted with his own problems, and so emotionally off balance after his release from custody, he would have demanded answers earlier, on the way over to the lodge where she was staying, when he'd first noticed she had been so jittery. But just now, when she had kissed him, he'd sensed her tensing, holding back—and when his younger brother Rafe walked over and gently tapped on the car window, she nearly jumped out of her skin, her body coiling into what he recognized as a fight-or-flight posture.

But there was no time for questions now, not with his joy overriding all else as he bailed out of the car to embrace the chief financial officer of Colton Oil, whom Ace had not only grown up with, but also worked with closely throughout their adult lives.

"Not so hard, man. You may've heard I've got some stitches," Ace reminded him, laughing with relief when his blond sibling's bear hug finally eased.

"Sorry, but it's just so damned good to have you back, Ace," Rafe said, backing off to clap him—somewhat more carefully—on the shoulder. "And we've missed you so much. You've had us all so worried."

"I'm sorry, so sorry for taking off without a word like that," Ace said, more choked up than he'd imagined at the concern in his brother's blue eyes. Uncomfortable with the emotion, he cleared his throat and abruptly changed the subject. "Allow me to introduce Sierra Madden, the woman who tracked me down and then pulled the pin out of that garbage case against me."

"*Helped* a little," Sierra corrected. "And Rafe and I have met, when I was interviewing various family members, trying to figure out your whereabouts."

Her mention of family brought to mind the pictures she'd shown him of his family members. Including one of Nova. His stomach flipped as he wondered, would his—his mind could still barely form the word—*daughter* really be here this evening? "Should we—should we all go on up, then?"

"Absolutely," Rafe said. "I came down to run off any reporters, but it seems the coast is clear for now—and Ainsley and Grayson have covered up those big windows of yours with enough sheets so no one should be able to sneak any photos through them, either."

"That's great," Ace said, wondering how celebrities survived the feeling of being stalked like big game, year after year, by paparazzi, when the past few months had worn so badly on him and his family.

Feeling like a stranger returning to his own place after so long away, Ace went to the recently replaced digital access pad that allowed them into the garage. There, a glance assured him that the car he usually drove around town remained, still covered, in his corner parking spot in the underground parking lot. He led them to the elevator and keyed in the code that took them to the third floor, which was solely occupied by a modern-styled unit he'd had built back when things like exposed brick, towering, floor-to-ceiling windows and a custom spiral staircase had mattered to him. He'd wanted a private place to entertain his more sophisticated friends and out-of-town business associates who often passed through Mustang Valley.

Sierra, who evidently hadn't seen the place, murmured, "Gorgeous," the moment the doors opened to reveal the bold splashes of color, large-format modern paintings and several sumptuous hand-woven rugs, along with an art-glass chandelier that offset the colder metallic surfaces, exposed brick and the gleaming white quartz of the generous space.

But Ace was beyond responding, his eyes locked on his sister Ainsley, who had risen from the long, curved sectional, her light eyes filling with tears and her chestnut hair flying behind her as she ran to throw herself into his arms.

"You're home! You're finally home," she kept saying, her tears—and all the tears he knew she must have shed on his account since he'd left—only deepening his guilt.

For the next few minutes they were all talking at once, with Ace stammering apologies for his flight, to Ainsley and his dark-haired brother Grayson, who greeted him first with a firm handshake and then overcame his natural reticence to hug him, too. As Ace's three siblings who were present argued that there was no more need for regrets and they were only glad to have him home in one piece, Ace caught a glimpse between Ainsley's head and Grayson's broad shoulder of Sierra by the island that separated the living space from the large, eat-in kitchen. With that deceptively gentle face of hers in profile, she placed a calming hand on the shoulder of a smaller and clearly younger blonde, who was being supported by a tall, slender man with tan skin and dark brown curls.

But it was the young woman's face that captured all of Ace's attention, a face as pale as milk as she stared at him with wide green eyes.

Ace felt an electric jolt zing through him and heard a buzzing in his ears as Sierra looked from the man with the dark curls to the clearly nervous young woman, whose striped dress showed an unmistakable baby bump.

A hush fell as, all at once, his siblings and Sierra all noticed him looking at his daughter, too, saw him take the first step forward, and then heard him force the first shaky words from his mouth. "You're as lovely as your mother, Nova."

Her breath hitched in answer, her nose growing pink as her eyes shone with emotion.

Sierra removed her arm and stepped aside, offering quiet words of reassurance. "This is going to be all right, Nova, and is it…?"

"Nikolas Slater," the man supporting her supplied with a nod.

Looking back toward Ace, Sierra nodded her head at

Slater before telling the couple, "You'll both see. He's a good man."

With Ace's next step, his heart pounded even harder, his world narrowing to the young woman who had somehow believed in him, if what Sierra had said had been true, before he'd even known of her existence. Because of the love his siblings still had for him, love that had transcended both DNA and doubts.

"I've only just heard about you recently," Ace told her, "and I'm grieving. Grieving for the time we've lost, but so grateful that you've come. Grateful for the chance to prove myself a decent man, to learn to be a decent father, to do whatever it takes to welcome you, and that little one you're expecting, into my life now."

After a last glance back at Nikolas, who offered her a reassuring smile, Nova took the first hesitant step forward, the hope in her face tinged with trepidation. "I—I'm so happy to finally get to meet you…sir."

Ace winced to hear her call him that, as if he were some stranger, though he knew it was the case. "Please don't call me *sir*—and *Mr. Colton* would be even worse, so let's just—how about *Ace*? For now, at least."

She nodded. "All right. *Ace*, then."

"Until I earn an upgrade." He tried for a smile—and hoped it didn't look like a pained grimace, as nervous as he felt. "*If* I ever do. I'm not saying it's going to be easy, after all these years I've missed, all the things there are for me to get to know about you. I'm only telling you I want to, and that I'd be honored as hell if you'd allow me."

Nova's pretty face suffused with color—a face in

which he was delighted to recognize the resemblance, in the eyes, that Sierra had mentioned earlier. A resemblance that swept aside any lingering, paranoid suspicions that this incredible story of a secret daughter had been some elaborate hoax whipped up by his siblings and the bounty hunter to trick him into coming home.

Damned if this girl isn't mine, and carrying my grandchild, too, he thought, his throat tightening as the miracle of this unexpected gift of a biological connection, after so much had been taken from him, truly sank in. Especially seeing it witnessed like this, blessed and aided by three of his siblings and the woman he prayed he could convince to become a part of his life moving forward.

But he'd be damned if he allowed his daughter's first impression of him to be that of a sobbing sentimentalist, so with some difficulty, Ace pulled himself together by grabbing a box of tissues from the countertop and offering it to Nova before her tears began to spill.

Instead of taking one, however, she sniffled softly and then abruptly ducked beneath his outstretched arm. Nova then wrapped Ace in a hug that had him wondering what he'd ever done in this life to deserve such grace.

WHILE ACE, NOVA, and Nikolas were speaking privately in the study, getting to know one another, Sierra and Ainsley sat in the main living area talking, while Grayson wandered over to examine the contents of the built-in bar just off the main living area.

"I don't know about the rest of you," Grayson said, a

relieved smile slanting across his handsome face, "but I sure could use a stiff drink right about now."

"I'll second that," agreed Rafe, who'd been leaning against the kitchen island returning a text message to his fiancée. "Though a cold beer sounds good about now."

"Sierra?" Grayson asked.

"I'd be good with sparkling water," she responded, since she felt the need to keep her wits about her.

"Coming right up. What about you, Ainsley?"

Ainsley nodded. "I'll have a glass of chardonnay, if there's any chilled, please. I'm completely wrung out from trying to keep all our other siblings from rushing right over here before Ace had the chance to spend any time with Nova. If Bowie hadn't surprised Marlowe with that overnight getaway, I'm pretty sure she would've been pounding down the door right now."

Sierra smiled, recalling from her research that that particular sibling had a condo in this same complex.

"You might want something stronger," Grayson suggested, "if you're going to break the news to Ace tonight about Micheline Anderson being his real mother."

Sierra, who'd been distracted by the surprising discovery that the PI she'd spoken to about Ace's case earlier was romantically involved with Nova, looked up sharply. *"Who?"* Though the name rang a bell—a warning Klaxon, for some reason—she couldn't place it for a moment. And then she remembered the photo she'd seen in the shop window, the one thanking the Affirmation Alliance Group founder for her help with earthquake recovery efforts.

"Wait a minute," Sierra blurted, staring in Ainsley's

direction. "Weren't you the one who warned me, right after I arrived in Mustang Valley, when I said I was looking for an out-of-the-way place to lodge, to stay as far as humanly possible from the AAG Center—and anything to do with Micheline Anderson and her 'Being Your Best You' groupies?"

"I did, and for good reason," Ainsley admitted, lines creasing her forehead.

"What?" Sierra asked. "Is she another one of those slick self-help gurus who help themselves to the contents of their followers' bank accounts?"

She mouthed a quick thanks to Grayson as he handed her the sparkling water she'd requested.

"Far worse." Ainsley accepted the glass of wine her brother offered but set it down, untouched. "We already had reason to suspect Micheline might have once gone by the name of Luella Smith, the nurse believed to have switched the babies. Then my fiancé, Santiago, and I uncovered evidence Micheline might also be connected to this phony Marriage Institute scheme, where they were promising couples counseling but actually taking payoffs from one side to tip the scales."

"Sounds like a nightmare." Sierra could all too easily able to imagine the horrific potential for abuse.

"The real nightmare," Rafe put in, looking at his sister, "is imagining what could've happened if your and Santiago's scheme to play a married couple and infiltrate that crooked institute had gone wrong."

"It very nearly did," Ainsley admitted with a shudder. "Fortunately, we were able to get that scheme shut down, but from what I overheard Micheline say during a phone call, I'm absolutely certain she's planning something that means big trouble."

"And now," Grayson said, "to have to tell Ace that a woman like that might really be his—"

Grimacing, Ainsley shook her head at him. "I can't tell him, not *now*. I've been a nervous wreck all day as it is, worrying how Ace would take instant fatherhood after everything else he'd been contending with. Nova would've been heartbroken, after everything she's gone through, if he'd rejected her."

Ainsley's brothers let the subject drop.

Sierra told them, "I don't think rejecting Nova ever entered Ace's mind. It was a shock, of course, when he first heard about her, and I know he still has a lot of questions about why the mother—what was her name?—never told him she was pregnant. I'm sure he'd love to ask her."

"Allegra Ellis," Ainsley said. "But I'm afraid Nova's mother's passed away, so Nova and Ace are left now to figure out their own truths...and how they want their story to end."

Grayson looked around. "Shall we all drink a toast to *happily ever afters*?"

"To *happily-ever-afters*," Ainsley said, reaching to pick up and raise her elegant crystal wineglass, "or at least as near to it as we all can hope to come."

Agreeing to that, they quickly drank, and afterward the brothers started talking, awkwardly, to Sierra's ears, about the impact of the recent earthquake on the town's economy. While Grayson explained something about the early emergency response to Rafe, Ainsley sipped at her wine and looked toward Sierra with a look worthy of her reputation as one of the shrewdest corporate lawyers in the state.

"So tell me, Sierra," Ainsley asked, dropping her voice and canting her head in a conspiratorial manner, "is there any chance, any chance at all, that our brother's *happily-ever-after might* possibly include *you*?"

Sierra sputtered on the fizzy mouthful of sparkling water she'd been swallowing. *"Me?"* Was it that obvious to others that she and Ace had slept together? Belatedly struggling to pull together her poker face, she coughed into her hand and asked, "What on earth would make you say that?"

"Because you're still here, for one thing," Ainsley pointed out. "And more than that, I'm not blind. I've seen the way he looks at you—and I've noticed your concern for him, ever since that awful ordeal with those men who ambushed the two of you."

"I needed to make things right, that's all," Sierra insisted, telling herself that it would be best—or at least less painful for Ace when she disappeared—if she didn't let on how close the two of them had gotten. "I felt bad about buying into Selina's story in the first place about why she wanted to hire me and even worse about getting Ace hurt when we ran into my—ah—those troublemakers that were trailing me." Hating the idea of near-strangers judging her father's gambling addiction, Sierra had offered scant details to anyone but Sergeant Spencer Colton about Ice Veins and his associates, explaining to the other Coltons only that as a bounty hunter, she occasionally dealt with the type of clientele inclined to hold grudges.

"You sure it's *only* that?" asked Ainsley, whose perceptive eyes narrowed over the rim of her wineglass.

"Badgering the witness!" Grayson accused his sister with a teasing grin. "Just because you and Santiago are all hot and heavy these days doesn't mean you have to fix up every single person within reach, too."

Blushing, Ainsley sent a pillow sailing toward her brother, but he caught it neatly with Rafe chuckling and Sierra trying to figure out a graceful way to change the subject.

Never famous for her tact, she went straight for the proverbial elephant in the living room. "So how's your father? Any change?" Noticing the siblings' exchange of startled looks, she shrugged an explanation. "Ace has been asking and asking, trying to find out anything he can regarding his father's condition—and yes, he absolutely does still consider Payne Colton his real dad. I've asked around, too, at the hospital, but you know how they are with all their privacy laws and blah, blah, blah."

Grayson, who'd long worked as a first responder, smiled while Ainsley shook her head and lectured, "You know, those federal laws exist for everyone's protection."

"Especially with reporters out there gunning for a story," Rafe added, his blue eyes serious, "*and* whoever really shot our father is still out there."

"Well, I'm not the press *or* the shooter," Sierra said impatiently, "so will you *please* just tell me how he is?

What should Ace expect when I take him there to see him later?"

Grayson shook his head. "To the hospital? As in *to-night*? Ah, Sierra, I'm not sure that's such a good idea."

"Why on earth not?" Sierra asked the three of them, feeling the weight of their collective disapproval. "Of *course* Ace wants to see his father. If you had any idea how worried he's been—"

"We've *all* been worried." Ainsley straightened so abruptly, the wine nearly overlapped the edge of her glass. "But you can't. If anyone sees him there—our stepmother, for one thing—I'd hate to see her any more upset."

"Because she still believes Ace might be guilty?"

"I don't exactly know what she does or doesn't think," Ainsley continued, "only that she's been confused, pulled in so many directions, with her husband lying in a coma all these months—though they've been seeing signs of improvement lately. Signs the neurologist is telling us he's beginning to regain consciousness."

"He's *waking up*?" Rafe asked. "I hadn't heard that."

"He's *beginning* to respond to stimuli and simple requests," Ainsley explained. "But he's not coherent yet, not talking."

"Coming out of a long coma's not like flipping the lights back on," said Grayson, who, with his first responder's training, had more medical knowledge than the others. "It's more like a very slow computer re-boot—only you're never sure which circuits will come back, or in what order. Or which information and abilities might be lost forever."

"And Genevieve's not going to want anything, any upset, to possibly interfere with his recovery," Ainsley said. "But it's not only her."

"Who else?" Ace demanded, appearing unexpectedly outside the study's doorway. "Who else in the family still believes I'd really shoot Dad? Outside of Selina, that is?"

Grayson curled a lip and shook his head. "Don't tell me you're counting *her* as family now."

"Yeah," Rafe said, a growl in his voice. "Since when?"

"You know that's *not* what I meant," Ace said, clearly struggling to control his temper. "I just need to know, after everything that's happened, who it is that's got my back now."

"*We* do, and Marlowe, Asher, all your siblings, Ace," Ainsley insisted. "Believe me when I tell you, if I hadn't figured it would have overwhelmed you, this place would've been packed to the rafters with your supporters tonight. I promise you, it was all I could do to fend the others off."

Sierra caught Ace glancing at his brothers, who nodded to confirm Ainsley's claim, and her heart ached, imagining what the past months' uncertainty must have been like for a man used to being a leader in the boardroom and among his younger siblings.

Grimacing, Ace glanced back over his shoulder before quietly closing the study door behind him. "Nova and I—we had a really good first talk, and Nikolas was a real rock for her. He mostly stayed quiet, but he seems like a solid guy."

"They're great together," Ainsley assured him. "But how's Nova?"

"She's a little worn out after everything, so she's resting on the sofa in there under an afghan. Nikolas is staying with her in case she needs anything."

While Sierra wondered whether pregnancy or the emotional meeting with her father was the real cause of Nova's fatigue, Ainsley nodded, a look of sympathy softening her expression.

Rising from the sofa, she approached Ace. "It wasn't our brothers and sisters I was worried about," she explained, "when Sierra mentioned taking you to see our father. Other than Genevieve—"

"It'll be late by the time we get there," Ace broke in. "Surely, she'll be back at home then. They aren't letting her sleep up at the hospital, are they?"

"I can't imagine they are, but reporters never sleep," Ainsley reminded him. "They just plant stringers around the lobby, with their little cameras, to keep an eye out for your appearance."

"You let Sierra and me worry about getting around the damned reporters," Ace said, glancing Sierra's way for support.

This would be the time, Sierra realized, a flutter of trepidation mingling with the chilled bubbles in her stomach. *The time to say I'm bowing out now. I've gotten him back home, out of jail and reunited with his family like I promised.*

But the thought of blindsiding him with the news

that she was taking off tonight, so soon after he'd come right out and told her he wanted her to be part of his life forever, had her nails digging into the palm of her free hand as she told him, "I'll get you in there, Ace. You have my word on it."

Ainsley frowned, head shaking at them. "Be realistic, Ace. Do you really think the hospital's going to *allow* you two in our father's room after visiting hours, unsupervised, especially when everybody knows you were accused of shooting him?"

"Why not wait?" Rafe suggested. "Get a good night's sleep tonight first, and I'll take you tomorrow."

"That's right," Ainsley pleaded, "and it'll give me a chance to make a few calls in the morning, smooth things over before you go."

Sierra had to force herself not to roll her eyes at their advice. The kind of advice one might expect from cautious, sensible people like a chief financial officer and a corporate attorney.

But not a bounty hunter. Or not one like *her*, at any rate, who couldn't afford to waste time cooling her heels around Nowheresville, Arizona, waiting to get her *i*'s dotted and her *t*'s crossed.

After tossing back the last swallow of her sparkling water, she rose from the sectional and dug the car keys from her pocket. Ignoring the others' startled glances toward the jingling, she looked directly into Ace's confused eyes and said, "C'mon, cowboy, stick with me—and let's find out the rewards that can come with a willingness to seek forgiveness rather than permission."

Chapter Ten

"How about if I drive?" Ace asked as they stepped out of the elevator into the underground garage. He pulled the keys to his silver Porsche, which he'd grabbed from his study, from the pocket of the leather jacket he'd had at the condo. "My car hasn't been driven in over a month, and it's not good for the engine to let it sit too long."

In truth, he suspected that one of his brothers—probably Rafe, who knew how much Ace prized the convertible—had probably taken it on a spin or two to keep the car in good running order for him, but Ace was itching to get behind the wheel again. To once more feel some semblance of control in his own life.

"Much as I'd love to humor you," Sierra said, "you have to know, reporters will be on the lookout for a vehicle you're known to drive. Which doesn't exactly make it a good choice when we're trying to keep a low profile. But if you want to drive my beater…" Tossing him her Chevy's keys, she turned toward the garage exit. "You're more than welcome to show off your superior driving skills."

"Hey, I'm not the one who recently mowed down Bambi's cousin."

Her pretty mouth thinned, her eyes narrowing. "That was a low blow, cowboy."

"Probably," he admitted with a half smile.

"Lucky for you, I happen to appreciate a man who can deliver a decent counterpunch from time to time."

Knowing she was right about the Porsche attracting unwanted attention, he followed her out beneath a sky where countless stars stood out against the blackness bright as ice chips. Sierra's head jerked toward a furtive movement hugging the ground in the shadow of the warehouse across the street.

"Coyote, probably down out of the foothills," he said, identifying it with a glance.

"Predators are always so much closer than we imagine," she said, zipping her jacket a little higher, "but as long as they stick to hunting things that creep and crawl, it's not the hairy ones that worry me."

As they approached her car, he pushed the button to unlock it, wondering what she was hinting at and why she still seemed so skittish.

Before he could ask, she abruptly changed the subject, saying, "So tell me about Nova. What was your first impression?"

Buckling in, he smiled to himself, warmed by the thought of his expectant flesh-and-blood daughter—*his child, carrying his grandchild*—curled up fast asleep on the sofa in his study. "That I've somehow won the lottery without realizing I'd ever bought a ticket. I realize of course it's early days, but she seems to have an amazing spirit—and a generous heart, to welcome a father into it who hasn't been in her life up until now."

"You're right," Sierra said over the sound of the engine starting. "Those kinds of situations can be tricky. But it sounds as if she's accepted that it wasn't your fault that her mother chose to keep her existence from you."

"Maybe it was, in part. I had a girlfriend, after all, and her mother knew it, so maybe she was scared I would reject her or—" With a grunt of disgust at his younger self, Ace put the car in gear and started driving. "I owned up and begged Nova to forgive me for it. But she said her mother had never seemed too bothered by it. Apparently, she quickly moved on and later burned her way through her own family fortune in Europe, where the family fled to avoid any gossip over the pregnancy."

"You jet-setting rich kids sure had different ways of solving problems than those of us from my side of the tracks," Sierra commented, sounding more amazed—or possibly amused—than resentful.

"Unfortunately, Nova hasn't always had an easy time of it—the money ran out some time ago and then she accidentally discovered that the father of the child she's carrying, this guy named Ferdy, wasn't only emotionally abusive. He was a dangerous criminal as well."

"I heard something about that," Sierra said, "about him following her from New York here to try to kill her."

"I wish I could have been there for her then, could have protected her from that creep." He swallowed past the regret lodged in his throat. "If it weren't for

Nikolas—I owe him and the police both, for ending that threat and saving my daughter and granddaughter's lives."

"Granddaughter? The baby's a girl?"

He broke out in a grin. "Not just any girl, but the perfect little girl. I'm sure of it."

Throwing her head back, Sierra laughed. "Listen to you already! When that little one comes along, you're going to be insufferable. I can just see it."

As they passed a security light, he glanced her way. "*Will* you?"

"Will I what?" She shook her head.

"Will you be around to see it, Sierra? By my side, because that's what I want—yet I can't shake this feeling that you're more likely to bolt than be in my life a week from now, much less when I'm holding my first grandchild."

"Ace, you know—you know this isn't for me, don't you?" She flung an impatient gesture in the direction of the condo. "The whole family deal, with all these clinging strands, like spiders' webs *stick, stick, sticking* to a person, until you're wrapped up so tight, you can hardly breathe. I—I've enjoyed our time together, but the truth is, I'm a loner. It's my nature. Maybe I got it from my mother. She couldn't hack that whole scene, either."

He heard the flippancy in her voice, the disdain and the dismissal, but he wasn't buying any of it—not after having seen her drop her guard to let him see through—to touch, to hold, to make love to the real her.

"I think you're fooling yourself, if that's what you believe. You're alone because you've had to be, not because it suits you. You're warm and compassionate, Sierra. And soft beneath that hard-ass facade. A loving woman who deserves to be loved back."

"You don't understand. I *have* to go," she insisted, emotion clogging her voice.

"You're scared," he said. "And I understand that. This has been so sudden, this thing blazing up between us, and you're right. My family situation is a lot to wrap *my* head around, so I can only imagine how it must feel to an outsider."

"Outsider," she echoed. "That's what I'd always be here. Some lowlife Vegas bounty hunter they'll all take for a dirty gold digger. You know it and I know it, so let's nip this little fantasy of ours, this idea that we could maybe have a future, in the bud right now before someone ends up really hurt."

This time there was no mistaking the bitterness in her words. But there was something else, as well, an edge of desperation.

That was when it hit him, how badly she wanted to make him believe what she was saying. How terrified she was he wouldn't.

Too distracted to drive any farther, he quickly pulled over, alongside a barn-size metal building where custom Southwestern-style furnishings were manufactured.

"Not here," she warned, sweeping the Dumpsters, parked delivery trucks and alleyway with an anxious gaze. "If we *really* need to talk about this, at least pick somewhere with better lighting. Or someplace more open."

"Not until you tell me what's really going on. And why you've been lying to me."

"I'm not—"

"Stop it, Sierra," he said sharply. "I'm not playing games here. Tell me what you're really up to."

Glowering at him, she blurted, "Maybe I'm trying to make sure I don't get you stabbed again, you stubborn jerk! Now let's get out of here before I take back my offer to let you drive my car."

"Your car, yes. The one with the Arizona plates I'm sure aren't registered to you. What's up with that, Sierra?" he asked. "Was the transaction even legal?"

There was no answer but the sound of her rapid breathing as she braced her hands against the dash.

"Just answer me this," he said, "and please, if you care for me at all, be honest. Ice Veins's death wasn't the end of your issue with him, was it?"

He caught the faint gleam of a tear, reflected off the dash illumination, as it traced its slow path down her cheek.

Shaking her head, she whispered, "My cop friend in the organized crime division back home thinks it might've been Ice Veins's nephew who's responsible, that he put out the word from the hospital where he went after he was stabbed. Or possibly some other associate. But word on the street is there's a hit out on me."

"A contract? So you're not planning to return there," he said. "You never were at all."

"Not since I heard, no. I—Las Vegas is no longer a safe place for me. I have my doubts it ever will be."

"Then stay here, in Mustang Valley," he said, dark

visions of the thugs he'd witnessed hurting her parading through his head. He damned well wouldn't, couldn't, let those kind of scum ever hurt her like that—or worse—again. "Stay with me, not in the condo, but at the Triple R. Security there is top-notch."

"Against mob hitmen? I don't think so. What you've seen so far—those thugs were only out to hurt me, Ace, teach me a lesson," she said, shaking her head. "Now it's only a matter of time before some enterprising killer—some serious assassin—tracks me to the location of my last known job."

"We can keep you safe. *I* can."

"How can you," she demanded, "when you haven't even been able to figure out who's pulling the strings behind these attacks against your own family? Or confront the woman who switched you with Payne and Tessa Colton's real firstborn son and find out what her game is?"

"I know there's a lot on my plate right now, but Sierra, you need to trust me."

"No, Ace," she said. "You need to trust *me* on this. I know the threat I'm dealing with, the criminal underworld and how it operates, far better than you can ever hope to. I've already delayed leaving too long as it is, but after we see Payne this evening I can't—I won't put it off any longer."

He fought back the desire to argue with her, the *need* to swear that he'd do anything, face any threat, to free her of the need to live in fear. But he had obligations, too—a family counting on him, a father who deserved justice for the shooting that had left him in a coma for months.

A lump thickening his throat, he felt the loss of her tearing a hole in him as he asked, "But where will you go? How will you live? And will I ever—will you ever come back?"

She hesitated for so long he thought she wouldn't answer before finally saying, "It's probably safer for us both if you don't know the answer to any of those questions."

"Then I'll wait," he vowed. "I'll wait for you. When the time is right, when it's safe again, you'll reach out, come to me, and we'll be together. I promise you, we'll—"

"Don't wait on me," she told him, her words choked with emotion. "And promise me, Ace, you won't ever postpone a shot at happiness. Because we never have any way of knowing when it's the last one that we'll get."

GLIDING THROUGH THE dark streets, Ace clenched his jaw to keep from shouting in frustration. To keep from arguing that he damned well wasn't going to accept that, now that he'd finally found a woman who made him want to play for keeps, the two of them had zero chance of ending up together. As he struggled to come up with alternatives that wouldn't involve abandoning the family he both needed and wanted to do right by, his thoughts chased themselves in endless circles, like a dog running after its tail.

"Ace," Sierra was telling him, her voice seeming to come from a great distance. "Ace!"

"What?" he ground out.

"Slow down, will you? You just blew through that stop sign. And getting the two of us or someone else killed isn't going to fix a thing."

"You're right," he conceded as he eased off the accelerator. "I'm sorry if I scared you. I just—I'd fight a war to save you. Don't you know that?"

"You're already fighting a war of your own on more than one front right now," she reminded him, "so you're going to have to trust me to handle my own battles."

He felt torn in two, thinking of failing her when she most needed him, whether or not she was willing to admit it. "Do you even have a weapon? Or money enough to finance an extended stay away from home?"

"I'll pick up something for self-defense, and I've got the money from Selina. Most of it's in the bank, of course, but I'll make an ATM withdrawal to get me started."

"That's not going to be enough. Not for—"

"I'm used to living by my wits," she insisted.

"It's the thought of your *dying* by them that scares the hell out of me," he said. "So at least let me help you, will you? Make sure you leave Mustang Valley armed and with plenty of cold, hard cash in hand. I have a good amount, you know, buried in a cache not far from the bunker."

"You *do*?" Sierra shook her head. "Why on earth didn't you say so earlier, when Ice Veins's goons were threatening to blow my leg off over that missed payment?"

"I thought about it," he said as the lights of Mustang Valley General Hospital came into view. "But at first, I didn't trust you—no offense."

"None taken," she said, "being as I figured you for a wannabe murderer yourself. An incredibly hot one, as it turned out, but still."

"And after those thugs showed up—and Ice Veins himself, later—I figured if I mentioned I have cash, rather using my accounts to buy us some more time until the police arrived, they'd march us at gunpoint to get it and then leave two dead bodies where the money used to be."

She exhaled noisily. "You might've been raised in privileged surroundings, but I'll give you this. You're a pretty quick study when it comes to dealing with the criminal element."

As they pulled into the parking lot, he said, "So then the plan is this, right? After we see my father, we'll head back up to the bunker and get you the cash you'll need." If he thought he could hide her there, he would, but they were both all too aware that the location could never again be considered safe or secret.

"I don't want to take your money, Ace. I can't—can't say when or if I'd be able to pay you back."

"I don't give a damn about the money," he said. "You'll *take* it, and there's a gun there, too, buried in the footlocker."

Sierra snorted, shaking her head. "So you were holding out on me about the weapon, too? For *shame*, you desperado."

He shrugged. "You never gave me half a chance to

get to it, but yeah, I've got another handgun squirreled away up there."

"You know, if you don't end up going back to the high-roller CEO life, I'm pretty sure you could have a future as a bounty hunter…or a felon."

"And if you ever give up the bounty hunter business—" a smile tugged at one corner of his mouth, as well as at his heart "—maybe you could be a stand-up comic, because that's the most hilarious suggestion I've heard all night."

She chuckled as he put the car in Park, but when their eyes met, Ace felt fear, as cold and wet as fresh-poured concrete, filling up his chest and lungs. Fear of losing the woman who'd not only found but also resurrected him from the closed coffin of his life in hiding.

She must have felt it, too, for his last glimpse, as she turned from him, was of the tears gleaming on her lashes. Then she flung open the passenger door and stepped out of the car.

Following suit, he hurried after her, calling, "Sierra, don't. Please. Let's figure out a way that we can—"

"Ace, look out!" she warned him, started as a small and wiry man rose from between two cars, springing toward them, aiming something at—at *Ace*?

Camera, he realized, blinded by the flash as the man wearing black sweats, a ratty ponytail and round, steel-rimmed glasses, snapped away. With a curse, Ace raised an arm to block his camera shot, spinning away to hide his face.

"Give me that! I'll take that memory card!" Sierra advanced on the photographer, a man Ace suspected was a stringer hoping to sell dirt on him to whichever news outlet would pay the highest dollar for the images.

"No! Hey, let go of my camera! You can't—this is public property!" Short and scrawny as he looked, he held on to the strap for dear life as she fought to jerk it away.

"I'll give it right back. I promise," she said.

"Let it go. Let him go!" Ace called to her, worried she'd be injured—or possibly haul off and slug the photographer in her frustration.

Several parking spaces over, a commotion erupted. A woman screamed, and an older man yelled, "Security!"

The sounds were Ace's only warnings before he heard the roar of an engine and the triple *crack* that he instantly recognized as gunfire. A *clunk-clunk* followed—the sound of a body or bodies slamming the side of a vehicle as both Sierra and the man she'd been struggling with went down in a writhing tangle of limbs.

His pulse booming in his ears, Ace shouted Sierra's name and lurched forward but was cut off as a dark-colored luxury car—the shooters'—pulled between him and the pair.

Two more rounds exploded before the sedan peeled away, wheels squealing. As the black Mercedes fishtailed, Ace turned his head in time to glimpse a gun barrel swinging toward him. As he dove, another burst popped against the sheet metal of a parked SUV behind him and Sierra's earlier words ran through his mind. *In their line of business, witnesses are liabilities.*

But with the shrieks and cries of witnesses multiplying, the shooters didn't stick around to make sure.

Pushing himself back to his feet, Ace scrambled to the spot where he'd seen Sierra and the photographer tumble down beside the truck.

Neither one remained there, but there was a dark gleam on the otherwise dry pavement that had his heart plunging through the soles of his boots. A thick, crimson smear that led behind the pickup's front tire.

"Sierra, are you under there?" he called, wanting to cough up his own pounding heart. "They're gone now, and help's on the way."

At least he presumed that was the case, judging from the sounds of fast-approaching sirens. But it all faded to background noise as he dropped onto his knees and crawled forward, not caring about the dampness on his palms and knees as he lowered himself to peer at the limp arm flung out before him.

"Sierra!" he screamed.

The hairy arm jerked away—the photographer it belonged to groaning as he drew himself into a fetal position. At the same time someone laid a hand on his back, saying, "I'm here, Ace. Right here. But let's get him help. He's been hit, I think..."

Turning abruptly, Ace pushed himself onto his knees to where Sierra had knelt behind him. Squeezing her tight, he said, "I was—was sure you'd been shot. Are you—I thought they'd killed you."

"I'm—I'll be fine. It's just, when I fell, I hit my—" She pushed back from him, pain tightening her face as she cupped a hand over the back of her head. "Hurts so—"

Her green eyes rolled back, shuttering as she collapsed.

"Sierra!" he yelled, catching her and lowering her limp form to the pavement—and praying he wouldn't find a bullet wound that he had missed at first.

Chapter Eleven

With the night strobe-lit by the flashing lights of emergency vehicles, Ace tuned out the sounds behind him. The frantic voices, running footsteps and the engine sounds all faded as his senses focused in on the essentials. Was Sierra bleeding? Breathing? Was that her heartbeat throbbing beneath his fingertips or his own leaping pulse?

Though he found little in the way of blood, one thing was for damned sure. She wasn't responding to his desperate pleas—"Open your eyes, *look* at me!"—any more than she did when he shook her roughly by the shoulders to try to rouse her.

Feeling as helpless as he ever had in his life, he remembered the loud thumps he'd heard when she and the photographer dove for the pavement along with her pained look when she'd reached to touch the back of her head. Before he could check for an injury, however, someone touched his shoulder.

A red-haired man in a blue uniform was holding some sort of medical kit, his younger female partner a half step behind him. "We need you to step back, sir.

I'm an EMT, and she's a paramedic. Our ambulance was just leaving when we heard the shots, but we've got the vic—is this your wife?—from here."

Now that the danger appeared to have passed, others were rushing to help, as well, Ace saw, heroic men and women coming out of the hospital in scrubs, street clothes and uniforms. But his focus was on the man's startling question. What the hell did it matter what Sierra was to him when he couldn't even tell if she was still alive?

"Just help her, please! I don't know if she's breathing!"

The smaller paramedic, with her curly, dark hair and a birthmark partly covering her face, squeezed between the men, kneeling to check Sierra's vitals before giving her partner the pulse, respiration and blood pressure results. Ace felt his own breath hitch, what felt like his heart restarting. *She hasn't died on me. Thank God.*

Recovering his voice, he explained, "She slammed her head pretty hard. Against that truck, I think," as the pair continued their examination. "And the man wedged underneath—I believe he's been shot."

When he glanced over, he saw the photographer had been moved, and two women, one in a lab coat and another wearing scrubs, were tending to the injured man. He was lying on his back, clutching his right shoulder as he wailed in pain.

Someone else grabbed Ace's arm, turning him around. "I need you to come with me. Now."

Ace blinked, his daze evaporating at the sight of Sergeant Spencer Colton in uniform, his normally boyish face aged both by tension and the flashing red-and-white lights of his K-9 SUV parked at an angle nearby, its driver's-side door thrown open.

Still shaking, Ace pulled away. "I can't leave. Those bastards in the black Mercedes—they hurt Sierra, maybe bad. She needs me here, in case they come back for her."

"Are you a doctor or a bodyguard?" Spencer demanded bluntly. "Because unless you're either, there's nothing you can do for her right now—nothing more important than getting in this car and helping me catch these shooters right now. As far as I know, you're the only one who got a good look at them."

"Bodyguard... I should call Callum," Ace stammered, thinking of his brother. But still in shock, he hesitated, his feet rooted like tree trunks as Sierra jerked partly upright with a groan, rolled onto her side and started retching. With the two medics in his way, he couldn't tell if she was fully conscious, only that she was seriously hurting.

"Come on," Spencer said gruffly. "There's no time to make calls at the moment, and she's in good hands here. I'll leave an officer standing guard. Hospital security, too, and the ER's right here, filled with all the machines and medicine and expertise she needs. Now, let's go and help her in the one way only *you* can—by stopping these people before they have a chance to strike again."

Ace nodded numbly before calling to Sierra, "I'll be back soon," though he seriously doubted she was in any shape to register his words. Still, he needed to say them, if only to assure himself that he would find his way back to her. That he would find her well again and safe.

Inside Spencer's SUV unit, which smelled faintly of the dark brown K-9 Ace had spotted riding in a cage in the rear, the sergeant asked as he drove, "Just how good a look did you get? Maybe a license plate? A partial?"

"You've got to be kidding. They were too damned fast—and I was too busy dodging bullets. I got a glimpse, at best, of both the driver and the shooter—both white males with dark hair, one with a goatee maybe—but nothing I could swear to."

"It'll have to be enough. And I'd bet my next paycheck the car'll turn out to be stolen anyway," Spencer said. "We had a patrol in pursuit, but they lost sight of the vehicle somewhere near the industrial area. We're going to see if we can intercept them, maybe heading out of town."

Fresh fear tightened Ace's gut. "The industrial area? I need to call my family." Fumbling for his cell phone, he said, "I have to warn them, in case these shooters have somehow connected Sierra to me and know about my condo there." An image of his sleeping daughter flashed before his eyes.

"Why would they want to go there?" Spencer darted a glance his way, his hazel eyes intense. "Do you think you might be a target of these— It's the Las Vegas underworld again, isn't it? This has their filthy fingerprints all over it, and after the motel shooting, Sierra told me how she's tied up with those gangsters."

Bristling at his tone, Ace said, "She might've been in over her head, but she's no criminal, Spencer. She was working her tail off—honestly and legally—to pay off her father's gambling debts when Ice Veins came after her once he'd passed. She only ran into real trouble when she refused to allow herself to be corrupted."

"So she's a bounty hunter with a code," Spencer allowed, still sounding dubious. "But she's still mixed up with the wrong people. People intent on turning my town into a war zone, leaving heaven only knows how many innocents as collateral damage if that's what it takes to punish her. Including maybe you and whoever's at your place if they suspect Sierra might've escaped their drive-by shooting and they head over there to hunt her down."

"Speaking of which, I'm making this call now," Ace said gruffly, pushing a number from his phone's list of frequent contacts. Moments later he was briefly explaining the situation to Grayson, who was fortunately still at the condo with Rafe, Ainsley, Nova and Nikolas. Grayson was able to quickly grasp Ace's concerns regarding security. He then promised to take charge of making certain the property and everyone inside it remained secure until Ace or Spencer assured them that the threat had passed.

As Ace disconnected, a call came over Spencer's police radio, the dispatcher reporting a vehicle fire in progress at an address only a few blocks from their location.

Cursing in frustration, Spencer goosed the accelerator before taking the next corner fast enough that his police dog barked in alarm from his crate.

"Sorry, Boris, buddy," Spencer called back before

turning his attention to Ace. “That’ll be the shooters’ car, I’m betting. Dumped and torched in favor of whatever getaway vehicle they had stashed and waiting. Which means they’re one step ahead of us.”

“That’s the car, all right,” Ace said as the two of them came upon the flames, which were leaping high enough that he had no doubt the someone had doused the black Mercedes in an accelerant before setting it ablaze. With its front doors standing open, it had been abandoned along the street outside the security fencing surrounding the metal sheds that comprised a local storage facility.

“Could be they stole it out of one of those storage garages in the first place.” Spencer drove past the burning car to point his headlights at what turned out to be a cut chain on the lot’s main gate. “Mostly, the larger bays at these facilities are used for recreational vehicles and boats and such, but occasionally, somebody’ll tuck a vehicle away for long-term storage.”

“An almost-new, high-end Mercedes?” Ace asked, glancing back toward the burning sedan and hearing sirens in the distance.

“Could belong to a drug dealer. Which would make this theft a crook-on-crook crime. Right now, though, I’m more worried about the shooting than any property crime.”

“But how will we find them now that they’ve switched vehicles?”

“It could take some legwork—and a little luck,” Spencer admitted as the first fire engine came into view down the street. “I’ll call in Kerry,” he added, referring to Rafe’s detective fiancée, “have her drag the facility’s owner out of bed to review the security camera footage, assuming any of them are actually operational. Though by the time we get all that accomplished, these guys'll likely be long gone. Unless they decide it's worth sticking around to try again."

"Surely they won't risk that," said Ace, a slippery feeling low in his gut as he remembered being cut off from Sierra as the shots rang out, "not after shooting up a parking lot in front of witnesses." After talking to Grayson on the phone, he'd nearly convinced himself that he'd been overreacting with his earlier fear that the killers might head over to his condo. Or maybe—he had no idea—his overblown fear of something happening to his newly discovered daughter was a normal part of this whole parenting routine.

"Like you said yourself before, they were in and out too fast to see much. Maybe they'll figure they were quick enough to chance it. What else can you tell me?"

Ace frowned, remembering his final, frustrating conversation with Sierra before all hell had broken loose. "She'd just told me she needed to take off, run from Mustang Valley before she got me or anyone I cared for hurt. Her cop friend in Vegas had told her there might've been a hit put out on her because of Ice Veins. By his nephew, most likely."

The hydraulic air brakes of the fire truck momentarily captured their attention, its flashing emergency lights splashing the streets in garish illumination that competed with the leaping flames.

"Detective Stratford from the organized crime bureau?" Spencer asked as the crew came off the pumper.

"She called me to vouch for Sierra earlier, after the motel shooting."

"Sierra didn't mention the name," Ace said, "but you're probably right."

"I'll give the detective a call, see if I can get anything more on what we're dealing with. But right now I'm damned worried. Because my instincts tell me that these kinds of hired killers aren't the type that give up easy—that until Sierra's dead, they'll keep on coming, no matter who stands in their way, to collect the bounty on your bounty hunter."

Ace opened his mouth, meaning to argue, *She's not my bounty hunter*, only to shut it firmly as an idea struck him. An idea that just might be the solution to their problem, if only they could pull it off.

"So what if somehow we *did* convince these hit men, and everyone else, that tonight's attack in the parking lot *succeeded* in its mission?" Ace suggested. "What if we somehow coordinated things with the hospital and Detective Stratford and then you set up a press conference—a news briefing condemning Sierra Madden's *murder* right here in Mustang Valley?"

"You're talking about faking Sierra's death? Do you have any idea how hard something like that really is to pull off? How many levels of authority I'd need to run this past, how many people would have to sign off to coordinate—"

"Let me ask you, then, Spencer, these so-called *authorities*, are they going to be the ones cleaning up the bloody mess, putting out the fires and notifying next of kin when more people end up hurt or killed in the crossfire? And are they going to be ready to deal with *me* if I do end up losing a woman I've very much come to care for, after I've already lost so much?"

SIERRA COULDN'T UNDERSTAND WHY, before they'd buried her, no one had made sure her mouth was somehow sealed shut. Dry and dusty as her throat was, she imagined it was full of grave dust. The dirty, gritty taste of it, along with a sudden, overwhelming revulsion, woke her, stomach heaving, and a firm but steady hand helped her as she rolled to one side.

"That's it. Just take a sip of water, and you'll feel so much better," said a female voice, kind and reassuring and definitely alive, the same as she apparently was.

Still, the sound exploded in her head and the room's lights—so many lights in this room—felt like spikes of pure pain driven through the back of her skull. She threw up into a shallow basin held by a woman in large glasses and matching raspberry-pink scrubs, whose platinum-streaked hair was shaved on one side of her head and chin length on the other.

When the nurse, whose lopsided hairstyle confused Sierra's vision somehow, started talking again, the words looped back onto themselves and tangled into gibberish. The one word she did make out, *concussion*, had her shaking her throbbing head and struggling to rise from what she realized was a hospital bed, which took up most of a small room, whose lack of windows left her even more disoriented, not knowing whether it was day or night.

"I can't just lie around here, waiting for a bunch of

tests and—what if someone else ends up hurt?" Images streaked like meteors through her memory: black car, gun muzzle flashes, a shiny dark smear on the pavement. Her pulse bumped at her throat.

"Where's Ace?" she cried, panicked at the thought there was something she was forgetting. Something bigger, something worse. "Where is he? Is he—did they—" Staccato bursts of gunfire echoing in her ears, she couldn't stop the hot tears from streaming down her face. "They shot him, didn't they? Was he—is he still—"

Firm hands pushed her gently back down. "Settle down, Miss Higgins. Now, don't you remember? We've been through all this before already. Mr. Colton's fine. He's just stepped out for a few minutes to make a phone call. You're in a secure room at the hospital. There's no need for you to be frightened. I'm here to stay with you until he gets back."

Sierra didn't remember any previous discussion and couldn't understand for the life of her why this woman was calling her by a stranger's name. But Sierra was distracted from that question by the thought of a male boxer from her gym, who'd ended up sidelined for weeks, unable to drive or work at his day job or even watch TV or read the paper after a serious concussion.

Her blood ran cold at the thought of being so helpless—a sitting duck for whoever walked through that door, intent on finishing what the gunmen in the parking lot had started.

"I have to get out of here," she said, breaking free of the nurse's grip and attempting to thrust her feet over the bedside. A raised railing blocked her, so she pushed herself upright, explaining, "I have to leave before they—"

With the abrupt change of her head's elevation, a dark wave overrode her doubled vision. Pain and nausea collided, and she grasped the railing and closed her eyes, needing a moment to ride out the churning storm.

"They'll hurt you, too, when they barge in. Get away from me," she warned, forcing her eyes open.

The nurse moved fast—a raspberry-pink blur—through the doorway to call into the corridor, "I need some help here—another sedative!"

Ace passed her, saying, "That won't be necessary. I've got this."

His gaze latching on to Sierra, he raised his palms, his expression both concerned and calming. "You're fine now. We're safe. I'm right here with you, and that's where I intend to stay."

Though it still beat much too quickly, her heart resettled into her chest when he came close, so warm and real and solid as he enfolded her hand in his and squeezed it gently.

"I thought—" she began, voice breaking with emotion. "I thought the nurse was lying. I thought I'd gotten you killed, just like I did that guy with the camera."

"I ran into that photographer's husband out in the parking lot, while I was out making my call where I could get a halfway decent cell signal," Ace told her, "and he said how grateful he was that you helped him hide underneath that pickup. He came out of surgery just fine last night."

"Last night?" she interrupted.

Ace nodded, scrubbing a hand over a lightly shadowed jaw. "You were out briefly at first, sleeping off and on since. But it's almost eight-thirty in the morning."

As she grappled with the loss of time—and wondered if part of her wooziness and memory issue might be related to some drug or another she'd been given, Ace continued speaking.

"The cameraman's recovering from a gunshot wound to the shoulder, but he *will* recover—because of your quick thinking."

"He never would've been shot if I hadn't hung around here longer than I should have." She raised her voice, needing to make certain she was getting through the noise inside her head. "Which is why I have to go, right now, before it's too late. What if it's *you* next time? I couldn't—I couldn't live with that."

Grabbing the railing, she threw one foot over with the intention of climbing. But Ace surprised her, trapping her wrist in one hand and producing a zip tie—which he must have swiped out of her street clothes—and securing her arm to the railing before she could get out a whimper.

"You're confused right now and groggy, so let me explain. Here's how things are at the moment," he told her, while she gaped in shock at the betrayal. "According to the doctor, you need to stay at least another day here, if not longer, so that smack to the head you took can be properly assessed and you can begin the healing process. In your current state, you're not safe to drive or care for yourself—and you certainly aren't fit to make decisions."

"I'm not an invalid, or a child, either," she insisted, her face burning as she yanked helplessly at the zip tie. "I'm fine—or I will be. As soon as I'm clear of you and some nurse who can't even get my name straight. So let me out of here."

"Uh, about that name thing," Ace said, grimacing as his eyes avoided hers. "There's something else I have to tell you. A decision that's been made."

Shaking with outrage, she said, "There's nothing I want to hear from you except, 'I'm sorry. I've overstepped here big time. Now let me cut this zip tie, and here's the keys to your car so you can get on down the road.'"

He winced. "I *am* sorry, for the record, but I'm not about to let you walk out of here, Sierra. For one thing, the doctors think you'll be okay, that this is only a mild to moderate concussion, but they haven't completely ruled out a more serious brain injury."

"I'd have to be brain *dead* to want to be tied up here, helpless, while those killers are out there somewhere, circling like sharks," she said. "And anyway, don't you still have plenty of troubles of your own to deal with? Have you even visited your father yet? Or looked any more into this thing about—"

"I've been a little busy, Miss Higgins," he said sharply, countering her attempts at distraction by throwing out that odd name again, "handling the details of your unfortunate demise."

"Demise?" she echoed, her skin creeping with the

memory of waking to the feeling that she'd been choking on a mouthful of grave dirt. "You mean, like *death*? Are you sure you didn't get knocked upside the head, too, Ace? I mean, please correct me if I'm wrong here, but I'm still kicking."

"Not, I'm afraid, according to the press conference given by Sergeant Spencer Colton last night, condemning this outrageous act of violence and asking the public for assistance in bringing your killers to justice. Which is why, for the time being, you're going to be referred to by the name of Iris Higgins."

She blinked hard. "*Iris Higgins?* That's the best you could do? Sounds like somebody's great-aunt who smells of mothballs. The kind whose tuna casseroles go untouched at family reunions." Not that she'd ever experienced such a gathering, but she had definitely heard things. Terrifying things that made her glad she'd never been forced to hang out with people she had nothing in common with but the tiniest trace of DNA.

Ace chuckled at that. "Sorry, Sierra. It was three in the morning, and anyway, I happen to have known a very kindhearted older lady named Iris, whose casseroles were very well regarded."

"Don't make a joke of this—of me," she said, feeling sick, helpless and frustrated, all of which left her furious—and scared out of her wits. "We're both going to end up dead if those killers figure out you've got me sitting here trussed up like this year's Thanksgiving turkey for them."

"There's a guard keeping watch outside in the hall, and anyway, the shooters are long gone," he told her.

"While you were, um, out of it, Spencer—Sergeant Colton—and I found the Mercedes, torched, in the industrial area."

A different fear pulsed through her as she thought of Nova and the siblings who'd met with them last night. "Not near your condo? Is your family all right?"

"Not too close, but I warned them just in case. They're fine. Worried about you, mainly."

"But not mourning me, I take it?" she asked before it occurred to her that though her "death" might cause brief shock and perhaps the same momentary sadness many felt whenever someone in her early thirties bought it, there were few who'd seriously grieve her. Not even the half-feral cat that had shared her home, as long as her friend Brie kept popping open the tops of his canned food and fluffing his favorite pillow now and then.

"I decided to let some of my family in on it," Ace told her, "just those who needed to know, since I'm going to need their help to keep you hidden, and Kerry, too, since she's working with Spencer on this. And all of them know how imperative it is that as far as anyone else is concerned, even the medical staff who first saw you when you first came in downstairs, you succumbed as a result of the injuries sustained in the parking lot last night."

"So you plan to keep me hidden?" Sierra echoed. "Or *prisoner*, you mean. How long do you imagine—"

"That depends on what your friend, Detective Stratford, tells us."

"*What?* Brie's in on this madness, too?" Sierra's eyes burned at what felt like another betrayal.

"She's one hundred percent in, Sierra—which is why she's put the word out both on the streets of Las Vegas through one of her confidential informants and through an LVMPD press release regarding your murder. Because otherwise, she assured me, the attempts would never end until you really were dead."

"No," Sierra said, head throbbing and hot tears spilling as she covered her eyes with her hands. "No, no, no. Tell me this is a nightmare."

"We only wanted to keep you *alive*, Sierra. You were helpless, hurt," Ace said, his warm brown eyes holding a plea for understanding as he passed her a box of tissues from the rolling table by her bed. Yet, in his voice, she heard, too, the set stubbornness of a man fully committed to his action. "I was terrified you really might die—and willing to sacrifice anything to keep that from happening."

Pulling free several tissues, she wiped at her eyes. "But don't you understand? Sacrificing my life, what I've made of it to this point—no matter what a mess it might look like by Colton standards—isn't a choice you were entitled to, you or Brie, the sergeant, or anybody but me. What about my home, my—"

"First off, I'm the last Colton in the world to judge what anybody else has going on in her life, especially someone like you. You were only trying to do the right thing by your father and then stick to your professional ethics when it came to Ice Veins's nephew."

"Such a brilliant decision on my part," she grumbled, though she knew in her heart that even if she could go back in time and amend that *misstep*, she'd still haul that piece of trash to jail—if only to wipe that smug sneer off his face.

"I'm so sorry to have to tell you this, but Detective Stratford informed us there's been a fire at your townhouse. The cause hasn't been determined yet, but—"

"Was—was anyone hurt?" Her stomach pitched again as she thought about her neighbors, along with any firefighters who might have stumbled into a blaze triggered by what she had little doubt would turn out to be arson.

"No one injured," Ace said, "but I'm—I'm afraid the place was gutted, the contents a total loss. There's—there's nothing left there to go back to. I've been asked to tell you that your cat is safe and doing very well with the detective."

Relieved as Sierra was to know that Rocky was all right, a lump thickened in her throat at the thought of everything she'd ever worked for, every memory collected—including irreplaceable photos of both the mother who had left when she was little and the father she had loved so dearly—stolen from her, along with her name. But she was too numb to shed any more tears.

Taking a step closer, he smoothed a few strands of hair off her face. "I've had a taste of what it's like, having an entire life, an identity, ripped out from under me. Of how hard it was to—"

"Don't compare us, compare this. You still have *family*," she said, her pain so blinding, she could only flail out at the nearest, the only, available target. "Hell, even some with your DNA. They've made it clear you're still a Colton, with a bank account, the fancy car and condo to go with it and a whole damned posse that has your back. Who do I have left now? What?"

"You have *me*, Sierra, for whatever that's worth," he said, his tone giving the words the weight of a sacred vow. "And a safe place to rest and heal, for as long as you'll need it."

"And you have *me* freaking tied here," she fired back. "Cut me loose, and I'm gone—because you have totally crossed the line."

AS ACE STEPPED into the hallway, he did his damnedest not to look like a man who'd been absolutely gutted. Arranging his face in what he hoped would pass for a neutral expression, he murmured a greeting to his half brother Callum, knowing there was no one he could trust more than the former navy SEAL and bodyguard to watch over the comings and goings around this out-of-the-way third-floor room, one Spencer had talked a helpful hospital administrator into setting up for the hastily christened Iris Higgins.

"You okay?" Callum asked him, the concern in his bright blue eyes telling Ace he hadn't pulled off the casual look as well as he had hoped. "Or maybe I should ask, is she?" He nodded his reddish blond head in the direction of Sierra's room.

"I'll be fine, eventually," Ace assured him. "As for her, I've given her a lot to process, and she's not a bit happy about any of it. So please, keep a careful eye out for every possibility."

Callum reached out and shook his hand, promising, "You can count on me."

After leaving his brother with his thanks, Ace tried to tell himself that in suggesting the plan to fake her death, he'd only done what was necessary—what both Spencer and Sierra's detective friend from Las Vegas, along with Mustang Valley's police chief, had all agreed it was going to take to save Sierra. But the look of betrayal on her face, the hurt and loss he'd seen there, had him remembering all too painfully how he'd felt when all of his own choices had been taken from him. Had he, out of love and fear, done the same thing to her by jumping the gun too quickly instead of waiting until she'd been in the position to make the call herself?

Groaning at the answer—and the wrenching fear that Sierra might never forgive him for it—he pushed the elevator's button to take him downstairs.

When the door opened, Ainsley paused her pacing to look up at him. Though her dark hair was neatly pulled up and she was dressed in one of the stylish blouse, skirt and jacket combos she might wear to the office, he noted the subtle signs of stress—or at least sleep deprivation: an earring missing, eyeliner smudged and a slight puffiness beneath her eyes.

Figuring he looked even worse after his all-nighter, he asked simply, "Are you all right? I would've thought that after everything last night, you would've gone back home to get some rest."

Though Spencer had had a sweep done of the area around the condo to reassure everyone the assassins weren't lurking anywhere nearby, the events of last night had resulted in numerous calls among the siblings—and between Ace and Nova, too—as plans were made, details ironed out and nerves were soothed. Ace couldn't imagine any of them had gotten more than a few hours of broken sleep, at best.

"I'll be fine," she said, hoisting a take-out cup that he recognized as coming from Java Jane's, "and before you ask—Rafe, Grayson and Nova and Nikolas are all okay, too, this morning."

"Nova..." he echoed, his sleep-deprived brain once more jolted by his new reality—his responsibility—as the only surviving parent of a grown daughter.

"You've really impressed her, by the way." Ainsley's smile was approving. "From what I could see, you handled that first meeting really well."

"Not as much as she impressed me. And if I didn't botch things with her last night, it was totally beginner's luck," he said. "But I'm determined to muddle my way through the whole dad thing as best as I can."

"I always secretly suspected that you had it in you," she teased, "even all those years you spent playing the part of corporate shark and Arizona's most eligible bachelor."

"Well, I've been *retired* from the former role and I'm pretty sure that at this point in my life, I'm permanently out of the running for the latter *honor* anyway," he said, recalling the embarrassment—not to mention the teasing by his friends and siblings over being named man candy by some swanky lifestyle magazine out of Phoenix. "So is that all you came to see me about?"

She shook her head. "Actually, no. I was really hoping I might catch you before you went to see our father."

"I was on my way for a visit," he said, a mix of dread,

fatigue and anticipation swirling at the thought of seeing their once-strong and vibrant father diminished by months in a comatose condition. "But I have to tell you, I just caught a whiff of that coffee you're drinking, and it's calling my name big time. So if you want to talk, how about we head over to the cafeteria? It won't be half as good, but beggars can't be choosers."

"You're on, but I'm buying," she insisted. "And you're having breakfast while you're at it. Before you open that mouth of yours to argue, stop. You've already lost more weight than is good for you, and I'd bet my next paycheck you can't remember the last time you had an actual meal."

She would lose that bet, he knew, recalling the takeout dinner he'd shared with Sierra yesterday. A shared meal that had been a prelude to a conversation, and then a union that had torn his heart wide open…

"Ace? Don't tune me out like that," Ainsley warned, her eyes narrowing as she studied him intently. "Now, come on, big brother. Let's get some food in you."

"All right. You win, but only because it's too damn early in the morning to go arguing with a lawyer," he conceded, but as drained as he was feeling, he realized, too, how much he'd missed his sister's harping on him—a sure sign that she cared.

Inside the hospital's cafeteria, she waited until he was seated with a tray containing a large black coffee and a plate with scrambled eggs, bacon, wheat toast and a side of mixed fruit before asking him how Sierra was this morning.

"*Iris* is conscious, but she's hurting," he said, forcing

himself to use the name Sierra so detested, even though the other tables in the corner they had chosen were all empty. "More so once I told her what we—what *I* insisted that we do to save her."

Ainsley shook her head. "I can't imagine waking up hurt and terrified after that ordeal, only to find out that everyone you've ever known has just gotten the news that you've been murdered. She must be—I don't even—"

"She's frightened and bewildered—and furious with me for doing this to her," he said, what little appetite he had dying at the thought.

"With *you*? But you meant—you were only trying to save her life."

He waved off her argument. "It doesn't matter. What matters is that she's alive now. If that means alive and hating my guts, I guess I'll have to live with that."

Reaching past the small cranberry muffin she'd ordered, Ainsley touched the top of his hand. "Don't give up on her too quickly. Not if you're really in love with her."

"Who said anything about love?" he demanded. Except that *he* nearly had, spilling his guts to Sierra like some smitten teenager after they had had sex, and what was more, he'd meant it in the moment. And still felt it—and couldn't keep himself from feeling it even now.

"No need to bite my head off," Ainsley scolded. "I'll drop the subject for the moment—on the condition that you have some coffee and make a dent in that breakfast."

"I'm not in the mood to sit here and chow down like everything's just fine."

"Please, Ace," she said, her eyes, so much lighter than his own, implored…and reminded him of the tremendous debt he owed her, for standing by and helping him when few others would have. A debt that left him humbled and contrite.

"Sure, Ainsley, and I'm sorry," he said. "I'll eat."

By thinking of the food as fuel, he managed to get down most of it and all the coffee. Neither made up for the night's sleep he'd missed out on, but he had to admit that he felt more human for the effort.

After disposing of their trash and going for a refill on the coffee, he told his sister, "Thanks for that. And for coming here to see me."

Frowning, she blew out a breath. "You may not thank me after I've told you what I have to tell you."

At her serious expression, he felt a cold chill overtake him as his thoughts ran to his stepmother. "Genevieve wants me kept out, doesn't she?" he guessed. "She's refusing to let me see our father? I understand what she's been through, and it's only natural that she wants to protect him, but if I could only talk to her, make her understand, I'm sure she'll—"

"No, no," Ainsley assured him. "Marlowe's talked things over with her. Went over again why the clues have never really added up to you, from the height and size of the shooter seen on the video to that Sun Devils pin Dad's assistant found in the boardroom after he was shot—"

"Speaking of that pin," Ace said. "While I was… *away*, I spent some time online, searching Arizona Sun Devils alumni lists and forums. I kept hoping a name would jump out, or maybe I'd find out that our favorite *evil* stepmother was secretly some kind of closet Sun Devils groupie."

He smiled and raised his eyebrows to show he wasn't serious. Or not completely anyway.

"Selina?" Ainsley smiled. "That really is a stretch, big brother. As hateful as that woman is, she's made it crystal clear she'd never risk killing the golden goose for a moment's gratification. But getting back to Genevieve, Marlowe explained that even Spencer's now convinced that you were set up from the start."

The warmth of affection served to thaw some of his tension. "What would I do without my little sisters?"

"I won't promise you Genevieve's a hundred percent comfortable yet, but she's willing to try. She does ask, though, that you wait until—"

"But I've been *waiting* for months now. I won't be put off any longer," Ace said, sharply enough that a few diners some distance away turned to look, shifting uncomfortably in their seats.

Realizing he had startled them, Ace grimaced and raised his hands. "I'm sorry," he said before looking back at Ainsley and repeating the apology more quietly. "I didn't mean to take it out on you, but surely, you have to understand how big a deal this is for me. I haven't seen Dad since before—"

"Until *tomorrow*, I was about to say," Ainsley continued, "since he's being transferred to a room on the third floor this morning."

"Why would they do that?" Ace asked, realizing

his father might well end up close to where they'd stashed Sierra.

"I guess there's some kind of maintenance issue with his room that can't be safely addressed with a patient in there," Ainsley explained. "Not only that, but the specialist overseeing his treatment is coming by this morning to see if there's been any more progress. Or anything they can do to make his transition to full consciousness easier."

Anger falling away, Ace felt both soaring hope and deepening worry. "So they really think Dad's waking up? That he'll be—that he'll still be *him* once he comes out of it?"

Most of all, Ace wanted their father back, whole and well, wanted him to be fully present to hear Ace beg forgiveness for the harsh words they had exchanged not long before he'd been found shot in the boardroom. But Ace desperately wanted to know, too, who had pulled the trigger. Was it possible that his father would remember what had happened and could name the culprit?

"I pray he will," said Ainsley, "but I don't know. No one does, but we're really hoping the neurologist can give us a clearer idea after this assessment. So can I tell Marlowe you'll hold off? Maybe until tomorrow?"

Ace struggled to swallow, feeling as if a walnut had lodged inside his throat, shell and all. "Yeah," he said, his voice strained. "Of course I can do that. For Dad, and you and all of our siblings. And Genevieve, of course." Even if his stepmother didn't completely trust him again, he knew she'd been through hell of late and bore her no ill will.

Shaking it off, he asked, "So are you heading back to the ranch to get some rest now, or over to the office? Because if you don't mind, I could use a ride. I need to catch a shower and a few hours' sleep before I—"

"I'm afraid we aren't done here, Ace," she said, straightening in her seat and putting on what Ace recognized from all the years they'd lived and worked together as her lawyer face. Which often meant she was about to lay some hard truth on him.

Bracing himself, he asked, "What is it?"

"A lot happened while you were away," she said before cutting to the chase, "but specifically, we need to talk about—about your biological mother."

His heart kicked in his chest, since that was the last thing he'd expected. "You mean—you've found the nurse who switched me with—with our parents' real son?"

"We're almost one hundred percent positive we know who she is. Only she hasn't lived under the name Luella Smith in decades. And she's come a long way from the young maternity nurse and single mother she once—"

"Who is this woman? *Where* is she?" he demanded, his head spinning under a barrage of questions.

Her shoulders tense, Ainsley blew out an audible breath. "I know this is going to come as a tremendous shock, Ace, and I'm so sorry, especially after everything you've been through."

"Please don't pussyfoot around it. I need to know the truth. Now."

Her gaze softening, she nodded. "She's here, in Mustang Valley. She's been in the area for years now. And I'm afraid you know her."

"Her *name*, Ainsley," he said through clenched teeth.

"It's Micheline," she told him. "Micheline Anderson."

"But that's— That can't be right." The cafeteria's outer walls seemed to whirl around him. Or maybe it was just his head, because this was impossible. "That Being Your Best You motivational speaker woman? The one who owns the Affirmation Alliance Center just outside town?"

"Yes, I'm afraid that's her. And I'm sorry to tell you, the news is even worse than that. What she's been doing—the talks, the acts of charity, and her corporate training sessions—might all look good on the surface, but she's about helping herself and not self-help. Most of her followers have no idea. They're brainwashed to thinks it's all legit, but there's a core group that's been funneling money from various illegal schemes back to her."

A buzzing started in his ears as she told him about what she and Santiago had gone through at the Marriage Institute—and what they'd discovered. But as horrifying as it was to imagine his sister having been in danger, his brain still couldn't accept that the same woman he'd occasionally crossed paths with at cocktail parties for charitable events, an attractive, older blonde who dressed for success and always seemed to attract a horde of eager admirers.

Though he'd never been especially impressed by the platitudes she spouted as if they were nuggets of ancient wisdom, he had to ask himself, if she were really his biological mother, wouldn't she have at least have been curious enough to try to make conversation with him—or even occasionally look his way?

"Are you listening to me, Ace?" Ainsley was looking at him strangely. "I was just telling you how our IT guy, Daniel—"

"I know who Daniel is, for heaven's sake."

"—traced back that email saying that you're not a real Colton back to that dark web geek who sent it, Harley Watts. Spencer says Watts still isn't talking, but—"

His head spinning, Ace blurted, "How does any of this connect Micheline back to me?"

"Watts is one of those AAG cult members, it turns out. Micheline's not admitting that she knew anything to do with him sending out those emails or has any connection whatsoever, but there's no refuting those photographs. You can see for yourself from the photos, if you disregard the style and age changes, that Micheline is definitely Luella Smith."

"But if it's true, if she really switched me for the real Ace Colton—" It would never feel less than surreal to say that "—what could she be up to now, exposing her own crimes forty years later?"

"That's what terrified me so much about overhearing her saying it's time to put her big plan into motion. What does she have in store for us?"

"Whatever it is," Ace said grimly, "I have absolutely no doubt it's bad news for our family. And maybe not only the ones we know about."

"What do you mean?"

"I mean," he said, "that we still don't know what she's done with—with the child that she stole. Where the devil is our brother, and how does he figure into her scheme?"

Ace knew that his siblings had hired a private investigator in an attempt to find "Luella Smith's" missing son. They'd even come across someone claiming to be the true heir, but that guy had turned out to be nothing but a phony opportunist.

"We still haven't been able to track down our—our real brother," said Ainsley, "only I *can* tell you we've learned that Micheline did raise a son, Jake Anderson."

"Just the one child?" It had occurred to Ace that it was possible that he could have other siblings, siblings that his biological mother had chosen to raise.

"Only one," Ainsley confirmed, "a son whom she's estranged from—and who's missing from the area since he was seventeen."

"But this Jake Anderson was raised right here, in Mustang Valley?" Ace waited for his sister's nod before adding, "And he's my age?"

"As far as we can determine."

"That's odd. That I don't know him, I mean. You'd have thought we would've crossed paths growing up, wouldn't you? In school or playing sports? You know how it is around here. Small enough that everyone's at least aware of others in the same age range."

Ainsley nodded. "I do. But I also know how isolated, how insular those AAG people are. What I saw at the Marriage Institute…"

"Did someone actually hurt you there?" Ace asked,

his protective hackles rising as he realized that she must have glossed over some of the more harrowing details in her earlier account. "I would've thought I could at least trust Santiago to keep you safe." He knew that his sister and the PI had a past, but it had been obvious, even from his distracted vantage, that there were still lingering feelings between the two.

Ainsley waved off his concern. "Whatever we went through, it was more than worth it to figure out what those charlatans were really up to and how Micheline was connected. And as far as Santiago goes—he was... he is amazing."

"So you two are back together?" At her nod, he smiled. "Well that's some good news, at least. *Isn't* it?"

A little blush dawned in her cheeks. "The best."

"Then I'm glad for you both," he said, smiling to see his sister happy. She deserved that much and so much more, and Santiago was a good man. "But about this Jake Anderson—"

"What I was getting at," she hurried to add, "is that with the center so far from town and full of so many of her followers eager to do her bidding, I'm betting she kept her son isolated, had him homeschooled out there so we'd never meet him."

"Makes perfect sense, if she was trying to hide her crime—and a kidnapped child—right under our family's noses."

"But that still doesn't tell us why she took him in the first place," Ainsley said, "or how she's involved with what's been going on around here lately."

"Yet you're absolutely sure she is?"

"Oh, yes. If you'd been there to hear her, if you'd seen the sly look on that woman's face—" Sighing in frustration, Ainsley shook her head. "We think—our siblings and I—that somehow, Micheline's behind our father's shooting. She probably had one of her minions do it, just the way she must've put Watts up to sending out that email."

Ace's gut told him Ainsley might be right. Bizarre as it sounded, it made a kind of twisted sense that a woman who'd hated a man enough to steal his child might still despise him enough to try to kill him, even decades later. "Why now, though? And to what end?" he asked.

"We don't know. So far there've been no demands for money, no blackmail attempts or anything like that, so whatever this *big plan* is, we have no clue."

"Have you confronted her and questioned her directly? Has *anyone*?"

Ainsley made a face. "It's a complicated situation. I've spoken to the police, of course, about what I overheard, but they're telling me it's way too nebulous to act on. She might've been speaking of those seminars she does, or some other project related to her self-help business—"

"Her *cult*, you mean."

"Right," said Ainsley. "The police are looking into her background, keeping an eye on her activities, but until they have something solid, they'd rather we don't tip our hand by letting her know we're on to her."

"So we sit around waiting for this woman to do more damage?" Ace asked, hating the idea. And hating even more the idea that he might actually share this woman's DNA. And what about his biological father? He frowned, deciding he was better off never knowing which of her hangers-on had sired him, since neither the sperm donor nor Micheline had chosen to be his parent. Neither one had put in the sweat equity the way that his true mother and father, Payne and Tessa Colton, had.

"For now, we wait," Ainsley agreed, "and watch for her to make another mistake."

"Well, you'll have to forgive me," he said sarcastically, "but after forty years of her not slipping up, I wouldn't pin too much hope on Micheline Anderson suddenly tripping up and tipping her hand one minute before she's ready."

Chapter Twelve

Left alone inside her cramped room, Sierra fought a battle tougher than any opponent she'd ever gone up against in the ring.

But if she'd learned anything from the fugitives she'd spent so many years recapturing and taking into custody, it was that pleas, panic and desperation would only trigger the use of heavier restraints. And since she was under the care of medical practitioners convinced they were acting in her own best interest, that was likely to include some kind of drugs that would leave her in a stupor.

So gradually, she struggled to slow her breathing, to ride out the pain and nausea until they dissipated. The emotions were much more difficult to master, the shock, fury and the panic she felt at the idea of her home, her very life, destroyed while she lay here trapped and helpless to fight back. And helpless to prevent the violence from spilling over.

A fresh wave of dizziness engulfed her as her mind exploded with memories of last night's drive-by shooting. She heard the screeching of the black car's tires and saw the light reflected off a lowering window. She stiffened as gunfire erupted all around her. The next thing she knew, the back of her head was throbbing and the cameraman's blood was hot and slick on her hands. Blood that so easily could have been her own or even Ace's.

Her body started shaking, her imagination racked with what-ifs. The only way to keep herself from screaming was to take refuge in a memory of the love and support she'd felt among the siblings earlier last night in Ace's condo. She remembered the feelings of warmth and safety as she'd watched the way the family had enfolded itself around Ace's newly discovered, pregnant daughter and welcomed the young woman into the Colton clan like a protective hug. Remembered the little tug of envy she'd felt, wondering what it might be like to be claimed as Nova had been, and know she'd forever belong.

Closing her eyes, Sierra then recalled the feeling of Ace's strong, warm arms encircling her, the safety and the satisfaction she'd felt sleeping, bounded by his embrace. And how he'd admitted, right out loud, that he wanted a future with her. Words she could honestly never recall hearing and had, in fact, disdained, imagining them the stuff of drugstore greeting cards and made-for-TV movies. Not the kind of world she lived in, where people used such sticky sentiments only to get close enough to take advantage.

She shuddered as a more distant memory caught her unawares, her skin crawling before she was able to push thoughts of her childhood aside. Better to forget the past, and not to think too much about the future, either.

Instead, she savored the magic of those perfect moments she'd had with Ace, wrapping herself in daydreams of an entirely different kind of life. A life she knew that, for a woman like her, was no more realistic than the castle, crown and crinoline fantasies she knew so many girls indulged in when they were little. But they were pretty enough dreams, and they helped her arrange the mask she knew she'd need if she ever hoped to escape this hospital—and get away from Mustang Valley before even more trouble came calling.

What felt like hours later, she passed her first test, conducting herself calmly and reasonably when a dark-haired neurologist named Dr. Amir came to test her visual acuity, her reflexes and ask her some basic questions about the date and time of year, where she was, and what had brought her here to the hospital. Though her vision remained a bit blurred, with a tendency to double if she turned her head too quickly, the only thing that really gave her pause was when the man asked her to tell him her name.

Noticing how intently the nurse with the asymmetrical haircut was watching her from behind her glasses, Sierra frowned before reminding herself she had to play the game. "It's Iris. Iris Higgins."

She then cut a look to the nurse, who gave Sierra a small nod of approval. But Dr. Amir was frowning at the nurse.

"I see no signs of combativeness, no disorientation that would for a moment warrant the use of any form of restraints on this patient. And this—" he said, his voice faintly accented as he gestured angrily at the zip tie still attached to the railing. "If it's true, as you said, that a *visitor* placed it here, without medical direction, that visitor should have been removed from the facility at once—and the restraint immediately removed."

"Yes, of course." The nurse flushed fiercely. "I'm aware of our protocol on restraints, but I have a call in her admitting physician about a possible...alternative, because there were—there are extenuating circumstances. You may have noticed the guard standing watch outside her room."

"*My* room," Sierra protested. "Excuse me, both of you, I'm *right* here, so why not try including me in this conversation? You know, like a *person*?"

"My apologies." Dr. Amir's warm brown eyes looked convincingly remorseful. "I'm afraid it can be an occupational hazard since I deal with so many...incapacitated patients."

Returning his attention to the nurse, he said, "I didn't notice a police *uniform* on that guard, so that tells me this patient is no prisoner."

"No, it's nothing like that," the nurse explained, casting an apologetic glance Sierra's way. "It's just that the Coltons want her protected—and from what I was told by the police sergeant who stopped by this morning, they have very good reason to fear for what might happen if she were to...act rashly."

"Ah, the Coltons. I see," Dr. Amir said before shaking his head. "I'm aware of the family's recent...*difficulties,* and I have great appreciation for the generous endowment Colton Oil has given to the hospital in the past. But surely, that does not mean we can allow their desires to compromise our professional ethics. Now, I have another patient to assess, Nurse Bishop, or I would see to this matter myself now, but I *will* stop by before I leave the hospital, and when I do, I will certainly expect to find Miss Higgins here *completely* unrestrained. Do you understand?"

"I do, Doctor, but if you'd seen and heard her earlier, she was—"

"She's absolutely right. I was confused and disoriented when I first woke up," Sierra cut in, throwing the nurse a bone in the hope of getting the woman on her side. "But my head's clear now. I'm feeling so much better. And I—I completely understand that everyone here has my best interest at heart."

Dr. Amir smiled and nodded. "We're agreed, then. I'd like you to stay another night for observation, rest and to reassess you neurologically to make certain everything's still heading in the right direction. Mostly, it's a precaution, since your CT scan looked clear. However, if you continue to improve at this rate, I believe you can expect to be released tomorrow."

Continuing to play the role of the world's most cooperative patient, Sierra offered her most angelic smile and thanked him, knowing she had no intention of hanging around waiting for anybody—not even the best intentioned—to decide her future.

THOUGH ACE HATED to leave Sierra on her own at the hospital, he knew that she'd be safe, under Callum's watchful eye. More than that, she needed rest and time to cool off and come to grips with her new reality. He trusted she'd be safe, as well, since the nurse he'd spoken to outside her room had promised to wait until she was settled—or preferably out cold before cutting the zip tie that kept her from once more attempting to climb out of her bed.

Since he, too, needed rest, along with a shave, a shower and a change of clothes, he asked Ainsley to drop him at his now-vacant condo on her way to Colton Oil, where she insisted she had a couple of pressing work issues she needed to deal with. Though he'd tried convincing his sister that no one would fault her for taking a personal day in light of what had happened, she only smiled and told him, "It'll be fine. Marlowe's cutting short her maternity leave to help out."

"That's generous of her. I hope neither of you are working yourselves to death, though."

"Just get some sleep, and I've had the refrigerator at your place stocked, so you should be good to go for at least a few days. And Asher's said he'll see to your wing at the Triple R, whenever you're ready to head that way," she added, referring to their younger brother, who worked as the ranch foreman.

Grateful anew for his siblings' thoughtfulness, he thanked her and promised to touch base by text that evening.

It was late afternoon before he headed out again, throwing caution to the wind and uncovering his Porsche after spotting no reporters anywhere around. As he'd hoped, the silver convertible thrummed to life without a hiccup, and Ace felt exhilarated once more having its power and speed at his command. Most of all, he loved reclaiming his independence and felt more like himself now that he was rested, clean and freshly shaven. Though his clothes were on the loose side, he found a pair of jeans that fit decently, along with a clean button-down shirt and blazer. He'd even taken time to eat one of the premade wrap-style sandwiches he found in the fridge to forestall any sisterly nagging if he happened to encounter Ainsley.

But it wasn't any of his siblings he ran into as he headed into a florist's shop downtown in the hope of finding a bouquet extravagant enough to win Sierra's forgiveness when he returned to the hospital to check on her. Instead, he had to stop short to keep from being run over by a woman charging out the front door, her chin down and her designer handbag tucked beneath one arm.

When she drew up short, too, his breath caught, his stomach plunging with a horrifying certainty. *Micheline!* The so-called *mother* who'd rejected him from the moment of his birth.

Grimacing, he scrambled back a step just as she looked up.

He blinked, the breath escaping his lungs, realizing his mistake. It wasn't Micheline at all, but another horror gaping up at him. His father's second wife, Selina. The same Selina who'd tried to pass herself off as a concerned stepmother when hiring Sierra to bring him in to the police.

And judging by the speed with which her look of surprise turned to thinly veiled hostility, she was no happier with this surprise encounter than he was.

"Selina," he said, recovering from his shock a beat more quickly. "I see you're here ordering the flowers for that welcome-home surprise party I'm sure you'll be throwing for me, since you're so *heavily invested* in my safe return."

He half expected her to try to sell the lie, attempting to convince him that she'd actually cared enough about his welfare. But maybe she knew that only a stranger to the family, like Sierra, would ever buy it coming from her.

Or perhaps his dig regarding the twenty-five grand she'd blown in the hopes of seeing him locked up was too much for Selina. Whichever was the case, she stiffened before haughtily tossing her expertly tinted light brown hair behind her shoulders. "Why, Ace, I can't *believe* you'd have the nerve to show your face on the streets," she said before looking up and down the currently vacant sidewalk. "Aren't you *terrified* that people will start shouting about a dangerous fugitive on the loose, or maybe some concerned citizen will even try to take matters into his own hands, since so many of them carry concealed weapons these days."

A spark of gleeful menace lit her smile at this suggestion.

Ace gave a grunt of disgust. "I'm sure you'd love it if someone shot me. It'd save you the risk of the real truth coming out at any trial, but all charges against me were dismissed."

She lifted her nose in the air, reminding her of how

she'd looked down on him since childhood, a habit that she'd continued long after he'd grown tall enough to tower over her. "What so-called *truth* is that?" she asked.

"Whatever you were trying to hide by seeing my father's shooting pinned on me. Whether it's that you were somehow behind it yourself, or something else is involved, I have no idea, but I—"

"Your father was always so ridiculously proud of you," she said, her searing gaze burning through him. "Boasted how his *firstborn* was so brilliant, so shrewd when it came to the business, and listen to you. Ha!" Her mocking laughter echoed beneath the awnings of the connected shops along the street. "You certainly make me glad I never wasted my precious time and energy on children."

Ace's own laugh was equally devoid of humor. "I imagine any potential spawn of yours would be grateful, too, to be spared of having such a mother. I certainly know that my siblings and I cannot *wait* for the day when we can talk our father into seeing you for what you really are and can evict you from the ranch, Colton Oil and our lives for good."

"Mark my words," she told him, "*that* is never going to happen. As long as he is living, your father will never dare to cross me—and I suggest that you don't, either."

"Why, Selina? Why? What is it you're holding over Dad? I know it's certainly not affection. If you ever cared about him at all, beyond what his money and his family name could get you, those days are long over. So what is it? Are you flat-out blackmailing him, or—"

Laughing, she turned her high-heeled shoes to walk away from him. But before she did, she tossed off a few last words, almost carelessly, over one stylishly dressed shoulder. "Wouldn't you like to know, Ace? Wouldn't all of you just die to..."

STILL STEAMING FROM his encounter with Selina, Ace did his level best to tell himself the woman wasn't worth getting rattled over. But he must've been more upset than he'd imagined, because as he was walking through the parking lot and into the hospital lobby with the large arrangement of white flowers he'd grabbed and purchased, thrusting his credit card at the cashier in stony silence, he couldn't help noticing the odd looks he was getting. Enough that he began to wonder if people recognized him from news reports and wondered what the notorious Ace Colton was doing walking free.

But no, that couldn't be it, because the looks weren't hostile or frightened, more...*bewildered.*

Looking about himself in confusion, Ace finally caught the eye of the older woman in a volunteer's smock sitting behind the lobby's information desk, who at first blinked in surprise before her mouth rounded into what appeared to be an *O* of comprehension. Smiling discreetly, she beckoned to him with a crook of her finger.

"Yes?" he asked her, more confused than ever as he set the arrangement on top of her desk.

"May I ask," she said politely, arranging her face pleasantly, "if these absolutely beautiful flowers are meant for one of our patients here?"

"Of course they're for a patient," he said, his irritation boiling over. "Is it really that unusual to try to cheer someone up with a few flowers when they're in the hospital?"

"Not at all," she said, arching one golden eyebrow, "but it *is* rather unusual for someone to walk into a hospital with an arrangement with that *particular* message."

Following the direction of her nod, he took a careful look—his first, apparently—at the front of the basket, then surprised himself with a loud bark of laughter as he finally saw his mistake.

"Whoa, boy. If I thought I was in trouble with my—with my lady friend *before*," he said, his face burning as he removed the silk banner he'd completely missed before. The one reading Rest in Peace. "I would've been resting in *pieces* if you hadn't saved me. Thank you so much."

Giggling like a teenager, she waved off his gratitude. "You're more than welcome. After all, it's not very often we hospital volunteers get a chance to save a life."

After thanking her one more time, he headed for the elevator, deciding that his boneheaded mistake had at least given him the gift of a decent story to tell on himself. One he hoped to turn to his advantage, using his own chagrin to get Sierra smiling. Or laughing at him, perhaps. He didn't care, if only it might somehow pave the way to her forgiveness.

But the moment he stepped off the elevator, his stomach clenched, somehow grasping ahead of his brain that something was amiss as various personnel hurried from room to room, poking their heads into doorways, looking behind the nurses' station and inside the supply closet.

When Ace spotted Callum among them, he caught his breath, shocked to imagine that, even with a concussion, Sierra had managed to figure out a way around the imposing man.

"How'd she manage it?" Ace asked him, knowing his brother was far too experienced to be easily outmaneuvered. "Because I know there's no way you'd let an outsider take her."

Regret darkening his blue eyes, Callum sighed. "I'm sorry, Ace. Damned sorry. She's slippery as a basket of eels, and about a hundred times as clever. She faked a convincing seizure and none of the medical staff answered the call button, so I ran to find help for her."

A nurse, alerted by Ace's tone, interrupted her own search to join them near the counter, where Ace had set down the flowers. A fiftyish woman with a no-nonsense set to her jaw, she gave him a look that all but dared him to try to pin this mess on her. "Your Ms. Higgins planned her moment, clearly," she said. "She waited until she heard the alarm. Another patient had coded just down the hall, so we all went running to help."

"Did she take her belongings? Her clothes?" *Her car keys*, he thought, recalling the Chevy still parked in the lot. Though surely, Sierra wasn't foolish enough to try to drive it very far, he could easily imagine her using it to make a getaway before ditching it elsewhere.

Sure enough, inside her windowless room, they found the plastic bag with her belongings missing from the storage locker. But when he went downstairs and looked outside, the Chevy remained where she had left it the previous evening.

Perhaps she'd feared another GPS tracker, or even a bomb, considering last night's attempt on her life. Or maybe she was still somewhere inside the hospital.

But according to Callum, he and the hospital staff had been searching the floor for her, after positioning staff to watch both the elevator and the stairwell entry, for the past half hour.

"And before that?" Ace demanded. "How long would she have had to get dressed and get out of here?"

"Five or six minutes, tops," Callum said decisively, with the nurse beside him nodding her agreement. "Things were hectic down the hall there, where that other patient coded."

"Wait a minute," Ace said, his heart skipping a beat as he remembered what he'd heard about his father being transferred to this floor earlier. "*What* patient?"

"I'm afraid I'm not at liberty to say," the nurse told him. "We *do* have privacy laws here."

"What room is our father in? You can tell us that much, can't you?"

Chapter Thirteen

When Ace entered the hospital room ahead of Callum, he cried out, shock colliding with relief at seeing his father again—seeing him sitting alone in his bed with the head elevated. A blanket had been pulled to his chest and his eyelids were at half-mast as he watched a wall-mounted television playing at low volume. As a hospital benefactor, he'd been placed in a private suite with a small divided seating area for waiting family, far larger than the cramped, windowless room where Sierra had been hidden away.

But the silver-haired family patriarch—the same Payne Colton whose tough and rugged good looks had been compared to a classic Western movie idol whose black-and-white image was now galloping across the screen on horseback—didn't startle at Ace's outburst. Nor did he turn his head, or even his gaze, to look in his direction.

"Dad?" Ace's voice broke, his vision blurring as he blinked away a hot haze of tears. Because despite the absence of the guard he'd expected to find at the door, the catch in his throat told him this was truly his fa-

ther, breathing and alive, though pale and frailer—and older-looking, too, with scarcely a hint of the powerful life force that had for sixty-eight years animated his expression.

Months after his father's shooting, Ace spotted no obvious bandages or other evidence of the bullet wounds that had initially been the doctors' greatest concern. But as Ace moved closer, he was able to make out a variety of tubes and an IV pole, plastic tendrils snaking around the once-formidable man.

"I'll just give you two a few minutes." Callum touched Ace's shoulder before his tone turned more serious. "Right now, though, I'm going to track down that guard who's supposed to be on duty watching Dad's door and give him a piece of my mind for leaving his post."

Ace nodded mutely, his gaze still glued to his father as he struggled to collect himself before speaking.

"Dad, it's me, your son, Ace." He was shaking head to toe now, aching to reach out, to gather his father in his arms yet terrified to touch him. "I—I've wanted for so long to come see you, to tell you how—how much I love you—and how I'll always—how you'll always be the only father I—"

At the sound of footsteps just behind him, he sharply turned his head, thinking Callum had returned already. Instead, it was the same nurse he'd just spoken to, the one with the severe, dark haircut. Only as she turned up the room's lights, Ace noticed that her stern expression had melted into one of sympathy.

"Go on," she urged gently as she reached for the remote and switched off the television. "There's a good chance he can hear you, at least, though so far his responses have been minimal."

"But minimal means that there's been something, right? And he was watching TV, wasn't he? I mean, he's always liked old movies like that." Ace knew that he was reaching, that Genevieve or anyone who really knew his father could've turned the channel on to soften the heartbreak of seeing his unfocused staring.

When the nurse only nodded, Ace turned a pleading look back to his father. "I'm here. Right here, if you could blink—or look at me or..." He glanced again at the nurse. "Is it all right if I take his hand?"

"You should do that," she assured him. "Why don't you stay with him a while? And I'll come and notify you the moment that we've found Miss Higgins."

Ace felt a twinge of guilt, since the shock of this reunion, a reunion he had dreamed of, prayed for, yet also somehow dreaded for so long had driven every other thought from his brain. Including the reality of how much trouble Sierra could get into on her own.

But if she spotted him looking for her, he knew damned well how she'd react, after the way he'd bound her to that bedrail. Whether she ran or hid or even tried to fight him, he'd end up no closer to gaining her cooperation...

He would also be leaving his father here, alone and totally unguarded, a thought that filled Ace with a tingling apprehension. After all, if word had somehow gotten back to the real shooter that there had been signs that Payne Colton might be emerging from his coma, that could make him a risk to the shooter. A risk to be taken out before he could name the person who had harmed him.

"I will stay here until my brother gets back, Nurse Martinez," Ace agreed, finally looking at the nurse's name tag. "But if you do find Sier—Ms. Higgins," he corrected himself, "*please*, do everything you can to convince her to come back to the room for her own safety. No drugs or restraints, though. She needs to understand that we're trying to help her."

"I'll do my best," she assured him before hurrying out and closing the room's door behind her.

Ace had more to say to his father—so much more—but the problems of Sierra's disappearance and the missing guard had him worried and suspicious. What if both were somehow connected?

Before he could press the screen, the door of the suite's attached bathroom swung open slightly. And he spotted a pair of legs and black shoes lying on the floor inside. A man, down!

Rushing to push the door farther open, he found the missing guard, lying motionless and bleeding profusely from the head on the tiled floor inside.

"Help!" Ace yelled toward the hallway. "We need help inside here!"

At his shout, a movement caught his eye. It was the blanket, sliding down his father's chest as he jerked, his head turning and his eyes widening.

His own heart skipping a beat, Ace murmured, *"Dad?"* And heard his father make a strangled sound as he struggled to lift his hand—*to point at him?*

Reading the absolute terror in his father's eyes, Ace felt his heart break to imagine that he, recalling their last argument but perhaps not what came after, might well fear him. But with the guard lying injured, or possibly worse, on the floor behind him, there was no time to—

His father gave another, far more urgent grunt, only this time an electric jolt of comprehension fired along Ace's nerve endings as he realized that his dad wasn't staring so much *at* as *past* him. Instinct taking over, Ace whirled around…

And came face-to-face with a slightly built stranger wearing an Arizona Sun Devils sweatshirt, a man in his midtwenties with a mop of wild, dark hair. But the look in his eyes was even wilder as he aimed his shaking gun directly at Ace's chest.

"I'm sick of waiting for you to leave, and I'm running out of time here," he ground out through clenched jaws, "so I guess I'll be staging a murder-suicide instead of just finishing off what I started here today."

"You!" Ace roared. "*You're* the man who shot my father? Who the hell even *are* you?" Although there was something vaguely familiar about that face. But why would he—

"Sh-shot me!" Payne was breathing heavily, the effort to speak, after months of silence, clearly costing him. "Him—*he* did!"

"Shut up, old man!" yelled the stranger, who must have been hiding around the corner in the sitting area portion of the unusually large room.

As he shouted, his aim drifted from Ace to his father for an instant—an instant Ace seized upon to leap at the younger man.

The gunman cried out in alarm, backpedaling to keep from being knocked off his feet as Ace slammed his shoulder and sent the gun flying. It clattered to the floor, along with the phone Ace had been holding.

Younger and apparently more agile, the stranger twisted around like a trapped animal and dove for the loose weapon. But before his hand closed on the pistol's grip, Ace's booted foot caught his jaw.

The kick snapped the intruder's head backward with a loud *Oomph!* As he recoiled from the blow, Ace, now seeing a clear path, leaped, his arm stretching toward the gun. His first desperate grab, though, only sent it spinning another two feet farther. It took another leap onto his stomach—and what felt like a few popped stitches from the chest wound Ice Veins had given him—before Ace finally had the weapon in his hand…

A weapon that he swung around to aim at the empty air and the fast-fading sound of running footsteps down the hall outside the room.

Ten minutes earlier

Though Sierra had managed to dress in the now-rumpled outfit from the previous evening and had even found her keys and wallet still zipped inside her jacket's pocket, she hadn't gotten far before someone must have figured out that she was missing. Or at least that was what she figured when flashing lights and an unfamiliar code announcement—both of which made her head swim—sent hospital personnel scurrying into the hallways so quickly that Sierra had no choice but to duck into the first doorway she encountered.

It turned out to be a break room, with a couple of round table and chair groupings, a countertop microwave, sink, a small refrigerator and a half-full coffeepot, along with a number of insulated mugs, which sat on open shelving. But what immediately caught Sierra's eye was a white lab coat some careless employee had left draped over one of the chairs. Sierra decided on the spot it would make a good start on a disguise.

She was even more excited to see a hospital ID had been left clipped to the lapel. Though she had zero chance of passing as Dr. Jonathan Wong from the radiology department, the white coat fit her well, at least, and by flipping around the ID backward, donning a pair of tortoiseshell-framed reading glasses she discovered in a cubby, and winding her hair into a messy bun style, she decided she could pull off "harried medical professional" if spotted from a distance.

Or if there weren't an entire floor full of very real employees of this hospital, along with the very capable Callum Colton, looking for her specifically. The thought made Sierra's heartbeat quicken, as did the realization that a good number of those people might have seen Sergeant Colton on the television news last night or read about her so-called "murder" in the newspaper first thing this morning. In a community the size of Mustang Valley, such an event would be widely shared by friends and neighbors on social media, as well.

Fear splashed through her with the thought. Had photos of her—one of *those* photos—run with the coverage? Cringing at the thought, she remembered how her father had convinced her it would be great for business for her to do some feature with a glossy Las Vegas-area magazine last year and how they'd insisted on photographing her badass-babe style, holding various weapons, wearing a pair of outsized boxing gloves, and even straddling some chromed-out motorcycle she wouldn't have ridden on the job in a million years. If she weren't already supposedly dead, she'd keel over from humiliation to imagine those ridiculous pictures circulating widely.

Or would she be risking blowing the even better cover of her *murder* by allowing herself to be seen?

Realizing that she had little time for indecision, she peered out into the hallway to make sure the coast was clear before hurrying toward where she spotted a sign for the staircase—probably her best shot at getting outside the building undetected.

Voices around a corner alerted her someone was coming. Sierra caught the words *room by room search*, and ducked into what turned out to be a utility closet, mostly occupied by a large bin half-full of bags of soiled linens to be laundered. By the time someone came to check that closet, less than a minute later, Sierra was deep inside the bin, with several of the floppy cloth bags strategically arranged above her.

Holding her breath as the searcher rattled brooms, mops, buckets and other items around her, she strained her ears until she heard the male voice call, "Closet's cleared," an instant before the door slammed shut behind him.

Still, she stayed in her hiding place a while longer in case someone else came, her heart pounding in time with the aching of her head and injured ribs. When no one else arrived, she climbed out again, a painstakingly slow operation because of the room's near-total darkness and her fear of knocking over anything that would bring another searcher running. By the time she was peering through the door again, she was sticky with perspiration and feeling more than slightly claustrophobic.

But she reminded herself that, during her professional efforts to get the drop on fugitives, she'd hidden in far tighter spaces. Sure, she wasn't in peak form now, considering her injuries, but she was an athlete and a competitor—and absolutely determined to once more take charge of her own future. A future where she would never again have to be tempted by Ace Colton's all-too-handsome face into imagining she was something more than the same Sierra Madden whose own mother hadn't seen fit to hang around, whose father hadn't paid enough attention to protect her from…

She closed her eyes, pushing back against the pain of wounds she hadn't thought about in years, wounds that had more to do with her reaction to being forcibly corralled here than she would ever admit. Taking a deep breath, she let go of her angst for the time being, finally cautiously cracking the door open.

Peering through the narrow gap, she spotted the marked stairway door where she'd been heading when the commotion had broken out. She gave a low growl of frustration, seeing a woman she recognized as a nurse's assistant stationed near that exit, her glossy, high-set ponytail swinging back and forth as she looked up and down the hallway.

A moment later a muted male voice called out from farther down the corridor. Sierra didn't make out the words, but judging from the swing of the black ponytail and the way the nurse's assistant went sprinting off in that direction, it might've been a call for help.

Though the coast was clear, Sierra hesitated a moment longer, carefully opening the closet door wide enough to hear a series of short, sharp shouts and the slap of running feet.

Had someone thought they'd spotted her—or was another patient suffering a medical emergency? Either way, she seized on the distraction and broke from her hiding place, bolting toward the stairway as fast as she could run.

She had nearly made it when she heard the steps pounding and the sound of someone breathing hard coming up behind her—too fast for her to hide, to run, even to change course. All she could do was brace herself, turn her head just enough to make out the blur of a smallish, slim male, his head topped in a cap of messy, dark brown curls—and about to mow her down.

At the last instant he reached out, hooked her right shoulder with a hand. "Out of the way, bitch!" he yelled before giving her a hard shove sideways.

"Hey, jerk, watch it!" was all Sierra had time to shout as she toppled to the floor, the reading glasses flying. Mad as hell, she scrambled back up in time to see him disappearing through the stairwell door—

And Ace Colton barreling down the hallway, his face a mask of fury and a drawn gun in his hand.

Tough as Sierra liked to consider herself, she shrank back reflexively as the sight of Ace waving around the weapon.

"Get back to your room now!" he shouted at her, his brown eyes wide and his face flushed. "I found my father's shooter in his room! He was about to stage a murder-suicide with Dad and me when I grabbed his gun, but he's still dangerous."

Recovering her wits, she answered, "Let me help you catch him. And please point that barrel down, will you? You're giving me palpitations here—and not the good kind!"

"I said get back in your room. You have a head injury, and—"

"And you don't have nearly enough zip ties to keep me in this place." She glared a warning that she wasn't above demonstrating another left cross if he tried such a stunt again. "So unless you mean to shoot me with that thing, why not bring along someone with some experience at apprehending violent criminals?"

"There's no time to argue. He's getting away."

"Well, that's at least one thing we're agreed on," she said, hurrying to open the stairwell door and waving him in ahead of her. "So how about we call a temporary truce—just until we catch this guy and I can be on my way?"

ACE KNEW SIERRA was right about one thing. They couldn't afford to waste time, not with his father's shooter getting farther out of reach with every passing second.

Nodding, he forced himself to slow his breathing, manage his panicked thoughts and sort his priorities. "Just a second. I need to make sure Callum's watching my dad."

Though he'd flagged down a nurse who had called others to help deal with the bleeding and unconscious guard, there was no way his father could be left without security, in case the shooter had an accomplice…or somehow managed to double back for another attempt on the senior Colton's life.

Fortunately, the phone he'd picked up off the floor before sprinting down the hallway still worked, though the screen had been cracked when it had been knocked from his hand. After sending a terse message to his brother, Ace looked up to spot Sierra donning a pair of reading glasses, her hair wound up into a precarious-looking updo. Along with the white coat she was wearing, it made for a reasonable disguise—one that convinced him that the confusion he'd witnessed in her this morning had cleared up.

Raising his brows in appreciation of her quick thinking, he nodded his approval before once more pulling out the gun and starting for the stairs. Sierra ran after him, lagging behind only a little as he pounded down the steps.

They were still too late, just as he'd suspected they would be, considering the delay. Or at least he was certain they were as the two of them emerged into the long, slanting rays of the late-afternoon sunshine, where they looked around the parking lot frantically.

Seeing no one except a white-haired couple, a man using a walker, and a young woman pushing her child in a stroller toward the hospital's main entrance, Ace turned on Sierra. "If I hadn't been held up arguing with you, I might've caught him! I might have finally had the man that my father told me shot him—"

Sierra gaped at him. "Your father—he's *talking*?"

Ace nodded. "He's just starting to, yes."

"I'm glad to hear that, but if you could hold off on the jumping down my throat a second—"

Chagrin tightened his jaw. "You're right. That was out of line. I'd already been slowed down getting help for the injured guard and grabbing my phone, not to mention making sure Callum's back in the room with our dad—"

When she held up a hand for silence, he half expected her to tell him what he could do with his apology. Instead, she took the practical approach, rattling off priorities like the professional she was. "We need manpower—the cops and hospital security—to search the building, especially the first and second floors, in case he ducked out onto one of the lower floors and never left the building."

"Agreed," he said, reaching for his phone again, but before he could pull it out, her head turned abruptly toward the throaty revving of an engine. Following her gaze, he spotted a bright yellow coupe across the parking lot—some kind of muscle car—peeling out onto the road before squealing off down the street.

"That's gotta be him," Ace guessed, imagining that a young guy bold enough to commit the flagrant acts this shooter had would be drawn to the flash and power of such a vehicle—and too shaken by their physical altercation to make a quieter getaway. "Let's go."

He pointed out his silver Porsche, parked only a few rows away. "I'm over there."

He beat her to the convertible and was strapped inside and had it started by the time she joined him.

"You okay?" he asked, noticing her grimace as she pulled the seat belt out and across her body. "You look kind of pale."

Nodding impatiently, she explained, "That's just my game face. Now if you're done playing mother hen, try showing me what this fancy ride of yours can do. We don't want to lose this guy again."

Backing out, he wheeled around. Then the Porsche shot off like the finely tuned machine it was. But thanks to a school bus lumbering past to delay them from getting clear of the hospital exit, the yellow coupe's rear bumper was nearly out of sight by the time he was able to safely get around the traffic slowdown.

"There, he's turned off to the right! You see it? A canary yellow '69 Camaro," said Sierra, who had put her window down to crane her neck out the window. "Probably not another one in a town the size of this one."

He cut her the briefest of looks. "You know your muscle cars."

"Enough to know there could be some serious horsepower under that hood." She shrugged. "My dad used to drag me to all the classic car shows back in Vegas as a kid."

Though most of his attention was riveted on the tiny yellow dot ahead, he managed to pass her his phone. "Call Spencer, will you? Let him know you're with me and tell him we're in pursuit of a younger white male, midtwenties, slight build, with curly, dark hair and brown eyes. Tell him, too, about my father identifying him as the shooter."

"Sure, I will, but—Ace," Sierra said a moment later, as he watched the Camaro make a left into a residential neighborhood ahead. "Your phone just flashed twice, and now *nothing.* I think—yeah, it's definitely dead. Broken, maybe? I see the glass is cracked."

"Shooter knocked it out of my hand upstairs," he said, knowing the battery had been fully charged when he'd arrived at the hospital. "Must've damaged it worse than it first looked like. Do you have your phone on you?"

She reached underneath the lab coat before shaking her head. "It's not in any of my pockets. I don't know what happened to it. You didn't let the police take it last night, did you?"

"I didn't *let*— It was probably lost somewhere in the ER or the parking lot, Sierra, while people were trying to save your life." He tapped the brakes, slowing for a rangy black dog that ambled across the road as if it hadn't a care in the world. "A life that you seem damned determined to toss aside, running off like some petulant teenager this afternoon."

"I'd say you and Spencer and the rest have already

done a fine job of tossing away the life I had," she fired back, "so quit acting like I'm some ungrateful brat who needs to be corrected, or you can drop me off right here."

"*You're* the one who insisted on coming, helping me to find him."

"I told you before I meant to earn that money Selina paid me. Earn it helping you to clear your name. I'm not welching on that promise—or a chance to score a little payback."

"Payback?"

"Well, yeah," she said. "You did just say this guy's intent was to frame you and stage a murder-suicide, to kill both you and your father, right?"

"I don't think I was his primary target, but he did say that's what he meant to do," Ace said, his stomach squirming as it hit him how close he and his father had come to dying in that room together. "When I think of my family, my daughter, *you*, tricked into believing that I'd been so consumed by guilt that I'd shot myself after finishing off my father—I could kill that son of a bitch myself, if I ever get ahold of him—"

"No, you absolutely can't kill him," she argued. "Not if you ever want any answers—or to truly prove your innocence. You have to use your head. And besides..."

"Besides what?" he asked.

"I wouldn't have been tricked. I never would've bought you'd do anything like that—that you'd hurt your brothers and your sisters, and the daughter who believes in you, by doing something like that."

He swallowed past a lump, wanting to thank her but

unable to find the words as he slowed to take the left turn where he'd spotted the Camaro disappearing. The neighborhood was older, with a mix of brick, stucco and adobe one-story homes, most landscaped with the rock and drought-resistant plantings common to the region. But many of the houses had walls that obscured backyards, and garages with their doors down that could hide a vehicle. "Where *is* he? Do you see the car anywhere?"

They stared at the long and empty street ahead. Running slightly downhill, it was intersected by three or four smaller cross streets before eventually curving off to the right.

"I don't see him anywhere," she started, craning her neck as she looked past a variety of vehicles parked along the street, none of which resembled the Camaro. "But keep driving. Maybe we'll spot something, anything."

"Not if he's pulled behind one of those fences," he said, trying not to sweat the telltale orange-pink glow splashed along the bottoms of the gauzy clouds to their west. Surely, they'd have his father's shooter before sunset—or at least ahead of full dark. Ace vowed he wouldn't let this chance slip through his fingers.

Their gazes traveled along the smaller lanes and between houses, desperately searching out the slightest glimpse of canary-yellow paint.

"This neighborhood looks familiar," Sierra commented. "I think we're only about a half a block from the apartment where Destiny Jones lived, just over there."

She pointed partway down the street coming up on

their left, where about a dozen school-aged kids, their skin tones ranging from dark reddish-brown to freckled ivory, were playing. Ace suspected the after-school game had started as touch football but appeared to be deteriorating as one of the larger boys sent a younger kid sprawling, causing an angry-looking pair of girls to get up in the aggressor's face with their fists curled.

"Pull up," Sierra said. "Let's see if these kids saw anything."

Ace slanted a dubious look her way. "You really think they'll talk to us?"

With all the emphasis in the news on children avoiding strangers, Ace suspected this gaggle would scatter if approached by adults.

"Not you, most likely, but let me give it a shot in my doctor get-up—unless you have a better idea."

"Fresh out of those," he admitted as he pulled to the curb around the corner.

She jumped out and headed directly to the group of about ten, which looked to be anywhere from about eleven to maybe fourteen or fifteen years of age. Though a couple darted suspicious looks in his direction, most ignored him, sitting out of earshot about thirty yards away.

While Sierra talked, the two biggest boys continued tossing the football back and forth, spiraling it aggressively fast and close as if to let her know they didn't appreciate her barging into their domain uninvited.

That ended when Sierra deftly snatched the pigskin from the air and tucked it close to her white lab coat. After that she gained the whole group's full attention.

But over the course of their brief conversation, Ace saw the crossed arms and hostile faces give way to gestures toward the south and nods before a number of the kids started talking excitedly at once.

A few minutes later she nodded approvingly before tossing back the football to the tallest boy and trotting back toward the car. Several of the younger kids waved after her, big smiles on their faces, and the biggest girl pumped her fist and yelled, loudly enough for Ace to make out, "You go take out that trash, Doc!"

"Down that way," she said, pointing in the same direction the kids had pointed out. "They saw the Camaro speed past—almost hit the littlest boy there."

"You're sure it's the same guy?"

"Oh, yeah. I told them I was an ER doctor, and my detective friend and I were tracking down this guy who'd beat up his little girl and then skipped out on the hospital bill." Her seat belt snapped crisply into place.

"I see that once again," Ace said as he sped off, "I've *vastly* underestimated your skills. You're not only a genius when it comes to improvising, you're also not half-bad with kids."

"Kids are very cool. I've done some coaching with my friend Brie down at the gym." She winced. "I hope they aren't too upset when they hear that fake news report about my—my so-called murder."

"I'm sorry," he told her. "You coach boxing?"

"Sure. Cops've got a program in my neighborhood, and it's been a way to pay them back…for being there for me back when I needed them."

"After your mom took off? Weren't there any other relatives, or family friends to help look after you?"

Her face tightened. "Listen, Ace. I promised you, back after Ice Veins, that I'd earn that money that Selina gave me for bringing you in by helping to clear your name. But the personal part of this conversation is over."

"That's not what you want. You're just scared. Scared of getting in too deep. Afraid of being trapped."

"So let's just focus on getting your father's real shooter in custody," she went on, talking over his objection as if she hadn't heard it, "so I can be safely on my way."

Part of him wanted to shout at her, to tell her that she couldn't go. He'd be damned if he'd let her get herself killed just to prove a point. But right now they had a would-be murderer to track down, and a thick tangle of crucial questions that needed answering—questions of who this vaguely familiar-looking younger man was, why he wanted Payne Colton dead and what, if anything, he knew about the circumstances of the baby switch that had taken place forty years before, along with a mind-boggling string of other crimes.

Which meant, Ace reminded himself, that just as Sierra had reminded him earlier, he needed to keep his temper in check. To tamp down his fury—along with the desire to shoot the worthless piece of trash with his own gun the first chance that he had.

Chapter Fourteen

Five minutes became ten, neither of them daring to speak as the tension coiled in their bellies wound itself up ever tighter and the red needle on the Porsche's speedometer crept higher.

The longer they drove with no sign of the Camaro, the more worried Sierra grew that this chase had been nothing but a fool's errand—and even worse, one that was wasting valuable time as the sun slipped out of sight. Had she been working a job on her own, she would've known better than to blunder through town like this, rushing around after a high-stakes suspect that she no longer had eyes on.

The moment she'd realized that she didn't have her cell phone on her, she would've pulled over somewhere to alert the authorities, offering a description and her best estimate of speed and direction. Surely, in a case like this one, they'd quickly put a BOLO over the radio and have the whole department looking, giving them a far greater chance of taking the shooter into custody before anyone else could be hurt.

She knew she wasn't thinking rationally, hadn't been

since Ace had told her the man lurking in his father's room had intended not only to finish off Payne Colton and Ace himself, but also to plant the gun in Ace's own dead hand. The moment he had told her that, all her professionalism, her experience and objectivity, went flying out the window. She'd ignited from the inside, burning with the need to bring in this monster, even if it turned out to be her parting gift to a man she knew she'd never forget.

When she looked over at Ace, she saw that he was even further gone, his grip on the sports car's steering wheel white-knuckled and a muscle in his clenched jaw twitching as his fierce gaze swept the buildings they passed leaving the town center. In hunting mode, he'd lost sight of any possibility other than the outcome he so desperately desired.

She drew in a deep breath, knowing she needed to be the one to reel him in. "We need to turn around, Ace. It's past time we called for backup."

"He has to be out this way somewhere. You said yourself that's what those kids told you—unless you think they might've been lying?"

"Lying, no," she said, "but it's possible he's managed to peel off on one of these side streets, or pulled in behind somebody's shed or something and we missed him. Or maybe he's outrun us. But it'll be a lot harder for him to outrun the whole Mustang Valley PD."

"This isn't Las Vegas," Ace argued, pushing the accelerator harder. "It's a tiny department, and it'll be dark in another—"

"Watch out!" she barked, seeing he was about to blow

a stop sign—and cut off a pair of adult bicyclists, both wearing form-fitting jerseys and leggings with their helmets, entering the intersection.

Screeching to a halt, he gritted his teeth as the two riders safely cleared his path by a few feet.

"No, this isn't Vegas—" the edge in Sierra's voice was sharp enough to slice flesh "—which means you may be mowing down a friend or neighbor. Or maybe a family member, given how you're somehow related to half of this town, if you don't slow down and think."

"Point taken," he said gruffly, "damn it. But it just kills me giving up now, when back at the hospital, I was so close I could—well, so close I *did*—touch the bastard."

She touched his arm, sighing as she reminded him. "Let's not forget, you saved your father's life this afternoon, along with your own. Plus, you've seen this shooter and the car he's driving, so why don't you go back to that little standalone Mexican bakery we passed about two blocks back and ask to use their phone?"

With a growl of frustration, he conceded, and turned the car around. Just as he pulled in front of the small, tan stucco building, the bright yellow '69 Camaro came blasting out from behind it, spraying up gravel as it exited the unpaved lot.

The muscle car's passenger-side window was down, allowing Sierra a glimpse of the wild-eyed male driver on her side. And letting her see the barrel of his pistol swing to point at her.

"Gun!" she shrieked, flinging herself forward. Ducking her head, she heard the pop—along with the splintering of the glass just behind and to her right.

Then the Camaro was speeding past them in the same direction they'd just come from, leaving behind a circular hole in the passenger window next to where her head had been only seconds before.

"Are you hit? You all right, Sierra?" Ace shouted.

"F-fine," she managed, her teeth chattering with adrenaline—and the realization that the bullet must have passed only a few inches behind her before flying— Her heart nearly beat free of her chest to see an exit hole in the driver's side window, just in front of Ace's body. "H-holy—how are we both still *alive*?"

Ace executed a neat three-point turn and then floored the accelerator. "We're alive because we're *meant* to stop him—only this time, I'm not letting him out of my sight—or allowing him to get far enough ahead to try another ambush, either. I can't believe that jackass had another gun stashed in his car."

"That might not be the last surprise he has in store for us," Sierra warned him as she reached for the weapon he'd taken from the shooter, which he'd stowed in a compartment of the Porsche's center console.

"What are you doing?" Ace demanded, sounding irritated.

"Since you're a little busy right now breaking nine kinds of traffic laws, why don't you let me concentrate on the gunplay? Especially since I'm pretty sure I have way more training and experience than you've gotten in the boardroom."

"You also took the kind of knock to the head that

affects vision and coordination. Can you even shoot straight, *Iris*?"

She made a huffing sound. "Call me Iris again, cowboy, and you might find out exactly how straight I can shoot."

To her surprise, he laughed at that. "Sorry, Sierra. And I'm sorry about before, with the zip tie, too. I wish I'd handled things differently, but—"

"Hey, where's he going?" she asked, seeing the Camaro abruptly veer onto a dirt track leading toward the foothills. "What is this?"

They passed a sign that read: Warning—Ungraded Road. Four-Wheel Drive Recommended. Bring Tools, First Aid, Water, Phone.

"Looks like he's taking the abandoned mining road up into the desert mountains. That's crazy," Ace said. "The only things out that way are tumbleweeds and tarantulas and this tiny old ghost town by the name of Gila Gulch at the end of the road—where he'll be completely boxed in."

"So what do you want to do about it?" Sierra asked him.

"If you're with me, I say let's go get my father's shooter and bring him the hell in."

"I'm with you, but only on one condition," she said.

"What's that?"

"If you do happen to spot any of those horrible spiders you mentioned—" Her skin rippled with revulsion at the thought of the disturbingly large arachnids, whose hairy legs had always creeped her out "—you have to be the one to stomp the things into oblivion before I get a glimpse."

"This is a seriously bad idea," Sierra said, groaning and holding her stomach as they slammed and jolted their way along the punishing road.

Cutting a quick look her way, Ace winced to see how miserable she looked, bracing herself against the dash as they drove over rocks and potholes that were rattling every nut and bolt in the low-slung sports car. And the choking dust, kicked up by the Camaro, now only about thirty yards ahead, since both vehicles had been forced to halve their speed, was making it tough for Ace to see well enough to avoid ruts and obstructions in the deepening twilight.

"Maybe we should turn around, then," he said. "Considering your concussion—"

"Absolutely not," she insisted. "We aren't losing what might be our only shot, when we're so close. Not over a little carsickness."

It was more than carsickness and they both knew it. But as their climb grew steeper, Ace decided that, with their quarry in sight, she'd never forgive him if he made this decision for her. Just as he would never forgive himself if his choice to continue forward ended up hurting her in any way.

"Look out. Someone's coming," she warned, pointed out a pair of headlights coming down the rocky mountainside ahead of them on the narrow, one-lane road.

The Camaro moved to the right just in time to miss a Jeep. Ace had to shave a rock wall, knocking off his side view mirror and eliciting a startled yip from Sierra, to allow the driver to get past him. As he did, he recognized the shocked faces of the local outdoor adventure tour guide and his passengers, who were probably astonished to see the two low-clearance sports cars risking serious damage by attempting this rugged trek. Besides, with darkness falling, they had to know there could be no legitimate reason to visit the isolated ghost town.

Before Ace could make any comment, the road jogged abruptly to the left and the Porsche's right front end slammed down into a particularly deep washout.

Sierra moaned. "On the way back to town, please remind me to stop and pick up my teeth. I'm pretty sure I left a few back there."

"Sorry about that," Ace said, wishing like hell he'd had the four-wheel-drive pickup he used out at the ranch for this trip. But he had to keep his full attention on the road to negotiate what he was almost certain would be the final switchback before reaching what was left of the old mining town. "Not much farther now."

With that, the Porsche's engine made a loud clanking sound and died abruptly, every idiot light on the dash flashing on at once. He tried restarting it, again and again until Sierra finally reached out to grip his arm.

"Give it up, Ace. I'm no car guru, but even I know your formerly pampered, garage-kept ride's not going another inch without a tow."

"You're right," he admitted.

As she peered out through the rock-chipped and grimy windshield, Sierra asked, "So what do you think? Keep climbing on foot?"

Ace blew out a long breath, weighing the deepening gloom against the very long walk back down and the far shorter uphill climb to an armed assailant who certainly knew that they were coming. "He's trapped up there, right around that next switchback, since this road won't take him any farther and there's no hiking cross-country out of there, especially in this light. If he's smart, he'll try to take cover and wait to ambush us as soon as we clear the curve."

She peered out her side window at the steep slope rising above her, a collection of loose rock and coarse gravel that appeared to be anchored by stalk-like, spiny plants and the claw-like roots of a few gnarled and stunted trees. "Is there a way to bypass the road, maybe surprise him by climbing over this ridge?"

"I'm not exactly sure what we'll encounter on the other side. To be honest, I haven't been dragged up here since I was a teenager." Though a couple of his more adventurous siblings had found the place eerily fascinating, Ace could think of better ways to spend a day than poking around among a bunch of falling-down buildings, rusting mining implements and toppling, crudely hand-carved gravestones. "I do know, though, that the terrain's steep, and there could be nastier surprises out there than a few harmless spiders—"

"Let's not spoil the mood by bringing up anything eight-legged," she told him, her lip curling in a look of disgust.

Amusement tugged at one corner of his mouth at the discovery that the normally tough-as-nails Sierra Madden had at least one weakness. "Yes, ma'am. You have my word."

"I'm holding you to that," she insisted before nodding toward the ridge. "If we do try climbing up over that, it could be that he'll be so busy listening for the car that he won't hear us. And if we're really lucky, he'll figure we've thought better of our plan and gone back into town to get help."

"You sure you're up for it?"

She made a scoffing sound. "You think I put up with being bounced around until I want to toss my cookies just to wait here in the car? Maybe *you* should wait in the car, while I take care of business."

"Not a chance in the world," he told her, recalling the hatred burning in the gunman's eyes as he'd pointed his weapon at Ace's helpless father.

Unbuckling her seat belt, she put down the handgun she'd been holding and began removing the white lab coat. "Ow," she said, wincing as she twisted, moving awkwardly within the cramped space. "Can you give me a hand with this sleeve? Ribs are still a little sore, but he'd see me coming from a mile away in this get-up."

"Sure thing." As he helped her to remove the garment, his forearm accidentally brushed against the warm smoothness of her neck.

Her gaze snapped up to meet his, their faces so close that all he could think of was the softness of her lips, the taste of her mouth, so temptingly close, and the electricity coursing through his skin as their bodies had lain together, without a stitch between them.

As he looked into her beautiful eyes, a chasm opened up inside him, a deep ache at the thought that he may have already irrevocably lost her. But no loss could be as devastating, as permanent, as death, and he knew damned well that that might be what lay in wait for them, just over the ridgeline.

"Sierra..." he said quietly, his fingers smoothing a lock of hair as he tucked it carefully behind her ear, eliciting her sigh and then a subtle shiver. "What I'm here to do—you know what it means to me, what it will mean to my family, putting away my father's shooter, getting answers to all the questions that've been tearing us apart for so long. But the truth is, *you* mean more than that—so much more."

"You—you mean a lot to me, too," she whispered, looking more worried than happy about the admission.

"As much as I love your—your gutsiness—it was hell last night. You have no idea. I thought I'd watched you being gunned down before my very eyes, and then when you collapsed the way you did, I was sure you were dying—"

Frowning, she shook her head. "I-I'm really sorry you had to see that. And even more sorry that once again I endangered your life with my problems."

"Your problems are my problems," he insisted. "So forget that. But now the idea of risking your life again, of seeing you hurt on my account or worse— So please, what if you sat this one out. For me? If you—"

"That's awfully sweet, Ace, but this is what I do. What I will always do because I love it and I'm damned good at it—go in and dig out fugitives, sometimes even armed ones, from their hidey-holes. Just like I did with you." Her green eyes softened as she gently ruffled the hair at his temple, where he still had a slight lump from the left cross she'd landed in the pitch-dark the night the two of them had met. "You forget already?"

"But *that* was before you were injured. And before I fell for you. It's like—I can't explain it, how it feels. But watching you struggle, worrying about your health, your safety and your happiness—it's like the world has taken you as its hostage, and I can only be happy knowing you're all right...because that's how much you matter to me. How in love I am with you."

Wiping at her eyes, she shook her head. "No, you aren't. You can't be. Because I can't—I *can't* risk—"

She cut herself off, looking away and rocking forward. Distress radiated off her, but she couldn't seem to say more.

"You can't risk what, Sierra?" he pressed. "I've just taken my damn heart and laid it out on a platter for you so tell me. Use your words for once, damn it."

"You know I have to leave," she erupted, her rushed words edged with anger. "You know I'm putting your family in danger with every day and every minute that I linger. And anyway, is that what you want for me, to have to stay hidden, living under an assumed name and hoping that the people hunting me—who are no idiots, I can assure you—never put two and two together?"

"So live under *my* name, Sierra, under Colton protection on the ranch."

She stared at him in clear confusion, her lips slightly parted.

"*Marry* me," he told her, "and I swear I'll keep you safe—"

"*Safe?* You mean like zip-tied in an attic someplace?

Or wrapped in cotton in your secret bunker? Absolutely not," she told him before picking up the handgun. "Now, let's go and catch your father's killer, before we lose what little time and light that we have left."

YOU'RE HERE TO *earn a bounty. It's all you were ever here for.* Again and again, Sierra repeated the words to herself, struggling to focus on the mantra as she tuned out the dull throb in her head and the pain of her injured ribs and picked her way up the rocky ridge ahead of Ace. It was almost impossible to keep from turning to look—or maybe to shout—back at him, with the words of his confusing—frankly infuriating—proposal still running through her brain.

But as aggravated as she was by the idea of a man who'd spent his life as a boardroom warrior being so hell-bent on physically protecting her from danger, even when she didn't need it, the lump in her throat was more about the realization that, impossible as it seemed, Ace Colton truly imagined that he loved her.

Just as she loved him, heaven help her… But how long would that last once he realized that what he was feeling was partly lust and partly pity, mixed up with whatever spell their mutual survival of the Ice Veins situation had cast over them on that first fateful night? How would he fit her into his new life as family man and father when he found out who she really was, a lifelong loner whose own mother hadn't even cared enough to stick around? She clenched her jaw, thinking of that kid who'd had to toughen up fast to mostly raise herself, keeping both her inattentive father and everyone who'd ever tried to help at arm's length. She'd found that less painful than giving anyone else the power to ever wound her so deeply again. And remembering those few occasions when she *had* forgotten, a young girl alone and vulnerable without real friends and family to watch for her, occasions that had taught her even harsher lessons. Lessons that had left her more fit for the company of the fugitives she brought in than good people like the Coltons. And forget the whole idea of being anybody's wife or mother.

Blinking back the threat of tears, she heard Ace coming up behind her, his breath scraping as he struggled to keep pace. Moments later she spun, gasping, as a soccer ball-size rock she'd accidentally dislodged went clattering downslope behind her.

"Sorry!" she whispered urgently as it bounced past him. "I didn't mean to do that!"

They both flinched when they heard it crash into the side of his poor, abused sports car, which she feared would never be the same.

"Just be careful, *Iris*," he whispered up at her, his voice droll as he emphasized the detested name, "because I'd really hate it if that sorry excuse for a proposal ended up being your last memory of me."

"Duly noted," she said, biting back a smile. "Though right about now, you're seriously risking my *bowling* your sorry rear end off this hill with the Iris nonsense."

The sexy rumble of his chuckle all but curled her toes. And told her that leaving this man and this crazy bond that they shared behind was going to be the hardest thing she'd ever done.

As she reached the ridgeline, however, she pushed aside such thoughts to take in perhaps a dozen or so structures that made up what was left of the mining town of Gila Gulch some thirty or forty feet below. With a newly risen quarter moon adding its thin illumination to that of the emerging stars, she could barely discern a roofless building—a church, perhaps, given what looked like rough pews inside, and the most solid of the buildings, a squared-off adobe with barred windows—that once had to have been the town's jail—just across the dusty street. The others were in worse shape, many consisting of little more than foundations and a standing wall here and there—one of which, she noted with a thrill of excitement, partly concealed the parked Camaro.

As Ace arrived beside her, she pointed it out to him before gesturing her intention to head down and check out the church ruins, which were where she suspected the shooter might be waiting to ambush the two of them as they came up the road around the switchback.

Ace nodded to show that he understood her intention before pointing to his own chest and then gesturing to indicate that he meant to split off from her, to check out the more intact jail building. Fear clutching at her stomach at the thought of him being surprised by the shooter while he himself was unarmed, she shook her head emphatically.

"We need to stick together," she insisted in a low voice. "If I see movement in the darkness, I don't want to worry I might shoot you."

"I'm right behind you, then," he whispered. "Careful on your way down."

Sierra, whose practical boots had heavy tread, was more worried about Ace as she started down the treacherous slope. But in the poor light and unstable surface, it turned out that neither footwear nor experience stalking felons was the deciding factor.

Erosion was the culprit that made the loose scree beneath her feet collapse and sent Sierra skidding, sliding on her rear end, and finally tumbling head over heels downhill.

Chapter Fifteen

"Sierra!" Ace's heart kicked like a mule as a portion of the hillside gave way just beneath him, disappearing—along with Sierra—before she could so much as cry out in alarm.

There was no answer but tumbling stone and hissing sand and the roaring of his own blood in his ears. Was she hurt down there? Unconscious? Before he could find a way down to her on the slope, now steeper and more precarious than ever, three blasts echoed in quick succession. Gunshots that rang in the rocky gulch, offering him no clue as to where they'd come from or who had pulled the trigger.

Did Sierra even still have the pistol she'd been carrying when the hillside gave way beneath her? If so, was she shooting at his father's would-be killer—or had the noise from her fall drawn his fire?

Ace froze in place for what felt like an eternity but was probably in reality only a minute or two, straining his ears for any clue—a moan or cry, a breath or footstep, that might give him some idea of which way he should go.

With his mind churning out image after image of Sierra bleeding, possibly dying, struck by one or more of the shooter's bullets, Ace finally decided he could wait no longer to try to find and help her. Praying he wouldn't make the situation worse—or fall himself—he started downhill.

Almost immediately, the loose, round rock rolled beneath his feet, collapsing his left knee and sending him skidding downward. Rocking backward, he sat hard, only to pick up speed until he desperately snagged a twisted tree root with one hand, finally jerking to a stop near the hill's bottom.

Hissing through his teeth with the pain of the splinters driven into his palm, he shifted off a rock jabbing uncomfortably into his lower leg. But as he moved to push himself to his feet with his uninjured right hand, he felt something cool and flat beneath his touch. His heart leaped as his fingers curled around what he realized, with a surge of raw emotion, was the grip of the gun.

The same gun Sierra must have lost in her fall.

The same weapon Ace had taken from the shooter in his father's room at the hospital.

Whether fate, fortune, or even random chance had guided his own drop, it had once more come back to him.

Praying he didn't end up shooting himself before he reached the ghost town's street level, Ace kept his head low as he descended the final six feet or so to level ground, where he immediately heard someone running toward the jailhouse.

Was it Sierra? Or was she lying somewhere in the darkness—or even partly buried by debris and in desperate need of help?

With no way to know and little chance of finding her in the darkness without making enough noise to draw more fire, he made the wrenching decision to follow the footsteps before he lost track of them.

And if that decision led him to the shooter— Ace's jaw clenched and his grip on the gun tightened, liquid fire streaming through his muscles at the thought of the man who'd come so close to murdering his father and destroying Ace's own life, and who might very well have just put a bullet in the woman that he loved. To hell with getting answers. What he most wanted now was the chance to end the threat forever, to make the shooter pay.

As he approached the corner of the jail, the runner's footsteps ahead of him stopped abruptly, leaving only the sound of Ace's own movement to carry on the dry desert air. Realizing the danger just as an arm emerged ahead of him, Ace slid to a stop, throwing himself to one side.

The air exploded from Ace's lungs as the hard ground came up too fast to meet him, the whine of a bullet slicing the air above his head. Pushing himself to his feet, he held on to the gun but didn't try to use it as he made for the closest cover available, the freestanding adobe wall of some small structure. He could only pray that it was thick enough to stop another bullet as he raised the gun in his hand, watching for his target to edge from behind cover to attempt another shot.

Willing his breathing to slow and his shaking muscles to stillness, he warned himself that he might well only get one chance at this. One shot at taking down a monster and getting back to help Sierra before it was too late to save her.

Ace startled as a shout of alarm—a man's voice—echoed from inside the walls of the jail. Hearing the thuds and grunts of a struggle, he quickly bolted from his hiding place, running toward the building.

"I *warned* you, stay down!" he heard Sierra order before she called out, "Hey, Ace? A little help in here? It's darker than a grifter's conscience—*Ooofff!*"

Ace reached the open doorway in time to make out the gunman elbowing Sierra in the midsection before breaking for the exit. Relieved as Ace was to see Sierra alive—and apparently in no need of anybody's rescue—he didn't fire on the shooter. But that didn't stop him from hauling off and landing the kind of punch he hadn't thrown since high school—a blow that caught the shooter's chin hard enough to lift him off his feet.

This time, the assailant stayed down, not moving a muscle.

"Nice one," Sierra said to Ace as she strode over, the gun she must have taken from the shooter in her hand. After checking on the shooter, she said, "You knocked him out cold, and with your left, too. You a southpaw?"

"No, but I figured if I clubbed him with the gun I'm holding in my right hand, I might—never mind that. Are you okay? You scared the devil out of me when you went tumbling down that hillside."

"It wasn't my plan for an entrance, either," she said, "but in the end, we got our man."

"*You* got him, you mean."

"Probably would've lost him, though, without that timely assist from you, so *go, team*," she said cheerfully, as, at Ace's feet, the curly haired shooter groaned, beginning to come around.

Grabbing him by one arm, Ace hauled the smaller man to his feet.

"Never get in the boxing ring, buddy," Sierra advised him. "You've got a heck of a glass jaw there."

"Let go of me!" he protested, struggling to break free.

"After what you've done?" Ace asked, incredulous. "You're damned well lucky I don't hit you again—or put as many bullets in you as you did my father."

"Police! Hold it right there, all of you!" boomed a familiar voice, a split second before Ace was blinded by the light of a pair of bright tactical flashlights. "Keep your hands up where we can see them!"

"Can you lower the beam, at least, for pity's sake?" Sierra asked, squinting as a uniformed male officer relieved her of the weapon she was holding. "I can't see a thing."

Moments later the blinding beams were redirected. Ace, too, willingly surrendered the weapon he'd been holding as soon as Spencer, who appeared to have come without his K-9 this time, cuffed the suspect's hands behind his back and patted down his pockets.

"Not that I'm not glad to see you," Ace asked his

distant cousin, "but how on earth did you manage to find us out here?"

"The hospital had already called to report what they knew, so we were on the lookout. Then one of the guides from Hidden Arizona Jeep tours got worried and called when he saw two cars speeding up to Gila Gulch this time of night," Spencer said. "Are you two both all right?"

"More or less," Sierra said.

"No thanks to him," Ace said, scowling at the prisoner, whose murderous brown eyes burned into him. Familiar brown eyes, somehow, reinforcing the suspicion that he knew this man, or once had. "I caught him in my father's hospital room, where he'd just wounded the private duty guard—"

"*Killed* the guard," Spencer reported grimly. "We received a radio dispatch updating us that the poor man passed away in surgery." Turning a harsh look toward his prisoner, he added, "So now you'll be facing murder charges."

His bleeding jaw clenching, the suspect turned away his sullen face.

"Just like he meant to finish off my father," Ace said.

"After what he did to my family, I only wish to hell I had killed him!" the prisoner erupted, struggling against Spencer's grip to spit in Ace's direction.

"That's enough of that," Spencer warned, jerking him backward firmly. "We can finish this conversation at the station, O'Neill. If you'll come with me, we'll—"

"To your *family*?" Ace demanded, talking over Spence. "What the hell—who *are* you?"

"Don't you get it, Colton?" the suspect ranted. "My mother worshipped your old man—thought he hung the moon, even after he utterly destroyed our family, taking advantage of her with their sordid workplace affair."

"You getting this?" Spencer asked the uniformed officer, who was holding up a cell phone.

The younger cop nodded, which Ace took to mean that he was recording the unprompted outburst. He was dimly aware, too, that Sierra had stepped in just behind him, to lightly grip his arm and shoulder.

"Easy," she warned, perhaps worried he might be considering throwing another punch at the shooter's face.

But right now Ace was too rattled by what the murderer was saying to focus on anything else. "What *sordid affair*?" he demanded, racking his brain to think of anyone, any woman his father had worked with at Colton Oil with whom he might have been involved.

"And it would've served him right if I'd paid him back for breaking up my parents' marriage," the shooter went on, "and driving away the father that I loved, by finishing what I'd started and making it look like *you'd* actually done the deed before killing yourself over his dead body."

"You—your *mother*..." Ace's eyes widened as a memory suddenly sprang to life—the image of a mop-haired kid, seemingly always underfoot, and then in later years, a teenager dragged along despite his obvious reluctance, to the annual summer employee barbecue events his family had hosted for years. A kid Ace mentally connected to his father's devoted longtime assistant, the always capable Olive O'Neill, who had succumbed to lymphoma several months ago.

"Wait, I know who you are," Ace blurted. "It's *Kyle*, right? Kyle O'Neill. Olive's son—" The one he'd heard more recently who could never seem to keep a job and still spent most of his days locked in his bedroom shooting up virtual opponents in video games. "I'd been meaning to reach out to you, after the funeral, to see if there was anything you needed."

But then all hell had broken loose within his own family.

"But you were always too *busy*, weren't you, with your fancy parties and resort meetings, too damned *important*, playing the big shot over at that damned company, weren't you? All of you! My mother was good enough to work for your father all her life, to destroy her own marriage for him when he was lonely between his divorce from Selina and when he finally married Genevieve—"

"Then he didn't—he wasn't breaking his own marriage vows?" Ace didn't know why, under the circumstances, that came as such a relief, yet somehow it did matter to him.

"That's all you care about. Your own father's precious reputation, his so-called honor, not my mother's."

"Of course I'm concerned, and I'm sorry I didn't make the time. I'm sorry, too, for what happened with her and with your family. It's a sad thing, but still, that gave you no right to—"

"You're just as bad as your father was, making his excuses when I went to the boardroom and demanded that he hand over all the raises that my poor, stupidly deluded, foolishly loyal mother had always been too meek to ask for while she was alive."

"Demanded with a *gun*?" Ace asked, thinking that if Kyle had approached his father differently, with a job application in hand maybe, Payne Colton would have surely, under the circumstances, shown compassion for the clearly troubled and newly bereaved young man.

"You know what he did? Your f-father?" Kyle was sobbing now, snot and tears making a mess of a face twisted with anguish. "He *laughed* at me, told me this wasn't one of my stupid video games when I pointed my pistol at him. Said I was nothing but an embarrassment, a damned waste of potential. Th-that my mother—the mother he'd used until he had no more use for, had confessed she was *ashamed* of what I had be-become…"

Sobs punctuated the confession, at once piteous and revolting.

"And that was when I shot him," he burst out, sticking out his chest and telling Ace triumphantly. "When I shot him and I shot him—only this was so much better than any game I've played."

As he explained it, Kyle's eyes went so wide with excitement that Ace made out the rings of white around the darker irises. It was that detail that would haunt him later, whenever he thought back to the final words of O'Neill's confession. Words he knew would stay with him forever.

"The hot spatter of your enemy's hot blood on your skin—the smell of it, the *taste* of that red mist on the air,"

O'Neill said, his voice going deadly calm. "There's freaking nothing like it, Colton. Nothing like it in this world."

SIERRA PRESSED HER hand to Ace's back, where she felt the pounding of his heart, the shaking in his muscles. At any moment, she feared, his control would snap and he would launch himself at this unhinged little nut job who had caused his family so much pain.

"Take a breath. Step away now," she murmured.

At the same time, Spencer pulled Kyle backward. "Okay, O'Neill. We've heard plenty from you for now." He then proceeded to advise him of his rights before adding, "We've got a bit of a walk back to our SUVs—since a Porsche is blocking the road just downhill."

"That'd be our ride, broken down, I'm afraid," Sierra explained to the officers, since Ace seemed too stunned to respond. "O'Neill's in the yellow Camaro over behind that wall—"

"I'm betting that's gonna turn out to be that stolen classic, Sergeant," said the younger officer. "Remember that '69 Fred Newcomb reported missing from his garage?"

"It's a '69 for sure," Sierra confirmed, holding on to Ace's arm as the two of them followed both officers, who escorted their defeated-looking charge toward the police vehicles.

"We can sort that all out back at the station—"

"I've got nothing to say to you pigs," the prisoner blurted.

Neither officer responded, but Sierra suspected that both were smiling inside, since, from what she understood of the law, O'Neill's uncoerced, recorded confession was more than enough to hold him while they gathered physical evidence from the hospital and ghost town crime scenes to shore up their case against him.

Trailing behind, Sierra nudged Ace, keeping her voice low as she asked him, "You hanging in there all right? I know it must be hard, hearing how—"

"I have to tell them. All of them. My—my family needs to know. They need to understand what happened, that it was all—I don't know—misplaced grief mixed up with resentment for—" He shook his head. "But I still don't understand how any of this could be related to the email sent about the switch-up in the hospital with the real Ace Colton or my birth mother being Micheline Anderson—"

"Micheline Anderson," Sierra echoed, not letting on for the moment that she'd already heard of the woman from Ainsley and his brothers at Ace's condo.

"Ainsley told me earlier they'd figured it out while I was still in hiding."

Sierra heaved a sighed, wondered how he was holding it together. "That's a lot to absorb, I'm sure, but let's say we table that discussion for now and focus on watching our steps walking through here. I don't know about you, but I've taken enough tumbles for one day." She wrapped her arm around his waist, realizing that he needed her support now more than ever to deal with the emotional shock of these revelations. At least until she could get him back to his family, so he could digest O'Neill's confession and the identity of his biological mother before taking stock of the questions still hanging over him.

Questions whose answers she wouldn't be around to help him deal with. But he had his siblings, a wealth of them, and a daughter, too, now. So why were her eyes filling at the thought of her own absence?

She didn't have long to focus on that before they reached the two police vehicles and Spencer asked Officer Donovan to transport O'Neill back to the station.

"I'll be taking these two separately," he told the younger officer.

"Yes, sir," Donovan replied before loading the still-cuffed and silent prisoner into the rear of his own unit.

"You, in the front with me," Spencer said, pointing to Sierra with a look that had her stomach tightening. "We have some things we need to talk about."

"I see my running off from the hospital hasn't much improved his opinion about bounty hunters," she said to Ace after he strode toward the driver's side. "He looks plenty mad."

This time it was Ace who clapped a hand onto her shoulder before leaning down to kiss her, just above the ear. "He does have reason. You have no idea what he went through, getting permission to run that phony press event to announce your supposed murder last night. All to ensure you wouldn't really end up on a refrigerated slab."

Grimacing, she shrugged off his touch, gritting her teeth at the reminder that he still thought he knew best how to protect her.

"Hey," Ace said. "I'm still on your side, remember?"

As he opened the door for her, the SUV's interior light lit his face. Though in need of a shave and lined with strain, it still held traces of the confidence and optimism of the man who'd once led a billion-dollar oil corporation. The man who'd claimed to love her. "Still hoping you'll give me another chance to convince you that I meant what I said before, about wanting to make a life with you. We don't have to rush things if you don't want, but I'd still love nothing more than—"

"We'll talk later, Ace," she promised as she climbed inside.

They weren't long underway, the ride far less punishing in the four-wheel-drive SUV, before Spencer spoke. But to her surprise he began by asking, "How are you feeling? Head doing any better?"

She cut a suspicious look his way. "I'll live, but what gives? Trying to soften me up before you chew me out?"

"Oh, you deserve a chewing out, all right, scaring the nursing supervisor who'd been sworn to keep your secret and several of us at the station half to death when we heard you'd gone missing," Spencer said irritably before blowing out a noisy breath. "But then, I got to thinking how I would've felt about it if I'd gotten knocked out after getting shot at, only to come around and find out the authorities had taken it upon themselves to tell everybody I'd been murdered. Oh, and by the way, my home had just been burned to ashes, and I'm going to have to go by some name I've never heard of and hide myself away for life. It's a hell of a lot to expect anyone to deal with all at once."

"So you're saying you forgive me?" It was a big ask, she knew, but a girl could dream.

"I'm telling you I understand, let's put it that way. That's not to say you haven't made a damned fine mess of things, since you were seen leaving the hospital by some upstanding citizen who snapped your photo on a cell phone and decided to call in a hot tip to the TV news producer I phoned last night about how she'd been duped about your so-called murder."

Sierra sucked in a startled breath, her pulse fluttering at the realization that whatever safe span of time she'd thought their cover story might have bought her had been blown.

"Which, by the way," Spencer continued, "has dropped my future credibility with the local media into the toilet."

"Have they reported Sierra's still alive yet?" Ace blurted, sounding rattled from his spot in the backseat.

"No, no, they haven't," Spencer said, "but it took my promise of my next big exclusive, a cashed-in favor the producer had forgotten and an all-out plea for Sierra's life to get her to hold off."

"Thank you," both Sierra and Ace said at once.

"Save your thanks," Spencer said gruffly. "Because I'm afraid that idiot, that guy that snapped your photo in the first place, is like a dog with a bone with what he's decided is his big scoop. He's posted it all over all social media, yelling about fake news, a police conspiracy to only make it seem like some shady secret government operative named Sierra Madden has been murdered."

"Government operative?" Sierra echoed. "Where on earth did he come up with that nonsense?"

"Turns out this guy's big time into conspiracy theories, and he's thrilled to have stumbled onto a little of what passes for social currency in his online circles."

From the rear seat, Ace cursed over the implications, and looking back at him, Sierra said, "My sentiments, exactly. For what it's worth, I'm sorry for making your job harder, Sergeant, and sorry to you both for being so ungrateful when I do understand that you've—you've been doing the best that you know how to help me."

"It's only because you're well worth saving." Though there was a metal gridded divider separating the front seat from the back, the sincerity in Ace's voice came through loud and clear. "Never forget that for a moment."

Glancing back, she saw in his eyes how much he believed it. But how would he feel when more killers came for her, endangering the family he had loved far longer?

Chapter Sixteen

Though Ace had nothing to hide, Michael Seaver nonetheless arrived at the police station later that night to guide Ace through that evening's police interview. As sharply dressed as ever, in one of his trademark designer suits and glasses, Seaver deftly steered Ace around any legal gray areas that he might be wading into while recounting the events that had taken place that afternoon and evening. He also helped to refocus Ace when his mind repeatedly drifted during questioning.

"Sorry. It's been a hell of a day," Ace said, pushing back the mostly untouched coffee he'd been offered to look from Seaver to veteran Detective P.J. Doherty, who'd been called in to handle his interview. Though it wasn't a stretch to say he was still reeling from recent events, Ace was far more distracted by the thought of what might be going on with Sierra in the next room.

Once she'd finished answering questions, would they tell her she was free to go?

After all, just before coming in here, he'd managed to pull aside Spencer, who'd been on his way to formally interview Kyle O'Neill, to ask, "So after Sierra's interviewed, will you take her back to the hospital since she was never officially released?"

Spencer's look had been dubious as he shook his head. "Is there really any point? You know damned well she'd just find her way out again, and considering the fact that her cover's been blown—"

"Then what about protective custody? Or *my* custody? I'll take her out to the ranch and keep her there, where she'll be safe." Though Ace still felt a little strange about returning to the mansion where he'd been raised after such a long absence, he was willing to put aside those feelings, and his lingering worries about any potential awkwardness with Genevieve, for the sake of Sierra's well-being.

Spencer made a scoffing sound. "Come on, man. No judge is signing off on that, nor should they. Your lady friend's a grown adult, more than capable of making her own decisions, and I see absolutely zero indication that she's a threat to her own welfare or that of others."

"But if she leaves, those hired goons'll hunt her down. As smart and resourceful as she is, we both know they'll *kill* her."

"And if you keep her here against her will, what'll *you* have killed, Ace?" Spencer had asked him quietly. "I think maybe you need to consider that, as well."

With a sinking feeling, Ace realized Spencer was one hundred percent right. But what consolation would that be if she ended up murdered when there was something he might've done to stop it?

By the time he'd finally finished with his own interview, Ace could see that his attorney's irritated glances had grown decidedly more pointed.

"I know you've got to be rattled after everything that's happened, but honestly, man, that was embarrassing, having to hear Detective Doherty repeat every question two or three times to get an answer," Seaver said as the two of them strode down the hall toward the station's front lobby and exit. "What's the matter with you? You should be celebrating."

"Celebrating?" Ace echoed dully.

"Now that O'Neill's blurted out that he was the one responsible for your father's shooting, it's obvious the police have no interest in giving you any further grief."

"I still don't understand how O'Neill managed to set me up to take the fall."

"More than likely, while watching your father to see when the best time would be to catch him alone at Colton Oil headquarters, he started picking up on your comings and goings, too—"

"And decided I'd make a damned fine scapegoat when he somehow heard about that email Harley Watts sent for whoever was pulling his strings at the AAG—"

"The AAG? So he's confessed?"

Ace shook his head. "He's not talking yet that I'm aware of, but getting back to O'Neill, after I'd been ousted from my position as Colton Oil CEO, he must have figured it was the perfect time to make his move."

Seaver shrugged. "Makes sense to me."

"Yeah, it does." Ace nodded. "Especially considering how at the hospital O'Neill was talking about setting it up to look as if I'd killed my father and then myself out of guilt as some kind of payback for driving his own father away from his family."

"That's some pretty twisted reasoning," Seaver agreed, "but in light of today's events, I'm sure Sergeant Colton and the DA will get it right this time."

"So my legal issues are over," Ace said, "but my family still has so many questions that need answering."

"Let's climb one mountain at a time, Ace," Seaver said, clapping him on the shoulder and offering one of those slick smiles he seemed to keep on hand for such occasions. "Can't you admit that today we've conquered Everest?"

Ace wasn't so certain about the *we* part, since he hadn't noticed Seaver helping Sierra and him chase down his father's would-be killer. But he let it go and nodded before spotting something in the lobby that had him blurting, "Thanks, Michael. We'll touch base tomorrow, but I've gotta run now."

"Hey, where're you going?" Seaver called after him as Ace took off.

But the words scarcely registered as Ace hurried toward Sierra, who was sitting with Ainsley in the lobby area. The two were leaning forward, their heads close. As he approached, he saw that his younger sister, dressed casually this evening in jeans and a striped sweater, was holding Sierra's hand, clearly offering her comfort.

Even more surprisingly, Sierra was accepting that kindness. But then, she looked utterly spent, her head drooping so that her tangled hair partially obscured her face. Her clothing, too, was dusty and rumpled and her shoulders slumped after her ordeal in the ghost town. Grateful as he was to see her still here, he forced himself to slow his approach, half-afraid that he might somehow frighten her into bolting—or stiffening her spine and insisting she was ready to take on all comers.

"Ace," Ainsley said when she spotted him before coming to her feet and wrapping him in a warm hug. "Sierra's filled me in on all the details. Are you—is it really true? Is this nightmare all over for you?"

"We can talk at home. I'm bushed."

"That's why I've come," Ainsley told them, "to take you back to the ranch, where everyone can be together. And before you give me any flak about it, I wanted to let you know that Genevieve's given her blessing. She—she's heard about what happened today at the hospital, how you saved Dad from that horrible man—and she says it's long past time that you came home."

"That—that's wonderful," he said, gratitude flowing through his veins like cool rain on the parched desert. Still, he couldn't keep his worried gaze from moving to Sierra.

"And I'm happy to say Sierra's already accepted my invitation," Ainsley added.

A warm burst of relief flowing through him, Ace reached out to offer her his hand. When she let him help her to her feet, he embraced her, murmuring, "Thank you," into her ear. "Thank you for still being here. You don't know how worried I was that you'd simply cut and run."

"I'm half-starved and exhausted and miles from my car, which for all I know is by now rigged up with more explosives than July Fourth in a theme park castle," she admitted, her voice hoarse with either fatigue or the dust she'd swallowed during her earlier fall. "So like it or not, I'm afraid that I'm not going anywhere quite yet."

A WEEK AFTER the arrest of Kyle O'Neill, Sierra found herself walking between two of the long, white barns outside the sprawling guest ranch-style Colton mansion early one beautiful, clear morning that hinted at the warmer days to come. Simply walking, she felt the pleasant stretching of tight muscles and her lungs expanding to take in the scents of fresh, green grass and open sky, which smelled as clean as her clothing now was, thanks to efforts of the ranch's pleasant and efficient staff.

Pleasant or not, she'd meant to be long gone by now, and surely would have been, had Ace not insisted on summoning a doctor to examine her here the night of their arrival—because apparently house calls were still a thing for people rich enough to own their own oil company. After politely but firmly ordering Ace to quit hovering and leave the tastefully plush and private guest suite where she'd been put up, the long-time family retainer had checked Sierra over head to toe.

A bosomy older woman with a warm, informal manner, she'd quickly put Sierra at ease, assuring her that she could expect to make a full recovery. With her mind already skipping ahead to fretting over where she could get her hands on another set of wheels and where she might go next, Sierra found herself caught off guard when the doctor had solemnly added the words, "In time."

Frowning, Sierra shook her head. "What do you mean, *in time*?"

The doctor's blue eyes captured and held her gaze, drawing out the pause before she spoke. "It's very clear that, between the healing ribs, this concussion and all the other scrapes and bruises, your body's account is badly overdrawn, and the payment's now come due—in the form of long soaks in the bath, plenty of sleep, preferably in a quiet, dark room such as this one, and nourishing, wholesome meals on a regular schedule. Home-cooked would be my recommendation."

"What kind of half-baked prescription do you call that?" asked Sierra, who couldn't recall the last home-cooked meal she'd eaten. "They pay you extra for the country doctor routine? Did *Ace* bribe you?"

But the truth was, she hadn't had much fight left in her, and Ace had been smart enough—or possibly distracted by his reunion with so many family members—to give her the space she needed to accept what both Dr. Earth Mother and her own body were telling her in no uncertain terms. When she'd finally passed out in what turned out to be the most comfortable bed she'd ever slept in, she'd remained asleep for the better part of the next two days.

But she could only lie around resting for so long, even with Ace hand-delivering trays of food and offering as much company and conversation as she cared for. But though she forced herself to eat and rest, to do what she needed to recover—including this attempt at light exercise—she could already feel herself withdrawing. Preparing herself for what she still knew in her heart was the right thing, the only thing that she could do. That was still as true now as it had been the night of her arrival in this haven, no matter how seven days and nights of soft, scented sheets, meals that didn't come with their own cardboard containers and complimentary grease blots, and the hundreds of acres of fenced pastureland surrounding what she'd come to think of as Colton Central had lulled her into a false sense of security…along with the three "hands" she'd already made as Ace's brothers Callum, ranch foreman Asher, and their distant cousin, Jarvis, whom she'd discovered, during her background research, worked as a ranch hand on the Triple R. But she went along with their charade, ignoring them as they pretended to fix a fence while discreetly monitoring her stroll, on Ace's instructions, no doubt, from a distance.

She had zero doubt all three were armed—something about the way they walked and periodically scanned the pastures, as if some eager hit man was likely to pop out from behind one of the grazing cattle to take a shot at her as any moment. Or maybe they were more worried she'd jump one of these neatly painted white fences, hop up onto the back of the nearest horse—she decided she liked the look of that flashy brown-and-white pinto with the wide, white blaze—and gallop off to parts unknown.

She chuckled to herself, imagining their dismay. And everyone's astonishment, once it was learned that her only previous equestrian experience involved a carousel ride at a now-defunct casino—and her swearing off champagne at the age of twenty-one.

The smile died on her lips when the phone in her pocket vibrated. Lost for days, the cell had been found inside her Chevy, which had been searched for any tracking devices or explosives by police before being towed from the parking lot of the hospital. Though Spencer had advised her not to risk driving the car again, he'd been kind enough to personally come to the ranch last night to deliver her lost phone, which she must have dropped inside the vehicle at some point. She'd been even more grateful when he hadn't brought up the fact that the car had never been legally registered in her name, though she could practically see him biting his tongue to keep from lecturing her about it.

After thanking him, she'd plugged in the cell to charge. But so far she'd been afraid to look at it—or her laptop—since the announcement of her so-called murder.

Dread filling her lungs, she forced herself to pick up the phone now, handling the thing as though it were a live bomb. And sighing to see it was her friend Brie, who had at least been in on the whole fake death scheme from the start.

Answering, Sierra said sarcastically, "Iris Higgins speaking."

"Whoever on earth came up with that name," the detective told her cheerfully, "you should probably kick him."

"Don't think I haven't thought of it," Sierra groused,

though the thought of repaying Ace's kindness and generosity in such a manner left a sour taste in her mouth.

She continued walking, so as not to worry the babysitters who were keeping a watchful eye on her. "How's Rocky doing?"

"Your cat's just fine where he is. More than fine. He and Max have gotten to be big buddies. Can you believe it? Who would've thought two reformed alley cats would turn out to have so much in common?" Brie asked, snorting at the mention of her boyfriend. "But I didn't call to talk about those two animals."

Sierra swallowed hard. "What then?"

"Well, you can forget the fake identity," Brie told her.

"I guess so, after Captain Conspiracy with the cell phone camera plastered my photo and his stupid little exposé all over social media," Sierra said, angry all over again about what the man had done. "I'll have to come up with something else—and the most convincing paperwork I buy off the black mark—"

She cut herself off, abruptly conscious she was talking to a cop and not just a friend.

"I'm going to forget you said that," Brie said. "And so can you, Sierra, because as of four-forty-six this morning, your situation's changed completely."

Giving up any pretense of walking, Sierra went to the fence and grabbed onto the top board with her free hand so hard the knuckles whitened. Because she heard an optimistic note in her friend's voice, one completely at odds with their last conversation. And of all the things Sierra had to fear, she was most afraid of allowing herself to get her hopes up, to imagine that this respite, the peace and the kindness—and even the love she had been offered—might possibly last…

ACE FOUND HER standing outside the south pasture, gripping the fence tightly as she stared off at the mountains. With her sunlit hair fluttering behind her in the breeze, she looked impossibly beautiful and fierce, yet somehow at the same time fragile, like a statue of a Viking warrior princess forged out of spun glass.

He cleared his throat so as not to startle her with his approach.

When she turned to look at him, he was relieved to see her cheeks were dry, though sunlight betrayed a few clumped lashes that hinted that Callum might have been right in telling him she'd appeared upset following the phone call she had taken some forty minutes earlier.

Instead of asking her about that, he decided on the indirect approach. "I've come bearing a gift. You look like maybe you could use this."

"I could always use fresh coffee. Thanks." Hand shaking slightly, she accepted the travel mug he offered.

When Sierra took her first sip of the mug's contents, her green eyes lit up. "Mm, what's in this? It's not the usual brew."

"It's Genevieve's secret blend," he told her as she drank some more. "Made with a splash of vanilla and some spices or other. Cinnamon, maybe? Nutmeg? She brewed it up special this morning to celebrate that the neurologist has confirmed my father is making slow but steady progress emerging from his coma."

"That's wonderful news," Sierra said before taking a second sip.

Her appreciative murmur took him straight back to the sounds of pleasure he'd coaxed from her when the two of them had been together—a memory that had him groaning in frustration before he could stop himself.

"What's wrong?" she asked, clearly unaware of how difficult it had been for him to focus on his father's ongoing recovery, the continuing search for the real Ace Colton and worries over what his birth mother might still have in store for the family.

"What's wrong," he admitted, "is that I can't keep up this charade any longer. Can't keep holding back my feelings for you and playing the genial, low-pressure host when I'm really worried sick that at any moment you're going to cut and run."

"I wouldn't—" she began. "I won't—not without telling you goodbye. And th-thanking you. For loving me. For healing me."

"But you're not healed yet, are you, Sierra?" he demanded, frustration hardening his voice. "Not if you're too scared to love anybody back. And not if you're still leaving, after what Detective Stratford told you about Ice Veins's nephew being murdered by a rival gangster this morning after being returned to jail awaiting trial."

Sucking in a startled breath, she choked and coughed on her drink. She still had tears in her eyes by the time she'd recovered enough to ask him, "Brie called you, too? I mean, Detective Stratford?"

"Don't act so put out," he said. "Your best friend

didn't rat you out. It was Spencer who called me after she'd informed him."

The color in her cheeks deepened, her nostrils flaring with sudden indignation. "Let's just back up a second, Ace. What do you mean, Brie didn't *rat me out*? Are you suggesting that after all you've done for me and everything we've been through together, I was intending to *keep* this news from you? And what? Just slink off somewhere one night? Is that what you think of me?"

"It isn't like you haven't warned me of your intentions to leave Mustang Valley."

"So you and your family wouldn't be in danger," she insisted, a fire igniting in her eyes.

"But we won't be in danger from your pursuers any longer, will we?" he asked. "Because without Eddie Harris alive to pay the price he'd offered on your head, you aren't going to have to worry about hit men any longer, are you?"

"I'll have to be careful for a while, and maybe stay clear of Las Vegas in case of close associates," she said, "but Brie doesn't think it will take long for word to get out that there's no money in the job to make going after me worth the risk or trouble."

"That's *wonderful* news, Sierra," he said. "You'll be safe again. And you'll have choices. Hell, you'll even get to return from the dead. How many people can say they've ever gotten that chance?"

"It's still sinking in, I guess. I suppose I'm still numb."

"Are you sure that's all?" he challenged. "Because you look more scared to me."

After balancing her mug on the fence post near her elbow, she turned up her palms, her eyes shining. "Of course I'm *scared.* More scared than I've ever been before."

Reaching out, he enfolded each of her hands in his. In spite of the morning's warmth and the coffee she had just been holding, they felt like ice.

"Are you afraid—afraid to tell me you don't feel about me the way that I do you?" he asked, something in him giving way at the thought of losing her now, when finally, the reason she'd been giving him for leaving had vanished. Or had that been an excuse all along? Had the tsunami of events they'd been swept up in, the one that had amplified her feelings for a time, left behind nothing but a clean-swept blankness when it receded?

"If that's the case," he told her, his throat thickening, "I'll do everything I can to help you start your life over anywhere you'd like. I promise you…even if it means you never want to see me again."

"Ace, *no*, that's not what I mean at all," she blurted, flinging her arms around his waist and pushing her head against his chest. "Don't you understand? It's not that I don't love you, far from it, or that I haven't been thinking about what you said about you and I being together. I—I want that. I want you, more than anything."

After squeezing her tight, he pulled back, enough to cup her face in his hands. That beautiful face, looking up at him completely stripped of its usual defensive layers.

"Then what on earth are you so afraid of, Sierra?"

"I—I'm scared that when you get to know the real

me, the girl who practically raised herself and has the battle scars to prove it, that there's no way you're going to like what you see."

"That's half of what I love about you, that you're smart, resourceful, tough," he said. "So different from the pampered princesses and the social climbers I've dated in the past that I can't believe I've wasted so many years chasing after the wrong women. Or more likely, the truth was, I wasted my life being the wrong man. But you've changed that for me, Sierra. You and what I've been through lately have helped change me forever. That's why I still want you. I want you to be my—"

She shook her head. "Please, just let me finish. I wasn't raised like this, Ace—" she gestured to the mansion, its architecture designed to blend into the beautiful terrain "—with a town place and some grand ranch like this out in the country and staff to anticipate my every need. Instead, I always had to be on my guard for people looking to take advantage—and sometimes I wasn't fast enough, good enough. Back when I was just a kid, there were a couple of men, gambling buddies of my father's. So-called family friends, who..."

Her gaze dropped, and heard the sound of her swallowing, saw her hands knotting into fists. The fists she'd made into weapons to protect herself. Because she'd had no other option.

"I'm sorry, Sierra. So damned sorry for what happened to you back then—and mad as hell to think of anybody hurting you or letting you be hurt when you damned well should have been protected."

"My—my father didn't—he had no idea. In his way,

he did his best, I think. And those men…" She shook her head, gaze drifting. "One's dead, and the other's in prison for another— It's all over. It's over, but it will always be a part of who I am."

"Listen to me, Sierra." Ace laid his hands on her shoulders and looked straight into her eyes, willing. "If you believe that what happened to you as a child could in any way diminish the way I feel about you, you've got things *completely* backward. You had no more choice in those crimes than I did when some nurse switched me out of a hospital when I was nothing but a newborn. The only thing your story does is make me admire even more what a damned strong, confident woman you've become."

She gave a little laugh. "Is that what it looks like from the outside? Because right now I don't mind telling you, I'd rather be in the ring, fighting a couple of classes over my weight, than having this conversation."

"Have you talked to anyone before about it?"

"I'm talking to you, now."

He kissed her forehead. "I'm honored you would trust me. But I hope you will keep talking. And not only to me, but to a trained counselor, or maybe even with other people who've been through this. People who will help you learn to be as proud of yourself as I am of you right now…and as I'd be as your husband, if you think a guy who was recently canned from his last job could possibly be good enough for a woman as brave and smart as—"

"*Fired* from his last job? But that ridiculous requirement that you have to have 'Colton blood' to be the CEO in the company bylaws certainly wasn't your fault," she erupted, sounding righteously indignant on his behalf.

"No, it definitely wasn't," he agreed, refusing to take any blame for Micheline Anderson's schemes. "But it does mean my future could be a lot different than I'd imagined. Less of this—" he gestured toward the mansion "—and something a lot more modest, based on how the firm for energy consulting I intend to set up after we finally get my family situation sorted, does—"

"With all your industry experience, it'll be a huge success. I know it," she said, her eyes burning with sincerity. With belief in him.

"But whether or not it is, I'll only be going through the motions, Sierra, unless I have you there by my side. So tell me, are you with me?"

The smile that warmed her eyes melted the iciest reaches of his own heart. "Didn't I tell you not long after we met, cowboy? You're well and truly stuck with me, for better or for worse."

Chapter Seventeen

"There's the lucky man," said Ainsley, running around her desk to give Ace an exuberant hug when he stepped inside her office at Colton Oil the following afternoon. "I didn't get to tell you in person before, with everyone else from the family gushing over the two of you, but I am *so* happy for you and Sierra. I *knew* there was something going on between the two of you!"

After giving his cheek a noisy kiss, she turned toward the doorway, where their blonde younger half sister, Marlowe, the current CEO, stood smiling, and offering her best wishes, too. "I've met her, and I think she's perfect for you. So are you two planning a long engagement?"

"Depends on how long it takes her to negotiate a signed contract with everybody that, after Nova's baby's born, she's not to be called Grandma before we get the chance to try for our own kids."

The two of them laughed, and Ace grinned, wondering when he'd ever been so happy and excited for the future, despite the questions still hanging over them—and the fact that he had come to finally clean out his desk…

and permanently walk away from a job he'd loved and taken pride in.

There was a tap at the door, and Ainsley's assistant was shaking her head. "I'm so sorry to interrupt, but—but there's a woman here, Micheline Anderson, insisting that she see you. All of you. I sent her into the conference room to wait."

Ace caught his sisters' wide-eyed looks of alarm, but his own shock was wrapped up in a white-hot ball of emotion. Curiosity. Rage. Dread over why the self-help guru—the former nurse who was believed to be his own biological mother—had come. Did she mean to finally reveal her end game? Or could Ace at least force her to admit, at last, and even to explain why she had switched him so soon after birth for his parents' true firstborn son?

Glancing anxiously from one face to the next, Ainsley's assistant shook her head. "Did I do the wrong thing? Should I have called security? Or the police?"

The siblings exchanged uncertain looks before Ace shook his head. "No. You're fine. We should hear her out, thanks."

"But stay close, if you will," Ainsley urged her. "If you hear raised voices from inside there, or anything alarming, don't hesitate to call for help." Looking from Marlowe to her brother, she added, "I don't think she's the type to get her own hands dirty with anything violent, but I definitely don't trust that woman."

As they walked past their father's office—the same room where he had been shot—on the way to the smaller conference room, Marlowe pulled out her cell phone and showed them both that she was switching on an app that would make a voice recording of their meeting.

Ace nodded in approval and tried to mask his emotions before stepping into the richly paneled room, where a long, mahogany table sat surrounded by comfortable rolling chairs.

Exquisitely dressed as ever, the elegant, blonde cult leader had seated herself at the head of the table, her long fingers interlaced and her features arranged in the self-satisfied expression of a woman who owned the place.

"What is it that brings you here?" Ace demanded. Ever since that email had arrived, they'd all been waiting anxiously, desperate to know whether the sender's true game would be money or some form of blackmail. Or was the real purpose of Micheline's visit something even darker?

Clearly oblivious to his mood, she smiled broadly and clapped her hands together. "I have some *wonderful* news to share with you today."

"Wonderful for *whom*?" asked Ainsley, perching on the edge of her seat as they all claimed chairs, each of the siblings keeping a safe distance from this uninvited guest.

Ignoring her, Micheline went on to say, "Finally, after that dreadful business with that horrible phony, Jace Smith, trying to cash in by pretending to be my son, I've found him. I've actually found my real son, my darling boy, Jake Anderson, and he's coming home soon! Isn't that *fantastic*?"

"Your real son?" Ace spat out. "Don't you mean Payne and Tessa Colton's stolen child?" Feeling sick, he knew then that he'd been holding out hope that Ainsley had been wrong about what she'd said back at the hospital about him having a biological connection to this woman.

"Well, you don't—you can't possibly understand." Micheline's painted nails splayed out to fan out over her chest.

"So you're finally admitting it?" Marlowe erupted. "You're confessing that you switched your *own* baby—" the mother of an infant son herself, she gave Ace a look brimming with emotion "—for a child that wasn't yours?"

"I—I—"

"After what you've just said, you might as well admit it," Ainsley said. "Anyway, we already had it figured out."

Micheline hung her head, a tear trickling down her cheek, creating a thin rivulet of dark mascara. "Of course you have." She sniffled. "And anyway, there's no point in holding it back any longer. Not when—not when I've been diagnosed with stage three bone cancer. It's why Jake's coming. To see me off, in case this last-ditch treatment doesn't offer the miracle I..."

She paused as if waiting for someone to offer the customary sympathy. But these weren't customary circumstances.

Even so, Ace finally forced himself to say, “Sorry you’re ill,” because his mother—the *real* mother who had loved and raised him—would have expected it of him.

Nodding an acknowledgment, Micheline said, “That’s a good man, so I’ll be very honest now. I did switch you with my newborn. It was a low point in my life, when I didn’t feel up to motherhood. I was all alone, and you were a strapping boy, so vigorous. When I saw how sickly the real Ace Colton was, I was sure he wouldn’t survive more than a day or two, and then I’d have my life back again.”

“So you just—you just *traded* them?” Marlowe’s horror was written in her eyes.

Her eyes damp, Micheline nodded. “I switched him with my biological son so he’d have excellent parents to grow up with and all the advantages I could never give him. And then I took the dying baby. I thought… I was certain I was doing a good thing. The right thing… for—for everyone.”

She burst into sobs and buried her face into a handful of tissues from the box that Ainsley pushed in her direction.

While Micheline wept, the siblings stared at one another, shock rippling over them like blast waves from a bomb that had detonated forty years before. Holy hell, Ace thought, as the details of her story sank in.

Still, something didn’t feel right. As he watched his biological mother’s continuing *performance*, he knew it in his bones. Micheline was still up to something nefarious. Something he sensed would come back to bite them when the real Jake Anderson finally turned up. But at least he'd have his family—the ones he'd grown up with, his newfound daughter and grandchild on the way, and Sierra. With them by his side, he knew could handle anything.

* * * * *